URGE
to KILL

JOHN
LUTZ

PINNACLE BOOKS
KENSINGTON PUBLISHING CORP.

PINNACLE BOOKS are published by

Kensington Publishing Corp.
119 West 40th Street
New York, NY 10018

ISBN: 978-1-61523-550-6

Printed in the United States of America

For Barbara,
As they all are

And to the memory of
John Mangosing,
A good friend gone too soon

AUTHOR'S NOTE

The author wishes to acknowledge the invaluable aid of Marilyn Davis and Sharon Huston.

PART I

They change their skies above them,
But not their hearts that roam.

—RUDYARD KIPLING,
The Native-Born

Why do I often meet your visage here?
Your eyes like agate lanterns—on and on
Below the toothpaste and the dandruff ads?

—HART CRANE, *The Tunnel*
(New York Subway)

1

In the long ago an eagle circled high above a rabbit burrow and would swoop down and lay on the ground a branch of ripe berries, and then climb high again into the sky.

The rabbit would see how high the eagle was and know there was time to leave the safety of the burrow to snatch the berries and return to the burrow before the eagle could reach him from up so high.

Again the next day the eagle would swoop down and leave a branch of berries, but this time a little farther from the burrow. Again the rabbit would see the eagle circling high in the clear sky and seize the berries and return to the burrow before the eagle might reach him.

For seven days this happened, each day the rabbit venturing farther from its burrow, and the eagle simply circled high overhead and looked very small against the pale blue top of the sky. The rabbit decided the berries were a gift, but still the eagle was an eagle and not to be trusted.

On the eighth day the branch of berries was still far from the burrow, but the eagle so small in the sky seemed no threat and like a mote in the rabbit's wary eye.

John Lutz

But as the rabbit left his burrow the eagle became larger, and it wasn't an eagle at all this time but a hawk that had seemed so high only because it was smaller than the eagle the rabbit usually saw. Too late the rabbit realized what had happened. There was no time to return to the safety of the burrow.

The weak things in the world have a time to die that is sooner than the strong. That is why the spirit made the weak and the strong. In its heart, the rabbit knew this and was still.

The hawk swooped down, and its wings spread wider and wider and covered the sun and made the sky black. The hawk's talons cut like blades into the rabbit's back, and the rabbit screamed as the hawk lifted it higher and higher into a blackness darker than the night. The screams became the wind and the beating of the hawk's great wings the thunder of the coming storms.

In the long-ago day, these things did happen.

2

New York, the present

Vera Doaks keyed the lock on her apartment door and told herself she needed to be patient.

She'd been in New York a little more than a month. That wasn't a long time, and already she'd placed an article in the airline magazine *Nation Travels* and sold a short story to a nationally published mystery magazine. Her MFA from Ohio State University was paying off. She told herself it wouldn't be long before she wouldn't have to wait tables in order to pay the rent. Some publisher would pay it for her.

She paused by the framed flea-market mirror in the entry hall and tilted her head to the side for a dust jacket publicity shot. The attractive redhead in the mirror smiled out at her, with wide cheekbones like a model's, intense brown eyes, slightly upturned nose, strong cleft chin, a knowing, confident grin.

Look intelligent now.

Her famous writer look. Vera practiced it frequently.

A career as a novelist was what really interested her. The

short story she'd sold was going to be the basis for her first book, a suspense novel set in her new city, New York.

She was from a small town, and she loved the hurricane of activity every day in the city, then the pulsing energy that maintained it through the nights. The theater (which she could barely afford), the delis and street vendors, the wandering transfixed tourists, the underground city of subways and tragic songs and sometimes dangerous people, the rich stepping over the poor, the poor rising up to be rich, the maelstrom of races and religions, of neighborhoods and languages and the uncertainties of life; she thrilled to all of it. Here, Vera knew, was the stuff of inspiration and of great fiction. Vera was positive she was capable of inspiration. She never gave up believing in herself. Nobody had ever explained to her satisfaction why she should.

She hadn't given up hope on the short story and article she'd submitted, and here she was, able to pay another month's rent on the Hell's Kitchen walk-up apartment she'd come to love.

Love, of the romantic sort, that was the one thing missing in her unfolding life of good fortune.

There's no need to give up hope for that, either.

She unlaced her joggers, worked her heels out of them, and kicked off the gray composite and canvas shoes so they bounced off a wall. Walked over to where her bed and a dresser were located behind a three-panel Chinese-print folding screen in the cramped efficiency apartment. From an apportioned space that passed for a closet, where one of the apartment's many exposed water pipes served as a hanger rod, she drew out the foundation of her wardrobe—a simple black dress. It seemed that every woman in New York owned a simple black dress and was in competition with every other woman over how to wear and accessorize it. She had uncomfortable but serviceable black high-heeled pumps to wear with the dress tonight, a white scarf and pearls, a matching knockoff Prada purse she'd bought from a street vendor. And she could do wonders with her shoulder-length red hair that was almost dark enough to be auburn. She wasn't pale, like a lot of red-heads. Her dark eyes were flecked with green. Not a ravishing beauty, to be sure, but she and her black dress could compete, and they could damn well win.

It was just that so far they hadn't.

She peeled off her faded jeans and Yankees T-shirt, then her Macy's panties, and padded barefoot to the sectioned-off bathroom area with its cramped shower stall.

Tonight might be the night. *Tonight, tonight . . .* The words were a melody in her mind.

What was that song from? She searched her memory.

Ah! *West Side Story.* A great musical, based on *Romeo and Juliet.* The ultimate lovers.

Well, she was on the West Side.

Vera adjusted the squeaky porcelain faucet handles and stepped beneath the water.

She picked up the smooth oblong sliver of soap and began to sing, knowing that out there in the night the city pulsed like her heart and waited, and the possibilities were endless.

Tonight, tonight . . .

3

Total darkness, total pain.

Where am I?

Vera tried to raise her head and look around, and a deep ache closed on the back of her neck like a claw. She let her head drop backward.

Backward?

That was when she realized she was hanging from her bound wrists and ankles. Her mind flashed on photos she'd seen of large dead animals, their lifeless heads dangling, being carried that way on horizontal poles by hunters. Only she wasn't being carried; she was stationary. The pain was from her cramped neck muscles, and from her body weight pulling down on her wrists and ankles. She could see nothing in the blackness. Hear nothing.

Her head, flush with the blood rushing to it, began to throb with almost unendurable pain behind her ears. She tried to ask if anyone was there, what was happening, but her mouth wouldn't open. Something, tape probably, was over her lips, sealing them together. She parted them with diffi-

culty but could only make a soft muffled sound halfway between a moan and a sob. She made the pitiful sound again.
Any sound was better than the darkness and silence, and the
pain.

She tried again to lift her head, but it weighed a thousand
pounds.

But with the thought of motion, and another stab of pain,
came memory.

Last night at Risqué Business, the man she'd had a couple
of drinks with . . . darkly handsome . . . well dressed in dark
pants and a gray sport jacket . . . a red tie . . . and with a cosmopolitan air, what used to be called smooth.

She tried to recall his name.

Had he ever told her?

Light!

Blinding her. She involuntarily clenched her eyes shut.

When Vera did manage to open her eyes wider than slits
she saw the bottom of a floor, rough wood planks running
one direction, joists another. Her wrists were tied together
with thick rope that had cut off circulation so that her fingers
were pale. She strained to see her ankles, her feet—*are they
as pale and bloodless as my hands?*—but couldn't pull them
into her field of vision. She did see several long fluorescent
fixtures, two glowing tubes in each. There must be lots of
fixtures. That was where all the light was coming from. And
the faint, crackling buzzing.

She realized she'd been able to raise her head slightly, almost to the horizontal, and with realization came another
shot of pain at the base of her neck. Her head dropped again,
dangling at a sharp angle from the thin stalk of her neck.

But she managed to turn her head slightly, before the pain
stopped her. She saw that she was in what looked like a large
basement. Gray concrete walls, wooden support beams, exposed steam and water pipes, round ductwork with shreds of
insulation hanging from some of it like grotesque stalactites.

Asbestos? Could be dangerous.

The pain became unbearable, and she tried not to move at all other than to blink away her tears.

In the glimpse she'd had of herself, confirmed by the lack of constriction on her upper arms and her legs, she knew she was nude.

Someone—*What's his name? I need to know it so I can plead, beg for him to stop whatever's going to happen!*—someone had done this to her, put something in her drink, perhaps. *Something* had caused her to black out, to awaken here, dangling from her bound wrists and ankles like a . . . She didn't want to know what. Or didn't want to think about it.

Tears welled again in her eyes and tracked downward along her temples, beneath her hairline. Tickling as if in cruel and obscene jest.

Motion caught her gaze, and there he was in her pain-blurred vision, the man from last night. She wasn't surprised to see him. He had to be responsible for this.

He was walking toward her, also nude, like a figure in a dream. Only it wasn't a dream. She could only pray that it might be. That she might wake up a second time, in her apartment, in her bed. Safe.

When she saw the knife in the man's hand her heart leaped. She did try to struggle then, but couldn't so much as squirm. Her hyperextended arms and legs were like lifeless tense cables preventing her from crashing to the concrete floor.

She saw that the man had an erection, and at that moment he reached up with the blade and must have sliced through the rope binding her wrists to the horizontal beam, because her upper body suddenly dropped.

She flinched as she swung downward. Surely her head was going to crack open on the hard floor.

But her body swung like a pendulum, swiveling slightly, her hair brushing the floor with each pass. Though her wrists were bound together, her arms were free now. She reached over her head—which was downward—and her fingertips scraped the concrete floor. There was no pain though, only numbness.

As she swung she saw something circular beneath her, a drain cover.

She dragged her numbed fingertips over the rough floor again, hearing them scrape, feeling her nails bend back and tear, as she tried to stop her body from swinging. If only she could stop she might support some of her weight by pressing her fingertips against the floor, reduce the pain in her ankles. The full burden of her weight was pulling on her ankles now, and she was swinging in lessening arcs. The rope must be digging into her flesh. She could feel something warm trickling down her calves, past her knees, along the insides of her thighs toward her crotch.

Blood!

The rope must have cut deeply into her ankles. She flashed a vision of her twisted, torn flesh.

Oh, God!

There was a sudden burning sensation on the right side of her neck. Then on the left. She caught a glimpse of a bloody knife blade and knew the man had slit her throat.

It wasn't *her* throat, though. It couldn't be.

Then she accepted that it was and lifted her arms, probed with her fingers, felt warm blood and something else.

It was when she heard the trickle of her blood in the drain that the real horror engulfed her. Her life was draining away, her remaining time, her remaining everything!

She panicked and tried to suck in air through her nose, and managed to raise her hands enough to rip the tape from her mouth. She drew in a breath to scream but inhaled only blood.

The man had waited until the pendulum arc of Vera's swinging body narrowed and was almost stopped before he cut the large carotid arteries of her neck.

He watched her.

Watched her.

After she'd tried to scream, he'd drawn the blade across her taut throat.

She wasn't alive when her body slowed to describe a small elliptical orbit above the drain and finally dangled motionless from the beam.

Nor was she alive to see the man, showered and neatly dressed, leave the building's basement, switching off the lights behind him.

She'd been dead for several hours when he returned to make sure she was completely bled out.

4

In the feeble light from his car's outmoded headlights, retired NYPD homicide detective Frank Quinn didn't see the damned thing. Not soon enough, anyway.

His old black Lincoln Town Car jounced and rattled over a pothole the size of a bomb crater, and he wondered if he'd chipped a tooth. He lifted what was left of his Cuban cigar from the ashtray and chomped down on it to use it as a mouthpiece so it might at least pad another such impact of upper and lower jaws.

He knew cigars were bad for him and had pretty much given them up, but the Cubans were too much of a temptation. Or maybe part of the appeal was that they were illegal, and he used to be a cop.

He smiled, knowing a cop was never something you used to be. He'd always figured small transgressions forestalled larger ones, so the cigars were okay.

Quinn cursed silently at traffic on Broadway as he jockeyed the big car north toward West Seventy-fifth Street and his apartment. The windows were up, and the air conditioner was humming away in its struggle with the hot summer evening. There was a slight persistent vibration of metal on metal—possibly a bearing in the blower fan motor going out. Quinn made a mental note to have it looked at. This would be a bad time of year for the car to lose its air-conditioning.

A traffic signal changed a block up, and a string of cars near the curb accelerated and made the sharp right turn onto the cross street. This created a break in the heavy traffic, and Quinn gratefully took advantage of all that barren pavement before him and ran the car up to about forty-five—a fast clip for most Manhattan streets.

Feeling pretty good, he puffed on his cigar and almost smiled. This was his poker night with five other retired or almost retired NYPD cops, and he'd won over a hundred dollars. It hadn't been a high-stakes game, so he was far and away the big winner. Everybody but Quinn bitched when they stopped playing, as agreed upon, with the last hand dealt before ten o'clock sharp. Quinn always felt unreasonably triumphant after coming out ahead at poker, even though at the level of skill where he was playing luck had everything to do with the outcome. Still, his life had left him at a point where he took his victories where he could find them.

Light glinted brightly for a moment in the Lincoln's left outside mirror. Headlights behind him. Despite the car's brisk speed, the trailing traffic was catching up. Quinn squinted and checked the rearview mirror, but didn't see much. The thick cigar smoke was doing something to the rear window, fogging it up so he couldn't see out.

Is it doing that to my lungs?

He *could* see well enough to know the car behind was too damned close.

Tailgaters always ticked him off. He ran the Lincoln up over fifty.

Almost immediately the big car's black leather interior was bathed in alternating flashes of red, making it damned difficult to see anything outside.

Irritated, Quinn braked down to about ten miles per hour

and peered through the windshield to find a space where he could veer in and stop at the curb.

There didn't seem to be a space.

Hell with it, he thought, and was about to double-park when a cab pulled out into traffic ahead of him, vacating a space. Quinn steered in close to the curb and saw that there was a fire hydrant there. That was the only reason there was a parking space in this part of town, and it was illegal. He braked to a halt anyway.

If there's a fire, I'll move.

The reflected flashing lights grew brighter, the headlights blinding, as the police car wedged in at an angle behind him. He let the Lincoln roll forward a few feet, giving the driver behind him as much room as possible.

Quinn knew better than to get out of the car. He sat still, his hands high on the steering wheel where they could be seen, and watched in the rearview mirror. In the whirligig haze of reflected light behind him, he saw doors open on both sides of the police car. Darkly silhouetted figures climbed out and advanced on the Lincoln, seeming to move jerkily in the alternating light show.

This shouldn't take long. Quinn might even know one or both of the uniforms. And the cops might know him. He could easily talk his way out of a ticket. Quinn was much respected in the NYPD. He even occasionally heard the word "legend." He prepared himself to exchange some friendly words and be on his way.

In the mirror he saw one of the silhouetted cops turn back toward the police car. Quinn figured the uniform was going to run a check on the Lincoln's plates.

Odd, Quinn thought. They could have both waited in the car while the plates were run. It was also odd that the cop on the driver's side had returned to the police car. It would make more sense for that cop to approach the Lincoln and talk to Quinn through the lowered window.

The one on the right side of the Lincoln, who should have

been doing the license check, kept coming, then passed briefly from view at the edge of the mirror.

Quinn felt a prickly sensation on the back of his neck. Something was wrong here.

Brightness slid to the side, out of the mirrors, and the radio car that had pulled Quinn over *whooshed* past him and continued down the street, its roof bar lights no longer flashing.

The passenger-side door of the Lincoln swung open, and the cop who'd approached on that side slid into the seat.

He wasn't wearing a uniform. Instead he had on an unbuttoned light raincoat, though it wasn't raining, and beneath it a suit and tie. A big man, in his late forties, overweight and with dark bags beneath his eyes. His jowls and the flesh beneath his chin sagged, making him look like nothing so much as a pensive bloodhound.

Quinn recognized him immediately, but the prickly sensation didn't go away.

The man who'd slid out of the night and into his car was New York City Police Commissioner Harley Renz.

Renz smiled, not doing a thing for the bloodhound look, and glanced around. "Smells like hell in here."

Quinn knew Renz was right. The cigar smoke odor had seeped into the upholstery and every cranny of the car. Even Quinn sometimes found it offensive, and he was used to it.

"You can get out as easy as you got in," he said. He and Renz had always gotten along, but not in the friendliest manner, each knowing the other perhaps too well.

"You smoking one of those illegal Cuban cigars you like so much?"

"Venezuelan," Quinn said.

"If you insist." Renz settled back in his plush seat, still looking over at Quinn. "You got an extra?"

"No," Quinn said. "You can finish this one."

"It'll finish you first." Renz upped the amperage on his smile. His effort at charm. Still a bloodhound. His eyes had gotten droopier since Quinn had last seen him, slanting downward more at the outer corners as if weights were attached to the sagging flesh. He held his insincere smile as he stared at Quinn. "How'd you do?"

"Do?"

"At the poker game."

"Won."

"Ah. Really, all that means is you quit soon enough not to lose."

"That why you stopped me? You riding in one of the traffic cars so you can collect graft from poker winners?"

"Seeing as I've become police commissioner, you should speak more respectfully to me."

Quinn didn't bother answering. He was wondering why Harley Renz would be interested enough in his poker night to follow him when he left the game.

"So what's this about?" Quinn asked. "You want in?"

"I know some of those guys you're playing cards with, Quinn. They cheat."

"Your kind of game."

"Even so . . ."

Quinn waited, tired of word games. He actually did have a sliver of respect for Renz, even though Renz represented authority and bureaucracy. Renz had at one time been a tough and effective homicide detective, and now and then it showed. And both men knew Renz was commissioner because of Quinn's work on the Torso murders, for which Renz had skillfully garnered most of the credit. Quinn didn't care about that. In fact, it had been part of the arrangement. The enthusiastically devious and ambitious Renz had used his newfound fame to become the most popular police commissioner in the city's history. A media darling of monstrous proportions, his high standing in the polls translated into leverage he didn't hesitate to use.

"I want to tell you a story," Renz said.

"About speeding?"

Renz waved a hand dismissively. "You were going way too fast, but we can forget about that."

Quinn pressed a button, and the window on his side of the Lincoln glided down. Sultry night air mingled with exhaust fumes tumbled into the car. He took a final pull on the cigar and tossed the glowing butt out into the street, watching it bounce and spark like a miniature fireworks display.

"Littering," Renz said. "Illicit cigars, gambling, speeding, and now this. Jesus, Quinn! You're a one-man crime wave."

"It gives me something to do in retirement." Quinn sighed and brushed cigar ash off his shirt. "It's still hot out there."

"Hotter than you know."

Quinn left the window down to let in plenty of heat so maybe Renz would leave sooner and the car would air out. He leaned forward so he could reach the ignition key and killed the motor.

"This story of yours," Quinn said. "Go ahead and tell it. And try not to be so cryptic."

5

The car was uncomfortably hot within minutes. Quinn
suffered gladly, knowing it would hasten Renz's departure.
He had a hunch what kind of story he was about to hear, and
where it would lead. Quinn was uneasy about that last part,
where it would lead.

"A month ago," Renz began, "a hedge fund manager
named George Manders was shot to death in a crowded
SoHo club."

"Never heard of him," Quinn said. Maybe he could hurry
Renz along.

"That's okay, you're not a suspect." Renz made a face and
wrinkled up his nose. It was probably a reaction to the cigar
smoke smell in the car, somehow made stronger by the
humid night air. Maybe Renz had a bloodhound nose as well
as the looks of the breed. "At the time of the shooting," Renz
continued, "Manders was dancing with a woman he didn't
know. At least according to her. They'd just met ten minutes
ago, and he'd asked her to dance. The dance floor was illuminated by those colored strobe lights that make everything

look fast and herky-jerky, and the music was so loud nobody heard the shot from a small-caliber gun."

"How small?" Quinn asked.

"Twenty-five caliber."

It wasn't an *un*common size bullet, but more rare than a .22 caliber when it came to small handguns.

Renz said, "The way the light was flickering, and the sound of the shot being drowned out by all that noise that passes for music, nobody realized at first that Manders had been shot. When he went down, they thought maybe it was some kinda tricky dance step and he was gonna pop right back up. Then witnesses said they saw someone bend over him—they thought to talk to him, maybe make sure he was okay—and the guy reached in and removed something from Manders's suit coat pocket and then shag-assed outta the club."

"This is the same guy that shot him?" Quinn asked, wanting to keep the facts straight.

"Far as we know," Renz said. "Nobody actually saw a gun. Hardly anyone even noticed there was something wrong. The music went on for another minute or so after Manders went down, and people kept dancing."

"Can anyone identify this guy who ran from the club?"

Renz shook his head no. "It all happened too fast, under conditions where it'd take a while for people to react. Half of them were juiced up on one substance or another anyway. So we got no positive ID in the offing. And nobody knows what was removed from the victim's pocket. His wallet, stuffed with cash, was intact, as was his Rolex watch and gold ring."

"Wedding ring?"

"No. Manders was divorced five years ago. He was living alone, like you."

"What kinda club was it?" Quinn asked, ignoring the barb.

"Straight clientele, upper to upper-upper class, looking for action."

"So that's what Manders was doing," Quinn said, "and he got a different kind of action than he was looking for."

"Could be."

"And maybe whoever bent over him wasn't the shooter but really *was* somebody wanting to help him, and when he realized Manders was dead he ran out of there so he wouldn't be involved."

"So what was taken from the victim's pocket?"

Quinn shrugged. "Maybe nothing. Maybe the guy bending over him was feeling for a heartbeat. Coulda been a doctor stepping out on his wife and didn't want any record that he was there."

Renz had to grin. His canine teeth were longer than most people's, and tinged yellow. "That's pretty good, the heartbeat thing with the philandering cardiologist. Why you're such an ace detective. Trouble is, there's more to my story."

It began to rain, hard. "I'm sorry to hear that." Quinn worked the buttons and raised all the windows, making it even warmer in the car. The windows blurred immediately, isolating Quinn and Renz from the outside world. There was a musty smell now to go with the stale tobacco scent. Nothing moved the sultry air.

Renz didn't seem at all discomfited. "Last week an insurance executive, Alan Weeks, was shot to death in Central Park, in front of witnesses too far away to see the killer's face. They did see the killer lean over the victim and remove something from his pocket before disappearing into the woods."

"Not his wallet?"

"Nope," Renz said. "Not his expensive pocket watch, either. The bullet that killed Weeks was fired from a twenty-five-caliber handgun, but *not* the same gun that killed Manders. Nothing about the murders seems to connect Weeks and Manders, other than bullets in the head. And possibly whatever was removed from their pockets."

Quinn drummed his fingertips for a while on the steering

wheel, making a sound something like the rain pattering on the car roof.

"Maybe coincidence," he said, not believing it. He'd been conditioned not to believe it. Coincidence and detective work were incompatible.

Renz flashed another canine smile in the wavering light making its way through the rain-washed windows. "Like it was coincidental we bumped into each other tonight."

Quinn stopped with the fingers. "Fate?"

Renz shook his head no. "Design." The grin stayed. "Another homicide like the first two," he said, "and we've definitely got ourselves a serial killer and all the media hype that goes with it. I need you and your team ready to go in the event that happens. Usual terms."

For particularly difficult and sensitive cases, the clever and immensely ambitious Renz called on Quinn and his team of former NYPD detectives, Pearl Kasner and Larry Fedderman, to act as his personal investigators. Their work-for-hire status provided them use of NYPD resources, but they suffered few of the department's hindrances.

Quinn knew this wasn't only because Renz wanted serious crimes solved on his watch. Quinn understood the bureaucracy and still held a grudge against it from when it had turned on him. He didn't have to be told that an important part of his job would be covering Renz's ass.

"You could call it a standby basis," Renz said, "but we both know it won't be standby very long."

"That's what my gut tells me."

"Your gut tell you to take the job?"

"Tells me not to touch it."

"How about your head?"

"My head says run from it fast as I can."

"But you're going to call Pearl and Fedderman? Be ready to go after this sicko?"

"Yes," Quinn said.

Renz stared at him for a while, studying him.

"Your heart must be telling you what to do," he said. He grinned hugely, all incisors and canine teeth gleaming in the night's reflected light. "How sweet."

"Get out of the car."

"Can't," Renz said. "You mighta noticed the radio car I was riding in has driven away, and now it's raining. I need a lift home."

"You shoulda thought ahead."

"If I hadn't been thinking ahead, Quinn, I wouldn't be here talking with you. I want us to be ready for the media shit storm."

"You still live over on East Fifty-first?"

"Same place," Renz said. "Newly decorated, though."

"It's kinda far from here," Quinn said.

"That's why I asked a friend."

Quinn started the car's big engine. Before pulling away from the curb, he drew a cigar from an inside pocket and fired it up with the Lincoln's lighter. If Renz was riding with him, he was going to suffer. If the smoke didn't get to Renz, it would only be because he was a cigar smoker himself and knew good tobacco when he smelled it.

"I thought you said you were smoking your last one," Renz said.

"This is the last one," Quinn said.

Renz stared ahead quietly, obviously pissed off. Made Quinn smile.

He would have offered Renz a cigar if they weren't Cuban.

6

Quinn figured it wasn't midnight yet, so Pearl might still be awake.

She wasn't a night owl in the sense that she liked to roam around the city after dark. It was simply that Pearl couldn't sleep. She was probably pacing the stifling confines of her apartment, counting the steps. Or maybe bouncing off the walls. She'd always been like that, even when living with Quinn. He'd wake up at 3:00 A.M. and find her in the living room, eating potato chips and watching television news or an old movie. She was partial to the old Busby Berkeley musicals, where every time a dancer takes an initial step a thousand other dancers appear.

He was right about her being awake. She picked up halfway through the second ring.

"Watching an old movie?" Quinn asked.

"Quinn. What are you doing, spying on me with a telescope?"

"I would if I could see you from here."

"*Babes on Broadway*," she said.

"I'd spy on them, too."

"That's the movie I'm watching, *Babes on Broadway*."

"Mickey Rooney?"

"Not here."

"Don't wanna talk to him anyway," Quinn said. "Wanna talk to you."

"Talk."

"You should be in bed sleeping."

"Like you should. You didn't call me about sleeping."

"Being in bed, though . . ."

"Have a good reason for being on the line, Quinn, or I'm hanging up so I can watch the dancing."

He told her about Renz's visit and job offer.

"I'm still working at Sixth National," she said when he was finished. "They need me."

"Pearl, Sixth National Bank hasn't been held up since nineteen twenty-seven."

"Overdue."

"You can get a leave of absence."

"I know," she said. "That's our arrangement. It's just . . ."

"What?"

"You start these things, these murder cases, and they take over your life. You understand. I know you do. It's a strain on mind and body, Quinn. It becomes a goddamned obsession."

"There are good obsessions, Pearl."

"Are there? I can't think of any."

"All right," Quinn said, tired of arguing with her. "We're slaves to ourselves all the way to the grave."

"Slaves to something," Pearl said.

"You in?" Quinn asked.

She didn't answer right away. He could hear lively dance music in the background.

"Pearl?"

"I'm in," she said.

Slaves to something.

* * *

After the conversation with Pearl, Quinn decided not to call Fedderman until morning. Retirees went to bed early, didn't they?

Quinn decided they did and went to bed himself.

He had trouble falling asleep. Maybe Pearl was right about obsessions. The hunt wasn't only in his mind, though. It was in every cell of his being. It seemed a kind of destiny that he and whoever was on a killing spree should share a common struggle.

There was little doubt in Quinn's mind that there was a serial killer out there in the city, playing out the drama he'd chosen for himself, making Quinn a part of it. Quinn would be the part the killer would regret. Old juices were starting to flow again. The hunt was in body and blood.

"Locked in," Quinn actually muttered, and finally fell asleep.

7

In the morning, Quinn put Mr. Coffee to work so he could have his caffeine fix before walking over to the Lotus Diner for breakfast. He showered and shaved, then dressed and combed his hair. He noticed he needed a haircut but figured it could wait.

Feeling much more awake after a restless night, he carried the wireless phone into the kitchen and sat at the table with his coffee off to the side within easy reach. Nine thirty. Fedderman should be awake by now. Maybe he was even on the links, or out on the wide ocean casting for marlin. Or he might be sitting in some diner swapping lies with other retired cops. Stories that sounded like lies to anyone listening, anyway.

Fedderman answered his phone on the second ring and was no problem. No Pearl-like discourses out of Feds, the voice of pure practicality.

"So we got a new hobby," Fedderman said over the phone, when Quinn was done relating what Renz had said. That was one way police described a long-lasting serial killer investigation. "One that should keep us busy for a while. It gives me a reason for living so I don't ride a bullet outta here."

Quinn sampled his coffee. *Yeow!* Still too hot to drink. "Things that bad, Feds?"

"Naw, things are just things. Living alone at my age, not gainfully employed, stretching my pension money with coupons and early-bird specials. It's okay for some people, but not for me."

"There are plenty of people who lead active lives after retirement," Quinn said, but he knew exactly what Fedderman meant, how he felt. Quinn had the same feeling sometimes, woke up with it lying heavily enough on his body that it felt like one of those lead bibs dentists lay over your chest to protect against X-ray damage. It made it hard to breathe.

"I tried golf," Fedderman said, "tried fishing. Golf just makes you mad, fishing disappointed."

"Rich widows down there," Quinn reminded him.

"Widows looking for rich husbands," Fedderman said, "not for bloodstained ex-cops. They get a sniff of my past and don't want much to do with me."

"Jesus, I'm glad I called."

"Me, too, Quinn."

Quinn's mind flashed an image of Fedderman, balding, gangly, paunchy, able to make the most expensive suit look as if it had just been stripped off a wino. Not tempting widow bait, Fedderman.

I should talk.

"You and Pearl still on the outs?" Fedderman asked, as if reading Quinn's mind over the phone.

"Yeah. Pearl's got her own place, and she's still working that bank guard job at Sixth National."

"Job for guys in their eighties," Fedderman said. "Banks

don't get robbed anymore in ways a guard might prevent. Usually it's done by computer. Robber might never even see the inside of the place."

"Technology."

"Who the hell understands it, Quinn?"

"Everybody under thirty."

"Not us," Fedderman said.

Quinn took a cautious sip of his coffee. It was still almost hot enough to singe his tongue. Mr. Coffee needed some adjustment.

"You want me to fly up there?" Fedderman asked. "I can close down the condo, put my convertible in storage."

"You drive a convertible?"

"Uh-huh. Lot of guys around here do. Reliving their youth. Place down here sells new cars made in emerging nations at reasonable prices 'cause of the low labor costs. I got a red Sockoto Senior Special. Front seat swivels and kinda lifts you so you can get out easy."

That was disturbing to Quinn. "You're in your fifties, Feds. You don't need that kinda crap."

"Nice, though. Makes things easier. You're still a young man, Quinn, comparatively. You got it made with early retirement, but you'll find out how it is."

Early retirement, Quinn thought. *A false accusation of child molestation, then a bullet in the leg. Some way to retire.*

"Not that you haven't earned it," Fedderman said, reading Quinn's mind again. "You want me to fly up there?"

"Not yet. Renz is waiting for confirmation and for the media wolves to start howling in unison. Then he'll give us the go-ahead."

"Confirmation?"

"Officially there's no serial killer yet. Not enough definitive evidence to link the murders."

"From what you told me, he's out there."

"Renz still has hope there won't be another victim. Busy building his fool's paradise. You know how he is."

"So we sit back and wait for the next victim?"

"Not much else we can do," Quinn said.

"I guess not. And I'd like to be with Renz on this one, thinking there might not be a next victim, but I know better."

"We all do."

Quinn added some milk to his coffee and tested it. Cool enough now to be bearable. Coffee could be a trial to drink, but he liked to use the coffeemaker now and then just to fill the kitchen with the warm scent of fresh grounds.

"Aren't you gonna ask me what Renz is paying this time?" he asked.

"Screw the money," Fedderman said. "You know what I mean?"

"Sure. It's the game."

"I know Pearl feels the same way. That's why I always figured you two'd stay together."

"Fire and ice," Quinn said. "Sometimes it makes lots of smoke but not much in the way of flames."

"Long as there's embers," Fedderman said.

Quinn wondered if, in Pearl's heart, there were even embers.

Fedderman was quiet for a while; then he said, "Can you feel him out there, Quinn?"

He couldn't help it; there was a note of hope in his voice. Fedderman knew Quinn was notorious for splicing into the thought processes of the mad and dangerous men who killed over and over. Quinn understood them from their work, from the pain they caused and the pain they left behind. He could read their handiwork the way a hunter reads a spoor, and then set off in the right direction.

"Quinn?"

The voice on the phone was faint, as if Florida were drift-ing away from the rest of the continent.

"He's out there," Quinn said.

After hanging up the phone he sat and drank some more coffee. It was making him hungry.

8

Pearl sat on the park bench with her cell phone in her hand, wondering if she'd done the right thing. It wasn't the bank; she knew they'd take her back when the NYPD and Quinn cut her loose. It was Quinn himself. She was certainly over him, but did he know it? Would he act accordingly?

Had Pearl made a mistake? Should she phone Quinn and back out of her agreement to become a cop again, just for a while?

Questions. Too many of them. When they reached a certain critical number, Pearl usually decided to ignore them and charge blindly ahead.

This time was no exception. She slipped her cell phone back into her purse and settled back on the bench. It was on the edge of the park, facing the street, so there was lots of pedestrian traffic.

A compact, dark-haired woman with a kind of vibrancy even when sitting still, Pearl was drawing male stares. She ignored them.

Right now she didn't feel beautiful, and the hot sun beating down on her didn't help to improve her mood. A bead of perspiration trickled erratically down her back beneath her shirt and into the waistband of her jeans. She admitted to herself that she felt like crap. Usually she felt better after making up her mind, when there was no turning back. Not this time. She hoped it wasn't an omen.

She felt suddenly as if she were suffocating in the heat; she breathed in some exhaust fumes, and didn't feel much better. But the next few deep breaths moved her away from the edge of panic. Manhattan air—whatever its quality, she could live on the stuff. Millions of other people did.

A squirrel with a gnarly tail that looked as if it might have been run over by a tire ventured close to the bench, where someone had scattered some peanut shells. It began to gnaw at one of the larger fragments of shell, then hunched its tightly sprung body and was very still.

There was the slightest of sounds; then a shadow passed nearby, and the squirrel shot away from Pearl and into some trees.

Pearl looked upward and saw the hawk. Its speed, the way it wheeled on the wind and soared higher, took her breath away.

"Falcon!" she heard someone nearby say.

Pearl squinted as the ascending bird crossed the brilliance of the sun.

Like a lot of other New Yorkers, she'd read in the papers about how people would sit and watch peregrine falcons that nested high on skyscrapers as if they were mountain crags. Residents of the buildings sometimes wanted the falcons killed or captured because of the mess they made defecating on and around the entrances. And hailing a cab in front of the buildings could be dangerous for the doormen and their cleaning bills. Sometimes canvas sheets were mounted several stories high on the buildings as makeshift awnings to shield the sidewalk below, but these were only temporary measures.

Pearl had read that there were over a dozen known families of falcons in New York City. Also that they fed on smaller birds such as sparrows and pigeons. So maybe this falcon was only curious and the squirrel had nothing to fear. But then, squirrels must have something to fear always, as did most animals that were the natural prey of carnivores.

Several passersby had also seen the swooping falcon and were standing and peering skyward, shielding their eyes with their hands as if holding salutes. A man accompanied by a boy about ten stopped to see what people were looking at. The man pointed, grinning, while the boy stood with his head tilted back and his mouth open.

The falcon veered, spread its wings wide to brake to a near halt in midair, and found its perch out of sight high on a building.

"That was something," a voice said next to Pearl.

A fortyish man in a gray business suit had sat down next to her on the bench. He had a brown paper bag in one hand, almost certainly his lunch, and an unopened plastic water bottle in the other. His hairline had receded, and he'd dealt with it by affecting a tousled, forward-combed hairdo that made him look as if he'd just tumbled out of bed. On the hand holding the bottle was a wedding ring. He grinned at Pearl in a way not at all like a married man.

"Something," she agreed pleasantly, and got up and walked away without looking back.

The man said nothing behind her.

There were plenty of men in the city, but Pearl was particular. Maybe too particular.

For the time being she contented herself with living alone and infrequently going to select dating bars, looking, but not for anything serious.

Still, if the right guy happened along . . .

Pearl smiled at her own naïveté. Right guy, wrong guy, like lyrics in a musical. It was all so much more complicated than that. She supposed that was why musicals were popular.

She found a comfortable stride and began in earnest the

walk to her subway stop. In motion she drew even more admiring glances, but she ignored them.

There was a slight rushing sound on the edge of her consciousness, and a shadow flitted like a spirit alongside her on
the sidewalk, then was gone.

Pearl ignored that, too. She walked on, determined through
her apprehension, refusing to be intimidated by her doubts.

Lavern Neeson lay as if asleep and listened to the apartment door open and close. The sounds were distinct, a faint
grating noise as key meshed in lock, then the soft sigh of the
door sweep crossing carpet, another sigh as the door closed,
and the click of the latch. Last came the rattle of the chain
lock as her husband Hobbs fastened it, locking them in together. Lavern shivered beneath the thin sheet.

Hobbs clattered about in the bathroom for a few minutes.
She heard the seemingly endless trickle as he relieved himself, the flush of the toilet, the pinging and rush of water in
the building's old pipes. He seemed steady in his move-
ments; he wasn't drunk tonight. He wasn't drunk as often as
she liked to think. Alcohol would at least provide some excuse for what he did, and for her allowing it.

Not that she had any choice. Her options had been taken
from her one by one over the seven years of their marriage.

No, alcohol wasn't the problem.

Something she'd done? Had kept doing? There must be
some solid reason for the guilt that weighed her down. Guilt
needed at least some soil in which to grow.

My fault.

That wasn't what she concluded whenever she carefully
analyzed her dilemma, but it was always what she *felt,* and
that was what made her powerless. She couldn't let this continue, yet she couldn't stop it. Every time it happened she
was more helpless to prevent it. Hobbs used to discuss the
problem with her, seeming to listen very carefully to what

she was saying, but she knew now it had been a ruse while he manipulated her, neutralized her defenses one after another.

What's wrong with us?

She'd asked the question more than once. Kept asking it. Now Hobbs no longer even pretended to listen politely or care and consider.

Lavern knew now that he didn't have the answer. Or maybe he was as fearful of the answer as she was. Perhaps he feared merely the question.

Where is this taking us?

The bedroom light winked on, blinding her at first, so she clenched her eyes tightly closed and pressed her face into the pillow. She kept her eyes shut and didn't move.

Hobbs knew she was awake. He knew all her evasive tricks.

"Lavern?"

She sighed, opened her eyes, and sat up blinking in the light. She was an attractive woman with honey-blond hair and blue eyes. Her slender figure was shapely but without much of a bust. (Years ago she'd considered breast implants, and was glad now she hadn't gotten them. They'd be another vulnerability.) Her features were a bit too long to be beautiful, her lips full and not quite meeting because of a slight overbite Hobbs used to tell her was sexy. Her pink nightgown slid down one shoulder, almost exposing one breast that truly was the size of a teacup.

Hobbs loomed over her, all six feet of him; he was almost forty now but was still burly and hard from playing college football until he'd blown out his right knee. Still had the buzz cut that made his angular features seem as cruel as a Roman emperor's. That harshness of countenance was made even more extreme by the coldness in his eyes that were almost exactly the same shade of blue as his wife's. But while Lavern's eyes were soft and resigned, Hobbs's eyes were as hard and reflecting as diamonds.

Lavern hadn't known Hobbs in college, though she'd been aware of him. They'd met on First Avenue six years later when sharing a cab out of necessity during a downpour; they were two people unfortunate enough to be going the same way—though of course they'd both thought it lucky at the time. They had so much in common—or so she'd been led to believe—and at first the sex had been undeniably great.

The relationship *had* worked for a while. Long enough for them to marry with romantic feigned impetuousness, helped along by a night of hard drinking during a weekend in Las Vegas.

It was after the marriage that they came to know each other better. That was when the real Hobbs emerged. Or possibly he'd been there all along and Lavern had loved him too much to notice the signs.

He'd removed his shirt, but hadn't taken off his pants. She noticed the empty belt loops and knew he'd removed his leather belt. There it was in his right hand, dangling and doubled and portending pain.

What have I done now?

His voice was level, but still carried a quiet menace. "The towels, Lavern."

Her mind danced frantically. She had no idea what he was talking about. "What towels?"

"In the bathroom. I take a piss, wash my hands, and the goddamned towels are filthy. You didn't even hang them up straight. Damned things were bunched under the towel rack so they'd stay damp. That's how disease spreads, Lavern."

She was bewildered. He actually seemed serious.

"I'll go see," she said, and slid sideways to get out of bed.

The belt caught her in the ribs, but she didn't cry out. She knew better than to make noise. The neighbors mustn't be disturbed. The neighbors mustn't know.

She grunted with pain and bent low enough that her elbows rested on her knees.

"Stand up, Lavern. Take your medicine."

She knew then it wasn't really the towels that bothered Hobbs. It was his sickness, the thing inside his heart that made him hurt with a nameless rage that from time to time would be directed at her.

As she fought her agony and straightened her body, he surprised her by not using the belt. He used the flat of his hand instead, slapping her left cheek hard enough to spin her head so it felt as if it might snap from her spine. She tasted blood and saw a tiny red splatter on the dresser mirror all the way across the bedroom.

He gripped her by one arm and jerked her upright so she was standing straight again, as if teeing her up for another blow.

Violence came as easy to him as laughter. One of his friends had reminded Lavern that Hobbs had barely escaped being kicked out of college for almost killing another student with his fists in an argument over a movie. She vaguely remembered the incident, the talk on campus. He would have been expelled, only that was before he hurt his knee, and he could still bowl people over at football. Assault charges had been dropped, and the matter had been classified as an incident of boys being boys, when it should have been a clear warning.

Not that any of this was relevant to Lavern's present circumstances. She knew she wouldn't have heeded any warning. Not at that age. Not even when she was older. *Just Hobbs being Hobbs,* she had decided, along with the faculty. Like almost everyone else, she had excused him his youthful misbehavior. He *was* fun to watch on the football field. There was even talk of a possible pro contract. Lavern had wondered from time to time if there might be some way to meet him.

Then had come the knee injury, and soon thereafter she'd heard that he'd left school.

The mature Hobbs shoved her back into the bed and

wrestled her almost inert body around so she lay on her back.

Then he was on her, straddling her, his weight mashing her slight form into the mattress. His breath hissed in the quiet bedroom.

He began to beat her, not as hard as he could, but methodically, slapping, slapping, slapping. She let herself go limp and closed her eyes to the onslaught, closed her mind.

Finally he stopped.

He's going to kill me someday. He's going to kill somebody.

She felt his weight shift and heard the rasp of his zipper being undone.

At least the beating was over.

He's going to kill somebody.

9

Joseph Galin was conscious, but he wasn't thinking or seeing clearly. It had become a world without time or meaning. He had no memory of how he'd gotten where he was, sitting slouched and apparently in a car.

His car?

He couldn't move, and though there was no pain, there was an advancing numbness. It had begun with his feet, then his hands. Now he had no feeling at all in any of his extremities. He might as well have been floating like a balloon.

Galin could see out the windshield to the wide expanse of the car's hood, where a bird of some kind was walking around, pecking, maybe damaging the paint. And it was night out. Evening. Dark and getting darker. Way past dusk.

Then darkness fell completely, as if he were in a sealed room and someone had pulled down a shade. Odd. Strange also that he wasn't afraid. More curious. What the hell was happening?

Am I drunk?

He'd been on benders before and figured this wasn't one of them.

Some kind of stroke?

If I could only remember who I am . . .

He could smell leather and something that reminded him of dirty coins . . . pennies.

A penny for my thoughts . . .

He might have smiled.

The darkness was heavy on him, keeping him from opening his eyes now. Not that it made any difference. He heard himself let out a long breath. Heard the bird pecking on the car hood, still working even though it was so dark. He heard a car passing way out in the street, beyond the mouth of the alley.

Alley?

He began to remember and was afraid. His mind searched for light and found none.

The fear remained. Held on to him like a lost lover dying along with him.

Dying?

Without meaning to, he said loudly and in a clear voice, "Hawk."

The word meant nothing to him.

Then Galin saw nothing, became totally blind. He could no longer remember what he couldn't see. Could no longer smell the leather and tarnished copper or anything else, could hear nothing, feel nothing . . .

Nothing.

The phone chirping by the bed pulled Quinn out of deep sleep. His mouth and throat were dry. There was grit beneath his eyelids. He glanced at his watch to see the time. It was . . . dark. Why the hell didn't luminous hands work at the same brightness all the time?

He found the phone in the dark, lifted the receiver, and mashed it against his ear.

Damned chirping's stopped, anyway. Like a nattering bird.

"Quinn?"

Renz's voice. Great.

"Quinn," he confirmed. He reached out and switched on the reading lamp on the table alongside the bed. Saw the face of his watch. A few minutes past five o'clock.

"You were sleeping, right?" Renz said, as if he'd been asked to answer some kind of riddle.

"You guessed it. That why you called? To wake me up?"

"Yeah, but there's a deeper reason. Remember our conversation from a week ago?"

Quinn was almost all the way awake now. "I remember. We got another one?"

"'Fraid so. Remember Joe Galin?"

Quinn searched his memory. Found a stocky, gray-haired plainclothes cop with an easy smile that could turn hard. "Detective Joe Galin? Narcotics? Manhattan South?"

"The very one," Renz said.

"Galin's dead?"

"Or putting on a hell of an act."

Quinn was having difficulty processing this. "Our killer did a cop?"

"Sure did. Single small-caliber bullet to the head. Ex-cop, by the way. He was retired, like you."

"Like I was," Quinn said.

Despite the hour, Quinn phoned Pearl and Fedderman. Then he got dressed, went outside to where his car was parked, and in the glimmering dawn drove across town and over the Fifty-ninth Street Bridge into Queens.

It was a gray but bright morning when Quinn pulled the Lincoln to the curb and braked to a halt behind a parked radio car. There was another patrol car and what looked like an unmarked city car parked directly in front of a take-out pizza joint with PIZZA-RIO painted on its window. Beneath the name in smaller letters was *PIZZA WITH A SPANISH KICK.*

Might be good, Quinn thought, as he climbed out of the Lincoln. But not now. Not here. What he wanted was coffee. He knew he should have taken the time to swing by the Lotus Diner and get a go cup. It would have taken only a few more minutes. Several uniformed cops and two plainclothes detectives were standing around on the sidewalk in a circle. They were holding white foam cups, some of which had steam rising from them, and at least two were eating dough-nuts.

As Quinn walked toward the mouth of an alley where, ac-cording to Renz on the phone, the shooting had taken place, one of the plainclothes guys—the shorter of the two, with a gray buzz cut and a broad, florid face, spotted Quinn and walked toward him. He smiled. "Captain Quinn?"

Quinn nodded, noticing the man was holding two cups of coffee.

"I'm Detective Charlton Lewellyn. I've been with Com-missioner Renz on the phone. He said this one was yours." He held out one of the foam cups for Quinn to take, as if he'd been referring to it and not to what had happened in the alley.

Quinn accepted the cup, which had a white plastic lid on it to keep in the heat, and thanked Lewellyn. He sipped. Good coffee, cream, no sugar. Had Lewellyn checked with some-one to see how Quinn drank his coffee?

"I hope that's okay," Lewellyn said, as if he didn't want Quinn to think he was too clever.

Quinn took another sip. "Fine."

"We kept the scene frozen for you," Lewellyn said. He led the way toward the alley. The uniforms had moved away and taken up position to keep any passersby clear. One of them was seated in a radio car with the door hanging open, work-ing on some kind of form on a metal clipboard. The other plainclothes cop was standing nearby, as if the one filling out the form might need help. It occurred to Quinn that there wasn't much of a turnout here considering an ex-cop had been shot. But maybe that was Renz keeping a low profile. Or maybe Galin had been gone too long. About five years, Renz had said.

There was yellow crime scene tape strung across the mouth of the alley. Lewellyn lifted it high so Quinn could stoop and move beneath it, like a corner man helping a boxer into the ring.

A late-model red Buick was parked in the alley. Beyond it, Quinn saw three kids peering down the alley from the block at the opposite end. There was no crime scene tape, but there was at least one uniform posted there, keeping anyone from cutting through. He came into view and talked to the kids, and they all looked down the alley toward Quinn and hurriedly moved along.

As Quinn got closer to the car he saw a figure hunched over the steering wheel. "CSU been here?"

"Nobody," Lewellyn said. "We were keeping it fresh for you."

Quinn set his coffee cup on the ground out of the way, then got some crime scene gloves from a pocket and worked them onto his hands. He moved in closer to the Buick. All of the car's windows were up. The doors appeared to be unlocked.

"The engine and air conditioner were off," Lewellyn said.

"Ignition key in the off position?"

"Yes, sir. It wasn't all that hot last night. The victim might have sat a while with the windows up and still not gotten warm enough to lower them or turn the engine and AC back on."

"Or he might have just arrived and been about to get out of the car," Quinn said.

Lewellyn nodded.

"I like it your way, though," Quinn said, making friends. "He didn't park here in an alley for nothing."

Lewellyn nodded again, same way, same expression, not

giving away much or taking much. Quinn liked that about him.

Quinn leaned closer and peered into the lightly tinted front-side window, across the wide seat, at the dead man behind the steering wheel. He saw no sign of a bullet hole. The heavyset man with the wavy gray hair might have been taking a nap.

Not touching the car, Quinn moved around to the driver's side. Through the window he could see the dark bullet hole in Galin's temple.

Making as little contact with the handle as possible, he opened the door.

The wound looked nastier up close and without tinted glass filtering out the details.

"He wasn't wearing his seat belt," Lewellyn said. He'd moved in so he was standing just behind Quinn.

Quinn saw that that was true.

There was no sign of a gun, but they might still be looking at suicide. Then Quinn noticed the butt of what looked like a nine-millimeter handgun protruding from a belt holster beneath the victim's suit coat. The position of the holster, the way the gun butt was turned, indicated Galin was right handed.

Left temple wound. Small-caliber bullet. Not likely a suicide, even if the gun that fired the bullet was around, under the seat or something. And why would somebody serious about suicide favor a small-caliber weapon when he had a large-caliber one in his holster? If you really do go through with it and shoot yourself, you want to make sure.

Quinn noticed the right-hand jacket pocket in Galin's gray suit coat was turned inside out.

"No sign of a note," Lewellyn said.

"Sometimes they put them in the mail beforehand," Quinn said.

Lewellyn sipped his coffee, holding the cup with both

hands as if it were a cold morning instead of seventy degrees.

"You know him personally?" Quinn asked.

Lewellyn shook his head no. "He worked out of Manhattan. You?"

"Didn't exactly know him. I recall seeing him around. He was Narcotics. Worked undercover sometimes."

"Think that might have anything to do with him being shot?"

"It usually does," Quinn said. "But probably not this time."

"Guy walks some mean streets for years, then doesn't bother wearing his seat belt and something like this happens to him."

"Goes to show you," Quinn said, "but I'm not sure what."

Lewellyn silently sipped some more coffee, not knowing what, either.

Quinn wished he could help him, but couldn't.

10

Quinn wished he could take his eyes off Pearl.

He was behind his big cherrywood desk in his combination office and den. Pearl was slouched in the small armchair on the left, angled toward the desk. She was wearing a white blouse, black slacks, a gray blazer, and comfortable-looking black shoes with thick, slightly built-up heels. Not a sexy outfit, but she turned it into one. Her black hair was slightly mussed this morning, her full lips glossed a red that wasn't brilliant but looked so on her. Her dark eyes with the long dark lashes . . .

"Quinn, you concentrating?"

Fedderman's voice. Feds was seated in the large brown leather chair where Quinn often sat when he was alone and wanted to read.

"Concentrating," Quinn said.

Fedderman looked at him and shook his head slightly. He had antennae, did Feds.

"Something I'm missing?" Pearl asked.

"Not a chance," Fedderman said.

Pearl didn't answer. Gave him a look. Quinn could feel

the old chemistry returning to the team of detectives. There was tension here, almost all the time, but it tended to lead to results.

"What we have is a dead ex-cop," Quinn said.

"There's no such thing as an ex-cop," Fedderman said.

"Me," Pearl said. "From time to time."

"We still have a dead ex-cop," Quinn said. "For him, time's over." He looked at Fedderman. "You know Galin when he was on the job?"

"Knew of him," Fedderman said. He was wearing a gray suit like Galin's, only Galin's fit him better, even dead.

Gangly, paunchy Fedderman was one of those people who mystified tailors. Not that Fedderman ever went to one. He always looked as if he'd just shaken straw out of his sleeves and come from scaring away crows in a cornfield. His body parts didn't quite match, and nothing fit him well. Often one of his shirt cuffs was unbuttoned and flapping as he walked. Quinn wondered how that happened. It was usually after Fedderman had written something down. Quinn thought it might be because he dragged his hand a certain way when he used a pen or pencil and it worked the cuff button loose.

Fedderman ran his long, pianist's fingers through what was left of his light-colored hair. That seemed to remind him he was getting balder by the day. He lowered his hand and glanced at it as if he might find errant hair. "Galin was a guy kinda kept to himself," he said. "Seemed friendly enough, just . . . I dunno, private."

"I was in the two-oh doing a report a long time ago," Pearl said. "Galin walked past and pretended he'd pinched me on the ass. Made a big thing of it. It got him some laughs."

"Sure," Fedderman said.

"But he didn't really pinch you?" Quinn asked.

"I said he didn't."

"What'd you do?" Fedderman asked.

"Shoved him into a desk anyway. He had to wave his arms around to keep from falling. That got the biggest laugh. I heard the two-oh guys called him 'Windmill Galin' for a while after that."

"I take it you didn't like him," Quinn said.

Pearl shrugged. "He was no worse than most. They get kinda wild sometimes, the guys doing undercover. No way some of that shit doesn't rub off on you. You do that kinda work, you better have some . . ."

"Moral equilibrium," Fedderman suggested.

Pearl looked at him as if he were a lesser primate that had spoken. "That's exactly right, Feds. Good boy!"

She sat up straighter, making her large breasts strain the fabric of her white blouse. She clapped once, as if to suggest they return to business, then rubbed her hands together as if to warm them. "I guess we rule out suicide."

"No gun in the car," Quinn said, "other than the nine-millimeter in Galin's holster, and it hadn't been fired."

"Holster strap wasn't even unsnapped," Fedderman said. "Galin either knew who shot him, or he was taken completely by surprise."

"Our guy do this?" Pearl asked Quinn.

"I don't doubt it," Quinn said. "Nothing seems to have been stolen from Galin. His wallet had over ninety dollars in it and wasn't touched. He was still wearing his wristwatch."

"Piece of crap," Fedderman said. "Galin liked to shop down on Canal Street, buy imitation name-brand watches. His watch said Movado, but it was probably worth about ten bucks."

"Free to the shooter," Quinn said, "and he still left it." He leaned back in his desk chair, swiveled an inch or two this way and that. The chair's mechanism made a tiny squeak each time it moved clockwise. "That inside-out pocket in his suit coat. Something was snatched out of that pocket fast, probably after Galin was dead."

The desk phone jangled. The sudden noise made Fedderman jump. Pearl didn't move. Both detectives watched Quinn as he picked up the receiver, then said "yeah" six times and hung up.

"That was Renz," he said. "They got the slug out of Galin's head. Twenty-five caliber. Ballistics said it doesn't match either of the bullets removed from the two previous victims."

"It was a warm night," Fedderman said, "and with gas high as it is, it costs a bundle to sit in a parked car with the engine idling and the air conditioner running. Lots of retired cops live on the cheap. Galin might have been sitting there with his window down, taking what breeze there was, and the shooter just worked in close and shot him in the head."

"Then he raised the window?" Pearl said.

"Maybe. Before he died."

Quinn wasn't buying it, about the window. "More likely the shooter approached the car, yanked open the door, and shot him. Then slammed the door shut and left."

"More likely," Fedderman admitted. "But who the hell'd walk up on him and shoot him?"

"Somebody who knew how to move," Pearl said. "Galin spent time on the streets. It'd take somebody with skill to work in on him unseen and unheard, open his car door, and fire a bullet into his brain. The way the car was parked in that alley, the shooter couldn't have approached at much of an angle."

"Maybe he just walked up to the car," Fedderman said. "Maybe Galin went there to meet him and didn't suspect he was gonna get popped. Opened the door to get out of his car, then bang."

Pearl nodded. "We don't know what we're talking about. Not at this point. We're just wagging our jaws making noise."

"That's okay," Quinn said, "as long as we don't make up our minds about anything important yet."

"Galin's dead," Pearl said. "That's important."

"Not to him," Fedderman said. "Not anymore."

"He had a wife," Quinn said. "He was important to her. Still is."

"Maybe," Fedderman said.

"Either way," Quinn said, "we're gonna talk to her."

11

Her name was June.

Joe Galin's widow was in her forties and looked as if she'd had drastic cosmetic surgery done to her eyes. They were dark brown and slanted like a cat's, and would have been beautiful if she hadn't been sobbing most of the day. Though short, she had a high-fashion model's anorexic figure, and even wearing an oversized T-shirt, baggy brown shorts, and flip-flops, it was easy to imagine her strutting along a runway. The widow would have been stunning if she hadn't had a nose that appeared as though it belonged on a much larger face.

Do the nose next, Pearl thought, when she, Quinn, and Fedderman had introduced themselves. She took in the widow's eyes, the possibly collagened lips, the probably uplifted boobs, and wondered about June's priorities.

June invited them all the way into a surprisingly well-furnished and tastefully decorated home that was on a middle-class street of single-story houses with vinyl siding.

Quinn had noticed that the Galin home was the only

brick-fronted house on the block. He also was noticing the way Pearl was sizing up June, figuring that when the interview was over, Pearl would have something to say.

June offered them tea or coffee, and after the offer was declined motioned for them to sit. She sat down herself in a flower-patterned chair with wooden arms. Pearl took a more comfortable gray leather recliner, thinking it had probably been Joe Galin's favorite chair, the point from which he'd observed the narrowing world of the retired cop. Quinn and Fedderman remained standing.

"We're sorry for your loss, dear," Quinn began.

'Dear.' Starting with the phony Irish charm, Pearl thought. *So obvious.* But that was his talent, how he got people to confide in him. Pearl could see right through Quinn, and wondered why the suspects and witnesses he laid his phony bullshit on couldn't.

June didn't have a wadded tissue, but she nodded her thanks for his condolences and dabbed at her swollen eyes with a dainty knuckle. Pearl caught the flash of a gold wedding ring inlaid with tiny diamonds that might have been as phony as Quinn's charm, but maybe not.

"Did you know my husband?" June asked Quinn and Quinn only. He'd captured her full attention. They were players in the same drama; the others might join in if they so chose.

He nodded solemnly. "Oh, yes. You know how it is, dear, I'm sure. All of us on the job are brothers and sisters."

Siblings against crime. Pearl tried not to make a face. She caught Fedderman's eye. He looked quickly away. He was watching, analyzing, as she was.

The deal was, Quinn was going to handle the interview. Pearl and Fedderman were to make mental notes and, when it seemed wise, occasionally add momentum to the conversation, if any momentum developed. The object was to keep the talk flowing so at some point the tongue might get a little ahead of the brain. A prodding now and then from the sidelines could be very effective, as long as the subject of the questioning didn't realize he or she was being ganged up on.

"During the days leading up to his passing," Quinn said, "did your husband behave in any way unusual?"

June's tilted, tear-brimmed eyes suddenly appeared suspicious. Was this about screwing her out of Joe's death benefit?

"I mean," Quinn said, seeing the signs, "did he seem on guard, as if someone might be posing some kind of danger?"

"He'd been retired almost five years. After that much time, who'd be looking to get even for something he did on the job?"

"Somebody who'd been in prison five years," Fedderman suggested.

June thought and nodded. "I hadn't considered that."

"We're checking his old closed case files for just that kind of thing," Quinn said. "The work we do, the time we put in to keep this city safe . . . with a good cop like your husband, the years collect all sorts of things, including enemies."

"He put away a lot of bad types," Pearl said. "Unfortunately, not for life."

"Those people," June said, sniffling, "the ones he helped put away . . . Joe said they talk big sometimes, but they usually cool off during their time in prison."

"That's usually true," Quinn said. "And usually ex-cons don't shoot and kill ex-cops."

"Usually not," Fedderman said. "But sometimes."

"It could happen," Quinn said with a trace of reluctance, as if he really wished he could agree with June but had to acknowledge Fedderman's point.

June shrugged one bony shoulder and dabbed at her moist right eye with the back of a knuckle. "Joe didn't seem afraid. But then, he was never afraid of much."

"Isn't that the truth, dear," Quinn said. He made a fist with his right hand and ground it into his left. "A fine man like your husband. A good and true cop. And then some worth-less piece of—" He caught himself and forced a smile. "I'm sorry. It's just that all of us here, we bleed for a lost brother as you do for your lost husband. Your love." He crossed his arms and stood there like a compassionate figure climbed down from Mount Rushmore. "It's a fact there are all kinds of love. It's not too strong a word to use for the way many of us felt and still feel about Joe Galin. Your husband will be missed by a lot of people. Missed in all sorts of ways and for all sorts of reasons. The world is the worse for his leaving it."

June lowered her chin to her chest and began to sob.

Quinn went to her and gently patted her shoulder. "There, there, dear, I shouldn't have made you cry. But we so much want to find out what happened. If there's *anything* you could tell us . . ."

"Everything seemed normal," June insisted. "Joe was happy enough, even planning an elk-hunting trip with his buddies. They were going to drive up to Canada when the weather changed and elk were in season."

"Sounds great," Fedderman said. "You ever go with them?"

"Oh, no. It's a men's thing. I don't want to shoot any animal. Shoot any living being."

"Great to get out in the woods, though," Fedderman said. "Nature can be beautiful."

A slight smile glowed through the tears. "That's certainly true."

"I suppose you and your husband enjoyed nature together," Pearl said.

June seemed not to have heard her.

"If you can remember anything at all," Quinn urged, dragging June from the sylvan setting of her imagination and back to her agony.

Her body shook in another spasm of sobbing. Her nose began to drip uncontrollably.

Fedderman went to where a Kleenex box sat near a

cream-colored phone on a table and pulled several of the blossoming tissues from their slot. He presented the bulky and stemless white bouquet to the widow. June accepted it and began dabbing at her eyes and nose.

"Thanks so much," the widow told him, glancing up with reddened and grateful cat's eyes.

"Something like what happened to your husband," Fedderman said, "reminds us that we're all in this together." There was a catch in his voice.

Pearl observed all this and felt a stab of pride. *These guys are good. And I'm part of the team.* Just then, the idea of standing around in her gray uniform, hour after hour, in a walnut and marbled quiet bank lobby wasn't so appealing.

"He didn't seem exactly afraid," June muttered into the Kleenex between sniffles.

"Pardon me, dear?" Quinn sounded casual, even distracted, as if he might have misheard a remark about the weather.

"Not what I'd describe as afraid," June said, more clearly.

Quinn nodded his understanding. "But he must have felt something at least somewhat out of the ordinary. At least sometimes, or you wouldn't have brought it up."

"Yes," she admitted. "But—"

"What, then?" he asked gently.

"I don't know . . ." She sobbed some more, dabbed at her nose and eyes some more.

"Did he seem uneasy?" Quinn asked.

"No, not exactly."

"Anxious?" Fedderman suggested. "Did your husband seem anxious?"

The widow looked at him. "Well, yes . . . I suppose you *could* describe it that way. But 'uneasy' is more like it. Sometimes on a case he used to get like that."

There was something here. They could all sense it. Sitting there in Joe Galin's Barcalounger, Pearl was wondering how a guy like Galin would act if he were involved with another woman, having a hot affair. He might act suspiciously around his wife, even a guy his age, with his experience and the elbows and who knew what else he'd rubbed over the years. Retired narc in love. And secretly loving the danger. *Missing* the danger.

"Anxious how?" Fedderman asked.

"I didn't say—"

"Elated?" Pearl asked.

The widow's head snapped around. She'd known what Pearl was thinking, and had to admit she might be right.

"Elated," she said in a hoarse whisper. She'd almost strangled on the word. Then she made a face as if she didn't like its taste and was considering spitting it out. Instead, she swallowed.

Quinn moved closer and gently patted her shoulder. "It's all right, dear. You're with friends."

She gazed up at him with moist, surgically widened eyes. "If Joe was elated, it was about something he didn't share with me."

Pearl stared at her, feeling a strange pang of pity.

It isn't okay yet to hate your husband. Not with him so recently passed from this world of the living and still a resident of the morgue. It isn't allowed.

"Nervous," June said. She'd found a word, a concept, she could handle. "Yes, I suppose that's the best way to put it. The last week or so before his . . . his death, Joe seemed nervous. Not afraid, but nervous."

"Anxious," Fedderman said again.

She looked at him, defeated. "Anxious," she conceded.

Feds had worn her down.

Pearl showed a thin smile when the widow wasn't looking.

Elated.

Interesting.

12

Jerry Dunn remembered a time in London when he'd sat in his hotel room awaiting the arrival of a prostitute. It had felt something like this.

It wasn't morning then, as it was now. And he'd been sitting on the bed then, not in a chair as now. The chair was armless and uncomfortable, before a low wooden desk on which was a phone and a gold-embossed leather folder stuffed with flyers explaining the amenities at the Mayerling Hotel in Midtown Manhattan.

The Mayerling was almost plush enough to be called luxurious, with a vast blue-carpeted lobby and marbled steps leading to a long registration desk. Arranged about the lobby were half a dozen conversation groupings of high-quality cracked leather chairs and heavily grained wooden tables. The main elevators were almost invisible in a decorative wall of polished oak and veined marble. Beyond an array of potted plants was a discreet entrance to a lounge. Jerry had noted that the lounge also had a street door, so that you could enter or leave it without passing through the lobby. That was an important fact that Jerry logged in his memory.

Jerry had a good memory. A good mind. And he was damned good at writing advertising copy. He knew he looked like an average kind of guy—mid-forties, dark hair just beginning to thin, pleasant features, nice smile. Always up, was Jerry, at least on the outside. If they were casting him for movies he'd never be the leading man. He'd get the roles Tony Randall used to get, or Gig Young. Clean-cut, handsome guys, but not quite leading men. That was how Jerry figured people saw him, not quite ready for stardom, ever.

He glanced at his gold Rolex watch. It was an imitation Rolex with a quartz movement inside a gold-plated case. It didn't cost as much as a real Rolex, of course, but unless you examined it carefully it could pass for the real thing.

The real thing.

Is that was this is about? What I have to find out? Am I the real thing?

It was amazing. The heightening anticipation was almost the same as with the London prostitute. Heather had been her name. The name she'd used, anyway. She'd looked something like Sami, Jerry's wife. That had put Jerry off at first, but only at first.

He gazed out at the morning sunlight blasting through between the tall buildings across the street and making his eyes ache. It was still early. Sami would be back from driving the kids to school. Or maybe not. She might have stopped off somewhere, to pick up some groceries, or maybe to have a coffee at Starbucks with her friend Joan. Sami of suburbia.

Jerry made a soft, snorting sound. He shouldn't feel that way, he knew. He should like their life out in the burbs. He *did* like it. And where else were you going to raise kids? Not in this shitpot city. The things that happened here . . .

He laughed nervously. *You should talk.*

The room was cool enough, but he realized he was perspiring.

Damn that sun! They oughta tint those windows.

He stood up, walked over, and closed the heavy drapes

just enough to block the direct light. Then he sat down again at the desk and thought about Sami, putting her in Starbucks, seated at a table sipping a mocha latte, a medium one, or whatever Starbucks was calling medium these days. Maybe leisurely leafing through a newspaper, browsing for sales.

She thought he was at an advertising convention in Los Angeles. The convenient thing was that there actually *was* an advertising convention in that city at the time of Jerry's stay in New York, and his firm of Fleishman and Gilliam was represented. Mathers was there. The Beave would cover for him if Sami did happen to phone L.A. The Beave would tell Sami her husband was on a side trip with some reps, or off to some other place where he couldn't be reached. Sure, he'd tell Jerry to call her when he saw him. Might not be right away, though, since the convention hotel was overbooked and Jerry was at another hotel a few blocks away.

Jerry smiled. The Beave would think of something, and would know how to elaborate on his lie so it would be believable. Most of the other people from the firm would do the same. The guys, anyway. They were used to covering for ol' Jer'. They'd figure he was off on another of his sexual escapades and provide a good story for Sami, stay in tight with him. They knew Jerry might be called upon to do the same for them someday. Those advertising conventions were fuckfests. Some of them, anyway.

He looked again at his watch. It was almost time to leave the hotel.

He began to tremble.

Since he still had a few minutes, he went into the bathroom and emptied his bladder. He should have known better than to drink so much morning coffee.

He zipped up and then washed his hands, looking at his image in the mirror as he dried them. He forced himself to smile and said aloud to his image a line from a song in one of his favorite musicals.

"I believe in you."
His image tilted up its chin and smiled back.
I believe in you.
When he left the room, the trembling began again.

13

Pedestrian traffic was heavy and moving fast. Everyone on Manhattan Island seemed to walk fast. It amused Pearl sometimes to think that if everyone just kept walking fast the direction they were going, it wouldn't take long for all of them to reach the water. Then what would they do? Simply keep going like lemmings and all drown? Or mill about until the mood grew ugly and violence would ensue? The smokers would die first.

Pearl was irritated. Fedderman was supposed to have picked her up this morning in an unmarked and driven her to Quinn's apartment, where the three of them were to discuss developments and plan the day.

But Fedderman hadn't shown. Most likely he'd overslept, having drunk himself to sleep last night. Not that Pearl knew or had heard anything about Fedderman being in the bottle, but why wouldn't he be? Pearl figured that in his place she'd probably become an alky herself, living a solitary life in some ten-by-ten condo in Florida, going outside now and then so the sun could bake your brain.

Different strokes . . .

She wished she could stroke Fedderman with a baseball bat.

Pearl had taken the subway uptown, and was now walking the remaining few blocks to Quinn's apartment. It was a hot morning. The sun seemed to burn with an extra fierceness and cast long, stark shadows that emphasized angles. Traffic gleamed like multicolored gems strung along streets. Bagged trash was still piled curbside. Some of the plastic bags had burst or been cut open to get to the contents. New York could smell sweet and rotten on a morning like this.

She was standing with half a dozen other people waiting for a traffic light to change, everyone starting to perspire like her in the building morning heat, when her cell phone played its four solemn notes from the old *Dragnet* TV show. She fished it from her pocket and answered it a second before checking caller ID to see who was on the other end of the connection.

She was a second too late. She'd expected Quinn, wondering where she was and what was keeping her. Instead she saw letters spelling out Sunset Assisted Living. Pearl's mother was calling from her modest but specially equipped apartment.

"Milton Kahn says you have something on your neck," her mother said, without preamble. "Just behind your ear."

Pearl wasn't surprised. It was the way her mother often began phone conversations.

"I've got Milton Kahn on my back," Pearl said, about the former lover she was trying to shed.

"He cares deeply about you, dear."

"Mom, we tried. We're simply not compatible. It wasn't a take. *Kaput!* It's over."

"What are you trying to tell me, Pearl?"

"That I'm at work and don't have time to talk."

"Even about your future, God willing that you have one."

Huh? "What's that supposed to mean?"

"The thing on your neck, Pearl—Milton Kahn says it might be serious, and he of all people should know, the necks he looks at. Not that it's critical now, but such things should be kept in check, dear, through regular visits to your doctor."

"In this case my doctor would be Milton," Pearl said. She knew the game. Milton Kahn was a dermatologist. He and Pearl had been the object of a matchmaking maneuver involving Milton's aunt, also a resident of Sunset Assisted Living, and Pearl's mother.

"Milton and I had a fling," Pearl said, "that's all. It can never be anything more."

"Fling, schming," her mother said.

"Almost all schming," Pearl said, not even knowing what she meant.

Actually Pearl had enjoyed their brief, exploratory affair, but Milton Kahn could never be the steady lover of a cop, much less the husband that his aunt and Pearl's mother envisioned. Pearl had broken off the affair. Milton didn't want it to stay broken. Now he was apparently plotting to get Pearl concerned about what appeared to be a simple brown mole on her neck, just behind her right ear. The last time they'd seen each other, at a mutual friend's daughter's bat mitzvah, he'd brought the mole to her attention, feigning what she now knew to be great concern. The tiny mole had been there—well, she didn't know how long. How often does anyone look behind his or her right ear? Knowing her medical insurance was scant, Milton was hoping to lure her to his office and place her under his care, then under him.

Pearl smiled as the light changed and she stepped down off the curb to follow the herd across the intersection. Dr. Milton Kahn only thought he was devious.

"Pearl?"

"I'm here, Mom. The mole on my neck hasn't killed me yet."

"Of these things you shouldn't joke, Pearl. Mrs. Edna Langstrom—I don't think you ever met her—didn't have the chance, poor thing. She was a resident here in the nursing home—"

"Assisted living," Pearl reminded her.

"Assisted hell, is what. But she was a resident like me, and she had this reddish rash on her neck, not far from where Milton says your mole is, and she tried to alert the medical staff here, but naturally they were too busy to pay attention—or so they claimed, though I often see them in their lounge drinking coffee—and the rash became larger and started to itch, and before dinner one night—pot roast night, your favorite—she fell over dead."

"From the rash?"

"From a car backing up the driveway to let out Mrs. Lois Grahamson, another resident. The car was driven by her grandson Evan, poor man."

"A car killed Mrs. Langstrom?"

"While she was distracted scratching her rash."

"The point being?"

"That you should be careful, Pearl. Take precautions, such as seeing your doctor."

"My doctor being Milton Kahn."

"He's a dermatologist, Pearl. You could do worse if you had a rash. You could do worse in many other respects."

"I don't have a rash."

"A mole could become a rash, or worse, if you don't take—"

"Mom, Milton Kahn tried and tried hard. He doesn't do anything to scratch my itch."

"Pearl!"

"He and I aren't a match. We made an effort. It wasn't a bad idea. It simply didn't work."

"Milton thinks it might yet."

"Milton is wrong."

"But you will do something about your rash."

"I don't have a rash."

"Yet."

"I've got to hang up now, Mom. Crime calls."

"Don't joke about your health, Pearl."

"You're breaking up, Mom."

"Nothing is funny."

Pearl held the phone away from her head, but didn't raise her voice. "Mom, you're brea . . ."

She broke the connection, figuring her mother had it wrong. It was Pearl's *mental* health that concerned Pearl. She expected and even thrived on the pressure of the job she'd taken on, but she didn't like the additional pressure applied by her mother, and now by Milton Kahn. He had a nerve, trying to use her mother so he could get back into her pants. Pearl's pants.

Pearl realized she was on Quinn's block. She made herself slow down. She'd been walking faster and faster as she talked on the phone, taking long strides for such a short woman. Now her heart was pounding away, and she was slightly out of breath. Unconsciously, she raised her right hand to her neck as she walked, tracing the area of the mole with her fingertips. The mole was there, all right. She could barely feel it.

She put it out of her mind.

"Traffic," Fedderman said, seated in his usual chair in Quinn's den, enjoying a cup of coffee.

"That's why you didn't come by my apartment and pick me up?" Pearl said. "You were caught in traffic?" She'd been about to sit down, but continued standing, as if considering springing at Fedderman. "You could have called."

"I tried," Fedderman said. "Got the machine at your place. You must have already given up on me and left. I couldn't get through on your cell, either. You oughta keep the line clear when you know somebody might be trying to reach you."

Pearl glared at him, then sat down and seethed.

"Something wrong, Pearl?" Quinn asked from behind his desk.

Pearl didn't look at him. "My mother."

"She okay?" Quinn asked in a concerned voice, misunderstanding.

"She is. I'm not."

"Oh." Quinn knew about the relationship between Pearl and her mother. "Why don't you go into the kitchen and pour yourself a cup of coffee? It'll help you calm down."

Now Pearl aimed her laser look at him. "Coffee does that? Calms you down?"

Fedderman was grinning. He held up his own cup, and then held out his free hand to demonstrate its steadiness.

"If you don't want a cup, then we'll get down to business," Quinn said in a voice that Pearl knew. His warning voice. She could take her bad mood further and risk serious confrontation, or she could back off. He shot a look at Fedderman, too, causing the grin to fade. "Either one of you seen the papers this morning?"

"Haven't had time," Pearl said. "Had to subway and walk all the damned way over here."

Quinn stared at the folded newspapers on his desk, as if the sight of Pearl might be too much for him. "Feds?"

"Haven't seen them, either. Had to drive, fight traffic, call on the cell phone," Fedderman explained, looking at Pearl.

"What you can do with your cell phone—"

"Did you say hello to your mother for me?" Quinn interrupted. That was his calm-but-about-to-explode tone.

Pearl seemed to adjust herself to a calmer setting. "I always do," she lied.

Quinn looked at her, regretting that she was so damned beautiful when she got her ire up. Seeing her that way reminded him of what he'd lost.

"Okay," he said, and opened the top paper, the *Post,* and held it up so the headline showed: .25-CALIBER KILLER STALKS CITY. Then Quinn held up the *Times* to demonstrate the same news in a less sensational fashion.

"Leaky NYPD," Pearl said.

"It didn't take the media long to give our guy a moniker," Fedderman said. "Next we'll see an artist's depiction of the killer, even though nobody's seen him."

"The artist will be working off Helen Iman's description," Quinn said. Helen was the police profiler he knew would sooner or later be in on the case. While he wasn't a fan of profilers, in truth he had to admit that Helen might be an exception.

"So the media shit storm Renz feared is on us," Fedderman said. "What now?"

"We drive over and look at 149 West Seventy-ninth Street," Quinn said.

"What's that?" Pearl asked.

"The city-paid-for office space Renz promised us." He stood up from behind his desk. "We ready?"

"Ready for anything," Fedderman said. He gulped down the remainder of his coffee and put cup and saucer aside.

"I already put the murder books and notes in a box in the trunk of my car," Quinn said. "We can drive it over, come back for the unmarked later if we need it. Parking's hell in that part of town."

Pearl and Fedderman stood up. Pearl wished they could stop somewhere so she could get a cup of coffee, but decided against mentioning it.

They moved toward the living room and the door.

"I always liked your mother," Fedderman said as they were leaving. "The few times we met, she seemed like a real lady."

"She mentioned to me she hated your guts," Pearl said.

She didn't look at Fedderman as they went outside into the heat. There was no doubt in her mind the bastard would be smiling.

Quinn, she noticed, had both newspapers folded under his arm. He was irked, but at the same time oddly energized by the sharper focus of the media and the name they'd attached to the murderer. The .25-Caliber Killer.

Name something and make it real. Make it more threatening.

The dial had been turned up. The pressure increased.

It was the kind of pressure Quinn feasted on.

14

Quinn was having difficulty concentrating on his driving. Having Pearl so near him in the car was affecting him more than he'd imagined.

He understood why she felt the way she did about her mother, but Quinn rather liked the woman. She could be a pest, insistent and insufferable, but she had her finer points. Would Pearl be like her when she grew older? Maybe. Would Quinn still love Pearl? Probably. Simply being so near to Pearl, smelling the subtle combination of her soap and shampoo, being aware of the energy that seemed to emanate from her compact and curvaceous form, made him understand that he would never really get over her. That didn't mean they'd ever be able to coexist as lovers, but he'd always feel something for her. As for Pearl, it seemed to Quinn that she'd completely gotten over him. He wondered if he could do anything about that.

"You missed your turn," Fedderman said from the backseat.

His thoughts interrupted, Quinn glanced over and saw that he'd passed West Seventy-ninth Street.

"Woolgathering?" Pearl asked.

"Whatever that means," Quinn said.

He drove around the block and parked by a fireplug in front of the building where Renz had found them city-provided office space.

The three detectives climbed out of the Lincoln and stood in the heat, looking up at the three-story brick and stone structure. The windows on the top two floors were boarded up. The first-floor windows had aluminum frames and looked new.

"Renz said the place used to be a meth lab," Quinn said. "There was an explosion on the second floor that damaged a lot of the building, including the third floor and the roof. First floor's okay, Renz says. That's us."

Pearl shook her head. "You gotta admire the way Renz keeps finding us cheaper and cheaper space in a city like New York."

"The city actually owns this building," Quinn said. "It was confiscated from the perps running the meth lab."

They went up half a dozen worn concrete steps and entered the vestibule. Lots of cracked gray tile there, and a bank of tarnished brass mailboxes. Also some black spray graffiti that was illegible but might have been some kind of gang code none of them knew. It was hard to keep up with the city's gangs. For some of them, graffiti was their lives.

Pearl wrinkled her nose. "Jesus! You smell that?"

Fedderman and Quinn sniffed. There was a slight but acrid scent in the still, warm air.

"I told you," Quinn said, "it used to be a meth lab. There was what Renz called a minor explosion."

"Smells like it might explode again," Pearl said.

They went up another short flight of stairs to the first-floor apartments, one on each side. Quinn tried the door on 1B and found it unlocked. He opened it to see a spacious apartment stripped down to lathing and wooden studs. The bare wood floor was littered with trash, and raw lumber was stacked high in the middle of what must once have been a living room. Several wooden sawhorses and a stack of metal folding chairs stood along the far wall.

"Tell me this isn't for us," Pearl said.

Quinn was thinking the same thing. He crossed the hall, tried the door to 1A , and found it unlocked.

It opened to an apartment whose interior walls had been removed except for the kitchen and bathroom. It was one large space, in need of paint to cover the grimy raw wallboard. There were unpainted vertical strips of rough concrete where interior walls had been detached. From inside the spacious room, the new windows appeared dirty and streaked. Some of them still had triangular blue stickers in their upper right corners with the name of the manufacturer. The acrid burnt wood and meth odor had permeated here, too.

"This is more like it," Quinn said dryly.

Along one wall were three gray steel desks with identical swivel chairs sitting on top of them. Two dented three-drawer black file cabinets sat nearby. Also on each desk was a computer. Lettering on cardboard boxes alongside the desks indicated they were from a used electronics shop in Times Square. Renz doing it on the cheap.

They pushed all the way inside.

"Busy, busy," Pearl said.

She was talking about the four people in work clothes, three men and a woman, scurrying about with tools and ladders. They ignored the three detectives, concentrating on running wires across the scarred wood floor and taping them tightly so no one would trip over them. The woman, young and wearing a Red Sox cap with her blond ponytail flouncing out the back above the plastic size-adjustment band, was up on an aluminum stepladder with both arms above her head, fiddling with a light fixture.

One of the workers, a handsome guy with lots of curly black hair and a serious cast to his eyes, stood up from where he'd been applying duct tape to run wiring and looked inquisitively at the three detectives.

"Help you?" he asked.

"That's what you were doing when we came in," Quinn said. He explained who they were.

"I'm Rusty," said the man with coal black hair. "We got another four hours' work here, then the place is all yours. Gotta finish running wiring to where the desks are gonna sit, then put in some ceiling fixtures. It'll all be crude, but it'll work and keep working."

"Like us," Fedderman said.

"We were told it's all temporary."

"Like us," Fedderman said again.

"You gonna set up the computers?" Pearl asked, thinking she might use her laptop.

Rusty shook his head no. "Somebody from the NYPD's gonna do all that, fix you up with Internet access, printer, fax machine, whatever. We're supposed to let him know when we're done here."

"It always smell like this?" Pearl asked.

Rusty looked confused. "Like what?"

"Never mind," Pearl said.

Rusty grinned. "Hope it isn't me."

"Not unless you're flammable."

His grin widened. "You never know, but there are ways to find out."

"You don't flirt with a cop," Pearl said. "You'll get run over so flat you'll never get back up."

Rusty looked surprised, then thoughtful. Then he nodded.

"We'll check back this afternoon," Quinn told him.

"But she won't have changed her mind," Fedderman told Rusty, as they were leaving.

Rusty, a fast learner, said nothing.

Quinn drove them to Pizza Rio in Queens, next to where Galin's body had been discovered in his parked car. Then he assigned Pearl and Fedderman to check with people in nearby buildings to find out if anyone had seen or heard anything unusual the night of the murder—in particular the sound of a shot. Much of this was double-checking, as they'd already read the responding officers' reports. But that was what police work was all about—double-, triple-checking. Then checking again.

Quinn went inside the pizza joint to see if whoever was in there had been working last night.

It was a small take-out place that smelled great. Quinn thought he might actually be able to reach out and feel the spicy garlic scent wafting from the ovens. There were only three small tables with chairs. They were more for people waiting for carryout orders than for sitting and enjoying a meal. One employee was working behind the counter, a young black guy in his twenties. He was bone thin and had a soul patch growing under his lower lip and a silver Maltese cross dangling from his left ear. He was wearing a stained white apron to protect a stained white shirt. He grinned hugely at Quinn with stained white teeth. The plastic name tag on his shirt said he was Mickey.

"Help you?" he asked.

"Second time today," Quinn said.

"Help you?" Mickey said louder, thinking Quinn hadn't heard him over the deafening rap music booming from the kitchen: *"Kill the bitch, do the snitch, got the itch, don' matter which . . ."*

Quinn smiled back and flashed his shield. "Turn that crap off."

Mickey looked injured, disappeared into the kitchen, then returned. The abrupt silence seemed to reverberate with a decibel life of its own. "You don't like rap?"

"Good rap's okay," Quinn said.

"Such as what?"

"Second offense, twenty to life."

"Never heard of 'em. They new artists?"

Quinn ignored the question, since he was here to ask, not answer. "Were you working here last night?"

"Sure was, but I don't know nothin' about that cop got hisself shot."

"How do you know he didn't shoot himself?"

Mickey shrugged so elaborately it might have been a dance step. "Now you speak of it, I don't. Did he?"

"What?"

"Shoot hisself?"

"How late did you work?"

"Came in at eight, worked till twelve. Do that five evenin's a week. Go to school durin' the day."

"College?"

"New York University. Gonna make it big in the music industry."

"You perform?"

"Plan to, in court. Gonna be an entertainment attorney. Represent lots of celebrities. Wear loud ties. Maybe get on TV in one of them little squares on talk shows."

It occurred to Quinn that Mickey might be putting him on. "So tell me how it went the night of the shooting."

Mickey did his little dance shrug again. "Been sayin' an' sayin', I was workin' the phone-in orders as usual, passin' 'em on to the delivery guys, when I noticed some commotion outside."

"Commotion?"

"People standin' around talkin'. Some of 'em pointin' toward the side of the building. Boss man wasn't here, so I figured I was in charge. Went out, seen this guy sittin' in his car parked in the alley. Walked closer an' seen how he was slumped over. Went to talk to him through his window and seen the window was up. Then I looked in closer, through the windshield, and saw he was dead."

"Shot?"

"Didn't seem so at the time. But I seen dead before, an' I knew he wasn't jus' nappin'."

"Where've you seen dead?"

"Iraq. Fourth Infantry."

"Good enough. You touch the car?"

"Naw. I watch TV an' know better'n to mess with no possible crime scene."

"You ever seen the victim before?"

"Naw. He wasn't no customer that I know of."

Quinn watched Mickey's face carefully. No change. He figured he was getting the truth here. "You didn't call the police."

"No reason," Mickey said. "I could see that some citizen with a cell phone already done that. I came back in here an' took some pizza orders, is what I did."

"You did right," Quinn said. "One thing, though: you said you were here when that cop got himself shot. He was an ex-cop. How'd you know that?"

"Tha's two things."

"I guess it is, technically. You got two answers?"

"Yeah. One: I read about it in the papers, seen TV news. Two: ain't really no such thing as an ex-cop."

Quinn chuckled down low in his throat. Mickey looked alarmed, not quite sure what he'd heard was laughter.

"True enough," Quinn said.

He talked with Mickey a while longer, making sure his story correlated with his earlier statement, then went outside, where it wasn't quite as warm as inside but didn't smell as good.

A couple of Hispanic teenagers were hanging around a bike rack at the opposite side of the building from where Galin's body was found. The bikes chained to the rack were beaten up, looked identical, and had oversized wire baskets attached behind their seats. Quinn realized the teenagers were waiting for instructions from Mickey, addresses where they should deliver pizzas.

"Either of you guys working last night?" Quinn asked.

"Depends if you're a cop," said the shorter of the two. He grinned and bounced around as he talked, in a way that suggested he had to do it. Lots of energy. Might have been on batteries.

Both boys wore baggy and low-slung gangbanger pants, but this one had what looked like a dirty athletic bandage around his right ankle, holding the voluminous pants leg in tight so it wouldn't snag in the bike's chain. The other boy said nothing. He was as tall as Quinn, wearing filthy jeans, a wifebeater shirt, and a sensitive, somber expression. He had coiled snakes tattooed on both skinny arms. Quinn didn't think he'd want either of these characters delivering his pizza.

"I'm a cop," Quinn said, "but nobody's in trouble here unless you guys shot someone."

"You mean *ever* shot someone?" the grinner asked. Then he bobbed around some more. "Jus' jokin', officer." He had a Spanish accent he laid on heavily to project a certain pride that came across as arrogance. Quinn understood it and didn't care.

"You see what happened here last night?"

"Guy gettin' shot? Never seen it happen. Or even heard it. I came back from makin' a delivery an' there was this buncha people." He put his hands on his hips and struck a mock indignant pose. "I tol' another officer all this."

"That's okay." Quinn looked at the taller boy, thinking he resembled the old movie actor Sal Mineo. "How about you?"

"I left right before the guy was found. What I know's what I seen in the papers next mornin'." His accent was lighter, or maybe he just wasn't hiding behind it so much.

"See the victim's photo?"

"Sure. Front page."

"Ever see him before?"

"No. I don't think he was from around here." Quinn saw something change in the liquid dark eyes. Only for an instant, but it had been there. *He's lying. He knows something.*

"Dead guy used to be a cop, right?" the short boy with the attitude said, possibly trying to change the subject, protect his friend.

"Used to be," Quinn said.

Both boys nodded, maybe sadly, probably too young to be pondering their own mortality. Again, something came over the tall one's handsome features.

Quinn took both boys' names. The short one was Jose Meayna. Sal Mineo's name was Jorge Valento.

"Anyone ever mention you look like Sal Mineo?" Quinn asked Jorge. *See if he lies again.*

"My mother. She's dead now."

No change of expression. Sal Mineo on Novocain.

Quinn peered more closely at Jorge's arms. "Nice tats. Look like real snakes."

"Thanks."

Quinn didn't mention the needle tracks that had nothing to do with tattoos. Possibly the snakes were there to disguise them.

He said good-bye to the boys, figuring he'd talk with Jorge again when they could be alone. Maybe the boy had simply been lying because he was talking to the police. In this kind of neighborhood, lots of people lied to the police.

But Quinn didn't think that was it. Jorge knew something, and sooner or later Quinn would know it.

This was a homicide investigation. Eventually and in myriad ways, everything would become known.

Everything.

15

Hettie liked bars at night.

She particularly liked the bar at Chico's, a tiny restaurant on West Forty-sixth Street that was handy for the theater crowd. It was dim yet bright enough to show off her good skin and strong bone structure. And every now and then somebody from one of the Broadway or near-Broadway shows wandered in.

Not that Hettie hadn't already been discovered, just not by the theater world. Since moving to New York, she'd had small speaking parts in half a dozen TV series, and was the voice of Dubba the Mermaid on a Saturday morning cartoon show that had lasted five weeks three years ago but was still in re-runs. She wished adults would watch things over and over the way kids did. It was simplistic things that sold to kids again and again, and it didn't necessarily have to be quality stuff.

She wasn't knocking Dubba. Maybe it was her part in that show that had landed her the detergent products commercial spot she was scheduled to shoot next week, wearing the skimpiest of bikinis.

Good clean work, she thought, like she'd promised her mother back in Idaho.

From the potato state or not, Hettie had a kind of wicked sexiness about her. She was five-ten and slender but curvaceous, and had those much sought and envied finely chiseled features with high cheekbones, bright dark eyes, and a full-lipped wide mouth that easily slipped into an arc of disdain even when she was thinking nice thoughts. She knew that men read all sorts of things into her, most of them carnal. That was fine. It meant she could play almost any role that came her way, from Gidget to black widow killer. Trouble was, not enough roles were coming her way.

So here she sat sipping a Cosmopolitan, having just come from an acting lesson, when she should be standing on a Broadway stage.

A guy down the bar gave her the look. Average height and weight, maybe well built inside the expensive blue suit. Wearing a white shirt and red and black tie with the knot slightly loosened as a concession to the heat outside. He was handsome enough to be an actor, with his thick black hair and symmetrical features. And just sitting there, he had a way about him. The kind of guy who seemed intelligent, viewed life with cynical humor, and took no shit. The kind of guy looking for a one-night romp but maybe more.

Hettie shifted on her bar stool and crossed her legs so her skirt hiked up another inch or so, putting on a leg show while sipping her Cosmo and studiously ignoring the guy.

He caught her eye in the back bar mirror and somehow gave her a smile without rearranging his features. Neat trick. Movie close-up stuff. He knew how to underplay, so maybe he *was* an actor.

She watched him in the mirror as he slid down off his stool and moved toward her with a casual grace, idly spinning empty bar stools as he advanced. He got up smoothly onto the stool next to her. It was almost as if they'd been playing some kind of game with the stools and now it was his turn on that stool.

That was when Hettie pretended to first notice him, but she held her silence. Whoever spoke first would be initiating the pickup, if that's where this was going.

"What are *you* doing here?" he asked, as if he knew her and was mildly surprised to have come across her tonight.

"Drinking."

He glanced at an oversized gold watch peeking from beneath his white shirt cuff. "You belong a few blocks downtown," he said, "acting, singing, or dancing on stage."

Amazing! Is he a mind reader?

She gave him a smile, trying to keep it low key as he had in the mirror. "Nobody's where they're supposed to be."

"Charles Manson."

"No," she said, "he should be in hell."

"Your point." He'd brought his drink with him. Looked like scotch rocks. He took a sip. "Really, if you aren't an actress, you should be."

"You say that to all the women you try to pick up?"

"Pretty much so."

She laughed. Couldn't help the way it just bubbled out of her. There was something about this guy. The word *disarming* came to mind.

He cocked his head to the side as if to examine her more closely to satisfy his curiosity. "But with you it's the truth, right? You really *are* an actress."

"Well, yeah." *Like half the women in this place.* "But I'm between roles right now. Except for a TV commercial shoot coming up. I'm gonna be in a bathtub full of detergent packages and bottles."

He grinned. "I can visualize that." Another sip of scotch, though now she noticed it smelled like bourbon. Another smile. *Handsome guy.* "Then you actually are in show business," he said.

"Sure am." The Cosmo was making her a little light-headed. Overconfident. And in this kind of game it was okay to exaggerate a bit. She decided to let herself go a little and find out where it might lead. "I've done quite a lot of TV work."

"Really? I'm impressed."

"You don't seem *that* impressed."

"What's your name?" he asked. "Let's see if I've heard of you."

"Hettie Davis."

He pretended to think. "It really does sound familiar. Especially to a guy who likes old movies."

"That's the idea," she said. "And it's better than my real name, Angela Obermeir."

He gave a little shrug without shrugging. *You're the one who should be an actor.*

"Oh, I dunno," he said. "They're both kind of glamorous names."

She smiled.

"For a woman with a glamorous smile," he added, leaning toward her. "I don't mean to sound flip, or too much like I'm some lounge lizard who does this all the time. Truth is, I looked at you and something clicked."

"Now, that's not very original."

"Well, I warned you. I'm not good at this. You know what I worry about now?"

"What's that?"

"That I might work this kind of shallow chatter too hard because I don't know how to really get through to you." He toyed with his glass, regarding the amber liquid. "That I might lose you when I've just found you."

"Kind of like yanking too hard on a fishing pole and breaking the line?"

"Kind of like," he admitted. He aimed those dark and deep eyes at her, at the center darker than her own. Becoming darker the longer she looked into them. "I'm trying to be honest with you, Hettie. I'd be dishonest if I thought it would help my cause."

"I like a little dishonesty now and then."

"Sure. But only now and then." He seemed absolutely serious.

"The object of your game," she said, "is for us to leave here together and go to your place or mine."

"Or to a hotel." He rotated slightly on his stool so he was facing her. "Listen, Hettie, half the men in here—no, more than half—would gladly cut off any appendage but one if they could leave here with you."

"I'm not crazy about hotels," she said.

"Neither am I."

She was liking this guy more and more. And the way he could look deep into you . . .

She had to think about this, but she was already 90 percent sure of her conclusion.

He must not have liked the way the conversation was flagging.

"Maybe I've seen you on TV or somewhere," he said. "What have you been in?"

She placed both elbows on the bar and leaned toward him and to the side, so their heads were almost touching and she could speak softly and directly.

"Ever heard of Dubba the Mermaid?"

"I might have," he said. "Refresh my memory."

Hettie smiled at him.

Maybe tomorrow when we wake up.

16

"Good thing the car's black," Fedderman said.

The weeks-long assault of hot weather was having its effect on the pavement. Fresh blacktop from where an early morning street crew had just patched a pothole spotted the windshield when it was thrown up from the tires of the truck ahead of Quinn's Lincoln. Quinn used the windshield squirts and wipers and got most of it off without leaving too much of a mess on the glass.

"They've got chemicals that'll take tar off," Quinn said. He wasn't worried about the car right now.

They were driving to a diner on First Avenue to talk to Vance Holstetter, a homicide detective who'd been Joe Galin's partner until shortly before Galin retired. Pearl wasn't in the car. She had listened to Quinn's account of his conversations at Pizza Rio and asked if she could go take a run at the two delivery riders, especially Jorge, the one Quinn thought might know something.

Quinn had figured there was nothing to lose, so he'd told her to take the unmarked and go. Pearl had a way with young guys sometimes, knew how they thought and how to manipulate them. He wondered if she'd grown up with brothers. He really didn't know much about her early life. Maybe he could ask her mother.

His cell phone chirped, and he drew it from his pocket and squinted at it cradled in his palm.

Renz calling.

He raised the phone to his ear. "Hello, Harley."

"Quinn, where are you?"

"Driving to meet Galin's old partner, Vance Holstetter."

"Something you should know: The lab's blood pattern guys got together with the medical examiner, and they all agree about Galin."

"That he's dead?"

"Quit trying to be funny. There's a complication. Galin wasn't shot where the car was parked. The bullet didn't kill him right away. He apparently drove to the alley by the pizza place after he took the slug."

Quinn said nothing, trying to digest this. It was a complication, all right. No wonder nobody inside or in the vicinity of Pizza Rio saw or heard anything around the time of the shooting. Galin had been murdered someplace else.

"He couldn't have driven far," Renz said. "Nift says the gunshot wound was probably inflicted somewhere in Manhattan, on the East Side, judging from where the body was discovered. Galin couldn't have lived very long after getting shot. It's likely he took the tunnel or drove over the Fifty-ninth Street Bridge into Queens before he got too weak to get any farther."

"Headed for home, maybe," Quinn said. "Running on instinct while his life bled out."

"Could be," Renz said. "Or maybe he had a strong yen for pizza."

The car bounced over a pothole the patching crew had missed, causing Quinn to juggle the phone and grip it tighter.

Renz must have interpreted the silence as disapproval of

his joking about a dead cop and made a stab at recovering his solemnity. "It's true you'd want to get someplace familiar if you knew you were dying," he said in a somber tone. "Way the human mind works. Even animal minds."

"That so?"

"Hell, I don't know. That's something for you to find out. You're the detective."

"What are you, Harley?"

"I'm a politician now," Renz said. "Best you keep that in mind."

He broke the connection.

Fedderman looked over from the passenger seat. "What?"

Quinn told him.

Neither man said anything for a while. Quinn realized he was driving one-handed and snapped the phone shut and slipped it back in his pocket.

"Complicates things," Fedderman said.

"Complications are pretty much our job," Quinn said.

He thought about calling Pearl and telling her never mind about talking to anyone at Pizza Rio. Then he remembered the guilty, knowing look in Jorge Valento's eyes and decided not to call.

The diner on First was on a corner across from a D'Agostino market. Quinn saw a parking space almost in front of it, cut across uptown traffic, and pulled to the curb, causing a delivery van driver who'd been about to park there to give him the finger. Quinn ignored the gesture. The man blew him a kiss. Still Quinn didn't react. The guy in the van drove farther down the street in search of parking. Fedderman thought the guy didn't know how lucky he was.

Inside, the diner was surprisingly spacious. Lots of maroon vinyl booths and maroon vinyl padded chairs. A counter and cash register were on the immediate right, tables and booths to the left. Toward the back there was a step up and even more maroon. The breakfast crowd was gone, and among the dozen or so customers, the guy at a back booth by a window was the only one who looked like a cop, even though he was in plain clothes.

Quinn and Fedderman walked back there. Quinn noticed that though the restaurant was cool enough, it was slightly warmer in back.

The man who was surely Holstetter stood up. He was wearing a gray suit with the coat unbuttoned and was tall and skinny, with pointed features and oversized pointy ears that stuck way out like open doors. All in all, he looked like an overgrown leprechaun.

When he grinned amiably with little sharp teeth he looked even more like a leprechaun, but a sad and resigned one who hadn't been let in on the secret of where the pot of gold was.

"Holstetter," he said, like an admission of guilt.

Quinn nodded and shook hands. "I'm Quinn. This is Larry Fedderman."

Fedderman and Holstetter shook hands, then everybody sat down. A waiter in white was there from out of nowhere, and Quinn and Fedderman ordered coffee. That was all Holstetter had in front of him on the table. Cops drinking coffee at 11 A.M. It was probably happening all over the world.

"You guys wanna order some doughnuts?" Holstetter asked. "They're good here."

"No, thanks," Quinn said. "I don't want to be a stereotype."

Holstetter flashed an oversized tired-pixie smile. "I thought since we got the coffee, we might as well go all the way."

Quinn figured Holstetter was treading water, stalling before getting to the Q-and-A part of the conversation. Quinn thought they were wasting time.

"Tell us about Galin," he said.

Holstetter used both hands to revolve his cup slowly on

its saucer, then he sat back in the maroon upholstery. "Me and Galin were friends. Know that right off."

Quinn nodded. "Two guys work together a while, it happens."

"I wouldn't be saying this at all, only Joe's dead, so what's it matter? He's got no family except his wife, and he wasn't crazy about her. Talked all the time about leaving her."

Quinn thought June Galin might be surprised to hear that.

"And what I'm about to tell you, it might not be true anyway," Holstetter said.

Nobody spoke for almost a minute.

"Go or no go?" Quinn asked.

"I think Galin might have been on the take," Holstetter said.

Quinn saw the hardness that came over his features. Cops didn't talk like this about their former partners unless they were dead certain it was true.

"I wouldn't say that, only it might help nail whoever did Galin."

"Might," Quinn agreed.

"The thing is, I've got no real proof of it. But Galin and I talked a lot with each other, confided some things. He never quite said he was taking protection money, but he came close. And once he was carrying a hell of a roll of cash. Flashing it like he kinda wanted me to ask where he got it, if you know what I mean."

Quinn nodded. "Did you?"

"Ask? No. I didn't want to know."

"But you knew."

"I guess so."

Still unwilling to be definite about his former partner. A good cop.

"This was when you were working narcotics?" Fedderman asked.

"Yeah. It woulda been so simple to go on the take. Drug money. Nasty stuff, floating all over the street in those days.

Both of us had our offers, but we always turned them down. At least I thought we both did. It wasn't easy."

"They know how to make it hard," Fedderman said. "Then when you take that first shitty dollar they own you."

"Maybe they owned Galin. That's all I'm saying, is maybe."

"But you think the odds are pretty good," Quinn said.

"I wouldn't be here otherwise."

"Got anybody in mind who might have had Galin in his pocket?"

"Maybe. A dealer name of Vernon Lake. I couldn't tell you why I think that. Just the way they talked or looked at each other sometimes, like they shared a secret. Hey, this was all a long time ago. I don't even know if Lake's still around. These guys have got life expectancies like fruit flies."

"Where'd Lake sell?"

"All over, but mostly down in the Village. Best friend of lots of college kids that hit the clubs down there."

"He live in the Village?"

"Doubt it. They don't like fouling their own nests. I think he lived over in Brooklyn or Queens. Far enough away so the heat wouldn't singe him."

"Did it strike you that Galin had a lifestyle beyond a cop's salary?"

Holstetter stared into his coffee cup, then looked up and met Quinn's gaze. "Yes and no. I mean, he had a modest enough house, didn't wear flashy or expensive clothes, or spend his vacations in Europe. But he had a Rolex watch, said it was a knockoff he bought down on Canal Street. I think it was genuine, worth over twenty thou."

"President?" Fedderman asked.

"Huh?"

"That's the expensive Rolex."

"Probably was. It had diamonds for numbers. Looked real to me, like the gold looked real. He didn't wear it all the time, just when he was trying to impress somebody. We'd go out at night sometimes, talk up women in bars or restaurants. Seldom led anywhere, though, except to trouble for me once. I think Galin just wanted to show off, know he could score if he wanted to."

"He never did score?"

"Couple of times. Not in any way meaningful. He'd throw money around, flash the watch and his gold cufflinks. He did have a few suits and jackets that'd put a strain on a cop's salary."

"He wasn't wearing an expensive watch when he was shot," Quinn said. "And there wasn't all this gold or a Rolex in his dresser drawers or mentioned when we talked to his wife."

Holstetter grinned. "June wouldn't have known about that stuff. Galin was planning on a life beyond early retirement that didn't include her."

"According to her, they were happy enough," Fedderman said.

"Maybe they were. Maybe Joe changed his mind. Life's complicated."

"We were talking about that on the drive over here," Fedderman said.

"Complicated as . . . shit," Holstetter said.

Quinn knew that for a fact. The most profound things in life happened in a place beyond words and easy explanations, behind a thick, impenetrable curtain. Now and then the curtain parted slightly to allow a glimpse. Sometimes it was horrifying.

"I never dreamed I'd ever be sitting someplace ratting out my dead partner," Holstetter said, "but it seems like the only thing I can do if I want his killer brought down."

"Always the rock and the hard place," Quinn said.

"Ain't that the damned truth?"

Quinn figured Holstetter had said all he was going to say that might be useful. He knew where the conversation was going now. It was time to leave. He'd been in these maudlin cop confabs too many times over the years. All that was missing here were the doughnuts.

"Death can be complicated, too," Fedderman said, joining in the glum philosophizing.

"Until you get right up to it," Holstetter said. "Then it's simple."

17

Hettie didn't exactly feel drunk. But it was a feeling close to being drunk. Maybe drunk with love.

She giggled.

"You okay?" he asked, raising his head so he could look down into her eyes.

They were in her bed, she realized, not even recalling how they'd gotten there. It seemed only minutes since they'd entered her apartment. She could barely remember walking from the lounge. He'd had her arm. She'd felt dizzy, disoriented, almost as if she were floating, being led, her feet not quite in contact with the ground. That was all she remembered, and how insubstantial and *small* she'd felt. No, wait . . . Hadn't there been a subway ride? She seemed to recall the sound, the roaring, clacking, steely clamor. Maybe she'd dozed off. Subways always made her drowsy.

Anyway, here they were. She was on her back. He'd been tickling her right nipple with his tongue.

"Okay," she said. " 'Cept you stopped to talk."

"No problem," he said with a smile, and resumed paying extraordinarily close and gentle attention to her nipple.

"You slip something in my drink?" she asked, not angrily, but in a have-you-been-naughty tone of voice.

"Uh-uh. Did you slip something in mine?"

She giggled again.

They were nude. She did recall how they'd removed each other's clothes, slowly, with soft caresses and frequent kisses. That had been his idea. A good one. This man was full of good ideas.

She lay with her eyes half closed, feeling his hand creep down along her stomach. She'd had no idea the flesh of her stomach was so sensitive. Down, down, closer, closer . . . when he began manipulating her she heard her own moan as if from a distance. How good he was at this! How he seemed to work his fingers in rhythms she rode up, up, up and then swiftly down . . . and then up again, each peak of emotion higher than the last. A knowing touch, gently tracing out the circular designs of a desire that turned her in on herself and consumed her very soul. The window air conditioner continued humming softly like an engine of her passion. A controlled and insidious sound. Irresistible . . . relentless . . .

She felt his softly circling fingers move away.

"No . . ." a woman pleaded, not wanting him to stop, knowing what would happen next. Her own voice. She pleaded again.

Not as if she really meant it.

You're not fooling anyone, she said in her mind to the woman with her voice. *Why don't you just be honest?*

He entered her slowly at first, unfolding her like a flower so she wouldn't be injured. In and out slightly then, not far, not far, twice, three times, no pain . . . and he was all the way into her in a single lengthened stroke that left her breathless.

She began to say something as he began a slow and rhythmic rocking motion that caused the headboard to bump against the wall. Without breaking rhythm, he kissed her on the lips, using his tongue, stilling her words. She had no idea what she'd been about to say.

Not that it mattered.

* * *

In the morning he was gone.

Hettie reached over and ran the flat of her hand over cool sheet, then the cool pillowcase.

She felt a stab of loneliness, then of guilt.

One date. That had been all it had taken to get into her pants and beyond. What must he think of her?

If he thought of her at all.

She'd slept all night in the raw and was cool now. While the morning outside was warm, the air conditioner had been set on high and was running hard, winning its battle against summer. Hettie had goose bumps. She pulled the thin sheet up beneath her chin and stared at the ceiling.

Get up. Take a shower. Wash last night away.

In truth she remembered little about how he'd somehow talked her into bringing him to her apartment. Letting him stay, then sleeping with her. Or had *she* talked *him* into it?

They'd talked a while after arriving; she did have some recollection of that, snatches of memory. He'd been interested in her apartment, in the exercise area behind a folding screen in a corner of her bedroom. She remembered him effortlessly chinning himself a few times on the chinning bar. It was a collapsible piece of equipment, the bar set up firmly on a tubular steel frame, and would support much more weight than Hettie demanded of it. He'd been pretending to test the bar but really showing off for her. And he had plenty to show off. He was average-sized but extremely muscular, no stranger to working out.

About their lovemaking she remembered everything.

Or did she?

The smile that had started to form on her face faded. What wonderful things might she *not* be recalling?

Don't be absurd.

The sheets still smelled of sex. *Leave that behind you. New day.*

But she didn't want to forget everything about last night. That's where the guilt crept in.

One cheap date!

She sat up in bed, and it was as if a headache had been waiting for her to make a move. It slammed her hard. The ache behind her eyes made her clench them shut.

Squinting, she climbed out of bed, felt the cool hardwood floor beneath her bare soles, and padded toward the bathroom.

Her gaze fell on her wristwatch on the corner of the dresser. Nine fifteen.

Jesus, what's he done to me? He . . . ?

She realized she still didn't know his name. *My God, what a whore!*

At least he didn't leave a wad of bills on the dresser. Not that I couldn't use it . . .

A loud knocking on the door made her heart skip. Was he back?

Not likely. Ever. He got what he came for.

Hettie changed course, went back into the bedroom, and found her white terry-cloth robe. She slipped it on and tied the sash, then on the way to the apartment door ducked into the tiny bathroom and did what she could to rearrange her hair so she didn't look like an escapee from Bedlam.

More knocking. Even louder.

She went to the door, peeked through the spy hole, and saw a man in a light-colored shirt cradling a long white box in his arm.

Leaving the chain on, she opened the door a few inches and peered out.

Big guy, dark mustache, a potato for a nose.

He smiled at her. "Flowers for Hettie Davis. That you?"

"It's me."

"Gonna open the door so I can deliver these, get you to sign for them?"

"Who are they from?"

"I don't know." He opened the box and held it so she could see inside. Pink roses. Lush and beautiful against soft white tissue. A dozen of them. "There's a card, but it's inside an envelope." He shifted his weight and glanced at his watch. "Listen, lady, I don't blame you for being scared. Hasn't been that long ago a white florist's box meant a dangerous killer to most of the women in New York. But I ain't no serial killer. This is on the level, and I've got lots more deliveries."

"Of course. Just a minute." She closed the door, then went to where she kept tip money in the kitchen and got two one-dollar bills. She went back to the door and removed the chain, then opened the door.

These are from him. They must be!

She accepted the flowers and tipped the deliveryman, who gave her another smile and left, his descending footfalls clattering on the wooden stairs. As she closed and relocked her apartment door, she heard the street door down below *whoosh* open, then close.

After laying the box on the kitchen table, she opened it and fumbled to remove the small white envelope attached to a stem with a white ribbon tied in a bow. She opened the unsealed flap and withdrew the stiff white card, holding it to the light so she could make out the handwriting in dark blue ink.

> *Sorry I had to leave early.*
> *Last night was too wonderful*
> *not to repeat. I'll call you soon*
> *to see if you agree.*

There was no signature.

A weight lifted from Hettie, and her headache magically disappeared. She still didn't know his name, but he'd call, surely, or he wouldn't have bothered sending flowers. Maybe he was married. Wanted by the police. On the run from the

Mafia. She didn't care. She'd be waiting for him with open arms, not to mention legs.

Don't think that way, whore.

But she was grinning, immune from insults even from herself.

She found a tall glass vase for the flowers, and, after arranging them, hastily placed them in the center of the small Formica table. Then she put some coffee on to brew and plodded back toward the bathroom to shower.

The needles of warm water on her breasts rekindled her desire.

Of course it would be nice if she had his name, but you took what you could get in this mixed-up and too-often-disappointing world. He'd already revealed so much of himself to her that eventually he'd tell her his name. She could wait. Hettie was patient, and maybe on the very edge of a love affair like none she'd ever known.

18

The late-morning sun beat down on Queens from a cloudless sky, shortening tempers as well as stark shadows. Already the temperature was almost ninety. As she drove, Pearl watched the people on the littered sidewalks, reading their faces and body language. Some of them trudged along looking beaten and resigned. Others scowled and swaggered, with fixed glares suggesting they were near the breaking point. Heat and the city.

Pearl was driving a dusty black four-door Ford. To anyone with a knowing eye it was obviously a city car.

A middle-aged man with a stomach paunch straining the silky material of a blindingly violet shirt glanced over at her from the sidewalk and frowned. *What the hell are you doing here, in my neighborhood?* Pearl gave him her dead-eyed look, but he continued to stare, unimpressed, as he absently unwrapped a piece of candy or stick of gum and tossed the wrapper on the sidewalk. That irritated Pearl. She considered stopping the car and bracing the arrogant bastard for littering. And that shirt must be in violation of some ordinance.

Forget it. Bigger fish to fry.

She turned up the blower on the car's air conditioner and made a left turn. In the rearview mirror she caught a glimpse of the guy in the luminescent shirt standing and staring at her with his fists on his hips. *Prick.*

Pearl pulled the car to the curb diagonally across the street from Pizza Rio. It was almost eleven o'clock. She was hungry enough to eat a pizza, so somebody else would soon crave an early lunch and pick up the phone to order takeout. Then one of the two teenage boys lounging near the bike rack across the street would place a cardboard box in a warmer on the wide basket on one of the ratty bicycles and leave to make a delivery. Pearl hoped it would be the shorter, heavier of the two, leaving her to talk privately with the tall one, who must be Jorge Valento. Knowing she was a movie buff like himself, Quinn had told Pearl to look for Sal Mineo. From this distance, the tall one filled the bill.

Pearl settled in, leaving the car's engine idling and the air conditioner on high. Even with the windows up she could smell the spicy scent of pizza being baked. It was making her hungry.

The two boys by the bike rack didn't seem to notice her. Jorge leaned with his back against the brick wall, his hands in the pockets of his baggy, torn jeans. Now and then he casually spat off to his left, away from the bikes. The shorter kid was doing all the talking, all the time jumping around a lot like a junkie needing a fix.

After about fifteen minutes, the jumpy one was suddenly still, and Jorge raised his head with a sideways tilt. Apparently a buzzer or some other kind of signal had sounded.

Pearl was in luck. It was the short boy who scurried into Pizza Rio and emerged almost immediately with a large, padded black pizza warmer. He used bungee cords to strap it to the wire basket behind a bicycle seat, then mounted the bike and rode off, standing on the pedals and leaning out over the handlebars as he gained speed.

Good at his job, Pearl thought, which meant she might not

have much time. She switched off the ignition and climbed out of the car.

Not moving from where he leaned against the wall, Jorge observed the woman from the car approaching in the corner of his vision. When she was within about ten feet, he pushed himself away from the wall and turned toward her.

Nice-looking piece, he thought. Compact, trim, good legs, great rack. Nice face on her, too. Long dark hair that'd be fun to yank on. Dark eyes. Maybe she was Hispanic, as he was. A sister. He might play that angle.

No, now that she was closer she looked Jewish. That was okay, too. It just required different moves.

He knew he had a beautiful smile. He aimed it at her.

"You're a cop," he said.

She didn't change expression. Not much would surprise this one.

She flashed her shield. "I'm Detective Kasner."

"And I'm not." *Play wise ass with her, see how she reacts.*

She seemed about to yawn. "You're Jorge Valento."

It kind of bothered him that the bitch knew his name. "How'd you know?"

"I came to talk to you about Joseph Galin, the man whose body was found here in a parked car night before last."

He made it a point to meet her direct stare, and then blatantly looked her up and down, lewdly appraising her.

She looked only mildly irritated.

"I don't know much about that," he said.

"Sure you do."

"I told everything I know to another cop, yesterday."

"Not everything."

"Who says?"

"Homicide Detective Frank Quinn."

"That the cop I talked to yesterday? Old icicle eyes?"

"Uh-hm. Those eyes are the windows to his soul."

"So why should I tell you anything I didn't tell him?"

"It'd be a lot easier to tell me. You see, in Quinn's mind, me asking you is just like him asking you. When people lie or refuse to talk to me, which is to say him, he gets impatient."

Jorge remembered the big cop, Quinn, the large hands with their knobby, scarred knuckles. Not a young guy, but you just knew he could still be mean, and that it was his way sometimes. Jorge felt nervous. It had to show. He mentally put his mask back on, rearranging his facial muscles so he looked bored.

"You look like Sal Mineo," the titty little cop said.

"That's what my mother says." *My mother, who died ten years ago of alcohol poisoning.*

"If you don't talk to me, you might not look like Sal Mineo much longer."

Jorge didn't like the way she'd said that, as if she meant it. "Is that a threat, Officer Kasner?"

"That's *Detective* Kasner. And yes, it's a threat."

He was surprised. Usually they didn't come right out and say it. "Cops ain't supposed to threaten people."

"People aren't supposed to use illegal drugs." She nodded toward the broken crack vials among the litter at his feet on the concrete.

"What drugs?" he asked.

"The ones in your pocket."

Jorge realized how hot the sun was. He began to perspire.

"That pizza sure smells good," Pearl said.

"You get used to it."

"That's 'cause you get to smell that way yourself. You'll sure smell good to the lifers in your cell block. Before you know it, you'll be Sally Mineo."

Jorge gave her a laugh he didn't feel. "You're pretty tough," he said.

"You don't know the half of it, Jorge."

"So how do I avoid learnin' the other half?"

"Tell me what you know about Galin."

"He was dirty," Jorge said.

He watched her face, how she looked not so much surprised as disappointed. Cops were a club whose members had to believe in each other. Not to believe hurt. And it was dangerous, when you couldn't trust the guy watching your back. The titty cop would be surprised if she knew that when he was a ten-year-old kid he'd considered trying to join that club. Before he got mixed up in the gang that saved his life.

"It's a dirty world," he said.

"We agree. How was Galin dirty? Was he your supplier?"

Jorge almost smiled. She didn't know much. "Naw, Galin never moved no stuff himself. He just watched over things, made sure nothin' went wrong."

"For the dealer?"

"Sure. Who else?"

She moved closer. For some reason she became scary. The eyes, maybe. Even the tits looked dangerous. "What I want now, Jorge, is the name."

"The dealer's name?"

"The name of whoever was paying Galin for protection."

"That could get me in real trouble," Jorge said, trying to find some leverage, an angle.

But the lady cop had all the leverage.

"You're five minutes away from being taken away from here in handcuffs," she said. "You'll give us the name or you'll see time behind walls."

He kept his voice level, no quaver. He was no pussy. "You scare the shit outta me, lady."

"Yes," she said. "That's probably because you're smarter than most of your asshole friends."

He stared at her. She had him, and they both knew it.

"Name you want's Legend Lawrence," Jorge said. It had slipped from between his lips almost on its own, but not surprising him. His mind had made the calculation without him realizing it. She wasn't bluffing. He had no choice but to give her something. Prison time—a real stretch in an adult lockup—scared the crap out of him.

"Don't screw around with me, Jorge."

"Well, that's his street name, anyways."

"What's his real name?"

"That I don't know. Honest."

The titty little cop sighed. He didn't like the way she sighed, as if she was giving up on him.

She turned, about to walk away. The big cop, Quinn, would be the next one he'd see, and there'd be no sense running and hiding from him. He was the kind who'd find you no matter where you went or how good you hid. Like a goddamned Doberman pinscher with a bloodhound nose. Fear washed over Jorge like cold water.

"Lawrence was shot by another dealer," he said.

That stopped her. "When was this?"

"Four days ago."

She took a few steps back toward him. "What dealer?"

"I dunno who shot him. That's what I heard, is all."

"This Legend Lawrence dead?"

"In a hospital's what I heard."

"Which hospital?"

"I dunno. But he's there under another name. Vernon Lake."

"That his real name?"

"I got no way of knowin' that."

She studied him, making him feel like a bug or something under a magnifying glass. This was a hard bitch.

"Okay, Jorge. We'll see about what you said."

"You won't tell where you got the information, will you?"

"I'll try not to."

"You seem like a nice lady."

"Don't shit me, Jorge. You gotta learn not to keep trying that." She walked away a few steps and then turned back to face him. "And quit lying to yourself, too."

"Everybody does that," he said.

She grinned with big beautiful white teeth, like a celebrity.

"Now you're learning," she said.

Jorge watched her walk back across the street to the dusty black Ford. Even scared as he was, he couldn't help admiring her ass.

When the car had turned the corner and she was indeed gone, Jorge swallowed hard and thought over his predicament. Cincinnati, he decided. He had cousins in Cincinnati who'd put him up for a while. Anyplace other than New York.

The bell mounted high on the brick wall gave two brief rings, signaling that a pizza was ready for delivery.

Jorge thought the hell with that, and climbed on the remaining bike.

Then he reconsidered, dismounted the bike, and went inside for the pizza and the delivery address.

Outside again, he crumpled the address slip and tossed it on the sidewalk before throwing his leg back over the bike. He took the pizza.

He didn't know when he'd get a chance to eat again.

Probably not soon.

19

Jerry Dunn took a cab from the city to his suburban home in Teaneck, New Jersey. He and his wife Sami had lived in the house for twenty-two years and raised a couple of kids there. It had memories. He liked living there. The neighborhood was tree-shaded and quiet, and only a short commute to and from his job in the city.

Land near New York City being relatively expensive at the time the houses were built, in the fifties, they were close together, but each had a single-car attached garage. Jerry and Sami's car was a white ten-year-old Toyota Camry, but neither liked to drive in the city, so it was used mainly for errands and trips to restaurants or to a nearby shopping mall.

After paying off the cab, Jerry entered the front door and picked up the scent of onions being fried. Sami was expecting him. They'd made a deal: he'd take a cab to and from LaGuardia so she didn't have to fight the airport traffic, and she'd have a hot meal waiting for him when he returned.

Of course, this time the cab hadn't come from the airport, but a deal was a deal.

He set his suitcase in the front entry hall, then followed the scent of onions to the kitchen.

There was Sami at the stove, barefoot and wearing jeans and a loose-fitting blue tunic. Her upswept dark hair was mussed in back in a way that made her neck look skinny. She was frying what looked like thinly cut steaks with some onions in sizzling oil. The table was already set for two.

Jerry knew she'd heard him come in, so he approached her from behind and kissed the nape of her neck, then pulled her to him so her back and generous rump were against him.

He realized he was getting an erection and felt like carrying her into the bedroom. Was it because of what had happened in the city? What he'd done?

My God, is it a turn-on?

"—was the convention?" she was asking, still concentrating on her cooking.

"Just what you'd expect. Information booths, panels, speeches, speeches, speeches . . ."

"Drinking," she added, flipping a steak with the wood-handled spatula in her right hand.

He moved back so their bodies weren't touching. "I went easy on that," he said.

He was sure she believed him. Whatever his other vices, he was a light drinker. As for women . . . well, Sami never questioned him about that, thank the Lord. From time to time he thought it might be because she was afraid of the answers, but lately he'd assumed she simply didn't know what a stud he was. Besides, his hotel quickie sex with almost-strangers meant nothing, really. Not that Sami wouldn't strongly disapprove. But surely she understood that Jerry had needs she didn't fill.

"Want iced tea with your steak?" she asked.

"Sounds perfect."

She propped the spatula against a trivet on the stove and turned and kissed him on the lips, then smiled up at him. "I'd rather have you home than away," she said.

He kissed her back, hard, and said, "That's where I'd rather be."

She turned back to the stove and sizzling canola oil.

"We gonna eat soon?" he asked.

" 'Bout fifteen minutes."

"I'll do some unpacking."

"You got time," she said. She opened a drawer and got out a can opener to use on a tin of green beans sitting on the sink counter.

Jerry patted her rump and went back to the entry hall for his luggage, congratulating himself on how calm he was. On how smoothly everything had gone.

After dinner, maybe some wine. Then maybe the bedroom. Or the sofa. It was odd how much he felt like sex. Like he was back in his twenties.

Hell, don't question it. Make the most of it.

Later that evening, he went out to the garage to put his suitcase up on the sheet of plywood over the rafters where the luggage was stored. His black nylon carry-on he took to his wooden workbench set up against the front wall of the garage.

He glanced at the closed door from the kitchen and stood still for a few seconds. He'd left Sami in bed, snoring lightly. He smiled, remembering. He'd exhausted her.

After dinner they'd watched part of a Yankees game on TV, then gone to bed early. They'd had sex every which way, and then read for a while in bed. Pleased and surprised, Sami had remarked that she'd never seen Jerry so passionate and so relaxed.

It was true, he realized. It was amazing how everything in the world seemed so much better, more vivid and *real*, once a man took control of his life.

He unzipped the carry-on and looked at the banded

stacks of dull green bills inside. A hundred thousand dollars in small denominations. Another fifty thousand would soon be given to him. That money would be profit after paying back the bridge loan he'd taken out at the bank. He had a personal credit line there and had taken out such loans before, for stock purchases or business deals. They'd known him for years, so all that was needed was his signature.

The money had been left for him in a tightly wrapped and taped brown package at the hotel desk. After checking in, Jerry had taken it up to his room, made sure the door was locked, and started to count the money. But he'd soon gotten bored and impatient. It was all there, he was sure, so he threw away the brown wrapping paper and stuffed the banded bills into his carry-on.

The question now was where to hide the money.

Jerry looked around the garage, trying to settle on a safe place of concealment, somewhere Sami would have no reason to look.

Finally he decided to take his suitcase back down and put the carry-on, still with the money in it, inside, then lock his suitcase before replacing it in storage. Sami had her own luggage and would probably never touch his large suitcase anyway. That was where he'd always hidden her Christmas gifts before wrapping them, and she'd never found them.

When he'd switched off the garage light and returned to the house and gone to bed, he lay beside his sleeping wife and calmly stared into the darkness.

He'd reached a new maturity. It was great the way he could set aside selective parts of the past so they didn't get in the way of the present. Compartmentalize.

When he thought back on what he'd so recently done in the city . . .

Sweet Jesus!

He held up his right hand and tried to see if it was trembling, but the darkness in the bedroom was so dense he couldn't tell. It sure *felt* steady.

He decided maybe there'd be a delayed reaction. But if that were true, it didn't seem it would hit him tonight. Jerry laced his fingers behind his head and sighed. He had no remorse, no regrets. He was sure he never would have.

But it took him forever to get to sleep.

He would dream without remembering.

20

"Dan Martin," he said, and Hettie knew the name of her lover.

She repeated the name, as if testing for taste.

"You never asked my name after the first time," he said.

They were in her bed, and had just had sex. Hettie was spent and sore, but if he wanted to go around again . . .

"You could wear me out," he said.

She grinned and moved her nude body against his on the perspiration-damp sheet. In the warm room their flesh seemed almost hot to the touch. "Did I hear a complaint?" she asked.

He smiled. His dark hair was damp and mussed, a lock dangling over his forehead and almost in his eyes. "You did not."

"Well, I'm complaining now," she said. "I'm thirsty."

She started to get up, but he gripped her shoulder gently and pulled her back down. "I'll get us something." He sat up and swiveled on the mattress so he was facing away from her. Twisting his muscular body, he looked over his shoulder at her. "What would you like? I'm having a beer."

"There's an open bottle of Pellegrino in the fridge. That'd suit me fine."

He turned some more so he could lean down and kiss her lightly on the lips. "Gonna miss me?"

She laughed deep in her throat. "I already do."

He kissed the top of her head, then stood up. She watched him as he walked from the bedroom. He'd have to cross the living room to get to the kitchen. She wondered if the blinds were closed.

He returned a few minutes later with the green glass Pellegrino bottle and an opened can of Busch Lite. She sat up on the bed and scooted back so her shoulders were against the cool headboard. When he handed her the bottle she immediately took several long swallows, aware of him watching her. Some of the cold water dribbled onto her warm breasts, sending a chill through her as it mixed with her perspiration.

Dan (as she was training herself to think of him) sat back down on the mattress, exactly where he'd been before, facing away from her. She watched a drop of perspiration drip from his damp hair as he tilted back his head to take a long pull on his beer.

Hot work, she thought. It called for cold drinks afterward.

Neither talked for a while, getting comfortable with each other's silence. The air conditioner had cycled off and was quiet. Hettie listened to the constant rush of traffic from the street below. A faraway car alarm warbled briefly, barely audible in the summer night. Closer, but still far away, a police or fire department siren called like a lonely banshee.

Loneliness. Hettie hated it. Maybe now, for her, it had ended.

She reached over and traced the fingers of her left hand down Dan's sweaty, muscular back.

He turned and grinned at her. "You trying to seduce me again?"

She smiled. "I could've sworn it was you who seduced me."

"A woman's convenient lie," he said, leaning back and kissing her softly, using his tongue, showing her that if she were willing . . .

She let out a long breath and pushed him away.

He moved his mouth to her ear. "What should we do now?" he whispered.

"It's almost three a.m.," she said. "Maybe we should try sleeping for a change."

He threw back his head and finished his beer in a series of long gulps, then swiveled on the mattress and let his upper body flop back so he was lying beside her. Hettie worked herself down so she was eye to eye with him in the damp bed, lying on her side.

"You finish your water?" he asked.

"Most of it. Why, you want some?"

"No. Want some of my beer?"

"Nope. I'm fine." She smiled. "Your beer's empty anyway."

"Tired?" he asked, looking over at her.

"Getting there," she said, just before she dozed off.

Hettie dreamed, saw the dark, muscular form of Dan Martin moving about the bedroom, heard a soft, metallic clinking sound. She couldn't imagine what was making that noise. Dim light then, shadows gliding like the wings of soaring birds.

Dan's voice: "Tired?"

Concerned about me. So sweet.

"Are you sleeping, Hettie? Hettie?"

She decided not to answer. Why should she? It was her dream.

* * *

When Hettie awoke she realized immediately what she was smelling. Perfumed soap. Her brand.

Her brain had barely registered that when pain erupted in her ankles.

What . . . ?

She was dumbfounded. Disoriented.

Full consciousness made its way through the thick layers of confusion, and with it came panic.

She fought the panic by concentrating on the pain, then by trying to accept the pain, to somehow push it aside.

Reason! Think!

How did I get here? Where?

It was almost completely dark.

Can't see! Can't move arms or legs!

She tried to call out. Call Dan's name. Her lips and the tip of her tongue worked helplessly on a rough, sticky surface she recognized as the adhesive side of tape.

Can't scream!

A headache she'd barely been aware of now struck her skull like an ax, and she realized she was dangling upside down. Her feet were tied together, bound to something, and her wrists were tied or taped to her thighs. She could move only her head, and that brought excruciating pain to her neck.

Her eyes were getting used to the dimness, and she made out folds of what looked like white plastic near her. *The shower curtain!* Nearby vertical tubular steel glinted dully to her left, and to her right. She recognized it and knew where she was—hanging upside down from her chinning bar that, along with its collapsible and portable supporting structure, had been moved from the exercise corner of her bedroom into the shower stall.

Dan! He did this! Must have planned it all along. Put something in my water bottle, something that made me sleep so he could do this. Oh, Jesus, I can pick them!

The pain in her head increased with the pressure of

blood-swollen veins and began to pulse. She made another attempt to scream but could barely hear the muted hum that found its way through the tape.

Dear God, If I ever—

A scuffing, building rhythm came to her, moving closer. Footsteps in the hall, near the open bathroom door. The lights blinked on, blinding her.

21

Sometimes it made sense to go back to the beginning.

It occurred to Quinn that they'd carefully investigated the
.25-Caliber Killer murders that had happened on their
watch, but the first two crimes, the murders of George Manders and Alan Weeks, had been given only slightly more than
a cursory examination.

He decided to start with the first victim, George Manders.

Quinn and his team had studied the murder book on Manders, read the statements of neighbors, friends, and relatives,
and looked into the life of Manders himself.

Manders seemed tailor-made to be an unlikely murder
victim, a maddening conundrum for the police.

They'd found nothing in his life that might lead to his
murder. But of course there must be something, because he
had been murdered.

Quinn sat at Fedderman's desk, where the light was brighter,
and propped the rectangular half-frames of his reading glasses
on the slightly crooked bridge of his nose. Patiently, and in a
pedantic pose that didn't suit him, he began to read.

The statements of people who knew Manders seemed to lead nowhere, and the revisited facts concerning his murder also yielded nothing new.

Manders had been a fairly successful hedge fund manager for a firm called Prudent Power, which specialized in shorting the market using exchange traded funds. Quinn could barely make himself read about that, so boring did it become. But he scanned it, learned something about puts and calls, then decided it probably had little to do with Manders's murder except in larger and general ways whose understanding didn't require an MBA from Harvard. He hoped.

He stood up, stretched, and then poured some of yesterday's coffee into a white foam cup. Tasting the horrid stuff and making a face, he snatched up the Manders file from Fedderman's desk, sat down at his own desk, and booted up his computer.

After a minute or so, and several acidic sips from the foam cup, he peered over the frames of his glasses at the glowing monitor. Where to look first but the *Wall Street Journal*?

Interesting. The price of Prudent Power had plunged as the market rose, losing a lot of value for its investors. But wasn't that what a hedge fund was supposed to do, move the opposite way of the stock market? Quinn wasn't sure. It might not be that simple, meaning the manager of Prudent Power might have made enemies by the thousands. It would take only one furious client crazy enough to kill him.

But would that same killer then have moved on to take more victims, people who, presumably, had nothing to do with his (her?) finances? And Quinn wondered, how many serial killers had there been who were wealthy enough to have holdings in hedge funds?

He phoned the police profiler, Helen Iman, and asked her that question.

"Maybe Jack the Ripper," she said. "But we'll never know for sure. That's about it. Don't bother barking up that tree, Quinn."

He was holding the phone to his ear with his left hand while leafing through papers in the file.

"What're you doing, Quinn?"

"Looking for another tree to bark up."

"I'm pretty busy here," Helen said.

"I'm leafing through witness statements as we talk," he said. "Not that there were really any witnesses."

"The usual friends and relatives talking about what a great guy the victim was, and how he had no enemies?"

"On target."

"Read me who they are."

Quinn found the statements list and began reading her the names of people either his team or the earlier investigators had interviewed.

"That last one," Helen said, interrupting him. "Same last name as the victim."

"Zoe Manders," Quinn said. "Sister."

"The name sounds familiar to me. She the one who's the psychologist?"

"Says here she's a psychoanalyst. Got an office over on Park Avenue."

"La-di-da. Well, maybe that's where I heard her name, some convention or other."

"Manders himself was no pauper. Lived on East Fifty-sixth Street, near Sutton Place."

"Prosperous siblings," Helen said.

"Like you and I would be, if we were related and had money."

"Talk to her again," Helen said.

"Says here she and her brother only saw each other half a dozen times a year, mostly on holidays. Didn't go to the same places or have the same friends. And sis is solid with alibi."

"She might know something she doesn't know she knows," Helen said.

"That's pretty goddamned cryptic."

"How old is Dr. Manders?"

"Forty-six," Quinn said, adjusting his reading glasses to peer more closely at the file.

"Victim was forty-three," Helen said. "They probably grew up together and were close. She was his big sister, and now she's a psychoanalyst. Most likely looked out for him when they were kids. She probably knows a lot about him."

"And being a shrink, she'd know how to root through her childhood memories in productive fashion."

"Exactly," Helen said. "All you have to do is get her to think like a cop, and she might tell you something illuminating about little brother. Dr. Manders might be a hidden undeclared asset."

Had Helen been reading the *Wall Street Journal*?

"One way to get to know something about the killer is to know his victims," Quinn said.

"You got it, Quinn. *Cherchez la* shrink."

"Always," Quinn said.

Hettie's almost constant muted screams were like insane musical accompaniment to her agony. While they were barely audible, *she* could hear them. Each one echoed in every dark corridor of her mind, each echo sharper and more painful than the last. Hettie had given up hope long ago.

What filled her mind now, along with the pain, was a question.

Why must it take so long to die?

22

Zoe Manders's fashionable Park Avenue office address, just off Fifty-ninth Street, whispered success. Standing in the towering building's glass and marble lobby, Quinn studied the directory and found that she was one of maybe a dozen doctors of one sort or another on the floors not occupied by corporations large and small. He walked over to where a uniformed security guard sat in a low chair behind a curved marble-topped counter and signed in. The marble was cold to the touch.

"Good to see you again, Captain."

Quinn glanced again at the guard and recognized the grinning, puffy face of former NYPD detective Ben Byrd. Byrd had worked out of Manhattan South homicide and been in a bad car accident while on the way to a crime scene . . . what, five years ago?

"You're looking good, Ben," Quinn said, shaking hands. Quinn meant it. He'd heard about how seriously Byrd was injured, the endless rounds of operations.

Byrd added a shrug to his smile. "I don't get around so well, but other than that there's no pain. It's pain that can wear you down, especially the back pain."

Quinn caught a glint of polished steel behind the counter and noticed for the first time that Byrd was seated in a wheelchair.

"I don't get up outta here by myself," Byrd said, but the grin didn't waver. "I can get around okay, though. Things turned out all right, considering."

"Better than what almost happened."

"That's what I tell myself, Captain." Byrd's gaze dropped to the building log on the marble counter. "I see you know Dr. Manders."

"Meeting her for the first time," Quinn said.

"Police business, I guess."

"Yeah. Thanks for assuming I'm not one of her patients."

"It wouldn't be an insult. I was one of 'em myself, after the accident."

"She must know her job," Quinn said, a bit awkwardly.

"I figured you were here 'cause of what happened to her brother. That Twenty-five-Caliber thing. How's it going on that one?"

"Slowly," Quinn said.

"So nothing's changed."

Quinn told him nothing had, then offered his hand again to shake.

Byrd, with a still-powerful grip, gave Quinn's hand a squeeze and said, "Take it easy on Dr. Manders. She's one of the good ones."

"In the building, you mean?"

"One of the good ones anywhere," Byrd said. "A class lady."

"Thanks for telling me." Quinn smiled. "She's not a suspect, Ben. Class ladies don't shoot people in the head."

"Most of them don't," Byrd said.

Quinn found the neatly disguised elevators and rode one to the ninth floor. At the end of a long, carpeted corridor, beyond the door to a law firm, was a plain wooden door simply lettered DR. ZOE MANDERS.

The door opened to a small anteroom that was tastefully furnished in grays and greens, with a brown leather sofa and two matching chairs. There were a lot of potted plants that looked artificial, but when Quinn touched one of the leaves he found it was real.

There was no receptionist and no place for one to sit and greet people. No phone in sight. The doctor must have an answering service. Next to a door beyond one of the brown leather chairs was a small illuminated button. Quinn had called ahead for an appointment, so he went over to the button and pressed it. A buzzer sounded behind the closed door.

Within a few seconds Dr. Zoe Manders opened the door and smiled at Quinn. She was a slim woman who looked too young to be in her forties, slightly taller than average, with brown eyes and short brown hair. Her features were even and radiated more health than delicacy. Maybe it was her wide cheekbones and wonderful smile, or maybe it was the fact that she was a psychoanalyst, that reminded Quinn of Ingrid Bergman, who'd played a psychiatrist in a Hitchcock movie.

"Detective Quinn?" she asked.

He'd been staring. "Yes, and you're Dr. Manders?"

"The introductions are out of the way," she said, still smiling, and stood aside so he could enter her office.

Simply being there made Quinn feel better, and he'd felt okay when he arrived. Gray and green in here, too, but with lighter tan leather. There were some heavy, shaded lamps with oversized bases on darkly grained wood tables, floor-to-ceiling bookshelves in matching wood, the books neatly arranged. The carpet was a plush beige two shades darker than the leather chairs. The heavy drapes that muffled the sounds of Park Avenue traffic nine stories below were the deep, velvety green of old moss. On two of the walls were framed prints of Monet garden paintings, containing almost every color but in a muted harmony that made them relaxing to gaze on.

Dr. Manders was wearing loose-fitting charcoal-gray slacks, a silky pale gray blouse with a white pattern that made it look almost lacy, and low-heeled shoes of a gray that matched the blouse. She led Quinn to one of the comfortable-looking leather chairs and motioned for him to sit down, then she sat behind a polished wood desk that had delicately carved legs and looked more like a table. The effect of the room with her in it was strangely soothing. It was all calculated, Quinn told himself, but it certainly worked.

"You came about George," she said. Her voice was unexpectedly low, also soothing.

At first Quinn didn't understand, then realized he'd been thinking of the victim, her brother, by only his last name. "I did."

"You're not the first."

"I know that, Dr. Manders. I mean I *really* came about George."

She appeared puzzled.

"As opposed to his killer," he said.

"You need to explain."

"You know who I am? I mean, beyond my name and NYPD identity?"

She nodded. "I read the papers, watch TV news. When I heard the city had put you in charge of the investigation, I was glad. Not just because of George, but for the other victims. A serial killer . . ."

"The way we search for them," Quinn said, "is figure out how they think, what passes for logic in their damaged minds. The more we can learn about them the better, even if it's not directly related to the murders."

"You mean you want my input as a psychoanalyst? I'm afraid you—"

"No, no," he interrupted, leaning forward, realizing for the first time she was wearing perfume, something subtle that carried the scent of lilacs. "What I mean is that, the next best thing to knowing the killer is to know the victim. It might seem that these are random killings, but to the murderer, they're not. Even if the killer thinks they are, they still might not be. The more I know about George, the more I can surmise about his killer. It's even possible that I'll be able to discern some sort of motive, even if your brother and his killer never crossed paths until the time of the murder." He studied her impassive features. "Does that make sense, Dr. Manders?"

She locked gazes with him and nodded. "Very much sense. And it's Zoe. We might as well be informal if I'm going to talk about George. It will make it easier for me." Her dark eyes remained trained on his, searching, maybe imploring. He didn't quite understand that. It came to him that there might be a lot about this woman that was beyond his understanding.

"All right, Zoe. If it's okay with you, I'll just sit back and you can tell me about your brother. Even the things that don't seem important. I need to have some idea of him."

She smiled. "Shouldn't we change places?"

"No," Quinn said seriously, "you're in control here."

"I sometimes wonder," she said, and leaned back in her chair. Her eyes fixed on some point above Quinn's head and behind him.

"I am—was—three years older than George," she began. "We grew up in a middle-class neighborhood, but a kind of tough one. For a while, I was his protector. Not that he wouldn't fight, but he was small for his age."

"Was he a magnet for bullies?"

"No more than any kid small for his age. And bullies didn't taunt him once they learned he was my little brother."

"So you were pretty tough."

She laughed. "No, just pretty. The boys wanted to stay on my good side."

"Easy to see why."

She ignored the compliment. "When I was sixteen and George was thirteen, our father died in an industrial accident."

"What kind of accident?"

"Chemical," she said. "He was a chemist, and someone at the plant where he worked for Montrose Insecticide and Feed used a wrong compound in a weed-killer, and it . . . killed my father. Our father." She looked at Quinn, then back at the point above his head. *What does she see there?*

"Poisoned him?"

"The fumes destroyed his lungs. It was a terrible way to die."

Tears glistened in her eyes. Quinn sat quietly, giving her time.

"When Dad died, it was as if a bomb had exploded in the family. Our mother raised us, never remarried. She had to work two jobs to keep the family going. Things changed between George and me. He became the protector. I became more of a . . . victim."

Quinn listened patiently for well over an hour while she went on to describe their home life, the pets they'd had, the arguments, how she and her brother had attended the same college, how George had an inborn skill with numbers, which carried him through business school. After working at a brokerage house he managed to attract investors and started a growth mutual fund, which evolved into a hedge fund, Prudent Power. Zoe meanwhile had gone on to postgraduate studies and earned her degree. She interned and worked for a while in a clinic, then as a corporate psychologist. Eight years ago she began her own practice.

"Obviously, you and George were both highly motivated."

"I suppose so." She smiled sadly. "To escape grief, perhaps."

"Sounds as if things were hard for you."

"Only to a degree. We were both good students, and we must have inherited ambition."

"Strange thing for a psychoanalyst to say."

"I suppose it is. But I think we both felt that things would work out okay for us."

"Is your mother—"

"She died twelve years ago. A heart attack."

"George never married?"

"He almost did, once. But the girl changed her mind."

"What about his sister?"

She looked startled. Then she smiled, understanding he was talking about her. "I almost did once, too. Only I changed my mind."

"George and you turned out to be overachievers."

"That'd be my diagnosis," she said.

"Because of your father's death?"

"Maybe. He was an overachiever, too, as was his father."

"In your genes."

"Yeah, maybe. So much is genetic. Do you think murder is genetic, that it's in your killer's genes?"

"I honestly don't know. That'd be your field."

"Well, Detective Quinn—" She seemed suddenly surprised at herself. "I forgot to get your first name."

"Just Quinn'll work."

"I thought we were on a first-name basis."

"We are, Zoe. My given name's Frank, but everyone calls me Quinn."

"Well, Quinn, I don't know, either. About the killer gene."

She sat farther back. He sat back. They regarded each other.

"Life's so goddamned short," she said.

"For some of us. Usually the wrong ones."

"Has this conversation been a help?" she asked.

"Has it helped you?"

She swallowed. "I suppose it has. It hasn't brought George back, though."

"It might help to catch his killer," Quinn said. "There's no way to know for sure at this point."

"If you really think you and I getting together might help," she said, "maybe we should do it again."

Quinn felt surprised and oddly embarrassed. He couldn't

contain his smile. "I thought you psychoanalysts were supposed to be obscure."

"That was me being obscure," she said. "What I really meant is that you intrigue me. Your methods, who you are. Maybe it's because you're trying to track my brother's killer. Maybe when you catch him, or kill him, you'll no longer intrigue me."

"That was direct enough," Quinn said.

"Often being direct is wise. Life offers only so many opportunities, it's a shame not to explore them. Believe me, I'm not being impulsive. I'd tell you I hardly ever do this kind of thing, only you already know that."

"I do know it," Quinn said.

"I don't take very many chances."

Oh, yes you do. Was your brother a gambler like you? A risk taker? Some people say that's in the genes.

"Neither do I," he said.

She crossed her arms, cocked her head to the side, and stared at him with hope and a certain vulnerability. He knew what courage it must take. But at the same time, the lady seemed to get off on risk. Quinn understood that; he often fought the same instinct in himself.

And sometimes he didn't fight it.

What the hell, since we're being direct: "How about dinner, then maybe later . . . ?"

"How about sooner," she said, "then maybe dinner?"

Later that night Quinn wondered, *is there a victim gene?*

23

It was almost like watching a wary exotic fish considering a variety of lures. The man in the unmarked blue baseball cap had watched her yesterday from across Broadway as
she meandered from shop to shop, looking in windows, regarding the bait. He knew she'd finally see something that
interested her and enter one of the shops. She would finally
bite.

Men and women thought quite differently. He understood
how women thought, had made a study of it. Certain women,
for certain reasons, he studied individually and closely.

That was because only certain women would do. It would
be wrong to call them all the same physical type. It was
more something about their bearing, the way they held
themselves and moved. The way they thought. The look in
their eyes.

That was something he hadn't yet seen. He hadn't looked
into this one's eyes.

She was certainly attractive, he thought, as he slowed and
stood with his hands in his pockets, staring across the street.
She was medium height, with long dark hair, long legs en-

cased in tight jeans, long and graceful arms that nonetheless looked strong. Even her neck was long and slender. What interested him most was her ballet dancer's tightly sprung body. It hinted at physical strength as well as grace, reminiscent of a wild and lovely animal that might bolt and be up to speed in seconds. A prey animal, like an elegant gazelle. Every slight movement she made was unconscious art.

She went into a mid-price fashion shop and, after about fifteen minutes, emerged carrying a small white shopping bag. From outside the shop he followed her back the way she'd come, along Broadway. She was walking now with a firm destination in mind, and he had to quicken his pace to keep up with her long, graceful strides.

Finally she took the concrete steps down a shadowed stairwell to a subway platform. Even descending the steps, had she wanted to, she could have balanced a book on her head.

Though the train was crowded, she managed to find a seat. He stood halfway down the car, holding on to a vertical steel bar, unobtrusively watching her.

They didn't ride far before exiting the subway and surfacing back into the bright sun. Like moles, he thought, blinking at the light. He was sure she still hadn't noticed him as he fell in behind her at a prudent distance.

He had to find out as much as possible about her, and where she lived was essential information.

It turned out to be a West Side apartment in an old brick building with phony green shutters and fancy grillwork on the ground-floor windows. He'd watched, but it was impossible to know which unit she'd entered. It was probably useless to cross the street and look at the mailboxes, and he might attract suspicion.

He'd be back tomorrow, though. And if things worked out as he suspected, he'd return here often. At least for a while. He'd find out what he needed to know. He always did.

He thought about the woman with the strong and elegant

ballerina's body, the way her hair flipped with each step as she strode with her long legs. So delicate and precise, with a grace one had to be blessed with at birth. He replayed the image over and over in his mind, studying it for meaning and vulnerability.

He was learning. He was stalking.

The next morning he found out where she worked.

He'd been waiting less than half an hour when she appeared outside her building, wearing jeans again (though these weren't as tight) and a T-shirt with some sort of lettering across the back. He was too far away to read what it said. Her graceful stride lengthened as she headed in the direction of the subway stop where they'd emerged last night. He fell in behind her as he'd done yesterday.

He followed her to an Office Tech, one of the big-box chain stores that retailed office supplies and electronics. It wasn't far from where she'd been shopping early yesterday evening.

Now he followed her into the store, along the aisles of electronics, seeing nothing in focus but her. Without hesitating she strode toward the rear of the store, occasionally nodding a good morning to some of her fellow employees. Closer to her now, he could read the lettering on the back of her T-shirt: PRACTICE RANDOM ACTS OF KINKINESS.

A joke. She thinks.

Her regal elegance was incongruous and somehow stimulating as she brushed through a swinging door into what must be a storage area. Apparently she didn't work on the sales floor.

Not quite ready to be disappointed, he decided to hang around for a while. He browsed about, pretending to study notebook computers, printers, various computer supplies. Twice he had to assure salespeople that he didn't need or want help. There were about half a dozen of them in the spacious store, all of them wearing identical pin-on green buttons with identical fake ink stains on them that, if you looked closely, resembled desktop computers. The Office Tech logo.

Ten minutes, and she hadn't come out of the storage area. He was becoming impatient. Close behind her, he'd been able to pick up her scent, the harbinger of her fear. Of her excitement.

Almost immediately they know without knowing.

He heard one of the salespeople, an older woman, ask a young clerk if "Terri" had come in yet.

"Few minutes ago," the clerk said. He was a skinny teenager with a wannabe mustache. "She's in back moving stock."

"I figured you'd notice," the woman said, and they both smiled.

The older woman, apparently a supervisor, walked toward the back of the store.

Going to check on Terri? Make sure she's working?

A small message board was mounted on the wall next to the door to the storeroom. It was one of those erasable ones of the sort you saw outside hospital rooms. The name "Terri Gaddis" was written on it, along with several other names. The woman used a writing instrument hanging on a string beside the board and put a checkmark next to Terri's name.

In his mind, the man in the blue baseball cap put a checkmark next to Terri's name.

Terri Gaddis.

He was about ready to give up for the morning and leave Office Tech when Terri emerged from the storeroom. She was wearing one of the green buttons with the logo ink stain.

So she did work on the sales floor.

It was still early, so there weren't many shoppers in the

gadget-lined aisles. She walked over and stood near a display of notebook computers, all with their screens glowing, and looked beautifully bored.

Well, he enjoyed shopping for computers, talking about them, learning. He enjoyed learning about almost anything. Who knew when any bit of knowledge might prove useful? So he wouldn't completely tune out what Terri was going to tell him while he was primarily learning about her. Studying her from only a few feet away. Looking into her eyes as he must so he could see in them the commitment they would make to each other on a deeper level than her conscious knowledge. Those who were prey always recognized the predators, always accepted what would surely occur. Often the premeditation in what the courts called premeditated murder took two.

He walked toward her, smiling.

Terri Gaddis didn't know it, but she was ready for her close-up.

24

"If I'd known it was going to be like this," Quinn said, "I'd have seen a shrink sooner."

They were in Zoe's bedroom, in her king-sized bed. The window treatments were white-stick blinds that were halfway down. Diaphanous white sheer curtains over them admitted soft morning light.

Her apartment was also on Park Avenue, two buildings down from her office. It was on a high floor in a pre-war brick and stone tower that admitted very little sound from outside. Not a large apartment, it was well and eclectically decorated. Zoe's dresser was a marble-topped French provincial work of art, while a large walnut wardrobe that supplemented her closet was an almost plain period piece. A chair near the bed was upholstered in maroon and had artfully turned wooden arms. The carpet that covered most of the polished hardwood floor was a multicolored Persian with an intricate design and variegated shading. Quinn knew a little about carpets and thought it was authentic. Everything looked expensive and should have appeared mismatched, but somehow it all went together.

"You had a great decorator," he said.

He thought she'd tell him she'd decorated the place herself, but she said, "It looks all right. You live in a place, you get used to anything."

She had a point. And he knew she hadn't grown up in professionally decorated rooms.

"You'll have to see my place," he said, figuring she'd laugh. She didn't disappoint him. "I did it myself," he said.

"Very good. It'll reflect *you*."

She shifted her weight on the mattress so she could see him better, causing a fold of white sheet to drop and expose her right breast. He couldn't swear she didn't do it on purpose. Women moved so easily through the world of convenient chance. He leaned forward and kissed her nipple, feeling her fingers run through the hair on the back of his head, gently at first, then roughly, pulling him closer.

When after a few minutes he leaned back, she said, "I'm glad we took the chance."

"It's unanimous."

He was about to get up when he heard the opening notes of "Don't Cry for Me Argentina."

"My cell phone," he said, sitting up. The sheet fell away as he stood. He was aware of her watching him as he went to his pants folded on the maroon chair and fished the phone out of a pocket. He flipped open the lid, staring at the caller's number on the tiny screen.

Pearl.

Just what I need.

"Yeah, Pearl."

"I called your apartment and didn't get an answer, so I figured you'd already left."

"On my way in," he said.

"Oh." He knew she wouldn't miss the fact that there were no traffic sounds in the background.

"Stopped for a bagel," he said.

"Ah."

Oh and *Ah*. It didn't take much for Pearl's antennae to pick up the slightest reason for suspicion. Or was Quinn simply feeling guilty and reading things into her tone?

Zoe was sitting up in bed, looking at him with one of her eyebrows arched. He shrugged helplessly. *Damned Pearl!*

"I talked to Jorge, the handsome pizza biker," Pearl said. "Shook something loose." She told him what Jorge had revealed about Joe Galin and his business relationship with the drug dealer Vernon Lake.

"We need to find out what hospital Lake's in," Quinn said

"That's what I was up all night doing. He's in Roosevelt, room six-twenty. I told them I was police, but since I wasn't there in person to flash my shield, the nurse I was talking to clammed up. I called back later and got a different nurse, told her I was Lake's sister Veronica. She told me the name was familiar, that she must have heard Lake talking about me."

"He's liable to rabbit outta there if he hears about your call."

"Lake's not going anywhere. He's got two bullet holes in him and he's on painkillers."

"He gonna die on us?"

"Might. The nurse that thought I was his sister sounded somber, but she wouldn't tell me much about Lake's condition over the phone. He's listed as critical but stable."

"Stable for now," Quinn said.

"Yeah."

"We've gotta get over there."

"Yeah."

"Leave now, and I'll be at the hospital waiting for you."

He regretted the words as soon as they were spoken. Pearl would know he wasn't on his way to work if he was closer to Roosevelt than she was.

"I'll be there soon as I can," she said. "You take your time. Finish your doughnut."

"Bagel," Quinn said.

"Whatever. They both have holes in the middle."

She broke the connection.

Sarcasm?

"Work?" Zoe asked from the bed.

" 'Fraid so. A policeman's lot." He padded barefoot over to the bed and kissed her. "Sorry. I was looking forward to us going out and having breakfast."

"I understand," she said, maneuvering her body so she was seated on the edge of the mattress. She tossed the wadded sheets behind her toward the center of the bed as she stood up. "You go ahead and get dressed, and I'll make you some breakfast."

"Don't go to any trouble."

"I won't. Just a bagel."

25

When Quinn, Pearl, and Fedderman asked at the nurses' station for Vernon Lake's room number, they soon found themselves face-to-face with a uniformed cop named Butterfield who knew Fedderman from his NYPD days. Butterfield had bad symmetry; he was built square and had a round, angelic face. The crow's-feet at the corners of his blue eyes and a head of thinning gray hair suggested he had to be near retirement age.

After exchanging pleasantries with Fedderman, he said, "You wanna see Lake, I'll have to take you to him. He's been charged and read his rights, but maybe it's his last rites he needs." A nearby nurse behind the counter had overheard and glared at him, then continued bustling about.

"We heard he'd been shot," Quinn said. "Bad?"

"Depends on whose point of view."

"Lake's."

"He'll get over the two bullet holes in him. What he hasn't been told yet is he's got pancreatic cancer and won't live more'n three months."

"Jesus," Pearl said.

Butterfield shrugged. "It'd be easier to feel sorry for him if he hadn't been living off kids' drug money for years."

"He in any condition to have a conversation?" Quinn asked.

"Sure. I wouldn't say he's eager to leap outta bed, or even able, but he's conscious and not in a lot of pain."

Butterfield led them to Room 620 and then told them to go on in and he'd wait out in the hall.

It was a small room with only one visitor's chair, and that with a stack of folded linens on it. Sunlight sneaked in through slatted blinds. It smelled as if someone had been hanging around there chewing spearmint gum.

The three detectives stood close to Vernon Lake's bed as he regarded them with rheumy brown eyes. He was an African American man in his thirties, with a powerful upper body and a sharply defined face of ebony planes made darker by black stubble. The bed was cranked up so he was almost in a sitting position. His midsection was swathed in white gauze, as was his right bicep. An IV unit with two plastic packets of medication hanging from its metal stand was feeding clear liquids into a vein on the back of his left hand. His wrists were handcuffed to the steel bedrails.

He didn't smile as he looked up at them. "You ain't doctors." He sounded tired, but didn't slur his words, obviously not too drugged up with painkillers to know what he was saying.

"Healers of society," Quinn said, flashing his shield.

"Not my society."

"We got some questions for you," Pearl said.

"Then maybe I oughta have my lawyer here."

"You got one?" Fedderman asked.

"Public defender. Name of Sophie Murray."

"She's a tough one," Quinn said. "You might wanna call

her at a certain point. All we want from you are a few answers about Joseph Galin."

"Don' know him."

"He's the guy you paid for protection while you were dealing. Back when he was a cop and we were all younger and better looking."

Lake pressed his head back into his pillow and said nothing.

"We can offer you a deal," Quinn said, "if you give us some answers and don't play the hard ass. You know Galin's been shot and killed. Maybe you even did it."

"Talk that way," Lake said, "an' I want my lawyer."

"Hear me out before you decide. We're not interested in pinning Galin on you. We know you're innocent. You know you're going up for a long time on the drug charges, not to mention trading shots with another dealer. He's gonna be okay, by the way, just like you."

"I been tol' he was dead."

"Then somebody's jerking you around."

"Wouldn't be the first time for that. All cops do, ain't it, jerk us plain folks around?"

"Some cops sometimes," Quinn admitted. "Not me, not now. All we want's some straight information about Galin. He's dead now, so if you owed him something, it doesn't matter."

"I din' owe that man nothin'."

"We want Galin's killer," Quinn said. "We've got no interest in you otherwise. What we'd like to know is, was he dirty?"

"Why should I—" Lake decided in mid-sentence to be silent. His powerful neck muscles flexed as he scrunched his head farther back into his pillow. He was obviously going to be stubborn.

" 'S'cuse me, please." Quinn stuck his head outside the

room's door and said something to Butterfield, then ducked back in.

Lake glared at him without moving his head. "Don' matter what you do. Till I get—"

"Shut up," Quinn said, hardening his tone. "Be a smart asshole for once and shut up till you know the game and decide whether to play."

Lake seemed to relax, but only slightly. This was the kind of cop talk he knew. His breathing was loud and rhythmic in the quiet room.

There was a knock on the door. Quinn went to it and was handed something, then closed the door and came back to stand again by Lake's bed. He was holding a Bible.

"You a religious shit-head?" he asked Lake.

"Long-ago Baptist, if it be any of your business."

"I'm a religious man, through and through. It's why I'm a cop. I don't miss church on Sundays, and I try to live by the good book. You believe me?"

"Don' believe a thing you say."

"That hurts me. I'm gonna offer you a trade. You don't want it, then we can do the lawyer thing and you can talk or go mum or whatever, but the deal will be off the table."

"That legal?"

"For Christ's sake, I'm a cop."

"Yeah, that's what I be thinkin'."

Quinn held the Bible out flat in his left hand and rested his right palm on it. "I'm gonna tell you this, and I'm swearing to it on the Bible. You tell us what we want to know about Galin, and . . . well, I can't guarantee you won't do some time on the charges against you, but I can and *do* guarantee, on this good book and by all I hold holy, that you won't serve more than eighteen months." He handed the Bible over for Pearl to hold. "Now, we can go that way, or we can do this by another book. You can call your lawyer in and we'll go through the usual bullshit, and maybe you'll do okay and only get fifteen to twenty years, but this offer will be off the table."

Lake closed his eyes, thinking about it.

Fedderman walked over and pretended to gaze out the window. Pearl held the Bible and looked at Quinn, standing there with his arms crossed, staring down at Lake. Beneath the medicinal minty scent in the room was the stench of Lake sweating under the white sheet that covered his lower body. Perspiration gleamed on his muscular chest and shoulders, on his broad forehead.

Lake, still with his eyes closed, said, "You can really do this?"

"I can do this."

"Guarantee me an eighteen-month cap?"

"Eighteen months or less, and you'll be out," Quinn assured him.

Pearl felt a queasiness, watching Quinn telling the truth yet misleading a dying man like this. Hard, hard bastard, Quinn. Believable as an emissary from God.

"We got us a deal," Lake said, opening his eyes. "But you best be tellin' me the truth."

"You'll know soon enough that I am," Quinn said. He didn't shake Lake's hand, but he reached down near the steel cuffs and touched it. Lake replied with a wriggle of his fingers.

The man in the bed sighed. He was going to unload. Quinn had pulled it off. Pearl felt a guilty elation.

"Galin was dirty," Lake said. "I paid him once a month to lay off my dealin's an' to let me know if somethin' heavy was movin' my direction. I do gotta say, he kep' to the deal."

"How much did you pay him?" Quinn asked.

"Ten thousand a month, then later on he wanted fifteen."

"He get it?"

Lake snorted a kind of laugh that hurt him and made him wince. "I paid. He be worth it."

"This go on till he retired?"

"No. Till six, seven years ago, when I went in for a short stretch. Nothin' to do with Galin, though. Got stopped for a traffic violation, had a trunk fulla product. Shitty luck, was all it was. What it usually is. When I got out, I knew Galin was gonna retire soon." He smiled. "An' of course I wasn't dealin' then anyways."

"No need to get into that," Quinn said.

"I wasn't surprised when I heard Galin was shot," Lake said.

"Why's that?"

"I always had the feelin' I wasn't the only one payin' him. I'd give you the other names if I knew 'em."

Quinn thought Lake might be lying, but he didn't want to push it. "You've told us what we wanted to know."

"I gotta ask again," the doomed Lake said, "you bein' straight with me? I can count on less'n eighteen months behind walls?"

Quinn took the Bible from Pearl, then gripped it tightly and held it out toward Lake, above the bed.

Pearl thought he looked like a faith healer ready to cast his spell. Was Lake going to rise up from the bed and walk, his handcuffs miraculously opened and dangling from his wrists?

"If you've been truthful to me," Quinn said, "I promise that you'll be free, Vernon. Within eighteen months, you'll be free."

"I been truthful. I swear to God I have."

"I believe you, son."

When they left the room, Quinn returned the Bible to Butterfield, who carried it back toward the nurse's station.

In the elevator going down, the three of them were alone.

Pearl said, "Sometimes you frighten me, Quinn."

"Vernon Lake's an asshole who killed his share of people," Fedderman said. "He knew something that could help us save lives. Quinn didn't actually lie to the man."

"That's what frightens me. And makes me a little queasy."

"Grow up, Pearl." Fedderman said.

"Yeah. Grow up, grow old, then die. Makes being born not seem worthwhile."

"Every right thing you do," Quinn said, "you don't feel good about it afterward."

26

Black Lake, Missouri, 1985

The bitter November air was sharp and full of scent. It froze the hair in Marty's nostrils and caught like a blade in his throat.

Eleven-year-old Marty Hawk stayed well to the side and slightly behind his father as they trudged up the snow-crusted rise toward the ridge of trees lined like silhouetted Halloween shapes against the gray sky. When the wind blew, it rattled the ice in the branches. Marty's breath fogged out ahead of him.

He held his rifle cradled in his arm, pointed at the ground as instructed. Marty had shot the rifle before, but not with the high-velocity rounds that were in its breach and magazine now.

The rifle was a Mossberg bolt-action 30-06 with Marty's name artfully carved into its wooden stock. It had been his birthday present last year. He'd practiced with it for months.

Now, finally, his father had decided he was ready.

As they approached the frozen ridge, his father shifted

his ancient Winchester rifle to his left hand, extended his right arm to the side, and made a downward motion with the flat of his palm. Man and boy slowed their pace and moved as silently as possible through the snow to the top of the ridge.

The trees and some bent and frozen underbrush lent them cover as they surveyed the lay of lightly wooded land beyond them. Through the trees they could see the wide flatness of the lake, not quite frozen but with sheets of ice in its dark water.

There was movement ahead, and Marty and his father hunkered lower. Marty almost slipped and slid back down the rise, but his father reached over to grab his wrist and steady him. His father raised his gloved hand to his face and held a forefinger in front of his mouth, in a signal for Marty to be silent. Marty watched the steam of his father's hot breath swirl around the raised finger and nodded. The rifle was getting heavy. He hefted it slightly higher so the tip of its barrel wouldn't touch the snow.

Marty's father pointed toward a doe and a large buck with a fine stand of antlers less than a hundred yards away. The two animals had their heads down, feeding on some grass they'd managed to find beneath the layer of snow. The buck raised his head, as if to show off his antlers, sniffed the air, then resumed feeding.

Marty felt his father's hand squeeze his shoulder, and his father pointed to him, then to the buck.

Marty's head swam. He didn't want to kill this beautiful animal, but he knew his father saw it as food as well as prey.

It *was* food.

And it was prey. And Marty was a hunter. At least he would be. He knew what his father expected of him. Marty would do almost anything not to disappoint his father.

His father squeezed his shoulder again, brushing his back as he removed his hand.

Marty raised the rifle and sighted down its barrel at the

peacefully grazing buck. He centered the sights on the deer's large chest, just above the left leg. A heart shot.

The steam of Marty's own breath rose in the icy air, for a second obscuring his vision. His heart slammed against his ribs and his blood rushed hotly through his veins. The blackened gun sight before him trembled.

He drew a deep breath, as he'd been taught, then slowly and quietly exhaled. They were downwind of the deer, and he knew he could take his time. The animals couldn't pick up their scent. If he and his father simply were still enough, the deer wouldn't bolt.

The end of the barrel was now steady. Marty adjusted his aim ever so slightly to the left, allowing for the winter breeze, and ever so gently squeezed the trigger.

The rifle's sharp report cracked through the still morning, and the stock kicked back hard against Marty's shoulder. He had to catch himself again to keep from sliding downhill.

When he looked for the deer he saw it beginning to run and was sure he'd missed. He didn't know whether to be sorry or glad.

Then the deer stumbled, struggled up again, took a few more leggy strides on limbs that refused to work, and collapsed.

"We won't have to track after that one," Marty's father said beside him. Then he laughed and hugged Marty, who found himself laughing and crying simultaneously, and hugging back.

He saw that the Mossberg was lying in the snow and dutifully stooped to pick it up, brushing snow off its bolt action. Should he have worked the rifle's bolt and readied it for a second or even third shot?

"You did good!" his father said beside him. "How do you feel?"

Marty thought about the question and decided. "Good."

He looked about and saw that the doe was nowhere in

sight. There were tracks in the snow, leading off toward the lake.

His father noticed that Marty had seen the doe's tracks. He didn't smile, but he nodded his approval.

Marty and his father topped the ridge and trudged downhill through the snow toward the dead deer, their weight back on their heels. There was no breeze now, and the air was like still crystal that shattered each time their boots broke through the crust of snow. Marty had forgotten to put his gloves back on and his hands were cold. Through the trees, he caught glimpses of brilliant red near the dead buck, like scattered jewels in the snow.

The buck lay on its side, its neck twisted so that its head was at a sharp angle. Its eyes were open and blank. When they were close enough, Marty stooped low and reached toward the animal and petted it.

"A fine shot," his father said proudly. "Damned fine!"

Marty would never forget that morning. Not so much because of what had happened, but because of what was to follow.

27

New York, the present

Quinn reminded himself that June Galin had a bad heart. She stood squarely in the doorway of her house in Queens, as if braced to defend her home against invaders. A bee droned close by, abruptly changed direction, and passed within inches of her face. She ignored it.

"We need to look around the place," Quinn told her.

"You mean search it," she said.

"Yes. That's what we're asking you to let us do."

"What do you think you'll find?"

"We don't know. That's why we want to search."

June's gaze darted to Pearl and Fedderman, standing just behind Quinn, then to the radio car parked behind Quinn's big Lincoln at the curb.

"You have a warrant," she said, "or you wouldn't have brought people with you to help search."

"We do have a warrant, dear. We thought we'd ask and might not have to use it. We were hoping for your cooperation, considering it was your husband who was murdered."

She flinched when she heard it so bluntly stated.

"You won't have to serve the warrant," she said, stepping back. "Come on in. Just try not to mess things up too much."

Quinn waved for the two uniforms waiting in the radio car to join them, then led the way past June Galin into the house. Though she'd made room for them to enter, they still had to edge past her. It was as if she was putting up a token defense for her dead husband.

"We'll try to be neat," Pearl assured her as she squeezed past, the two uniforms at her heels. They were officers Nancy Weaver and Vern Shults. Shults was near retirement and could be sitting behind a desk, but he preferred to be out in the field. Weaver had worked her way up to detective rank, but had screwed up again somehow and was back in uniform. She was a talented detective, but she liked to sleep around, especially with other cops. It had been good for her libido, but bad for her career.

June Galin walked to the sofa and sat down squarely on the middle cushion. She picked up a throw pillow and held it in her lap, hugging it, as the five invaders began what, in her mind, must be a vandalizing of her home.

"Possibly we can find something that tells us who your husband met the night of his death," Quinn said.

"I've already searched for that," June said, not looking at him.

"Then you understand why we must."

She didn't answer. Almost certainly Joe Galin hadn't confided in his wife. She didn't know she was defending honor already lost.

Quinn began opening drawers. The warrant specified that the object of their search was evidence that might shed light on who'd been with Galin the night of his death. But out in the street, before they'd approached the house, Quinn had made it clear to everyone what they were searching for once they got inside. It was the same thing police auditors and bank examiners were trying to find, only they were searching in paper form or on the Internet, or for a safety deposit box. Everyone was looking for Joe Galin's secret cache.

Looking for money.

Across the bridge, in Manhattan, something else had been found.

"Go on in and take a look," the uniform in the hall said. He was a young man with old eyes. His uniform was a size too large for him. He was pale, slender, with a prominent Adam's apple. Acne scars pitted both cheeks and the bridge of his nose. He could have passed for seventeen if it weren't for those eyes. "I'll go back in there if I have to, but I gotta say it ain't high on my want list."

Detective Sergeant Sal Vitali and his partner Harold Mishkin exchanged a glance.

"You say the super found her?" Mishkin asked. He was a small man in his fifties, with a receding chin and a sprout of gray mustache. He had arched gray eyebrows that gave him a perpetual expression of mild surprise. Vitali thought Mishkin always looked like a befuddled accountant interrupted at his work.

The uniform nodded, swallowing. "Yeah. In the bathroom. Said a neighbor complained about the smell and the flies."

"Flies?"

"Yeah. So many of them. Like thousands. They got into the ductwork, and some of them made it into the apartment upstairs."

"Where's the super now?" Vitali asked. He had a voice like gravel in a can, and a head of unruly curly black hair. He might have played Columbo if Peter Falk hadn't beaten him to it. Vitali traded on that in cold weather, wearing a wrinkled trench coat and squinting a lot. Mishkin let it pass without comment. Anyway, Sal wasn't nearly as subtle or polite as Columbo.

"The super?" the young cop asked, almost as if he was in a daze. "He's down in his basement apartment. He ain't feeling so well."

"What's your name?" Vitali asked.

"Henderson, sir. Ron Henderson."

"You ride with a partner?"

"No, but there's another of us here. Gary Mumford, he was nearby and did a follow-up on the squeal."

Vitali remembered two radio cars parked outside.

"Where's Mumford?"

"Went out to get some air. He ain't feeling so good, either." Henderson glanced at his watch, as if events were on some kind of schedule. "He oughta be back soon."

"You stay here in the hall," Vitali said. "Don't let anyone else in this apartment till we give you the go-ahead. Understood?"

Henderson nodded and swallowed. Vitali thought the young cop had the most prominent and hyperactive Adam's apple he'd ever seen.

Vitali looked at Mishkin. "You ready, Harold?"

"Almost," Mishkin said. He drew a small tube of mentholated cream from a pocket, squeezed a little on his finger, and applied it beneath his nose. "You want some?"

Vitali did, and followed suit. Usually he didn't bother, and it was only Mishkin, with his famously weak stomach, who used the menthol fumes to keep from upchucking. But after listening to young Henderson, Vitali figured this time should be an exception.

Mishkin held the tube out to the young cop. "This'll help," he said. "Used to be we lit up cigars at times like this, before they declared open season on smokers."

Henderson dabbed some of the cream beneath his nose and nodded his thanks to Mishkin. Another swallow, this time followed by a feeble smile.

Vitali was a little surprised by Henderson's reaction to this crime scene. Cops saw a lot, even young ones like this. And what about the other one, Mumford? What had so badly shaken up these guys?

Time to find out.

"Let's do it, Harold," Vitali growled, and led the way inside.

Mishkin drew a deep breath and followed.

Their first impression was that the apartment was quiet.

No, not quiet.

As they moved farther into the living room they could hear a faint but persistent buzzing.

Both Vitali and Mishkin had heard the sound before and knew instantly what it was. The flies Henderson had mentioned. Hundreds, maybe even thousands of flies.

The mentholated cream was making Vitali's eyes water as they made their way toward the short hall that must lead to the bathroom. With each step the buzzing got louder.

As they approached the open doorway they began to notice flies in the hall, all around them. Mishkin slapped one away from his face. Another threatened to fly into Vitali's right nostril. He brushed at it and saw it circle away.

Where have you been, you little bastard?

The buzzing coming from the bathroom was very loud now, filling every chamber of Vitali's brain with noise.

Just outside the bathroom's open door, he and Mishkin looked at each other. Then Vitali stepped closer to the doorway and leaned forward so he could see into the bathroom.

No, no, no, no, no . . .

"Sweet Jesus!" he muttered.

He felt Mishkin move up to stand alongside him.

"Awww," was all Mishkin said, as if he was terribly disappointed in someone or something.

The plastic shower curtain had been flung aside, maybe by the super, to reveal what was left of the woman. She was hanging upside down from some kind of metal contraption set up over the tub, covered with flies. They swarmed over her like a moving blue-black carpet, and their buzzing roared through Vitali's consciousness. There was something fierce and frightening in the sheer volume of their collective, constant drone. They were in charge now. It was their turn.

The woman had been slit open wide from pubis to throat. Her internal organs had been removed. Through the undulating carpet of flies Vitali could see her spine and the backside of her rib cage.

Bile rose in his throat. He made himself move closer on numbed legs and peer into the bathtub.

Her entrails were there in a bloody pile. More flies, so many the mass of them flexed and shifted like one huge creature intent on its feast.

Vitali jerked back away from the tub, bumping into Mishkin, who stared at him in surprise. Fear glittered in Mishkin's mild blue eyes.

"You don't have to look at that, Harold."

But Mishkin did, edging closer to the tub. When he turned back toward Vitali there was an expression of horror on his pasty face that Vitali would remember on his deathbed.

A fly bounced against Vitali's cheek, found its way back, and crawled into his ear. He slapped at it and felt it fall out. He was sure he felt it fall out.

"Let's get outta here, Sal," Mishkin said calmly.

Vitali backed out first, then turned and almost ran toward the living room and the door to the hall. Mishkin was behind him at a fast walk.

Back out in the hall, they closed the door tightly so none of the flies, none of the horror, would follow them out.

Young Henderson was leaning against the opposite wall, looking somberly at them with his old eyes. *You've seen it, too,* the eyes said. *Welcome to the club. There's no way to resign.* There went the Adam's apple.

"Call for a CSU, Harold," Vitali said. "Tell them about the flies. They'll need to get rid of the damned things before they can get her out."

Mishkin didn't answer, but pulled his cell phone from his pocket and walked down to the end of the hall. He tried to open the window there, but it was jammed tightly closed, so he contented himself with standing, staring outside, as he made his call. Considering his own reaction, Vitali was surprised that Mishkin had managed to keep down his breakfast.

"Stick here," Vitali told Henderson. "Keep the scene frozen. That means you don't go in there, either."

"I was just about to go check out that bathroom again," Henderson said.

Vitali had to smile. Humor, no less. The kid with the old eyes was going to be okay. For a second Vitali considered explaining to Henderson how they were going to have to put what they'd seen somewhere in the dark cellars of their minds and not look at it or think about it, never let it escape back into the light. It wasn't exactly forgetting, but it passed. Then he realized none of this would be news to the young cop. Besides, it wasn't the kind of thing easily put into words.

"Don't you even *think* of going back in there," he growled at the kid, shaking a finger at him.

Then he went to get Mishkin so they could talk to some of the neighbors before the crime scene unit showed up.

"They're on the way," Mishkin said, still staring out the window at the end of the hall. "I was thinking, Sal, how this one looks like it could be habitual."

Mishkin knew what he meant. A murder like this one, committed in such a brutal and bloody ritualistic manner, might not be the first such crime.

And it might not be the last.

28

"Here!" Fedderman said.

At first Quinn wondered where Fedderman had gotten the white board he was holding. Then he realized it was one of the bottom shelves of the floor-to-ceiling bookshelves. They were searching the Galin house's den, or family room, wherein was a large red leather sofa and matching recliner, as well as the oversized oak desk where all the family's bills were paid and correspondence was written.

Fedderman and Nancy Weaver had removed almost everything from the shelves, even the large encyclopedia set and coffee table art books on the bottom ones. One of the end-bottom shelves had a hole about half an inch in diameter drilled through it at a sharp angle toward the room, so that it was barely noticeable when the white enameled shelf was viewed by anyone facing it. But if it happened to be noticed, you could insert a finger at the angle of the hole, crook it, and easily lift out the shelf. The bottom shelves were set on a baseboard about five inches above the dark brown carpet, and in the space between this shelf and the floor had been hidden stacks of rubberbanded bills of large denominations.

Along with the money were several large, plain brown envelopes.

Pearl had also heard Fedderman and came over with Quinn to see what he'd found.

"Neat little hidey-hole," Fedderman said, nodding toward the space beneath the removed shelf.

"There's a small fortune there," Weaver said.

"Large fortune for a cop," Pearl said. She glanced over at Weaver's trancelike stare at the money. "Is it giving you ideas?" She and Weaver had never gotten along for more than minutes at a time.

Weaver's face reddened, but she said nothing and moved away.

"Don't start, Pearl," Quinn said softly.

She didn't bother to look at him.

Fedderman began opening the envelopes. Some of them contained more money, stacks of hundred-dollar bills. Others contained gold and silver jewelry. Even some gold coins.

"Looks like pirate treasure," Pearl said.

Still miffed at Pearl and feigning disinterest, Weaver had gone into another room where her partner Vern Shults was working. Quinn saw movement near the door and thought she might have calmed down and was returning, but June Galin entered the den.

She stared at the books stacked on the floor, then at the white shelf, which was now leaning against the wall. Then she saw what was going on, and her eyes widened. Quinn watched her closely. She really did seem surprised.

When she got closer and saw what had been hidden beneath the removed shelf, she seemed genuinely shocked. Quinn was afraid her legs might buckle and braced himself to be ready to catch her if she fell.

But she managed to maintain her equilibrium.

"I don't understand . . ." she said. But Quinn knew she did. The knowledge had come suddenly, and at a cost.

"Your husband never told you about this?" he asked.

She began to stammer and then clamped her lips shut. Obviously holding back tears, she looked bitterly up at him. "Who do you think he was hiding all this *from*?"

Quinn understood how she must feel, betrayed by her husband even after his death. Their relationship hadn't been as loving and trusting as she'd imagined. It had to be difficult for her.

"I don't know *what* to believe now," she said, rubbing the heel of a hand into her eye. "What else might not be true?"

"We're going to try to find out," Quinn said, as gently as he could. He believed—his years of experience and his gut told him—this woman was an innocent caught up in her dead husband's game.

She swiped the back of her hand across her nose, which had started to run. "I'm so goddamned confused . . ."

Quinn wasn't confused. What he felt was rage toward the late Joseph Galin, dirty cop, almost certainly planning on keeping his ill-gotten gains and at some point leaving his wife.

"I'm sure your husband loved you," he said, "whatever his faults."

Pearl gave him a look, letting him know this was no way to talk to a suspect. That's what June Galin had suddenly become, though Pearl had come to the same conclusion as Quinn: it was unlikely that June had known her husband Joe was a bent cop. The hiding place beneath the bottom shelf had been created mostly to keep her from finding that out.

June began sobbing in earnest now, and went to the red recliner and sat on its edge, her face buried in her hands.

Pearl and Fedderman both stared at Quinn, question marks in their eyes. Were they going to regard June Galin as a suspected coconspirator? Cuff her, read her her rights, and take her in?

Quinn, almost imperceptiblly, shook his head no.

Fedderman came over to stand near him, keeping his

voice low. "If Galin was dirty, it could be his murder's got nothing to do with the Twenty-five-Caliber Killer."

"Maybe," Quinn said, thinking the investigation was leaning in that direction. There was no shortage of motives when it came to who might have killed Galin.

Then he recalled that inside-out pocket in Galin's suit coat. And there was something else . . .

"Hey!" a woman's voice said.

Everyone turned to look at Nancy Weaver standing in the doorway. She was holding a six-foot-long oak board beneath her right arm, as if she might go surfing, but the surfboard was obviously a bookshelf. And she was grinning.

Quinn remembered the bookshelves in the living room, crowded with glass figurines and a pewter collection.

"There was one of those removable bottom shelves in the living room, too," Weaver said. "Come see."

The hiding place in the living room held more money and jewelry, along with an envelope containing three deposit box keys.

When the tally was completed the next day, it was determined that Joe Galin had hidden in his modest home two hundred thousand dollars in cash, as well as ninety thousand dollars' worth of jewelry. The three deposit boxes had held another fifty thousand and a coin collection that hadn't yet been appraised.

But what interested Quinn most was something found in the first hiding place they'd discovered. An empty yellow envelope that looked, by the way it was folded and impressed, as if it had once contained money.

Renz was telling Cindy Sellers over the phone whatever she wanted to know about the Hettie Davis murder. Sensational though it might be, it wasn't what Vitali and Mishkin feared, the opening act of another serial killer in the city. Not yet, anyway.

"The thing about the flies," Sellers said, obviously taking notes. "That's great."

"Yeah," Renz said, and swallowed. *Ice-hearted bitch.*

"Any additional comment?" Sellers asked.

"Just that we're working day and night and in between," Renz said. "And the killer should know we're getting closer with every breath he takes."

"That's good," Sellers said. "You decide to give up police work and politics, you should be a writer."

"Who'd believe any of it?" Renz said.

After the conversation, he hung up his desk phone, confident that Sellers wouldn't speculate in her paper about yet another serial killer, this one focusing on women. The way Hettie Davis was killed must have taken a lot of hate, a lot of sickness, a lot of evil.

He pushed the intercom button and told his assistant out in the anteroom that he didn't want to be disturbed, then got up from his desk chair and cracked the window a few inches. Then he sat back down in his chair and fired up a cigar. Not an illegal Cuban like the ones he knew Quinn was smoking, but a good cigar nonetheless. Smoking wasn't permitted in the office or anywhere else in the building. Damned near nowhere in the city. But what was the point in being police commissioner if he couldn't break the law?

He leaned back in his chair and smoked, thinking about Hettie Davis again. Her murder had shaken even two old pros like Vitali and Mishkin. It had to be hard stuff.

What was wrong with people out there in his city? Were they getting worse? Renz had seen plenty of all sorts of crime, most of it committed for the usual reasons: greed, passion, revenge, mental illness. . . . But sometimes the reason was simply evil. Not often, but sometimes. Renz believed in evil, and he knew Quinn believed in it. They'd both seen it and would see it again.

Renz swiveled his chair so more of the cigar smoke would drift out the window. He didn't want it to leave a tell-tale tobacco scent after he'd finished the cigar and sprayed the office with aerosol pine air freshener. He adjusted his position until he saw with satisfaction that the window was drawing well. Smoke seemed to be fleeing the office.

He rested his head against the chair's high back and blew a perfect smoke ring that dissolved quickly and headed for the polluted outdoors. He thought some more about evil. It was difficult to define, and though you might deny it even to yourself, you could feel it when you were in its presence. It did something to your flesh and stirred something long dormant in the minds of those whose job it was to deal with it. Genuine evil, the real deal, stuck to people, and it scared the hell out of them. Ask Vitali and Mishkin. Ask anyone who'd been anywhere near that crime scene.

Renz tried and failed to blow another smoke ring. In his cynical, self-serving way, he prayed there wouldn't be another Hettie Davis.

29

Black Lake, Missouri, 1985

The snow-painted woods were quiet after the reverberation of the rifle shot; then there was the crunching sound of boot soles breaking through the icy crust as Marty and his father made their way down the shallow grade toward the kill point.

They stood over the dead ten-point buck Marty had just shot. The action had quickened their blood, and despite the low temperature, neither of them felt the cold. Marty, in fact, was perspiring under his heavy coat.

"We draggin' it back now?" he asked, his breath fogging out before his face as he looked up at his father.

His father smiled. "We ain't got *my* deer yet."

Marty returned the smile tenuously. "We gonna just let him lay here, pick him up later?"

"Can't do that. We'll tree-hang him, cut him so he bleeds out, then come back later and field dress him proper."

"How we gonna do that?"

Marty's father drew a coil of thin nylon rope from a coat

pocket. "I'll help you string him up; then I'll show you what to do. Then you'll do it." He walked over to a tree about ten feet away and tossed one end of the rope over a thick branch about ten feet off the ground.

"I'm rememberin' when me an' my dad did this," Marty's father said.

"How old was you then?"

" 'Bout your age. Like he was when his father before him showed him how it was."

"Long time ago," Marty said.

"Not so long. Grab on, son."

Marty and his father clutched the deer by its antlers and dragged it over the snowy ground to the tree. It left a long red track of blood along the trail of their boot prints.

Marty's father made a large loop in the rope and pulled it tight to the branch so a single strand dangled from the tree. He held the dead animal's rear hooves together and wrapped the rope around them in a weaving motion, around and in and out between the slender legs, so they were tied firmly together. Then he looked around for a stout fallen branch, found one, and broke it over his knee so it was about two feet long. This he inserted in the slack in the rope and began to wind it, tightening as one would a tourniquet. The rope drew taut, and as Marty's father rotated the branch, his arms well above his head, the deer raised off the ground.

"There's a wire gizmo called a gambrel you can use to fasten the rear legs," Marty's father said. "We use rope. Always have, always will."

When the deer's antlers had cleared the ground, Marty's father looped rope around the piece of branch so it was firmly fixed. He stood back, breathing hard, his breath steaming, and surveyed his work. The deer dangled awkwardly upside down, but the knots were tight and the rope would hold.

"Ain't goin' nowheres," he said.

"Guess not," Marty said.

His father unbuttoned his coat and reached inside. He

drew out his long bowie knife from the sheath on his belt, and with one swift, powerful motion slit the deer's throat.

Blood spurted from the great severed arteries, brilliant red and steaming on the white snow. The shock and stink of it made Marty gasp and step back.

"Mind you don't get none on you," his father said.

Marty felt sick to his stomach. He swallowed and tried to keep his voice as deep as possible, but it still broke when he spoke. "We goin' lookin' for your buck now?"

Marty's father peered closely at him, as if trying to see into him, and smiled, then looked away, almost as if to see if there was anyone else in this part of the woods.

"Ordinarily we would," he said, "but there's somethin' you gotta do first. Let's jus' take a little walk, wait for this fine animal to bleed out."

Marty followed, not at all unhappy to be leaving the scene. As they walked away he could hear blood pattering on the ground. The sound of it, the scent and vivid red of the blood on the pure white snow, would never leave him.

They walked down to the lake, then along the frozen shoreline. Winter had hit with the lake level high, and the dark water that was flecked with ice looked to be halfway up some of the smaller trees. There was no sound in the winter woods other than the crunch of their boots in the snow, and sometimes in the frozen mud.

"There's somethin' Alma an' me don't much talk about," Marty's father said. Alma was his wife, Marty's mother. He and Marty referred to her by her first name, because that's what she demanded. His father looked over at him with a faint smile as he spoke. "The both of us—you an' me—are from a family of hunters, descendents of Red Hawk, who was the most renowned hunter in the Chippewa nation."

This wasn't news to Marty. He'd even used the fact to earn some respect at school. Aside from family whispers, he had heard others mention Red Hawk and his father's Chippewa lineage. He'd even read in some of the books in the school library about his ancestor, the legendary Red Hawk.

"You proud of who you are?" his father asked.

" 'Course I am. Always been."

"When my father was young, his father took him huntin' when he was just about your age, an' it was the same way with *his* father, all the way back to Red Hawk."

"Family tradition," Marty said.

"Oh, it's somethin' even more'n that."

They'd left the lake and circled around and were back near where the dead deer hung from the stout tree branch.

When they approached the deer, Marty couldn't believe how much blood was on the ground beneath the ugly jagged slice in its neck. There was so much blood around the gash itself that it made the cut look even deeper than it was, so it appeared as if the great animal's head might fall off from its weight and the weight of the antlers.

Marty's father reached beneath his jacket and drew out a different knife, large, with a sharp blade. About an inch from the knife's point was a curved barb, jutting out about half an inch like a steel tooth.

"Take off your clothes," he said to Marty.

"Wha—"

His father smiled. "Don't be frightened. Jus' go ahead an' undress."

Marty did as he was told, hanging his clothes over some nearby tree limbs, letting his boots sit on the ground with his socks in them. What had seemed a slight breeze became more brisk now, as if taking advantage of Marty's nakedness.

His father smiled at him again, then turned his attention to the deer. He inserted the point of the blade in between its rear legs, then grunted with effort and made a long incision all the way down, even cutting through breastbone, almost to the gashed throat.

The deer's stomach opened wide, and its entrails spilled out onto the ground. Marty recoiled from the fetid copper stench of blood and corruption. He could taste it along the edges of his tongue. A long gray section of intestine remained dangling from the body cavity.

His father flipped the knife around in his hand so he was holding it by the bloody blade. He extended the bone handle to Marty. "You finish the job. Ordinary way to do this is to lay the deer down, open it up more gentle, but we do it this way. This here's a gutting knife. Some hunters like this kind 'cause it's got a gut hook. You use that sharp barb on the blade to hook the deer's insides. That'll help you pull out the internal organs. You cut out the rectum an' tie it with this cord, else wise you can have a hell of a mess. You gotta clean that deer out good so nothin'll rot later on, so the meat'll cure okay. You understand?"

Marty had never felt so naked and addled. His stomach was on a roller coaster. Bile rose bitterly in his throat. At first he thought he could stop it, but he had to turn away suddenly and vomit. His bare toes were splashed, and he moved back out of the way. That was when he noticed he was standing with his feet in blood. All around him was blood now mixed with vomit.

"Dad . . ."

His father moved the knife closer to him, and Marty took the bone handle and trudged through the snow and blood to the deer. He had goose bumps and was shivering, but not entirely from the cold.

The stench and heat of the deer almost overwhelmed him, and made him vomit again. But he steeled himself and found surprising resolve deep within him. A place in his mind he didn't even know existed.

He did something like turning off his mind, and set to work with the knife.

"Use your hands," his father said. "Both of 'em if you have to."

Marty continued gripping slippery, sometimes still-warm internal organs, cutting them free and pulling them from the bloody cavity, dropping them to the saturated ground at his feet.

"Hollow him out good," his father said encouragingly.

Marty worked harder and harder, not so much minding the blood now. What he wanted to do—what he *had* to do—was finish field dressing this deer so he had the approval of his father. Of his father's father . . .

When the carcass was nearly hollowed out, he heard his father say, "Now rub the blood on yourself, Marty. All over yourself."

And Marty, sobbing quietly from his stress and effort, did exactly that, painting himself with blood.

War paint. Like putting on war paint.

His father came to him, dipped a hand inside the deer, and rubbed more blood on Marty's forehead. The tip of his forefinger moved with slow purpose above Marty's closed eyes, tracing some kind of design, a symbol. Then he removed the knife from his son's hand and stuck it into the deer. Still holding Marty's hand, he led him down to the lake.

Marty washed in the icy water, rinsing the blood from his hair, splashing lake water coldly over his face. He was trying to shock himself back from what seemed like a dream.

Only he never made it all the way back. It hadn't been a dream.

His father told him to run ahead and get dressed, and Marty, shivering, made his way back to where the deer was strung up. He got his clothes down from where he'd draped them over branches. Fumbling with frozen fingers, he managed to dress himself.

He was still cold, even with his boots and coat on. He tried not to, but he began to shiver.

"You'll get used to field dressing game," his father said. "The way I did after my father had me do the same thing you jus' did."

Marty could only nod, still trembling from the cold.

"Think of it as an initiation. A rite of passage. Can you?"

"I can," Marty said. It didn't seem like enough. "I do."

His father gazed at the sky and pointed.

Marty looked and saw a large bird, maybe a hawk, circling high above. It was wheeling lazily, the way hawks do, as if they're more concerned about rising than falling.

"You're one of us now, son. A hunter."

A sudden flush of pride warmed Marty so that he not only stopped trembling, he barely felt the cold.

"A hunter," his father said again. But it didn't seem like his father's voice that time. Not exactly. It was almost like a third voice, inside Marty's head.

30

New York, the present

Pearl and Fedderman were out reinterviewing witnesses. Quinn had assigned them that task mainly because Renz had wanted to meet with him alone.

They were in the sparse but efficient office on West Seventy-ninth Street. Quinn was seated at his desk. Renz was standing across from him, leaning back with his butt propped against the edge of Pearl's desk, the way Pearl often stood. Quinn wondered if there was something about that spot, the way the two desks were arranged, that induced people to stand that way.

"The Hettie Davis murder," Renz said. "Hell of a mess."

"The job takes a strong stomach sometimes," Quinn said.

"I don't mean just that kind of mess," Renz said. "The sort of butchery that was done on the victim, that's usually not a one-time thing. The bastard treated her like she was some kind of animal he'd killed and was gonna make a rug out of, or something." He absently toyed with a cellophane-wrapped tip of a cigar protruding with a clipped pen from the pocket of his white shirt. "How likely is it that we've got two major psychotic serial killers operating at the same time in the same city?"

"In this city," Quinn said, "maybe not so unlikely. But whoever killed Hettie Davis might not be a serial killer."

"We both know better than that," Renz said. "By the way, she'd had sex, but some time before death. Impossible to know how long, but at least six hours. No sign of forcible entry. No semen, either, so no DNA. Traces of condom lubricant. Might have nothing to do with her murder and she was a random victim."

"Or maybe it was a crime of passion."

"Cold-blooded passion," Renz said. Both men knew there was such a thing. "I had a records search done, and there's nothing like that kind of killing happened here as far back as it went."

"So it would be his first," Quinn said. "At least in this city."

"All that doesn't change the fact that it's the kind of gory, ritualistic murder serial killers commit."

"But not *always* serial killers. Not even usually. Maybe she wasn't a random victim. Maybe there's something personal in this."

"Personal?" Renz asked, as if people murdering people they knew were a new concept.

"Killer and victim could have known each other," Quinn said, "could even have been lovers, and there was something between them that led up to the murder, maybe even over a period of years."

"I got a good team on it, checking all that out. Vitali and Mishkin."

Quinn knew both men, and they were top detectives. Sal Vitali was a pushy kind of guy, a hard driver. Harold Mishkin was almost timid, a deep thinker with a weak stomach. Together they got things done. "My guess is they'll find the victim had a history with the killer," Quinn said.

"Your guess and my hope. Two psycho freaks terrorizing the city at the same time's a nightmare scenario."

"We don't have that," Quinn reminded him, almost adding *yet.*

Renz seemed suddenly to become aware that he was fingering the cigar. "Okay to smoke in here?"

"Sure. Pearl'll find out—she can smell tobacco smoke at a mile and a half—but that's okay."

Quinn waited until Renz had used a thin gold lighter to fire up his cigar, then got one of his Cubans from a desk drawer and lit it with a book match. When Pearl got hissy about the air quality, as she almost certainly would, he could truthfully blame it on Renz.

The two men enjoyed their smokes for a while, not saying anything. Then Renz said, "I'm the goddamn police commissioner and whenever I light up anywhere in this city I feel like I'm back smoking in the boys' room in high school."

"You get to be mayor, Harley, and you can change that."

"Be at the top of my agenda," Renz said. "Right after bustin' balls in the NYPD so the murder rate drops. Between that and the smokers' vote, I don't see how I can't get elected."

Probably, Quinn thought, he was serious.

Renz tilted back his head and blew a series of imperfect smoke rings that created a white pall up near the ceiling. He laughed. "Pearl will be furious."

"At somebody," Quinn said.

He simply wasn't getting it, so Prudence Langton patiently explained it again to the apartment building's super, a grossly overweight man wearing a dirty gray uniform. He was sweating profusely, causing his dark chest hairs to glisten where the top two buttons of his shirt were unfastened. He was bald, smelled rancid, and wore what looked like a religious symbol on a silver chain around his thick neck. She didn't consider him dating material.

Prudence had on a fashionable gray pantsuit with a ruffled white blouse. She was wearing her usual Blind Obsession dabbed behind her ears and at the top of her cleavage, but its delicate scent was easily overwhelmed by that of the super. "I was Vera's roommate in college," she said. "I knew I was coming to New York on business and wanted to see her. I've been calling for two weeks and getting her machine. And I've been here twice knocking on her door, and nobody answers." She leaned toward him, trying not to breathe in. "You *do* know who I'm talking about?"

"Sure. Miz Doaks, Seven B. I ain't seen her in quite a while neither, runnin' in an' out like she usually does. A regular jogger. Keeps in shape, all right." His small gray eyes journeyed up and down Prudence as if they had a lascivious mind of their own. "She's an actress or somethin'. I just figured she had a job outta town. Summer stock theater, or whatever it is them kinda people do."

"I'm afraid it isn't that. I talked to her literary agent. He said he's been trying to get in touch with her, too, and hasn't had any luck. What I'd like is for you to unlock her apartment so we can see if anything's happened to her."

"You mean is she up there dead?"

Pru swallowed. *Dead? Not Vera. Not possible.* "I'd prefer to think that perhaps she's sick and unable to get to the phone. Or possibly she's taken a trip and there'll be some sign of that."

"Summer stock," the super said again. He used a filthy rag to wipe his gleaming face. He seemed to see for the first time the look of apprehension in this obviously refined woman's eyes. Maybe it was because of him. He didn't like it that his appearance might be scaring her. Slightly embarrassed, he forced a smile. "I been workin' on the plumbin'," he explained. "Dirty work."

"You don't have to go in yourself," Pru said, assuming he was concerned about smudging Vera's apartment. These were two people who definitely couldn't communicate on the same wavelength. It was more than frustrating for Pru. "I just want to glance around and make sure she isn't there."

"Then what?"

Pru's plan was to go to the police and see if they'd list Vera as a missing person, but she decided not to involve the super in that.

"Then I'll know," she said simply.

The super made a big show of considering. "I don't usually do something like that unless it's the police or somebody like that askin'. Or unless I know there's some kinda trouble in a unit."

"Well," Pru said, running out of patience, "I can get the police. But time might be important. If Vera's up there with some sort of health problem and the worst happens, I don't want to be in any way responsible. Nor do you, I'm sure."

The prospect of legal responsibility did the trick. "You got a point there." He untucked the dirty rag from his belt and used it to wipe his hands. "I'll go get my passkey, and we can take a look-see."

As they rode the elevator up, he said, "Miz Doaks is one of the nicer tenants here. I wouldn't want anything bad to happen to her, so I guess it is best we decided to look in on her."

Covering his ass. Not so dumb. "We have to look out for each other," Pru said.

"Used to be you didn't have to," the super said, "but now you do. In this city, you sure do."

After he unlocked the door he stood back, obviously intending to stay in the hall. His visitor's apprehension had proved contagious.

Pru opened the door to a stillness and staleness that suggested the apartment had been unoccupied for some time. She stepped inside, noting that Vera's home was functional and fairly well decorated.

Immediately she noticed the potted plants on a windowsill. They were brown and dead.

Pru's heart began to pound as she moved deeper into the small apartment. She held her breath as she glanced in each room.

No sign of Vera.

Now she wished the super had come in with her. She had to make herself open the door to the closet in the bedroom, and to another in the short hall. She had to make sure Vera wasn't in one of them, that someone hadn't locked or hidden her out of sight.

But Vera was in neither of the closets. The one in the hall held only linens; the one in the bedroom, what looked like Vera's full complement of clothes and shoes. Pru made herself peer under the bed. There was nothing there but dust bunnies and two suitcases, one large, one small, both with wheels. Both empty.

It seemed unlikely that Vera was traveling.

When Pru went into the kitchen and opened the refrigerator she found sour milk, and green mold on cheese and meat. In the produce drawer were limp brown celery stalks and two shriveled tomatoes.

This wasn't good. The dead plants, unpacked suitcases, closet full of clothes, and the obviously old contents of the refrigerator. Something was very wrong.

Pru went back into the living room and noticed the phone with its answering machine blinking red, signaling there were messages. She thought about playing the messages and then decided against it. Maybe she shouldn't touch anything in the apartment.

When she returned to the hall she watched as the super relocked the apartment.

"Satisfied?" he asked.

"Yes," Pru said. "She isn't in there."

But where is she?

She decided that her next stop would be the nearest NYPD precinct house.

* * *

Pearl stood staring at herself in the restroom mirror. She didn't like admitting that they were getting to her. At odd times of the day or night, she found herself wondering and had to check.

She leaned toward her mirror image and with her right hand bent her right ear forward, tilting her elbow in as she rotated her body to the left.

There, on the right side of her neck, was the mole, usually invisible behind her ear from this angle.

She leaned in closer, turning her head left at an extreme angle while looking right, so she might have a better view.

Larger.

The mole, or brown spot, or whatever it was, was definitely larger than it had been the last time she'd checked.

No. Not definitely.

She realized she was hurting her ear and released it and leaned back away from the mirror.

This was stupid, this constant self-examination. Her mother and Milton Kahn had driven her to this state of mind with their idiotic harping on the mole. Or spot. Or whatever it was. If she was going to keep examining it, she should wait at least a few days so it had time to become larger and she could actually see a difference.

As she started to turn away from the mirror, she couldn't help herself. She folded her right ear forward and looked again at the mole. Or spot. Or whatever it was.

Not larger.

Not definitely.

What is it?

Something to worry about. That was for sure. You go around day after day and think you're healthy and secure, and all the time something's working on you, against you, without you even suspecting it. It could appear harmless, simply a part of you that you've gotten used to, but it could kill you as surely as a safe falling on your head, and almost as suddenly. Like your own body deciding it had lived long enough so it was time to turn on you. On itself.

Pearl let her ear flop back in place.

Don't be so morose. Don't think that way.

But she knew it was true. Life could be like that, end like that.

In a boarded-up imported dry goods warehouse in the East Village, Vera Doaks's hollowed-out corpse dangled motionless in the darkness. Her internal organs were reduced to a coagulated hardened mass an inch thick on the concrete floor, inedible now even to the rats and insects. Other than considerable damage to the feet and hands, the corpse itself was only moderately eaten on, as it was a tricky task even for a resourceful New York rat to traverse the crossbeam and make its way down the rope that bound the ankles. What was left of Vera Doaks was beginning to take on the look of dry mummification.

31

Some rich men have a certain subtle sheen, as if over time gilt had rubbed off on them. Thomas Rhodes was such a man. He was accustomed to the best, and it showed. He looked like a component of the wealth and luxury surrounding him.

He drew a small white card from his pocket and checked again on the room number that had been given him, then rode the elevator to the thirtieth floor of the Eastin Hotel in Times Square. After decades of reversal, the Eastin had been recently renovated and brought up to its present high-end luxury standards. In fact, the décor was almost decadent. Gold-flocked wallpaper, wide crown molding, veined marble, and ornate chandeliers seemed to crowd one another even in the hotel's vast spaces. On one of the elevator walls was a Rubens print in what appeared to be a museum-quality gilded frame.

Now in his mid-fifties, Rhodes was still lean and fit, his graying hair combed straight back from a widow's peak, his tailored suit a black chalk-stripe material set off by his gold and black striped tie and the flash of white cuffs and gold cufflinks when he moved his arms. He looked exactly like what he was, a very successful banker.

There was another passenger in the elevator, a small man in a gray business suit, who obviously found himself in awe of Thomas Rhodes's near presence. Rhodes was used to such reaction and barely glanced at the man. The fellow's shoes were cheap imports, his watch a gold-plated imitation. He hardly mattered.

Rhodes set his wingtip Barker Black shoes in a wide stance and waited for the high-speed elevator to settle before striding from it out into the plushly carpeted hall. He looked neither left nor right.

Finding the room number he'd been given, he checked his Patek Philippe watch to make sure he was on time to the minute, then knocked.

The man who almost immediately opened the door was slightly shorter than Rhodes, slightly leaner, and had dark hair neatly trimmed and combed to the side from a perfect part. He was wearing a well-cut dark blue suit, a white shirt, and a blue and gray silk tie with a perfect Windsor knot. His face was as lean as his body—hawklike—even with hooded brown eyes. Despite his rather predatory features, there was a professorial aura about him. Even a courtliness.

The one thing, the pertinent thing that Thomas Rhodes noticed about him, was the way his eyes took in Rhodes standing in the doorway. They were unimpressed and unafraid.

Even standing out in the hall it was obvious to Rhodes that the room was very cool. The man ushered him in, smiling slightly and offering his hand. "Martin Hawk," he said.

"And you know who I am," Rhodes said. *Might as well get on top of this conversation from the start.*

"Oh, indeed I do," said Hawk in his softly modulated voice. "Thomas Rhodes, Stanford honor student, Harvard MBA, successful career at Cartner-Whimer, inventor of the bottom-up leveraged buyout, now president emeritus of Rhodes and Finkman Finance."

"Not so emeritus," Rhodes said pleasantly, careful not to show his surprise at this man knowing so much about him.

"Yes," Hawk said, "you're still quite active in the business, when you're not away on safari or stalking game in Canada or Alaska. No children. Married Gail Cromartie in nineteen ninety-two, divorced in ninety-nine. Presently Gail is living in London, while you reside here in New York in a condo in Benton Towers on the Upper East Side. You have homes in the Hamptons and in Sarasota, Florida, where your boat, *Striver II*, is docked."

"Yacht," Rhodes said.

Hawk smiled, his hooded eyes steady. "I stand corrected. The yacht is outfitted for deep-sea fishing as well as luxury. You hold the record for largest ocean pike, I believe."

"Have for twelve years." Rhodes felt his composure slip a notch. "You've done your research."

"I hope you're not offended."

"Not in the slightest."

"Please sit down, and we'll discuss the reason you're here."

Soon Rhodes was seated in a satin-upholstered wing chair across from Hawk, who sat relaxed with his legs crossed in a brown leather easy chair. His wristwatch was visible, an undoubtedly genuine Rolex. Rhodes was sure his shoes were Savile Row. Both men were sipping twenty-year-aged Macallan single-malt scotch whiskey that Hawk had already poured.

"You've been recommended by a former client of my company, Quest and Quarry, Mr. Rhodes," Martin Hawk said, in his level and cultivated voice—not an English accent but almost. The voice went with the man's obvious polish.

Rhodes resisted asking who was the source of the referral. Hawk almost imperceptibly nodded, as if to say he approved of Rhodes playing his cards close to the vest. It was unsettling.

"You are a hunter, Mr. Rhodes. On various safaris and expeditions, you've hunted the most dangerous animals on earth. Now you have the opportunity to hunt something even more dangerous than the tiger, the only animal that doubles back and lies in wait for its stalker. This tiger will be armed as you are—and also hunting you. Your, and his, expertise in the bush will be neutralized by the terrain, so you and your fellow hunter will start even, with identical weapons—small and untraceable twenty-five-caliber handguns. A condition of the hunt is that after you take your prey, you remove his weapon as your trophy and return it to Quest and Quarry, so there'll be no evidence of our involvement or unconventional business arrangement."

Rhodes sipped his scotch. "Well, that's quite a bit to take in."

Martin Hawk sat patiently and waited. At this point, a few clients had gotten up and walked out. Not that they knew anything they could prove. But their refusal to do business did necessitate changing hotels, being extra careful for a while. Hawk didn't figure Thomas Rhodes for one of the walkers.

"I've been reading the papers," Rhodes said, "watching the news."

"Have you now?"

Neither man mentioned the .25-Caliber Killer.

Rhodes took another sip of the excellent scotch and said, "So far so good. Tell me more."

"The terrain is Manhattan. You'll be in separate hotels that you must leave and not return to between nine a.m. and midnight. This is important: within your respective hotels, each of you is out of season and safe.

"Your prey will be a predator like yourself, a tiger who yearns for the ultimate hunting experience and is willing to pay for it. Participants pay a hundred thousand dollars each. When the survivor presents his trophy gun as proof of his opponent's death, returning it with his own weapon to Quest and Quarry, he receives a full refund plus fifty thousand dollars."

"The money is inconsequential," Rhodes said.

"Of course it is. Though not to some of our clients. But it isn't about the money."

"No, it isn't. Not to a certain type of man." Rhodes gently swirled the rich amber liquid in his glass, his gaze fixed on something outside the high window. Beyond the sun-touched buildings across the street was clear blue sky but for a few streaks of white cloud, like claw marks.

"I want you to think about this carefully, Mr. Rhodes, but I would like your answer before you leave this room. For both of us, I want you to be sure."

Rhodes finished his scotch and stood up. Being sure was what he was about.

Martin Hawk regarded him with mild curiosity.

"Whom do I kill?" Rhodes asked.

PART II

Oh, write of me not "Died in bitter pains,"
But "Emigrated to another star!"

—HELEN HUNT JACKSON,
Emigravit

32

Lavern Neeson made a halfhearted attempt to duck beneath her husband's slap. The flat of his hand stung her forehead instead of her cheek with a solid *whap!*

She put her mind, *herself,* on hold.

Just as well. There wasn't time to think about defending herself. The second slap was almost instantaneous, to her left cheek and ear, causing a thousand needles of pain, a ringing sound, and the salt taste of blood. The force of the blow whipped her head to the right. Blood escaped her mouth and splattered the dresser mirror. Alongside the blood was her own face staring back at her, a mask of horror that terrified her.

She didn't even have time to look away. In the mirror she saw Hobbs's hand clutch a fistful of her blond hair. The horror mask image flashed out of sight as Lavern was slung across the room and onto the bed.

The pillow again!

Bedsprings sang. Hobbs was on top of her, straddling her, pressing one of the pillows—her own—almost flat against her body with one hand. The other hand he balled into a fist, and he began pounding the pillow. Lavern almost cried out with pain, but she knew that would only make it worse. The pillow would prevent bruising while his fists caused agonizing internal injury. Her body, so damaged inside, would appear unmarked.

Not her face, though. Hobbs usually couldn't resist beginning one of Lavern's beatings by starting with a slap or two—"to get her attention," he'd once told her—before concentrating his righteous wrath on her body.

She kept her teeth clenched, her lips clamped, emitting only whimpers, as she heard him breathing harder with each blow. It would stop soon, she was sure. She often counted the blows, and usually somewhere between fifteen and twenty he'd become exhausted in limb or rage and stop pounding the pillow.

Eighteen!

Nineteen!

Finally spent, he gave her a final punch, just below her breasts, and then shifted his weight off her. He'd left her breasts themselves undamaged this time, knowing she was soon due for a mammogram. No point in doing something that might show up on an X-ray and prompt questions.

Lavern felt herself being turned onto her stomach, felt her slacks and panties being wrenched down. Hobbs removed her shoes. Then she heard stitches pop and felt her clothing other than her shirt being worked down over her calves and rigid feet, turning into a tangle and a clump, and yanked away, leaving her terribly exposed and vulnerable. There was a glimpse of something dark, like a great bird soaring across the room, which she knew was her wadded clothing being tossed into a corner.

Hobbs was on her then, lying full length on top of her. His right arm snaked around her neck, yanking her head back. If she tried to scream now he'd tighten his grip so she could only make a harsh rasping sound, like a crow cawing.

Lavern's mind drew back further away from what was

happening, into a quiet dark place of shelter and unknowing. A place of surrender and suspension that prey animals knew so well.

The woman being crushed into the bed felt something cold between her buttocks. Vaginal lubricant, or whatever kind of greasy substance Hobbs happened to come up with. Once it had been cooking oil. Her buttocks separated, and she felt his probing finger, then more fingers.

Wincing silently in pain, the woman understood why Hobbs abused her. In some twisted, debilitating way, while she loathed it, she couldn't simply walk away from it, couldn't escape it. The more he abused her, the more she must deserve it, and the more she deserved it, the more he'd abuse her. It was a cycle, like the rest of life. And like the rest of life, it had to be accepted because it simply *was*. Like the rest of life, it was a trap.

The woman knew that Hobbs was as helpless in the cycle as she was. Knowledge was supposed to be power, she thought. It didn't work that way for her. Knowledge was only more of a conundrum. As the one who understood, it was her responsibility to stop what was happening, yet she didn't. She couldn't. That meant, in an oblique but very real way, that she was the one to blame. The one who deserved to be punished.

Hobbs removed his left hand, and she watched from the corner of her eye as he wiped his greasy fingers on the bedsheet. Then he used the hand to grip himself. She felt his weight bear down harder on her, felt the pressure that was impossible to resist as he guided himself into her.

Hobbs preferred anal sex. It hurt more.

In the morning he'd assure her that he loved her, and she'd believe him because it was true. She knew it was true.

It had been a long time since a man had professed love for Rosa Pajaro, who was fat, forty, and tired. Lifting the stacks of sheets and pillowcases to the top shelves of the hotel storage closet sent a dull pain along the base of her spine.

She wondered sometimes how she'd come to this situation. It seemed that only yesterday she'd been one of the prettiest girls in her village of Tojano in Oaxaca, Mexico. Then had come her affair with the American engineer. A year after the affair had begun, her beautiful daughter Sara was born. Their daughter, though the American never claimed the girl publicly.

Then had come Sara's illness and the medical bills. The American was by then dead, after an infection from a wound incurred in an auto accident on a winding mountain road. He had been drunk, and on his way back to town after an assignation with a married woman. Rosa could never forgive the woman, but she'd long ago forgiven the American.

Rosa's mother was now watching and caring for Sara in Tojano. Rosa, her dark eyes dimmed and weary, her olive complexion coarsened and seamed, her black hair lank and graying, had made her way to America to work, having bought forged papers with money the American had left her.

Hard years had passed like cards being shuffled in a deck. Now here she was working as a maid in the Antonian Hotel in Manhattan, having replenished a storage room with freshly laundered linens. Ever the optimist, Rosa rubbed her sore back with both hands and reflected on how wonderful the fresh linens in the small room smelled from the perfumed detergent the hotel laundry used. Rosa liked that part of her job that dealt with the clean linens. The soiled linens were, of course, a different story.

She was about to go back out into the hall, when she heard a sound as if someone had been slapped, only louder.

The storage room was off a corridor that ran the length of the hotel's east side, where there was a little-used exit out into a passageway between it and the side of the Honeysuckle Restaurant next door. Rosa hesitated in pushing the storage room door open with the cart she'd used to transport the linens, and instead eased the door open about six inches with her hand and peered out into the quiet, carpeted hall.

So little used was this corridor that she expected to see no one. Instead she saw two men. One was on the floor, the other bending over him. As Rosa watched, the man who was standing lowered himself on one knee and removed something from one of the pockets of the man on the floor. She was sure it was a gun, and realized the sound that she'd heard had been a shot. The kneeling man placed the fallen man's gun in his own pocket. Then he straightened up and looked up and down the corridor.

And saw Rosa.

He didn't hesitate. He strode toward the storage room.

Rosa thought about screaming, but realized no one would hear her. Instead she decided to shut and lock the door.

But of course there was no lock on the inside of the storage room door.

It opened quickly, the knob yanked from her hand so suddenly and violently that it hurt.

He was tall and fierce looking. She saw that his big hands were empty. He'd left the gun he'd taken from the other man in his pocket. He simply stared at her with cold blue eyes.

Then he smiled. He raised his forefinger to his lips in a signal for her to be quiet, and to remain silent about what she'd seen. Then he turned and walked back toward the man on the hall floor.

As she watched, he again bent over the prone man, gripped him beneath each arm, and pulled him backward, toward the door leading outside. He glanced at Rosa and again raised his forefinger to his lips. Then he dragged the other man out through the doorway and into the night.

The door swung shut. She knew that it automatically locked and couldn't be opened from outside without a key.

She told herself she was safe, but she didn't feel safe.

Rosa stood trembling, staring at the empty corridor. It

had all been like a dream. *Had* she seen it? Had it actually happened?

She moved backward all the way into the storage room and, without thinking about it, resumed her work. She pushed the empty laundry cart out into the hall, bumping the door open, thinking of her mother and Sara in Mexico, of her forged papers and her job at the Antonian. Rosa was in charge of rooms 570 through 580 on the fifth floor. They were suites, and the tips were more than adequate. They were in dollars that soon became pesos.

She pushed the cart back along the corridor the way she'd come, listening to its squeaking rear wheel, telling herself that what she'd seen hadn't happened. She couldn't afford for it to have happened, so it hadn't.

It hadn't. She'd seen nothing, and she'd say nothing.

It hadn't happened.

She silently repeated her daughter's name to herself to the rhythm of the squeaking wheel, *Sara, Sara, Sara* . . .

It hadn't.

33

Sal Vitali knew this was going to be one of his worst days.

"I wanted to look the place over before my company seriously considered leasing it," Arnold Penington said. He gulped. "That's when I found it. Her, I mean."

It, Vitali thought, as he looked at what was left of the woman. She was hanging upside down from her bound ankles attached by rope to a beam, a long incision made from her pubis to her throat. She was opened up and hollowed out like Hettie Davis, only the long period of time had . . . Vitali, stared slack-mouthed at the dried, leathery state of her body. He could only think of it as cured meat.

The hardened mass on the concrete floor, beneath and alongside the woman's upside-down head and gracefully draped arms, was what was left of her internal organs. Her eyes were missing—thanks to the rats that lived in the long-abandoned warehouse—and three of her fingers on the dried hand that lay partly on the concrete floor had been nibbled to bare bone.

Vitali heard the warehouse's steel overhead door clatter

and clank up, then lower. His partner, Harold Mishkin, he of the turbulent stomach, had just entered the warehouse after talking to the uniforms outside who'd secured the scene.

Vitali considered telling Mishkin not to look at the dead woman, then thought better of it. Mishkin took pride in the fact that he could screw his courage tight and look at what homicide detectives too often saw without losing his lunch. Occasionally his stomach had its way.

Arnold Penington had moved well back and stood silently, not looking in the direction of the dangling body. Mishkin continued to advance. He was about twenty feet away, waving at the dirty, narrow windows lining the east wall of the building. "We oughta get more light in here, Sal."

"Maybe not, Harold," Vitali said in his gravel-box voice.

Mishkin stopped cold and stared at what was left of the woman dangling upside down from the warehouse beam. His hand floated up to his mustached mouth.

Almost immediately he gained control of himself and pretended he'd raised his hand to stroke his mustache.

He said, "Jesus, Sal."

"Him and his dad," Vitali, the lapsed Catholic, said. "I don't see how they could let something like this happen."

"Just like the other one," Mishkin said. "Hettie Davis."

Vitali could smell the menthol cream Mishkin always dabbed beneath his nostrils to help keep his food down at violent crime scenes.

"Gotta be the same guy," Vitali said. "She's been gutted and cleaned like some kinda game animal."

"Yeah, but . . . what else happened to her? I mean, her eyes and all . . ."

"Rats," Vitali said.

Mishkin turned away and bent over. He still didn't lose it, though. He turned back, straightened up slowly as if in pain, and wiped his forearm across his mouth.

Vitali was proud of him. Mishkin should have been in another business, or riding a desk at some precinct house in a gentler part of town. It was where he'd be if he weren't so damned good at his job.

Whatever the physical impact of what he saw, Mishkin's mind was still working, along with his commitment to the job. He paced off a slow circle around the upside-down, dangling body. There was a floor drain nearby, down which most of her blood must have flowed. It was obvious, too, that her throat had been slashed, probably while she was alive and hanging there. The things people did . . .

"First Hettie Davis, now this one," Vitali said. "We've got a set."

"Judging by the condition of the body, this one was killed way before Davis," Mishkin said.

"Yeah, but either way . . ."

"I know what you mean, Sal. We've got us a serial killer." He finished his slow circle and wound up standing near Vitali. After another glance at the dead woman, he shivered. "What's wrong with people, Sal?"

"Some people, you mean," Vitali said.

"Yeah. Thank God only some."

"I don't know what's wrong with them, Harold. Maybe that's why we do what we do, trying to figure it out."

"That and we like to get paid," Mishkin said, playing hard.

Sirens sounded outside.

"Reinforcements," Mishkin said, figuring more radio cars and a crime scene unit. Maybe an ambulance. More than once somebody assumed to be dead turned out to be alive. It wouldn't happen this time, though.

Neither Vitali nor Mishkin said anything for several minutes. Penington, even farther away now, remained silent. Then the steel overhead door at the other end of the warehouse rattled open again and let in a blast of bright light. Silhouetted against the afternoon brilliance, half a dozen figures entered the warehouse. Among them, Vitali recognized the short, chesty form of Dr. Julius Nift, the obnoxious little medical examiner.

"The little prick's here," Mishkin said.

"We've seen enough of the victim," Vitali said. He nodded toward the advancing figures. "She belongs to them now."

"No," Mishkin said, "she belongs to us."

34

Hobbs would kill her if he knew she was doing this, stopping for a drink at Melody's on her way home from the doctor. But she felt she had the right to stop, to steady her nerves and to celebrate her relief.

Though Lavern Neeson hadn't really expected a problem, she was nonetheless relieved. Her mammogram had turned out negative. Dr. Chivas hadn't seemed to notice any injury to her internally bruised torso, which she had held as stiff and still as possible. She did sense that he'd noticed the makeup covering her facial bruises, but he didn't say anything. There were all kinds of ways she might have gotten those marks, from a fall down the stairs to a quarrel with a neighbor. Anyway, Dr. Chivas wasn't the sort who pried. If his patients wanted him to know something, they'd tell him. Then he would act. He would do what he could to heal.

Lavern had left the medical clinic and walked only a few blocks toward her subway stop before spotting Melody's Lounge. She'd noticed it before, but had never gone inside. This afternoon, with something to drink to, and the city so hot, she did go in.

She was soon situated on a bar stool near the door. The lounge was dim, and there was a blues tune playing so you could barely hear it. Peggy Lee, one of her all-time favorite singers. There was a woman who'd overcome a rough youth, who'd had to cover her bruises with makeup. What a career Peggy Lee had enjoyed. What a life she'd led, after a stumbling start. Listening to her always made Lavern feel better.

Aside from a woman behind the bar, there were only three other people in Melody's. A couple sat at one of the tables along the wall, lost in the promise of each other's eyes. Halfway down the bar from Lavern a guy sat staring straight ahead, maybe at himself, in the back bar mirror, sipping something amber from an on-the-rocks glass. There were two identical empty glasses in front of him.

Kind of early for that kind of drinking, Lavern thought. Though the way Peggy was slowly meting out the blues, it might have been a gloomy two in the morning. The woman behind the bar, tall and with a top-bun hairdo that upped her to over six feet, approached and smiled a hello. Lavern ordered a Bloody Mary. Almost a health beverage.

Of course Hobbs would still object to it, as he objected to almost everything she did. He'd made her promise him she'd stop drinking, trying to get her to pretend along with him that she was developing a problem.

The tall woman—maybe Melody—had the drink before Lavern within a few minutes, then withdrew to the far end of the bar, where she'd been working on what looked like a crossword puzzle. Peggy Lee launched into a song warning her lover not to smoke in bed. Other than that it was quiet, with only soft traffic noises filtering in from outside.

Pleasant, Lavern thought. The alcohol relaxed her almost immediately, maybe because of the heat outside and the fact that she'd skipped lunch. She felt safe in here, isolated, her cell phone turned off and in the car, Hobbs at work for most of the rest of the day. She took a bite of the celery stalk that had been in her drink, then set it aside on a napkin. The crunching sound of her chewing the celery seemed unusually loud. Maybe it even attracted the attention of the guy down the bar.

He lowered his drink to its coaster and glanced over at her and smiled. *Wham!* This was a handsome one. In his thirties, dark hair and eyes, killer smile, wearing light tan slacks and a black sport coat, a red and black tie against a white shirt. Everything about him looked expensive.

Lavern thought about Hobbs.

He'd kill me.

If he knew.

She decided it wouldn't hurt anything if she flirted a little. Hobbs would never find out. Anyway, she'd be in enough trouble with Hobbs if he just knew she was here, drinking in the middle of the day. He didn't like it when he didn't know exactly where she was, and he especially wouldn't like it if he knew she was in a bar. Lounge, rather.

If she flirted a little, talked with this dark-haired guy and listened to his patter, it would make her feel better. Make her feel she was desirable as something other than a punching bag. She felt a pang of shame. A pang of anger. She smiled back at the man down the bar.

What the hell? It isn't like I'm gonna screw the guy.

What Hobbs would do if he discovered her in bed with another man was something her mind didn't want to comprehend.

In a kind of graceful manner the guy down the bar swiveled around on his stool and stood up, holding his drink steady and level in his right hand. She saw that he was about average height and well built beneath the nice clothes.

She liked the way he moved. He advanced toward her with a liquid, muscular walk, as if he might be some kind of athlete, absently spinning bar stools with his left hand with each step . . . two, three, five stools. They made a soft, ratchety whirring sound as they spun.

The closer he got, the handsomer he became. Heavy-lidded

eyes, the kind people sometimes called bedroom eyes, a sort of predatory but sexy cast to his lean features.

When he was about six feet from her the expression on his face changed. Lavern knew why. He'd noticed the bruises. The makeup could conceal them somewhat in the soft light, but not from a few feet away. The light in his brown eyes dimmed, and his smile lost its wattage. He knew what facial bruises probably meant: violence he wanted no part of. Lavern came with dangerous baggage, so why waste time talking her up? Lavern couldn't blame him.

When he was almost alongside her he widened his smile, raised his glass to her in a silent salute, then set it on the bar on his way out the door, as if he'd been headed there all the time and not down the bar to talk to her.

Letting me down easy.

"Too bad," a woman's voice said, as the door swung closed behind him, cutting off the glare of outside light. "I thought he was interested in you."

Lavern looked up and saw the woman who might be Melody behind the bar.

"I thought so, too," Lavern said. She took a sip of her Bloody Mary, then met Melody's eyes with her own. "Listen, you don't think I—"

"That you're in here working? Drinking a Bloody Mary and trolling for afternoon clients?" Melody shook her head, grinning. "Not hardly. But I do think our handsome friend was lookin' for a lady. He had that way about him."

"Yeah, he sure did."

"Oh, well. He'll never know what he missed."

"Shame," Lavern said.

But the woman who might have been Melody was already moving away behind the bar, returning to concentrate on what might have been her crossword puzzle. Lavern was left feeling, as she often did, that this was a world in which she couldn't quite connect.

It was strange, she thought, the way people's lives could

almost but not quite intersect, the way drastic changes could almost but not quite happen. She wondered if there were lots of parallel worlds where almost everything was different from the way it was in this one because different choices had been made. Different worlds with different, happy Laverns.

Not likely.

Fate, destiny, whatever. The hell with it.

Probably Hobbs would have found out and killed us both.

"Shame," Lavern said again, softly, to herself.

35

Probably to demonstrate to Quinn that he was a busy man, Renz wanted to meet him for a chat while on the way to an appointment. He'd said he had something to show Quinn.

They stood in the warmth of the sun at Rockefeller Center, beneath the colorful line of noisily whipping flags that were captives to the breezes flowing down the avenue. Now and then one of the flags would snap like the canvas of a sailboat suddenly billowing with air. Behind them, Renz's gleaming black limo sat at the curb, its engine idling, the barely discernable form of the driver behind the tinted windows sitting and staring patiently straight ahead.

Renz had on an expensive-looking blue pin-striped suit. His maroon tie had somehow found its way out from beneath his three-button coat and was frolicking in the breeze like the flags above. Backhanding the tie aside, he handed Quinn a large brown envelope and said nothing.

Obviously this was what he wanted to show Quinn, who undid the envelope's clasped flap and examined the contents.

They were crime scene and morgue photos of Vera Doaks.

"What's this world of ours come to?" Quinn said sadly.

"It's the same as ever," Renz said. "Story of life. We live, we become garbage, and they put us in a hole or burn us to ash."

"Somehow you live with that perspective," Quinn said.

"It's the only way I can live, being honest. You should try it, Quinn, instead of nurturing your weak spot."

"Which is?"

"You're a romantic. The world is shit. You fool yourself into thinking it isn't and try to clean it up while I recognize it for what it is and happily wallow in it. That's the difference between us."

"I'll stay a romantic," Quinn said.

Quinn knew what the photos meant, and there was no way to romanticize it. The killer the press had tabbed the Slicer had taken another victim. There was another serial killer in the city.

"On the surface it looks like we're dealing with two dangerous psychos," Renz said.

"On the surface?"

Quinn looked at the last photo and slid all of them back in the envelope. Then he reminded Renz of the common thread that seemed to connect the .25-Caliber Killer's victims. All of them had been hunters.

"And the two Slicer victims," Renz said, showing that he was a step ahead of Quinn, "were treated like game animals, gutted and strung up like meat put out to cure. Could be we got us one killer using two different MOs to throw us off the scent."

"Serial killers don't usually work that way," Quinn reminded Renz. "They act out of compulsion, and usually follow a ritual set in motion in childhood. These murders have all the earmarks of serial killer crimes, but it's doubtful they were committed by the same person."

"But possible."

"Barely."

Renz attempted to tuck his errant tie back beneath his buttoned coat, but it flapped right back out, reminding him it was an untidy world. "In this case," he said, ignoring the tie, "we're going to assume, publicly at least, that we have one serial killer using two different methods."

"And what links the murders is the hunting motif."

"Very good," Renz said.

"Flimsy."

"But convenient. Sal Vitali and Harold Mishkin will continue working on the Slicer murders, but under your direction."

"They won't like that."

Renz shrugged and made another futile attempt to tame his tie.

"Have you talked to Helen Iman about this?" Quinn asked. He was interested in what Helen the profiler had to say about tying the two cases together.

"She agrees with you," Renz said. "It's not likely the Slicer and the Twenty-five-Caliber Killer is the same person. Their methods aren't even similar. She thinks the hunting angle is thin, too."

"Helen's smart for a profiler," Quinn said. "You should listen to her."

"But like you she considered it possible, if not probable, that we've got one killer. When we began discussing odds, though, she started talking about a meteor striking us dead."

Quinn fixed a stare on Renz. "You don't think it's one killer either, do you, Harley?"

"I think it's politically expedient for it to be one killer. You might not like the necessity of handling these cases that way, but there *are* politics involved. That's something you should have realized earlier in your career, Quinn. You might have become police commissioner instead of me."

Quinn knew he was right. Still . . .

"Have you told all this to Vitali and Mishkin?" Quinn asked.

"An hour ago," Renz said.

"I'll bet they were overjoyed."

"They huffed and puffed, like you. But they took it. Like you. None of us has any real choice in this matter."

Quinn sighed and jammed his hands deep in his pockets so Renz wouldn't see that they were clenched in fists. "All of this for political expedience."

Renz smiled and stuffed his flapping tie inside his shirt between the top two buttons, where finally it remained trapped.

"All of this," he said, "for that."

36

Terri Gaddis wouldn't be surprised if he didn't show up. Handsome guy like Richard, he could have just about any woman he wanted, when he wanted.

How great it must be to be a man, rooting around among the trinkets, choosing then putting back down, instead of being one of the trinkets.

She took a sip of her rum and Coke and tried not to keep looking at the Magic Lounge's door. Now and then a wave of embarrassment and anger at herself would wash over her.

What am I doing here? Other than waiting to be stood up?

But she knew what she was doing. Trying to relieve the loneliness of working at Office Tech, then going home, sometimes stopping for drinks with one of the other women at the store, watching reality TV (*Survivor.* Boy, she could identify with that one), going to bed, getting up, and then climbing back on the treadmill. Day after numbing day.

Then all of a sudden there he was, tall enough and certainly dark and handsome, chatting her up among the printers and fax machines in aisle seven.

Lucky aisle seven.

He'd accidentally brushed his arm against her right breast when reaching to turn on a printer—she was sure it was accidental—and it felt as if wires ran from her nipple to the core of her sexual need, and another wire ran directly to her heart. Conduits of erotic electricity.

To look at his face you wouldn't think they'd made any contact at all, while her heart wouldn't slow down. Terri couldn't remember when a man had done that to her. If ever. Anyway, it was rare, and something you didn't just toss away in your life. She'd realized that the moment it had happened.

"This printer," she'd told him, "will print papers on any kind of photo."

He'd merely smiled at her awkwardness. "If I were dyslexic," he'd said, "I wouldn't have noticed that."

That was how they'd begun a long and increasingly personal conversation. He'd been so smooth, so obviously deeply interested in her, that she'd been the one to suggest they meet later here at the Magic Lounge for drinks and more talk. And he'd seemed pleased to accept her invitation.

Terri wasn't naïve. She knew that was a bullshitter's stock in trade, seeming to be just what people wanted or needed at the time. But if he was pretending, he was so, so good at it. Close enough to be the real thing, when emotion was there to fill in the blanks. What was fake and genuine was difficult enough to discern in this life, even if you looked closely. A person could see glass and throw away a diamond.

She wished he were here now to pretend, if that's what he was doing, instead of being sixteen minutes late. She'd pretend right along with him.

Other men in the lounge were getting interested in her, making her uneasy. All of them looked like losers, compared to Richard Crane.

Then the door opened, and there he was. Relief flooded through her and somehow morphed into a wash of desire. He was as handsome as he'd been in the store, wearing light tan slacks, a blue sport coat with brass buttons, a pale blue shirt open at the collar. Several women in the lounge looked at him and couldn't look away. Terri felt a tingle of excitement and possessiveness as he smiled and walked toward her.

"Been here long?" he asked, sliding onto the bar stool beside hers.

"Not very. Anyway, I had stuff to think about."

"Such as?" His gentle, hooded eyes held hers. He was truly interested in her thoughts. In everything about her.

"About how my life is going," she said. "One week after another in the store, stocking electronics, telling people about electronics, now and then selling electronics. It's . . ."

"Soul stifling," he said.

"Exactly." *He does understand.*

"Ever thought about quitting and trying something else?"

She had to laugh. "I don't have the nerve."

The bartender came over, and they ordered drinks. He a scotch rocks, she another rum and Coke.

"So rum's your drink. You could be a lady pirate," he said seriously.

She had to giggle. "Where do I apply?"

"Right here. I can see you in a pirate outfit. You'd look sexy. Boots, three-corner hat, sword . . ."

"Eye patch?"

He seemed to think about it. "Sure."

Their drinks arrived. She took a cautious sip of hers, remembering it was her second. If they stayed for a while here, he'd be a drink behind her. Dangerous.

"Boots and a sword," she said. "Are you a little kinky, Richard Crane?"

"Only if you want me to be." He tasted his scotch. "What turns me on is you. Just you."

They drank silently for a while, studying each other.

He said softly, "Take a chance, Terri Gaddis."

She felt her heart race.

"Have dinner with me tonight," he said.

"Is that taking a chance?"

"Depends on where we eat."

She smiled. "That eye patch thing is growing on me. Trouble is, I don't have one."

"We could make believe," he said. "Or you could keep one eye closed. That'd be enough for me."

Take a chance, Terri Gaddis.

"Let's finish our drinks," she said, "then go to my ship, and I'll make dinner in the galley."

"Sounds great. I'll buy the wine on the way there."

He wants to keep me drinking.

"Maybe we can have a treasure hunt," he said.

"I think it'd be better if we sailed around a bit first."

He wounded her with a smile, then sipped his scotch. "You're the pirate." He lowered his glass and regarded her. "If you're worried about the rape and plunder part," he said, "don't."

Terri smiled and rested a hand on his arm. "I would never plunder you," she said.

He downed his scotch and said, "Damn it!"

John Riley had finally drunk enough wine that the voices were stilled. An hour after it got dark, he made his shambling way into the passageway between the Honeysuckle Restaurant and the Antonian Hotel. There were some black plastic trash bags piled against the hotel's brick wall. Riley was pretty sure there wouldn't be much of value in them, but they might make a comfortable enough bed for the night.

He still had half a bottle of the cheap wine he'd bought with what he'd been able to beg on the street. Breakfast had been half a cheeseburger he'd seen someone throw away in the trash receptacle at the busy corner down the block, and he hadn't eaten since. The truth was, he wasn't hungry. Maybe it was the wine, or maybe the spot on his lung, the one that doctor had told him about last year, had developed into some kind of disease that was making him thin. Or maybe it was old age. Riley was what . . . sixty-three? Or four? Whatever, anything over fifty was old for the streets.

Riley stopped halfway down the passageway and grinned. This was good. It looked as if more plastic trash bags had been added since he'd cut through here yesterday. Or was it the day before? Time was losing its traction in John Riley's life. Why wouldn't it? Night was often day in this city.

Being in the passageway, the bags probably weren't part of the regular trash pickup, and the hotel would call now and then to have them taken away. Meanwhile, Riley could make good use of them.

He kicked with his right foot, chasing away two rats. Kicked at the bags again to make sure there weren't more of the rodents there, out of sight. He didn't kick so hard that the plastic would split, though, and release fluids or some foul odor that even he couldn't abide. Carefully, to accommodate arthritic knees, he lowered his aching body and lay back on the mounds of black plastic. He wriggled around so he wasn't in contact with anything hard, then uncapped his wine bottle and sighed. He was tired. If he was lucky, he wouldn't dream. He wouldn't hear the voices again until morning.

Riley took a deep draw on the bottle and felt the acidic liquid course down his throat. There'd been a time when he'd have sent this one back in a restaurant and ordered another vintage. In another life.

Some of the wine dribbled from his mouth and ran down his unshaven chin. Quickly he raised the bottle upright so he wouldn't lose more of its precious contents, and lowered it to his side. He shrugged a shoulder to wipe his chin against it and looked down at the bottle, about to raise it for another sip.

That's when he saw the hand.

At first he thought it might be a joke, someone hiding in among the trash bags. Or a fake hand. A mannequin's, maybe. Something like that.

But he knew it was human, even though it didn't look quite right.

Then he knew why it didn't look right. It was dead.

The voices screamed.

37

There were floodlights set up in the street and at each end of the passageway, so it was like day, only the glare was surrounded by darkness. Moths fluttered in and out of the brightness in warm night air so humid they might have been swimming.

"Same as the others," Fedderman said. He'd been closer and reached the scene ahead of Quinn and Pearl.

They were standing near the dead body that had been found beside the Antonian Hotel. Julius Nift, from the medical examiner's office, was over by his black city car parked among the NYPD radio cars, peeling off his latex gloves. The CSU techs were still gathering evidence in the blocked-off passageway. Nift glanced over at Quinn, smiled, and nodded.

Quinn nodded back, thinking, *Asshole.*

He thought about going over and talking to Nift, but the arrogant little ME was already climbing into his car, pulling the door closed. Quinn figured it didn't matter. As Fedderman had said, this one would be like the others. Cause of death: a small-caliber (which would later turn out to be a

.25) bullet to the head. Nift might have a time-of-death estimate, but it would be only that—an estimate. Quinn could
wait until tomorrow for the postmortem report.

He almost spat a foul taste and odor from the edges of his
tongue, then remembered this was a crime scene and swallowed instead. He was pretty sure most of the stench was
coming from the black plastic trash bags, but the dead man
was contributing.

Quinn looked back down at him. The man was in his late
forties or early fifties, dressed conservatively in neatly
pressed Dockers and a blue checked shirt, wearing a black
sport jacket that was twisted around his body because of the
way he was lying. He actually didn't look too bad except for
the way his eyes had sunk back in his skull, and of course the
hole in his forehead.

Fedderman had already searched the man's pockets and
found nothing other than a hotel key card. Galin had been
the only victim who hadn't had one of those on him. Galin,
in fact, was the odd piece in this puzzle, linked by method
and not much else.

"Looks like our killer shot this guy, then concealed the
body back against the brick wall under the trash bags so it
wouldn't be found right away," Fedderman said. "That
guy"—he pointed toward a ragged, bearded man yammering
and gesticulating wildly at a uniform from one of the radio
cars—"happened to notice a human hand protruding from
the trash while he was back here getting ready to sack out for
a while with his bottle of wine. That sent him screaming out
into the street, where he scared the shit out of people and
snarled up traffic. An ex-cop from Denver dragged him back
up on the sidewalk where he'd be safe and called us on his
cell, saying there was a crazy man running wild and yelling
about a dead body. Right on both counts." Fedderman
grinned at Pearl. "Why don't you go over and get Riley's
statement?"

"Riley the crazy guy?" Pearl asked.

"He's not the one with the uniform."

"Why don't you go?" Pearl said. "You're more likely to connect with him."

"I'll do it," Quinn said, to shut them up. This wasn't the time or place for one of their pissant quarrels. He pointed to a gray door set in the brick wall. "Where's that lead?"

"Into the hotel, I would imagine," Fedderman said, making Quinn wonder if Fedderman was messing with him. But then, it hadn't been the brightest of questions. "I tried it after I made sure the CSU people had dusted the knob for prints. It's locked."

"Lock automatically when it closes?"

"I don't know," Fedderman said. "Nobody's been in there yet."

"You go check out what's on the other side of that door," Quinn told Pearl. "Feds, let's the two of us go over and see what Mr. Riley has to say."

Pearl flashed a grin at Fedderman as she hurried away.

When Riley saw Quinn and Fedderman approach, he lost interest in the uniform. He was more than happy to confirm the story he'd told the first cops on the scene. Trouble was, he wouldn't stop confirming it.

"Should have given Pearl the job," Fedderman said, managing to get in a word that wasn't Riley's.

Quinn nodded.

"Pearl the lady with the big bazooms?" Riley asked, indicating big bazooms with both hands. His breath was terrible and might have been flammable.

"Let's not talk about that," Quinn said.

"Those, you mean," Riley corrected.

"Those," Quinn said, thinking if Fedderman laughed he was going to kick his ass all the way back into retirement.

"They're genuine, all right," Riley said.

Pearl was back within ten minutes, telling them the door led to a corridor and she'd found blood on the carpet. It looked like the dead man had been shot inside the hotel, then dragged outside and dumped behind the trash bags.

Riley's bleary eyes widened in alarm. "Shot? Blood? Holy, bejesus, bejesus, bejesus! I been told it's the End of Days. I been told."

"The dead man would agree with whoever told you," Pearl said, stepping to the side to avoid Riley's breath. To Quinn she said: "I've got the bloodstain cordoned off and a uniform posted to protect it."

Quinn nodded, not doubting that the blood would belong to the corpse lying next to the mound of stuffed trash bags. *This one is different. The other .25-Caliber Killer victims died where they were shot, or at least were never moved after death.*

Not exactly a break in the case, but something about it suggested to Quinn that it was important.

"Holy bejesus!" Riley said again.

Pearl said, "What the hell are you looking at?"

"Let's check inside," Quinn said. "Thanks for your help, Mr. Riley."

"The End of Days," Riley said.

"That's a good thing for you to be thinking about," Quinn said.

"I don't like that old jerk-off," Pearl said, as they were walking toward the front of the hotel.

"He seemed to like you okay," Fedderman said.

It didn't take long to learn which door in the Antonian the key card unlocked. After Quinn checked at the desk in the lobby, they took the elevator to the third floor.

The room was furnished like thousands of others in New York, an armchair that reclined, desk and matching chair, bed flanked by nightstands with lamps, an entertainment hutch, most of it in matching dark maple.

On a collapsible luggage stand was a suitcase with three changes of clothing. There was no luggage tag on the suitcase. The clothes were expensive casual and included a pair of designer jeans. There were three baseball caps, three different colors, each from a different team.

"Fickle fan," Pearl said.

Quinn looked in the tiny bathroom. There was a shaving kit and lineup of containers on the vanity. Also a coffee brewer that hadn't been used. The soap hadn't been unwrapped. No tissues, nothing, in the plastic-lined waste basket. The dead man hadn't been a hotel guest long enough to leave any stamp of personality.

Quinn took a wary look at himself in the vanity mirror and went back into the main room.

"A wallet," Fedderman said, standing at the open desk drawer. He thumbed through it. "We got us a Floyd Becker, SoHo address, fifty-one years old and will be forever." He riffled the money like a skilled bank teller. "Three hundred even."

"That's not the name he used when he checked in with cash at the front desk," Quinn said.

" 'Jones,' I'll bet," Fedderman said. "And he used his initial for his phony first name."

" 'Smith,' " Pearl said, "and no same initial."

Quinn shook his head. "You're both wrong. Answer's 'Bob Green.' "

"Shit!" Pearl said.

Fedderman chuckled nastily. "I was sure you said '*Smith*.' "

There was something unusual about this one, Quinn thought, despite Becker's lack of imagination in choosing a pseudonym. Something that deviated from the pattern in a meaningful way. Maybe it had to do with the body being dragged outside. Or maybe it was something else.

Terri Gaddis thought she'd found heaven. Her own Camelot, at least.

Richard Crane was the most gentle, skillful lover she'd ever experienced. She lay now in her bedroom, hungover and exhausted from the wine and sex, her head resting on Richard's bare chest. She could hear, could feel, his regular, coursing heartbeat. It must, she thought, be in rhythm with her own.

The pungent scent of their bodies, of their coupling, was still in the room, and she wished it would never leave. The air conditioner was humming, gradually catching up with the heat the two of them had generated. Soon, Terri knew, the room would return to normal, and so would her life.

Or would it?

Surely Richard had felt the same intensity she had, known the same revelation. *Yes! Two people can be this gloriously happy!*

He was the kind of man who would feel it. She knew that about him now. It was all she had to know.

Which reminded her that she didn't know very much. He'd mentioned that he worked for a Wall Street firm, but he didn't say which. Obviously he was successful, had money, or he couldn't dress the way he did, with the tailored suit and expensive gold watch and cuff links. And he took care of himself, judging by his muscularity and—she smiled—his endurance. She absently ran a hand over her right breast, her erect nipple.

We could do this again. And again and again and again.

She shifted her body and reached over to the nightstand where her half-full glass of wine sat and managed to wrap two fingers around the slender glass stem. After downing the rest of the wine to sate her thirst, she settled down again, snuggling against Richard's warm body. The last thing she remembered before falling asleep was his arm working its way beneath her neck and pulling her closer.

The room was cool when she awoke in the morning, and she was alone in the bed.

Terri sat up, looking around with something like alarm, and found herself the only one in the room.

"Richard . . . ?"

"In here, darling." He appeared in the doorway, buttoning his shirt that he hadn't yet tucked in. "I was getting dressed in the living room so I wouldn't wake you." His dark hair was wet, uncombed but smoothed back with his fingers, so he must have already showered. Terri had never been so relieved to see anyone.

"I thought we might go out for breakfast," he said. "Celebrate us."

"I can think of other ways to do that," Terri said.

He grinned. "It isn't either-or."

"Almost everything else is," she said.

The handsome grin stayed. "No, there are some things that are predestined. Nothing we do can change them."

"Are we predestined?"

"Most definitely."

"Then I can accept predestination." She climbed out of bed, unashamed of her nakedness in front of him. After what they'd done with each other . . . "I need to shower," she said. She padded barefoot to him, kissed him lightly on the lips, then squeezed past him and made her way into the bathroom.

She'd got under a hot shower, soaped up, and tilted back her head to rinse shampoo from her hair when she noticed the large metal hook screwed into the bathroom ceiling.

Surely it hadn't been there before.

Or had it? Maybe she simply hadn't noticed it.

No, impossible. I would have noticed.

Obviously, Richard had put it there while she was asleep.

She felt a deep dread. Why had he done such a thing? What the hell was it about? Some kind of kinky sex? Water sports? S&M? If it was that kind of stuff, Terri wasn't into it.

After last night and what had happened between them, was it going to turn into something dirty and violent? The thought of it made her stomach knot up with disappointment.

She shook her head. Dating in New York . . .

Then she felt a sudden flare of hope. *The super!* Jennison the building superintendent must have installed the hook yesterday, or even sometime over the past week, and she simply hadn't noticed it. That was it. Had to be. She'd been looking at the dark side again, jumping to disastrous conclusions. Her Camelot was safe.

When she got out of the shower, she'd mention the hook to Richard. He might even know what it was for.

38

Renz loved this kind of thing, a setting where he was in control.

He had them all in his office, Quinn, Pearl, Fedderman, and the team of Sal Vitali and Harold Mishner.

The office was hot because of the way sunlight was pouring in between the blind slats. Quinn knew the blinds would remain open because the deluge of morning brilliance was at Renz's back, putting his visitors at a disadvantage. Renz tended to play every card in his hand. Quinn also noticed the faint smell in the dust-mote-filled air: Renz had been secretly smoking cigars in his office again. If the mayor knew that, there'd soon be a new police commissioner.

Vitali and Mishner were reasonably friendly toward Quinn and his team, but Quinn could tell they didn't like the single-killer theory any more than . . . well, anyone liked it, other than Renz. And Renz liked it because it was politically expedient.

Still, Quinn had to admit it was possible that one serial killer in the city had, for whatever reason, committed two series of murders in different ways in order to forge, or satisfy, two separate identities.

Strategically silhouetted at his desk, Renz held up a folder. "This is more info on the Twenty-five-Caliber Killer's latest victim, Floyd Becker. He was wealthy from his construction company, Becker Synergies."

"Never heard of it," Quinn said.

"They aren't big in New York," the silhouette said. "They apparently built a lot of dams and such in South America. Anyway, he was well off, if not a Rockefeller."

"Liked to hunt, I'll bet," Quinn said.

"You got that right." If the silhouette was irritated by Quinn's remark, it didn't show it. "We still need to find out why he checked in at the Antonian under a phony name, and why he went out without carrying any identification." The silhouette laid the file on the desk and made a show of idly leafing through it. "No surprise to any of us that death was caused by a single twenty-five-caliber slug fired by the same make firearm—one we can't yet identify—but definitely not by the same gun."

"Maybe some make of target pistol with a changeable barrel," Vitali suggested.

"No," the silhouette said, "we checked that out. The firing pin strikes are slightly different. And you and Mishkin need to be focusing more on the Vera Doaks and Hettie Davis murders."

"If it's the same killer—"

"Call it a logical division of labor," said the silhouette. "Back to the facts: Becker was shot inside the hotel, in a corridor running the length of the building and with a door leading to the passageway outside. A spot of blood on the carpet tested out to be his. For some reason, after shooting Becker, the killer then dragged the body outside into the passageway and dumped it behind a pile of trash bags. The crime scene inside the hotel offered up little evidence other than the blood. The CSU team searched and vacuumed the surrounding carpet, came up with dirt and three human hairs. None of the hairs matches Becker's. One or more of them might be from the head of the killer. We'll know that when we nail the bastard." The silhouette turned its head toward Quinn. Strongly backlighted as it was, its hair looked like a hopeless tangle of wire. "The hotel staff have anything for us?"

"No," Quinn said. "We'll talk to them again today."

"Do that, and interview Becker's wife. She's been told about his murder, but was too shaken up to talk last night."

Quinn nodded and pretended to write something in his notepad.

"You two," said the silhouette to Vitali and Mishkin, "keep hard at the Slicer killings and report anything pertinent to Quinn. Have you got anything on the Vera Doaks murder?"

"She's still dead," Vitali said.

Here was a man, Quinn thought, without much of a future in the NYPD. But he was feeling a growing fondness for Vitali.

"If you're contacted by any of the media," said the silhouette, unfazed by sarcasm, "don't talk to them. I mean that. Tell them zilch."

"Even Cindy Sellers?" Fedderman asked.

The silhouette stared at him for a moment, trying to decide if this was more sarcasm. "Especially Sellers. I'll be the one to decide what she does or doesn't know, and when she knows it."

"Or doesn't," Quinn heard Pearl say beneath her breath. He hoped this meeting would end before she decided to jump in with Vitali and Fedderman and gang up on Renz. She could be captive to pack mentality.

The silhouette stood up and walked out from behind the desk, passing into the light and becoming Renz. "That's it for now," he said. "I've gotta meet soon with one of the mayor's aides. Keep the information flowing to me and to each other."

The five detectives assured Renz that they would, and he politely, but hurriedly, ushered them from his office.

Outside the building, in the glare of the already hot morning, Vitali put on a pair of fashionably tiny sunglasses and said, "Have you ever heard such bullshit?"

"Oh, sure," Quinn said. "But call me if you do have something on our murderous multitasker."

"I'll let you know if we apprehend either of his personalities," Vitali said.

He and Mishkin got into their unmarked, which was a later model than Quinn and his team had arrived in, and drove away. Mishkin smiled and gave them a slight wave through the passenger-side window.

"Vitali is obviously the wiseass of the two," Pearl said.

"I know Mishkin," Fedderman said. "He's almost mute and might faint at the sight of blood, but don't sell him short, even in a down market."

Pearl said, "Is the trail leading us to Wall Street?"

"Drive me back to the office and my car," Quinn said, "then Feds can take the unmarked and interview the hotel employees again. You and I, Pearl, will talk to Becker's widow."

Nerves were frayed, after the meeting with Renz. It was best to split these two up.

Quinn and Pearl's conversation with Floyd Becker's widow, a hefty, brunette with a bright pink face, yielded little of value other than to confirm that Becker was, like earlier .25-Caliber Killer victims, an avid hunter.

"He even has a lion," the widow had said. "Or what's left of one. It's down in basement storage someplace. For years we used it as a rug, complete with the head."

Pearl thought about that as she and Quinn drove through noontime Manhattan traffic toward the Antonian Hotel to join forces with Fedderman. She didn't know people still used animal skins for rugs. Wouldn't that prompt some kind of social outrage? It should, Pearl thought. In fact she felt quite vehement about it. She glanced down at her leather shoes, felt slightly foolish, then promptly righted herself and maintained her indignation. People needed shoes, damn it! They didn't *need* rugs. Especially rugs with heads on them.

"Wanna stop for some lunch?" Quinn asked.

"No. Not hungry."

Quinn glanced over at her as he drove. "You okay, Pearl?"

"Why shouldn't I be?" she snapped.

"I dunno. You look . . . angry."

"What I'd like to do," she said, "is catch this asshole we're after and have him made into a rug, head and all."

"We're pretty much of the same mind on that," Quinn told her.

"What's a lion but a big cat?"

"It's a big cat," Quinn said, making a right on Broadway.

He drove silently for a while, thinking, with Pearl fuming beside him.

She was a puzzle he'd never solve. Was that why he couldn't shake her from his dreams?

39

Later that day, Terri and Richard were eating lunch at Kazinski's on the Upper West Side. Terri was picking daintily at a romaine and walnut salad while Richard wolfed down his goulash.

She hadn't mentioned the hook in the bathroom ceiling. Hadn't thought it worth mentioning. When she saw the super she'd ask what it was for. Maybe to hang a bicycle by one of its wheels, get it out of the way for when guests came over. Not a bad idea for a tiny Manhattan apartment. Close the shower curtain and no one would ever guess they were sharing a bathroom with a Schwinn.

"I love to order goulash," Richard Crane said. "You never know what you're going to get."

Terri grinned and took a sip of her Chianti. "You obviously approve of that version."

"Yes. It's delicious. But maybe that's because I'm with you."

How can he always know exactly the right thing to say?

Terri had called Office Tech that morning and told them she wasn't feeling well. She was out of sick days, so the store manager allowed her to use one of her vacation days and said he hoped she'd feel better.

She'd felt like telling him she'd never felt better in her life, but instead politely closed the lid of her cell phone and continued her walk through the park with Richard Crane.

They'd played all morning, enjoying each other like lovers who'd been separated by life and somehow found each other. Maybe that's what they were, Terri thought. Maybe Richard was right in saying some things were predestined. Wasn't the study of genetics making that more and more obvious?

Human beings were so mysterious, Terri thought. So unpredictable. Didn't that make life wonderful?

Lavern winced as her friend Bess touched a damp washrag to the cut near her left eye. Bess held the washrag out and glanced at the blood, shook her head.

"This is happening more often," she said. There was anger in her voice.

Lavern could only nod. One of Hobbs's glancing blows had caught her in her throat, and it was still sore.

"You gotta do something," Bess said. "Make some kinda move."

Lavern began to cry. Bess touched the cool washrag to her injured eye again, and both women sat motionless for a while.

"Men," Bess said, finally. "They're never what we expect."

"Neither are we what they expect," Lavern said hoarsely.

"So everything's our fault?"

"Only most of the time," Lavern said.

Bess looked at her. "So you're goin' back to that piece of shit again?"

"Yeah. And I'd appreciate it if you wouldn't call him that."

"Ah, Lavern . . ."

"Really," Lavern said, and coughed, choking.

Now Bess began to cry.

Richard forked in some more goulash. "Would you like more bread?" he asked, while pouring her more wine.

She looked up from the topped-off wineglass and smiled. "Are you trying to get me drunk so you can take me home and have wild sex with me?"

"More like relaxed sex."

"No," she said.

He frowned.

"On the bread, I mean."

He grinned and somehow managed to add even more wine to her glass.

After lunch Terri went to the ladies' room and was surprised when she returned to find Richard holding a brown paper sack. He'd gone to the bar section of Kazinski's and bought a bottle of wine.

"Chardonnay this time," he said. "A particularly good vintage."

"Are you a wine expert?" Terri asked, as they left the restaurant and began walking through the warm afternoon toward a subway stop where a train would carry them south.

"Like everybody else," Richard said. He was joking, but Terri got the idea that he *did* know about wine. She suspected that Richard knew quite a lot about a number of things but was too polite to parade his knowledge.

"Every now and then," she said, "your good breeding shows."

"You object?"

"No. I like it. To most of the single men in Manhattan 'good breeding' signifies something else altogether."

He laughed. "Well, I like to think I know something about that, too."

"You should write a book," she said.

"I'd title it *Terri*."

Once inside her apartment, they drank to that.

"Around the time of the shooting," Fedderman said to Rosa Pajaro, "you loaded a cart with some clean laundry in the basement and brought it up in an elevator to lobby level."

"*Sí*. Yes. There is a storage room on this level where extra linens and other supplies are kept."

"It's near where Mr. Becker was shot."

He stared at her expectantly, even though he hadn't actually asked a question.

She returned his gaze for only a few seconds and then dropped her eyes to stare at the maroon carpet of the Antonian Hotel lobby. They were sitting and talking in what the management called a conversation nook. The maid was a terribly unskilled liar. Fedderman found himself liking her, and thought she must have been extremely attractive a few years and pounds ago. Rosa Pajaro was a woman who showed hard wear.

"Is right," she said, finally.

"When you rolled your cart toward the storage room, did you notice anyone or anything suspicious in the corridor?"

She shook her head no. "*Solitario*. I was alone with my job."

He had the impression she might speak English better than she was letting on. But that was a common ploy for illegal aliens, which Rosa Pajaro might very well be. In order to get her job here at the Antonian, she had to have papers, but papers could be forged.

"According to your records," Fedderman said, "you've been working here at the hotel for six years."

"Yes, that is so. I work hard."

"So it says here." The papers Fedderman consulted mentioned nothing of the sort, being a computer printout of directions and a restaurant menu. "You're rated as an excellent employee. One who would tell the truth."

"I am saying what is true. There is nothing to tell." Again she couldn't meet his eyes. "When this terrible thing happened, I must have been in the storage room."

"Or it might have happened before you arrived."

"*Sí*. Or even after I left."

"Did you notice any blood on the carpet near the door to outside?"

"No. Nothing."

"You're saying there was no blood?"

"I say only that I didn't notice any."

"Was the door to outside closed all the way and locked?"

"I couldn't say. I didn't pay attention to the door, only to my work."

Fedderman stared at her. He knew she was lying, but probably not about anything pertinent. Maybe she'd seen Becker's body before it was moved and then hightailed away. Or maybe she *had* seen the bloodstain, though on the maroon carpet it wouldn't have been very noticeable. He could take Rosa Pajaro in and lean on her, make her afraid, even suggest she was a suspect. But she couldn't be held, and when she got the opportunity she might run. If she was an illegal, so what? Fedderman didn't want to make trouble for her. There was really no reason to push her, he thought, unless she might be the killer, which was too unlikely to consider.

"I am in trouble?" she asked, alarmed by his thoughtful silence.

Fedderman smiled at her. "Not as long as you've told the truth."

"That's what I've done, I swear." She crossed herself. Fedderman wasn't sure, but he thought she might have done it backward.

40

Wow. Something's not right.

She knew she was beginning to slouch on the sofa, but she couldn't seem to make herself sit up straight.

The food, the wine, the walk from the subway stop to her apartment had made Terri Gaddis exhausted. After the third glass of wine, her eyes began involuntarily closing. It felt as if invisible fingers were pushing them shut.

She didn't want to feel this way. Richard expected some of that wild sex she'd mentioned at lunch. She'd *almost* promised him. He'd certainly be willing, but the wine was having its effect and she was fast losing her desire.

What's wrong with me? Why do I feel so . . .

Struggling not to fall asleep, she heard him rise from beside her on the sofa and cross the room, go into the kitchen.

When he returned, he lifted her head and gently placed the rim of a glass against her lips.

"Drink this, sweetheart. It'll fix you up."

His voice sounded far, far away. She sipped and was mildly surprised. She tasted the same wine she'd been drinking, one of the reasons she felt so tired.

"S'more chardonnay," she muttered.

"You say you want more?" he asked, amused.

He's deliberately misunderstanding.

"Same . . ." she murmured. She tried to say the word *chardonnay* again, but it was too difficult. Her tongue was getting numb, and there was no feeling in her cheeks. If she tried to touch them, they might not be there. They might be made of wood. She tried again. "Chardonnay." She heard something slurred and incomprehensible and realized it was her own voice.

Richard answered, she was sure, but she couldn't understand him as she dropped into a comforting warm darkness.

As she was keying the dead bolt on the door, Pearl heard the phone ringing inside her apartment. Which of course made her hurry and fumble and drop the key on the hall carpet.

By the time she'd opened the door and reached the phone, it had rung at least nine times. Maybe something important.

Too exhausted to be cautious and check caller ID, she took several long steps across the living room and scooped up the receiver.

"Pearl? Is that you, dear?"

Her mother, calling from Sunset Assisted Living in New Jersey. Pearl's heart took a dive.

"Pearl?"

"Me."

"It's your mother, Pearl, calling from Hades."

Pearl tried at least to keep a civil tone in her voice. "Assisted living isn't Hades, Mom."

"So purgatory then. A stop on the way down, just to torture. I've been calling and calling, and not even your machine answers anymore."

Pearl saw that the LED display on her answering machine was signaling that there was no more room for messages. It also indicated that she'd received fifteen messages. She stretched the phone cord so she could sit on the end of the sofa.

"Is something wrong, Mom?"

"I thought you'd never ask. Yes, wrong. I'm concerned, as a good mother should be, about my daughter, which is only natural and is why I'm calling, to find out some pertinent information about it."

Pearl didn't like this at all. She was worn down by the gauntlet of conversations she'd run all day with people who couldn't remember, didn't recall, didn't care, might be lying anyway. "What would *it* be, Mom?"

"The thing just behind your ear, dear. That's what *it* is, and it's more important than you, in your hectic and solitary life, seem to think."

"It's only a mole, Mom."

"You know this?"

"I'm sure enough of it that I'm not worried."

"So now you have medical opinions? Are you an actual medical doctor, like Dr. Milton Kahn? No, Pearl, you are not. It's not your place to examine a mole and just make up a diagnosis, not to mention a prognosis. This is a worry to me and to all who love you, and you should consider that and them."

"It's my mole," Pearl said, feeling at that moment the hopelessness of her position.

"So have you recently checked *your* mole?" her mother asked.

"Recently enough."

"And is it the same in shape, color, and size? Has it moved at all?"

Moved? "Everything looks the same, Mom." Pearl slipped her shoes off her aching feet and wriggled her toes. She wished she could hang up the phone, go into the bedroom, get naked, take a shower, and scrub off the lousy day

that she'd spent in the hole in the world left by violent un-
timely death. If people only knew, if they understood . . .

"Pearl," said her mother's voice on the phone, calling
from purgatory, "have you ever looked at a mole under a mi-
croscope?"

"No."

"They are not a pretty sight. And, I might add, it is the
consensus of medical experts that you might *think* you're
looking at a mole and be looking at something else very
much more dangerous."

"I'm not dying of mole poisoning, Mom."

"This is not a venue for humor, Pearl. A doctor, like
Dr. Milton Kahn, who would examine you free and avoid all
the expense and insurance nightmare, should be the one to
make that critical interpretation."

"Dr. Milton Kahn has pretty much examined all of me already," Pearl said, getting angrier by the second.

"Pearl!"

"I'm only trying to make a point, Mom. If Milton Kahn
thought the mole behind my ear was dangerous, he would
have mentioned it to me long ago."

"So you think he was concentrating on an out-of-the-way
spot behind your right ear while you two were—"

"Mom! Damn it!" The plastic receiver was getting slippery in Pearl's sweaty hand, as if it might slip from her grasp
like a watermelon seed and go zipping across the room.
She'd had about enough of this.

"So now impertinence and curse words are the answer?
Let me tell you, dear, they are the answer to nothing. When
your own mother calls and points out that you are in de-
nial—"

"I don't deny that I have a mole, Mom!"

"One you should regularly examine. If it *is* a mole."

"I have to turn my head to the side and bend my ear forward even to see it. It hurts to do that."

"Which is why you should have a doctor do the examining."

"I have an appointment with a doctor," Pearl lied. She'd had to call and cancel the appointment she'd made with the dermatologist who was not Milton Kahn. A murder investigation had gotten in the way.

There was surprise in Pearl's mother's voice. "Mrs. Kahn didn't say her nephew, Dr. Milton—"

"He's not the only dermatologist in New York!"

"For you, the only *free* one, dear. And one who cares for you already and will—"

Pearl cupped her hand over the earpiece, got up from the sofa, and placed the receiver in its cradle.

In the blessed silence she stood for a few minutes, waiting for the phone to ring. If her mother called back, as she sometimes did after such conversations, Pearl might apologize. Or she might not. Her mother was sticky and clever. She might trick Pearl into simply taking up the conversation where it had left off and getting angry all over again.

But her mother didn't call and apparently wasn't going to. Not this evening, anyway.

Pearl reverted to her plan to undress and shower before putting a Lean Cuisine in the microwave for dinner.

In the bathroom, while she was running the shower and waiting for the water to warm up, she stood before the medicine cabinet mirror, craned her neck painfully, and bent her right ear forward to examine the mole.

It appeared to be the same size as the last time she'd looked at it. Maybe a quarter of an inch in diameter. Maybe more.

She let her ear flop back in place and smiled. The mole wasn't any larger. Seemed to be the same shape and color. She was sure.

Reasonably sure.

In the shower she realized she hadn't checked to see if it had moved and had to laugh.

Briefly.

* * *

Terrible headache!

That was what woke Terri Gaddis.

Something was horribly wrong. Her head felt as if it were splitting wide open.

She attempted to swallow but couldn't. And she was breathing with difficulty, through her nose. She explored with her tongue and found that her mouth was stuck firmly closed, as if her lips were taped.

Her consciousness was quickly returning. She became aware of another pain.

My ankles! My ankles are on fire!

Only then did she realize her eyes were still closed. They seemed dry. Stuck firm. She tried to wipe them with her hands, but couldn't raise her arms. Couldn't move them.

Then she realized they were taped or tied to her waist and thighs, in tight to her body.

Fear gave her strength. She forced her eyes wide open in alarm, and through her pain realized what was causing such agony in her head and ankles.

She was mystified and horrified to find that she was hanging upside down.

The hook in the ceiling!

Terri knew she was in her bathroom, dangling head down over her bathtub, hanging from the hook.

She glanced about frantically. The plastic shower curtain was closed, and though the light was on in the bathroom, she couldn't see anything but her immediate porcelain, tile, and plastic surroundings. In a burst of panic she worked every muscle in her body, but nothing happened. Nothing!

Her struggles did cause her body to rotate slightly, and there were the stainless-steel faucet handles and spigot. The drain. Viewed so closely, she could see that the drain was starting to corrode and that a few of her hairs were caught on its cross braces from showers past.

How odd to notice something like that now.

Or is it? Is any of this real?

There was a slight sound on the other side of the plastic shower curtain, and she strained to see in that direction. Through the curtain she could make out the upside-down, shadowy shape of a man, growing larger, approaching.

Coming to help me, not to hurt me! Please!

When he was very near, the shadowy form on the curtain took on a paler, flesh-colored hue, and she realized the man was nude.

Kinky sex! That's all this is! Kinky sex!

"Richard!"

She was aware that she'd made only a soft humming sound.

She tried again, screaming his name in her mind. Something warm was trickling along her body, tickling her armpits. She could smell it. Urine. Hers. The ammonia stench of her mindless fear.

Oh, Richard! Please!

The curtain rattled open on its rod, and all she could look at was the knife.

41

Cindy Sellers sat on a bench near the Seventy-second Street entrance to Central Park and had what for her was a crisis of conscience.

Certainly she'd promised Harley Renz she wouldn't make public that the .25-Caliber Killer's latest victim had been shot inside his hotel and then dragged outside, to where the body was discovered. It was made clear to her that the police had settled on that detail being known only to them and the killer, so they could sort out the inevitable false confessions that were sure to interfere with the investigation.

But from Cindy's point of view, that curious fact was what gave the story its appeal. A question posed to her readers was always good for additional circulation. In this instance the question was simple and easy for her readers to understand: why was the body of this particular victim moved?

Only the killer knew the answer, and, as of now, the police were the only ones aware of the question. *So like a game,* Cindy thought, *and the police have an extra card in their hand.*

Of course, if she revealed that card the NYPD wanted to

keep close to its vest, she'd lose Renz's trust. She had to smile. She and Renz didn't *really* trust each other anyway. That was part of the game *they* played. Wolves on the prowl, both of them. And if she did include that inside-outside angle in her story, Renz would be angry, but he'd get over it. They were both forced to live with the fact that they were useful to each other.

Cindy was aware of the warm sun on her shoulders as she slumped forward and began tossing popcorn to the pigeons from a greasy bag she'd bought from a street vendor. The pigeons waddled cautiously toward the kernels at first, then rushed at them, nudging competitors out of the way. *Like people*, Cindy thought. Like newspaper readers elbowing each other aside to get to the next edition of *City Beat* before the rack was empty.

Fighting each other to be able to read *her* story.

If our situations were reversed, would Renz run the story with all the facts, including the one about how the body had been moved?

She knew the answer to that one.

Her fingers reached the bottom of the popcorn bag and found nothing but the grit of salt. She crumpled up the bag and tossed it to the pigeons. They began to peck at it and fight each other over it.

Cindy watched them. *Bird nature. Human nature. Maybe it's why I really don't like people.*

She brushed her hands together to rid them of most of the salt on her fingers, and then fished her cell phone out of her purse.

Her decision had been made. Already her conscience no longer bothered her.

How could she have even considered not running the entire story? It was strange how sometimes she questioned herself, when she knew her job and her purpose. She had enough on Renz to sink him anytime, if she so chose. At least, he thought she did.

The idea of leverage is when you have it, use it.

No more self-doubts, she vowed, as she pecked out the number that was a direct line to her editor. *I'm a professional practicing my profession.* A gray and white pigeon standing off from the others and watching her seemed to be bobbing its head in approval.

Zoe lifted her head from Quinn's bare chest and squinted at the clock by her bed. Almost nine o'clock. She had a ten o'clock appointment with a schizophrenic patient who was beginning to show distinct symptoms of paranoia.

Deciding to let Quinn sleep, she laid back the sheet that was covering her to the waist and gently lifted his arm, which lay heavily across her. As she moved the arm she could feel the strength in it, but it didn't resist her, as if it knew even as Quinn slept that she was something to be protected rather than harmed.

While Quinn was gentle in bed, he was the most physically powerful man she'd ever slept with, and a man who knew violence. A far cry from the postgraduates and professional intellectual types Zoe was used to. She wondered if it was the sense of danger, of potential violence, that intrigued her. No, she didn't wonder. She knew. She also knew she was safe with Quinn. The best of both worlds.

Smiling as a coconspirator with her own devilish self, she began sliding out of bed.

His big hand found her shoulder and closed on it, stopping her. Had he even been asleep?

"Gotta get up," she said, removing his hand. "Appointment."

"Some troubled soul like me?"

She laughed. "I don't see you as troubled. Not really."

"It troubles me that you're leaving," he said.

"That's just the sort of thing I mean." She managed to avoid his other hand that was snaking around her, and moved back out of reach. "I'm going to take a shower," she said. "You might consider joining me."

"Why? Are you coming apart?"

"For God's sake, Quinn!"

"Old joke," he said. He sat up in bed. "I'll join you, but I can't put you back together and make you any closer to perfect than you were. Are."

He'd just planted both bare feet on the floor when the phone rang. Instead of standing up, he watched Zoe walk to pick up the receiver, liking the way her breasts swayed with each hurried step. She had, he decided, the body of a much younger woman.

A shower. Not a bad idea . . .

"It's for you," she said, holding out the receiver for him as if it were a gift she regretted having to present. "Larry Fedderman."

"I gave him this number," Quinn said. His cell phone had been cutting out last night, and he knew there'd be no way to charge it in Zoe's apartment.

Zoe didn't seem to mind that Fedderman knew where to call. In fact, she seemed pleased that Quinn had told someone about them. She handed him the phone and then sat nude on the bed, watching him, understanding from his face that what he was hearing wasn't good.

"On my way," was all he said before hanging up.

He looked over at her. "There's been another Slicer murder. Our shower had better be a fast one."

She nodded. His job again. His guiding star. "You go first. I'll stay out of the way."

He smiled at her. "I'm sorry about this. It seems when we sleep together in your bed, I'm destined to get a phone call about a murder."

"That's right. It's just like last time . . ."

He'd only made a casual remark, but something changed in her eyes. He came to her, leaned down, and kissed the top of her head. He brushed his knuckles lightly across her cheek, studying her thoughtful expression.

"You okay?" he asked.

"Sure. Go take your shower."

But he knew something had occurred to her, disturbed her, and he didn't know what.

He didn't have time now to find out, but later he'd find the time.

42

A small, terrified-looking woman in her early twenties sat perched on a wrought-iron bench just down the hall from Terri Gaddis's apartment, where a stolid uniformed cop was standing guard. With her pinched features and pointed nose, she very much resembled a tiny, nervous bird. She'd obviously been crying, and barely glanced up at Quinn, Pearl, and Fedderman as they passed. There was fear in the glance, as well as sorrow. Quinn thought somebody should be looking after her.

The crime scene unit was already inside Terri Gaddis's cramped apartment, doing their white-glove ballet. Sal Vitali and Harold Mishkin were talking to Nift, the obnoxious ME, in a hall that probably led to a small bedroom and bathroom. Mishkin looked ill.

Vitali nodded a hello and motioned with his head. "In the bathroom," he said in his gravelly voice. Mishkin gave them a faint and sympathetic smile as they edged past, as if to warn them they weren't going to like what they were about to see.

Mishkin was right.

A tech who'd been dusting the toilet tank and vanity for prints saw them and got out of their way, leaving the tiny bathroom so they had a clear view of what was dangling from a hook in the ceiling.

It was what Quinn had braced himself to see, but it was still worse than he'd imagined. The woman's upside-down body was laid open from her pubis to the base of her neck. Her internal organs and entrails had been removed and were piled in the bathtub. Flies were beginning to feast.

Terri Gaddis had been an attractive woman. Her face, even with its horror-stricken expression, had somehow escaped being coated with blood and was in sharp contrast to the carnage.

Quinn looked up at the ceiling, almost as if to offer a prayer.

"Bicycle hook," Pearl said. "The killer located a wooden joist on the other side of the drywall so it would support plenty of weight. You do that if you've got a bike to hang."

Nift had halfway entered the tiny bathroom and was clucking his tongue. "She's no bicycle, but you can tell she was the kinda woman who'd give you a helluva ride." He leered at Pearl. "Hello, shweetheart." It was a bad Bogart imitation.

"Hi, ashhole."

"It's like the other victims," Nift said to Quinn, no longer Bogart and ignoring Pearl. "Same kind of knife was used. Looks like at pretty much the same angle. We'll know more once we get her to the morgue and I put her back together."

Why? Are you coming apart?

Quinn felt queasy as he recalled his joke with Zoe less than an hour ago.

"You can tell she had a pretty good rack on her," Nift said.

It was like something a hunter would say about a slain deer, and it made Pearl suddenly furious. "How does a prick like you become a doctor?"

Nift grinned. "People I work on never complain, so why should you?"

"Because you're a—"

"Pearl!"

Quinn's hand was on her shoulder, holding her back, and she realized she'd been advancing on Nift.

"Let's keep it professional," Quinn said. Then, to Nift: "Is everything there?" *If only you* could *put her back together.*

The cocky little ME seemed surprised by the question. Then he understood. "Yeah, I looked and made sure. And the organs have to be cut away from the peritoneum differently from the way it was done here if they're gonna be reusable. Nobody's doing this so they can get healthy organs to sell on the black market." He glanced at Pearl. "Shame. The killer's missing a bet, and he could maybe save somebody's life whenever he killed someone."

The stench in the stifling little room was beginning to get to Quinn. The stench and Nift.

He led the way, and they returned to where Sal and Mishkin were standing, watching the techs go over the living room.

"They won't find anything we can use," Mishkin said. "The guy works clean." He had so much mentholated cream all over his mustache he looked as if he had a bad cold.

Vitali noticed Quinn looking at his partner and said, "Harold does what works for him, just like the rest of us, even if he does smell like a walking meth lab."

"He smells better than the corpse," Quinn said.

"That's absolutely the nicest thing anyone's ever said about me," Mishkin told him. He had a deadpan, dry delivery. Quinn made a mental note that the innocuous-looking little guy might occasionally sting.

"Let's go out in the hall," Quinn suggested, in deference to Mishkin's weak stomach.

They dodged the techs and left the apartment, then moved down the hall so they were out of earshot of the cop posted at the door and the distraught young woman on the bench.

"Her name's Martha Swann," Vitali said. "She's the one found the body. When the victim, Terri Gaddis, didn't show up for work at one of those Office Tech stores and didn't answer her phone, they sent Martha here to see if Terri was all right."

"Terri wasn't," Mishkin said.

"You wanna talk to Martha?" Vitali asked. "That's the only reason we were still keeping her around."

"You got her full statement?" Quinn asked.

"Sure."

Quinn nodded to Pearl, who went down the hall and sat next to the woman, calming her and telling her she could leave, that a squad car would drive her back to work, or to where she lived, if she preferred.

"Poor kid won't forget this," Mishkin said.

"Her friend Terri already has," Vitali said. There was venom in his voice.

"Lighten up, Sal," Mishkin told him.

Partners for a long time, Quinn thought. He was glad they were on the Slicer end of the investigation and under his command. "Nift said all the organs are there," he said. "You guys check that on the other victims?"

"We did," Vitali growled. "Nobody's out there selling livers or kidneys. That'd make it too easy, give us a motive."

"Hunting," Mishkin said. "The bastard likes to stalk and kill, then field dress his game." He swallowed and absently moved his right hand across his stomach.

Pearl was back. Quinn looked down the hall and saw that Martha Swann was gone.

"She decided to go back in to work," Pearl said.

"Gutsy young lady," Fedderman said.

"Or one who needs the money," Vitali said.

There was a flurry of activity down the hall. Terri Gaddis was in a body bag on a gurney, being maneuvered out of her apartment. Also on the gurney was a black plastic bag twist-tied at the top. Quinn knew what was in it and thought it looked too much like a trash bag. Another defilement of a beautiful young woman.

"We told them they could take her after you had your look," Vitali said. "Hope you don't mind."

Quinn said he didn't.

As the remains of Terri Gaddis were wheeled past them, Nift, following the gurney, glanced over at the detectives.

"My examination told me there were times the lady looked a lot better on her back," he said, flashing his practiced leer at Pearl.

As the death procession was trying to fit itself into the elevator, Pearl said, "I wonder what makes Nift such an asshole."

"He makes those nasty cracks in an effort to stay sane," Mishkin said. "It isn't working."

"How's the other end of the investigation going?" Vitali asked.

Quinn filled him in.

"I thought we were gonna hold back that Becker was shot inside his hotel, then moved outside," Vitali said. "It's in all the papers."

"We tried," Quinn said. "The information leaked, and a reporter we had on our side double-crossed Renz."

"Cindy Sellers," Mishkin said. "Only a snake would trust somebody like her."

"Uh-huh," Pearl said.

"We can still use her," Quinn said. "Sometimes it works in our favor that she has no scruples."

"Any ideas as to why Becker's body was moved?" Vitali asked.

"None. Do you?"

"*No tengo ni noción.*"

The reply in Spanish was surprising, coming from the most Italian-looking man Quinn had ever seen.

The diversified city. He loved it.

"Anything in particular you want us to do now?" Vitali asked.

"Stay on the case," Quinn said. "And be careful."

"Have a good one," Pearl said, as the Vitali-Mishkin part of the team started toward the elevator.

Vitali gave a little wave. "*Ciao.*"

"Happy hunting," Fedderman said.

"*Shalom,*" Mishkin said over his shoulder.

Au revoir, Quinn thought.

Jerry Dunn chewed absently on a gin-soaked olive. He was nervous, but didn't know why. The man from Quest and Quarry had called and asked to meet him here, in Gillman's Bar on West Forty-second Street. It was about business, he'd said. Maybe that was why Dunn was nervous; he knew the business of Quest and Quarry, had in fact been part of it.

He swallowed what was left of the olive and wondered if he should mention the newspaper piece he'd read about the guy who'd been shot in the Antonian Hotel and then dragged outside. The latest victim of the .25-Caliber Killer. It had to have something to do with Quest and Quarry, but it might be a sensitive subject,

Here came the guy now, medium height, compact, clean cut, and thoughtful looking in a way that made him seem like a youthful college professor who hadn't yet burned out. But there was a grace and muscularity about him that attracted attention and suggested a lot of strength beneath that tailored blue suit. He gave his handsome smile and extended his hand to Jerry, who shook it and noticed how dry and strong it was.

Jerry had been drinking a Beefeater martini. The man from Quest and Quarry sat down opposite him in the wooden booth near the window and ordered a scotch rocks and a fresh drink for Jerry.

"I wanted to congratulate you on the fine hunt you conducted," he said, keeping his voice low. "Joseph Galin was a formidable quarry."

The drinks arrived, and both men were silent until the barmaid had left.

"I'm offering you another hunt," the college professor (as Jerry thought of him) said. "Same terms."

Jerry thought about it and sipped his fresh martini. "If I keep doing this I might wind up being a rich man."

"But that's not why you're going to say yes."

Jerry smiled. "We both know that."

"Do we have an agreement?"

Jerry nodded.

"This hunt will be slightly different," said the man from Quest and Quarry.

When he was finished explaining that difference, he said, "Your quarry will be a man named Thomas Rhodes."

After leaving Gillman's Bar, Martin Hawk took a cab to the block of Thomas Rhodes's West Side brownstone and got out at the corner. He put on the plain blue baseball cap he'd had in his suit coat pocket and adjusted the bill at a slight angle. Everyone in a baseball cap looked like everyone else in a baseball cap. He walked down the street and, without being noticed left a small, tightly wrapped package in the brownstone's mailbox.

He was smiling as he strode casually away. The package contained a small .25-caliber revolver. He knew that Rhodes would understand what it was for, and he knew how he'd react. Rhodes should never have discharged his weapon inside his opponent's hotel. It had been carefully explained to him that both hunters' hotels were safety zones. He'd broken the rules and the code of honor, and that was unforgivable, as well as dangerous.

Rhodes wouldn't contact the police, but he might try to

leave town with his life preserved, made silent by fear. Or he might feel that he had no choice but to take up the challenge.

Either way, Hawk had faith in Jerry Dunn. Also either way, Quest and Quarry would neutralize a former client who was a potential problem. This kind of pairing was Martin Hawk's way of sweeping up after himself.

He glanced at his watch. It was still early enough to see a woman who very much interested him. A special woman.

The special ones were getting closer together, he knew, and it was beginning to worry him. But there was no way to deny the need or the urgency. He really had no choice. And this woman . . . she was unique, like all of them, and the same, like all of them.

In the end, alike.

Simple puzzles. All of them.

He'd know how to deal with her, how to figure her out. He'd observe her and learn her thought processes and habits, and then take advantage of them. It was all in knowing when to move in. It was much like hunting.

It *was* hunting.

He stepped off the curb into the oil-stained street and hailed another cab.

43

Black Lake, Missouri, 1986

The old Chevy pickup was dented and rusty, but it was all determination as it snarled and rattled over the rough and uneven dirt drive leading to the dilapidated farmhouse and outbuildings.

During the year since his initiation rite at the lake, Marty had become the hunter his father had anticipated, keen of eye and eager. He was twelve now, taller, still skinny but filling out.

The truck needed exhaust work. Anybody within a quarter of a mile might have heard it. But there was a brisk wind to go with the subzero temperature, so there was nobody to hear and notice the pickup with the illegal deer in the bed. Most folks knew Carl Hawk and his son Marty hunted out of season anyway, and chose not to do anything about it. They were more than a little scared of Carl, and besides, the family needed the meat.

Carl was driving. Marty sat next to him with one hand on the door handle to brace himself, his teeth clenched, as the truck bucked and swayed. Their rifles were unloaded and fitted into brackets so they were stacked horizontally across the back window. The deer in the truck's bed was a dead six-point buck that Marty had shot three hours ago. Its throat was slashed and the animal had bled out where it hung in the woods while Carl and Marty had hunted some more, so it wasn't making much of a mess in the truck.

"We'll drive on into the barn," Carl said, "so's you can get right to it."

"Yes, sir." Marty's breath fogged like his father's in the cold truck, as the heater hadn't worked since he could remember. He'd thought some days that they might as well be driving with the windows down.

When they reached the barn, Marty climbed down out of the truck and used the cold, rusty hasp for a handle as he swung one of the big wooden doors open. The hinges squealed, and the wind tried to take control of the door, so he had to hold tight to keep it from blowing shut.

The old truck growled and spat as if clearing its throat as Marty's father bounced it over frozen ruts and inside the straw-littered building. Curtains briefly parted in one of the house's front windows, but neither Carl nor Marty noticed, being too cold and bent on their task.

As soon as the truck was clear, Marty leaned into the barn door and walked backward, letting it close of its own accord as a concession to the wind.

There was no electricity in the barn, but it was easy enough to see by the light slanting in through spaces between the boards. There wasn't much warmth, either, and eddies of winter wind found their way inside. There wasn't any livestock. The family was down to half a dozen chickens, huddled in their coop, and four hogs crowded together for warmth in the walled plywood lean-to attached to their pen.

There was more growling and grinding of gears as Carl maneuvered the truck so its bed was directly below the block and tackle attached to one of the barn's rafters.

Marty scampered up into the bed and got hold of the thick rope dangling from the pulley. He looped the rope around and between the deer's stiffened rear legs and fastened it with a solid bowline knot.

When he was finished, he hopped down off the truck and went over to where the rope was angled away from the overhead pulley and was wound about the spool of a steel winch. Marty clung to the winch handle and gave it several turns while his father edged the truck forward until the deer was hanging free of the opened tailgate.

The truck's engine gave a few mighty roars and died, and Carl got out and helped Marty work the winch another turn until the deer was hanging upside down with its antlers a few inches off the plank floor.

Carl brushed his gloved hands together, then stood off to the side and lit a cigar. He was watching Marty squinty-eyed through the smoke, a slight smile on his seamed face.

Marty knew what to do. He removed his jacket and draped it over the side of the truck bed, then rolled his shirt-sleeves up above his elbows. The gutting knife was hanging by its buckskin cord on one of the wood supporting beams. Marty took it down and ran a finger over its cutting edge to make sure it was sharp. Then he approached the deer, struck with the knife hard and straight between the deer's rear legs, and used his own body weight to make a ripping incision down the deer's swollen belly all the way to the base of its throat. He had to move back fast then, as undrained blood and the animal's intestines spilled out onto the floor.

Marty worked quickly and skillfully with the gutting knife, his arms inside the still-warm animal up to their elbows. Cold as the barn was, the deer's dwindling body warmth felt good. He tied off the anus, then sliced away the internal organs, making sure all the intestines were detached, letting the visceral matter drop to the floor where the initial mass of bloody innards lay. Marty and his father would later feed it to the hogs. Most of the rest of the deer they would store in the keep box outside the house, where it would remain frozen for weeks while the family gradually consumed it. Sometimes Carl would want the antlers saved, so he could mount them on one of the barn walls with dozens of other impressive racks of antlers. But this deer was merely a six point, so the antlers could also go to the hogs.

"You make sure you hose all that blood off you 'fore you come in the house," said a woman's voice.

Marty turned from his task and saw his mother, Alma.

Of course he hadn't been able to clean his arms and hands completely of blood. Not that Alma wouldn't have found blood, anyway. She always found something wrong.

That night, after Marty was in bed, she sighed and put down the Bible she'd been reading. He heard the faint squeaking of her chair's wooden rockers stop as she stood up from it.

She didn't delay. She came into the bedroom and yanked the T-shirt Marty slept in off him so hard that it tore. Then she took one of Carl's belts to Marty, and, as usual, Carl did nothing to stop her.

"You want the blood of the beast on you?" she asked, over and over as she lashed Marty, who was now wearing only his jockey shorts.

"No'm," he said, each time she asked, but she continued to strike with the belt, skillfully turning it at the end of some of the strokes so the edge of the leather cut flesh.

"I'll give you blood!" she said. "The Lord saith to give them that sins plenty of blood. I'll beat an' beat till you're washed in the blood of the lamb, and you'll be pure!"

When she was exhausted, she dropped the belt and staggered out of the bedroom, leaving behind Marty's lasting memory of his mother, a hunched, glum figure seen from the back, topped with a tangled mass of hair, trudging away from him.

Carl brought in the bottle of bourbon he'd been sipping

from and used some of the liquor for antiseptic, which he applied with what was left of the T-shirt Alma had ripped off Marty.

"Woman's got her scripture kinda misspoken," Carl said, dabbing with the saturated cloth as Marty gritted his teeth in pain.

"All in all," Marty said, "I like your religion better."

"Our religion," his father said, making sure there was plenty of alcohol on the welts he was treating. "Gonna kill us both, what she's gonna do. I think she's puttin' roach poison in my whiskey. It don't taste right. Hasn't for a while. An' it appears there's some poison missin' from the bottle out in the barn."

"No call for roach poison in the winter," Marty said.

His father nodded. "An' my gut most times feels like it's on fire."

Marty said nothing, trying not to whine as the alcohol contacted the welts.

"Woman's crazy," Carl muttered as he applied aid. "Somethin's gotta be done, is what. Somethin's gotta be done."

Marty knew there was no need to answer. It wasn't the first time for this. It was something he'd gotten used to, as much as you could say anyone ever got used to serious whalings with a belt. Marty could absorb pain without complaint, when he knew he must. And he knew this was one of those times, and that it would happen again.

This was family ritual.

44

New York, the present

Quinn and Zoe had just left D'Zello's Ristorante and were walking slowly along Broadway in the heat. He hadn't tried to talk to her at lunch about what was bothering him. If it led to an argument, he didn't want it to be where everyone could hear them.

They were moving faster than the traffic, which was backed up because one lane was closed for construction. Wooden sawhorses and yellow caution tape were everywhere, but it was impossible to tell what exactly was being done. Whatever it was involved a lot of digging, though no one could be seen at present doing work of any sort. Now and then a frustrated driver would lean hard on his horn. A siren yowled deafeningly and quickly faded, as if an emergency vehicle was going like hell a block over. Quinn knew it was probably bogged down in traffic and the driver was venting his frustration.

"Is there something you'd like to tell me?" he asked, as he strolled beside Zoe toward where his car was parked illegally with an NYPD placard on the lowered sun visor. A warm breeze kicked up, and he could feel the grit of construction dust on his teeth.

"About lunch?" she asked.

"You're the psychoanalyst," he said. "You think that's what I'm asking about?" Immediately he regretted the tone of his own voice; it was almost as if he were interrogating a suspect.

But damn it, she asked for it.

Or had she? Maybe he'd misinterpreted her words and facial expression.

After four more, slightly slower steps, she said, "What *are* you asking?"

"When we were together this morning and I joked about how I tended to get a phone call about a murder after we've had sex, the look on your face suggested something had crossed your mind."

"I'm that transparent?"

He smiled. " 'Fraid so."

They walked silently for a while. A hybrid bus accelerated away from a stop in the street alongside them, leaving a strong scent of environmentally proper exhaust. A new smell for the olfactory stew of New York.

"I hesitated mentioning what I thought," Zoe said, "because it's probably meaningless, and if I told you about it there might be unnecessary trouble."

"Should you be the judge of that?"

"Maybe. There's also a professional obligation."

They were at the parked Lincoln. Quinn slowed and stood beside the car. Sunlight glinted off its roof and obscured his vision so he had to move in order to see Zoe clearly. "This is about one of your patients," he said.

"No, nothing like that."

He rested a hand very gently on her back, spanning her shoulder blades beneath the thin material of her blouse with his long fingers. The slight contact made her heart thump, and not only from aroused sexual memory. There was something about Quinn that made people want to give up their secrets. She thought he would have made a damned good psychoanalyst. Better yet, a priest.

In a way, that's what he is.

"Zoe?" he said, as if reminding her that he was there, waiting for her explanation.

The words seemed to flow from her of their own accord. "When you mentioned the coincidence of learning about two of the murders when we were together, each time after we had sex, it made me think of someone."

"Someone you suspect?" He really didn't see how that was possible.

"Someone I . . . used to be involved with."

Ah . . . ! He didn't like where this might be going. "The way you're involved with me?"

"Not exactly. Not in any way. You and Alfred aren't at all alike."

Alfred? "But you were lovers?"

"Yes. For a brief while. It ended over a year ago."

"Who—"

"I ended it. Alfred . . . our sex was becoming more and more violent."

"He hurt you?"

"Sometimes. When he was in sexual thrall. Or when he became angry with me."

She seemed to be recalling the affair with the objectivity of her profession. She might have been talking about two other people, and to someone she barely knew. "Angry about what?" he asked.

"Anything and everything. Alfred had—probably still has—anger issues. Sometimes they find an outlet when they're sexually engaged. He's sadistic and admits it. He was looking for something in me I wasn't prepared to give him."

"How badly did he hurt you?"

"It was nothing serious. Minor bruises. Whip marks."

"*Whip marks?* Jesus, Zoe!"

"You've been a cop a long time, Quinn. You know the spectrum of human sexual activity, especially in this city. Alfred tried to persuade me to engage in things that left me cold, sometimes things that repulsed me. I hope I don't need to go into detail. In fact, I won't go into detail."

Quinn sensed her getting mad at him. So Zoe had her own anger issues. Well, maybe she had good reason.

"I'm not pressing you for any information you don't want to give. And I can see why, when the subject of women being murdered and defiled came up, you'd naturally think of . . . does he have a name beyond Alfred?"

"Beeker. Dr. Alfred Beeker. He's a psychoanalyst."

"Like you?"

"Not exactly. He's a cognitive analyst."

"And you are . . . ?"

"What you might call a creative Jungian."

Quinn thought he'd better take a different tack. "If Beeker's a psychologist, can't he figure out he needs help himself?"

"He's a psychiatrist, actually, who practices psychotherapy and augments it with drugs, and apparently he doesn't think he needs help. There are plenty of people out there playing the same games he plays, so he's not at a loss for partners."

"It can be a dangerous game."

"That's part of the allure. Listen, Quinn, Alfred moves in a world he considers normal. And for the people in it, maybe it *is* normal. No laws are being broken, and everything is consensual. But what it came down to was I wasn't part of that world and didn't want to be, and he couldn't accept that."

"I more or less agree with you about consensual adults, but what you described between the two of you didn't sound consensual."

She smiled in that gradual, quiet way that devastated him.

"The problem was that sometimes pretending to be forced was part of the game. It got so Alfred couldn't see the difference. As far as he was concerned, the game was always on."

"And for him it wasn't a game," Quinn said.

"For *me* it wasn't always a game." She moved away from Quinn and leaned with her buttocks against the car's sunwarmed fender, crossing her arms. "He didn't like it that I left him."

"You afraid of him?"

"Not anymore. I haven't even seen him in months. Maybe he doesn't think of me at all."

"That'd be a tough job for any man. What you were thinking this morning, Zoe? . . . Was it that he might know about you and me, might resent it, and it could somehow be tied in with the Slicer murders?"

Again Quinn surprised her with his nose for the truth, as if he were some sort of psychic bloodhound. He would get there sooner or later on his own, so she might as well tell him.

"He . . ." She tightened her grip on her elbows and swallowed. "He sometimes insisted on role playing, doing a scene where he raped me at knifepoint. He even wore a mask and pretended he'd just come in through my bedroom window. He took photographs with a digital camera. He told me he'd posted some on the Internet, though nothing too suggestive. But I was always afraid he'd . . . taken some I wasn't aware of."

"Hell, Zoe . . ."

"Back in college people said psych majors went into it because of their own crazy hang-ups. Maybe they were right."

Quinn shrugged. "I've heard the same thing about my profession. Maybe they were right, too."

"I know I was an idiot, but I went along with it. A few times, it went too far. He cut me."

"Cut you?*"*

"Not badly, and he always said it was an accident. But I associate dead women and knives with Alfred Beeker."

"I can see why. I'm going to talk to him, Zoe."

"That's what I was afraid of."

"I won't do anything drastic. But it wouldn't be a bad idea to feel Beeker out and see if he's still into those kinds of games, and if they've become even more violent."

"Quinn, I don't want you playing the protector-avenger role."

"I'm a cop, Zoe. Women are being murdered and butchered with a knife, and I've just learned about a sadist who likes to cut women. I need to look into him. I think you knew that, or you wouldn't have told me about him. Am I right?"

"I don't even know."

Quinn thought he knew. The city harbored more than a few sadists who liked to cut women, and he doubted that Beeker was the Slicer. Still, it wouldn't hurt to warn Beeker, to make sure the nutcase doctor knew there'd be consequences if he bothered Zoe again. Later, if necessary, would come the avenger part of Quinn's role.

He moved closer to her, leaned down, and kissed her cheek. She was wet with perspiration.

"Let's get in the car and get the air conditioner going," he said. "I'll drive you home."

"To my office," she said. "I've got a two o'clock appointment."

"With a psychotic killer?"

"With a man who's terrified of turning corners when he's walking alone."

"Oh," Quinn said, "that's all of us."

He opened the car door for her and watched her get in, thinking again how gracefully she moved and how beautiful she was. How much he already cared about her. She was becoming an addiction, his own illness and fixation.

So this is what it's like dating a psychoanalyst.

"What are you thinking?" she asked, as they pulled away from the curb.

"How glad I am I didn't bring up this subject in the restaurant," he said.

Later that same afternoon, Quinn found Dr. Alfred Beeker in the Manhattan phone directory. His office was on Park Avenue, about three blocks away from Zoe's.

Quinn thought he should see the doctor as soon as possible, with or without an appointment.

45

"So the doctor says, 'Not only have I never seen anyone get pregnant that way, I don't understand how it could happen.' "

Jackie Jameson's delivery was spot on the beat, and the punch line drew a good laugh from the Say What? audience. But Jameson's mind wasn't completely on his work. It used to be that New York comedy clubs were hazy with tobacco smoke, but not anymore, so from where Jackie stood onstage it was easy to read the expression on the face of the man trying to bore holes in Mitzi Lewis with his eyes.

Mitzi was a looker who attracted lots of the wrong kind of attention, with her spiky white blond hair, childlike features, and compact, curvaceous body. She was used to the attention, and her fellow comic Jackie was used to seeing it, but this guy seemed different. Much more intense. Like he wanted to have her right now with his Coke and fries.

Mitzi was scheduled to do the set after Jackie, so she was standing just offstage waiting to be introduced, visible only to a small part of the audience seated off to the side. The guy with the laser eyes and his tongue hanging out was alone at his table and had a perfect view.

Jackie took him in again with a sidelong glance while laying the groundwork for his final joke, the one about the man who thought he was a violin. The man at the table was handsome in a dark, predatory way, about average height and build, but there was something about him that suggested great physical strength. Though he wasn't the only guy in the club wearing a dark blue suit and white shirt with a tie, he was the only one who looked like he'd just stepped off the cover of *GQ*. And the only one who for some reason looked flat-ass rich. He had the high cheekbones, well-defined features, and thick black hair of a male model.

If I looked like that, Jackie thought, *I wouldn't be funny.*

But Jackie was funny, and headed for his own Comedy Channel special.

He continued his routine onstage without seeming to pay any attention to the man staring at Mitzi. But Jackie was still watching the guy. He was seated at one of the tiny tables that had been jammed in at the edges to accommodate maximum audiences. There was barely room on the thing for his elbows. The glass before him was empty. When a waiter approached and tried to push another drink on him, he made a flicking motion with his hand that somehow was a threat. The waiter retreated.

The longer Jackie watched the guy, the more he figured the handsome gawker was trouble and might want to do more than just look at Mitzi. Considering what was happening around town, with those women getting their throats sliced and their guts cut out, Jackie thought it might be wise to warn Mitzi about the guy.

Not that Jackie, who had his own plans for Mitzi, was the jealous type, but he did know that next to the dude in the blue business suit he looked like a troll. And a dumb one at that. Something else about the guy was that he looked intelligent even when sex starved, which was when Jackie looked his dumbest.

"I thought you meant sex and *violins*!" Jackie heard himself say.

He got his expected big laugh, told the audience they'd been great and that he loved them, and then strode off stage. Ted Tack, who owned and managed Say What?, passed him going the other way and gave him a big grin and a mock salute. The mood was on.

"Don't be obvious about it," Jackie said to Mitzi, "but check out the guy in the blue suit, sitting alone right of stage and eating you up with his eyes."

Mitzi leaned forward to peek as she was being introduced. "Yummy."

"If you like raw sewage."

"That's harsh," Mitizi said. "When I go on I'm gonna blow him a kiss."

"Don't be craz—"

But her intro was finished and she was gone, prancing toward the microphone and waving her arms.

Jackie wasn't surprised when she didn't blow the creep a kiss. She was too much of a pro for that, already into the moment, where the laughs were to be found.

"You guys are great! Anybody out there got a crazy uncle?"

Mitzi avoided looking at the man as she worked her way through her set. The folks out there grinning at her, already softened up by alcohol and Jackie Jameson, soon warmed to her. Then they were with her; then she was with them. Then she had them. *God, what a great feeling!* She deliberately avoided looking at Mr. Handsome in the blue suit, not letting anything get in the way of her timing and delivery.

But a part of her mind did wonder what Jackie was all worked up about. She didn't see anything wrong with the guy, and he sure wasn't the first to look at her with a hungry expression. She could recall catching Jackie himself staring at her in that cat-and-canary way, so what was the big deal?

She was halfway through her Seinfeld imitation, enjoying a big laugh, when she looked directly at Mr. Handsome.

Mistake.

Their eyes met, and she felt as if she'd been Tasered. *Whoa!* His hooded dark gaze took her breath away and made her legs rubbery. When she inhaled, her hot breath seemed to go straight to her stomach, making her weak.

Definitely something there.

She understood now what Jackie meant. There wasn't the slightest doubt in her mind what this man was thinking, what he was doing with her in *his* mind. And they both knew she was a willing participant.

Best of all, everything about him suggested he was thinking exclusively of her. Intensely.

Mitizi liked intensity. There was too little of it around these days.

Jackie was right: this man held a power over her that she could no more deny than understand. What passed between them was a dark promise of unexplored pains and pleasures. Creepy? Sure. Mitzi could see how Jackie would read it that way. And maybe he was right. Most definitely he was right. Here was the danger of deep water.

What Jackie didn't know—and what Mitzi was now discovering—was that she liked it.

God help me. I like it!

Doubt immediately began to creep in.

Is it only me? All in my mind? Is the guy simply stoned and only thinking about his wife and kids? Do I remind him of his sister?

She loused up the joke about the amorous mouse and the hot dog, but the audience was kind to her. They were still on her side and gave her a big hand, even a halfway standing O, as she left the stage.

She glanced back at Mr. Handsome, and he smiled and raised his empty glass in a silent toast. It was a smile and gesture that suggested they would meet again.

And they would.

46

Quinn was struggling to escape the huge bird that was pecking at his entrails. The gigantic eagle—if that's what it was—reared back its head and jerked it to the side to glance down at him with one huge and glittering eye, a string of something red oozing from its hooked beak.

As he rose toward full consciousness, Quinn thought he heard a muffled rustling sound, like the powerful beating of vast wings. Still and afraid, he lay in his dark and stifling bedroom while his mind fought to comprehend what was nightmare and what was real.

The illuminated red numerals on the clock near his bed read 1:27 A.M. Time was a measure of reality that helped to tilt his brain toward the familiar, where things were tangible, quantified, and understood.

Some things, anyway.

The sheets beneath him were soaked. The T-shirt and Jockey shorts he slept in were just as wet. He wiped the back of his hand across his forehead and was amazed by how heavily he was perspiring. The window air conditioner clicked from its low hum to a deeper tone, signaling that the compressor was now engaged and reassuring him that cold air and sanity were on the way.

He felt a wash of cool air across his bare legs. *Wonderful.* He was still breathing hard after his dream. What had brought on the nightmare? The gutting knife used on the Slicer victims? The gigantic bird's beak was that of a predator, strong and hooked so that it could easily tear flesh, not so unlike the knife the ME had described and then shown the detectives in a hunting supply catalog.

Too restless now even to close his eyes, he sat up in bed, reached into the darkness, and switched on the lamp, half expecting to see the terrible bird perched in a corner, its beak dripping with . . .

Beak . . .

Beeker. Quinn's conversation with Zoe about Alfred Beeker might have been part of why he'd had his nightmare. Dr. Alfred Beeker was another sort of predator, and a real one.

Quinn stood up from the damp bed and padded barefoot down the hall to the kitchen, which was noticeably warmer than the bedroom but smelled better. He got a carton of milk from the refrigerator, checked the date, then poured some in a glass. Wasn't drinking milk supposed to relax you and help you sleep?

Immediately after downing the milk, he wished he'd drunk scotch. That worked better, at least in the short run.

The hell with it. If he had to be awake, he might as well be awake all the way.

But what to do with his extra hours?

Do something!

Call Zoe?

He turned toward the phone in the kitchen and remembered the time. There was no point in disturbing Zoe's sleep just because he, Quinn, had experienced a nightmare. He wondered what Zoe would make of his bad dream. Probably something he wouldn't like.

Fedderman or Pearl? No, he needed them in top form to-morrow. And Pearl might get so pissed off she'd come over and berate him in person. It didn't make sense to wake any-one up just because he couldn't sleep and felt like having some company.

What did make sense was making himself useful, since he was going to be wide awake anyway. He decided to get dressed and go to the Seventy-ninth Street office, reread some murder files, maybe make use of his desk computer.

Do *something*!

He splashed cold water on his face and raked back his hair with his fingers. Then he put on a pair of pants, the shirt he'd worn today and dropped into the hamper, and moc-casins without socks.

As he was leaving the apartment he paused, ducked back in, and got a cigar. A prop to remind him that reality was so much better than his dream.

Quinn opened the office door and knew immediately that something was wrong. An old cop got to know about dark rooms, to be able to sense whether the air was moving or still, to distinguish the slightest sounds that *weren't* normal, maybe even detect body temperature.

Quinn *knew* he wasn't alone.

His hand darted toward the light switch, but didn't make it.

Something, probably a shoulder, slammed into his mid-section, and the air rushed from him as he bounced off the door and wall.

The door had slammed shut from the impact, and Quinn, fighting to breathe, saw the shadowed bulk of a man trying to open it. Quinn tried to get up, tried to stop the dark figure, but the spastic action of his lungs sucking in nothing kept his body curled in on itself; he was helpless.

Not quite.

He wasn't sure how he did it, but he was aware of his arm extending, his fingers closing on a handful of material. A cuff, the man's pants leg. He squeezed the wadded material harder, harder . . .

The leg jerked a few times in an effort to break free, and then the shadowed figure twisted and bent over Quinn.

There was a loud grunt, and something hard smashed into the side of Quinn's head. He felt his grasp on the pants cuff lose its strength. Then his hold on consciousness started to fade. *Lost him.* . . . He could breathe a little now, but he knew he was going to pass out.

He'd been intent on preventing the intruder from escaping, but now there was another possibility.

Is whoever attacked me still here? Ready to strike again?

Fear arrived, something real and palpable that began crushing down on him like a weight. He began to crawl, not even sure of his direction. His left shoulder brushed something hard. *One of the desks?*

He tried to stand up, but that only made him dizzy and wobbly. And closer to unconsciousness. It was like the condition brought on by that stuff they gave you intravenously in hospitals to calm you before the big hit of anesthetic in the OR. He became too woozy even to be afraid.

He sought the strength and will to stay conscious, but realized it was a losing battle. It had been from the beginning.

Slipping into darkness, the last thing he thought was that he didn't want to dream again about the gigantic bird.

Mitzi Lewis knew she was dying.

Perspiration ran down her face and stung the corners of her eyes, but she knew she couldn't rub them.

"He was so stupid," she said, "that he thought the *B* on elevator buttons meant *Backward*."

The audience's reaction was at best muted. A couple of

smiles here and there, but Mitzi knew they were due more to embarrassment than amusement. Embarrassment for her. She hated that strained and polite expression on people's faces. Right now she hated people in general, her profession, the human race, herself.

"You guys have been great!" she yelled through a frozen smile, her eyes glittering from sweat that might be taken for tears. She could feel waves of pity rolling up from the audience. She loathed pity. "Thank you, thank you, thank you!" She blew everyone a big kiss and did her trademark prance off the stage.

Thank God that's over!

"Don't take it so hard," Jackie Jameson told her as she finally made it offstage. It was obvious that the game little girl from Brooklyn was upset. "It wasn't you."

"It sure felt like me out there," Mitzi said, her shoulders slumping.

"It was the crowd. They'll laugh at those same jokes tomorrow night."

"You got a lot of laughs during *your* set," she said, wiping at her eyes. *Real tears now, dammit!*

"I pay them a lot of money," Jackie said, straight-faced.

Mitzi almost, but not quite, smiled at that. One corner of her mouth twitched upward. Jackie pointed at it and grinned.

"Bastard!" Mitizi said. "You won't even let me feel bad."

"Against the rules, Mitz."

She pushed past him and hurried into Say What?'s communal dressing room, where she rinsed off her face and put on some fresh makeup. She yanked up her white blond hair into longer and more defined spikes, then reassessed herself in the mirror.

Okay, she thought. *You'd never know I was run over by a train.*

She left the dressing room and went down the short corridor to the exit. Once she got through that door, she'd have to work her way—unnoticed, she hoped tonight—through the back of the crowd, around the bar, toward the club's street door.

She wished she were invisible. All she wanted right now was for tonight to be over.

Some loudmouth at the bar was holding court with a drunken story, creating something of a diversion, as she made herself small and edged toward the glowing red EXIT sign.

When she was almost at the door, a voice said, "*I* thought you were funny."

She turned and found herself looking into the dark, dark eyes of Mr. Handsome from last night. He had even more of an effect on her close up. Her throat tightened so she couldn't speak.

Not like me, to be at a loss for words.

"You must have been the only one who thought so," she finally said in a choked voice.

"The others were too busy thinking you were beautiful."

"That's . . . uh, very nice of you."

"Seriously, you were great. It was just a tough crowd."

"Like when I played Arlington," she said.

He looked blank for a moment. Blank, but still handsome. Then he smiled. "Oh, the cemetery. Sorry, you're a bit quicker than I am."

"I kind of doubt that." She was finding herself now. The guy was easy to talk to, and smooth enough that she knew she should be careful.

"Since you're convinced you died up there," he said, motioning with his head toward the stage, "why don't we go someplace else where we can have a drink and hold a proper requiem?"

She pretended to think about it, all the time knowing she was going to leave with him.

Gotta put up a front, signal that you're resisting. Every mother's advice, as if we were all born through immaculate conception.

He moved closer to her, as if she had emitted some kind of magnetic field.

Had she?

"I think you'll find," he said in a gentle voice, "that you didn't really die onstage. It was only a near-death experience."

She smiled at him and took the arm he offered. "That was pretty good," she said.

"Use it in your routine."

"I would if it was funny enough," she said honestly. "I have no scruples."

"Ah, we're a perfect match."

He pushed open the street door, and the damp heat of the night dared them to leave.

Mitzi thought she heard someone call her name, but she didn't look back.

47

The morning sunlight's warmth on his bare right arm woke Quinn. Something about the way it angled through the window made the flesh it contacted feel as if it might burst into flame. It was almost enough to take his mind off his terrific headache.

He didn't open his eyes, but right away he knew where he was, on the floor of the Seventy-ninth Street office. He wasn't exactly sure how he'd gotten there.

He lay motionless, curled on the hard, cool linoleum, or sheet goods, or whatever it was being called these days. Recollection came slowly, and then in a rush. He remembered unlocking and opening the office door late last night—early morning, actually, but a long way from daybreak. As soon as he'd stepped inside, even before he'd had a chance to flip the wall switch, something, some*one*, had slammed into him. There'd been a brief, confused struggle; he'd managed to crawl away from it, and then . . .

His headache flared as if to remind him that he'd been struck just above his left temple.

Beeker. He realized he'd been thinking about Dr. Alfred Beeker as he'd lost consciousness, and something about a giant bird.

The stuff dreams are made of.

Quinn gradually opened his eyes to the bright morning light. *Ouch!* His eyelids seemed to be dragging themselves across sandpaper. And the light was blinding.

Almost blinding.

Through the brilliance and swirling dust motes he could make out the form of a woman standing in the office's half bath with the door open. Washing her hands? No, not that. She was standing at the washbasin though, leaning forward so she could stare at herself in the mirror. In the blinding light and through his aching eyes she might have been an apparition. Like the bird. Was he still unconscious? Still dreaming? Had the blow to his head damaged his brain?

As he watched, the woman raised her hand to her right ear. She jerked her head quickly to the left, almost like a bird when something's caught its attention, and began toying with the ear, straining as if to examine it or look behind it.

Pearl!

"Pearl?" he said in a hoarse voice.

He heard her sharp inhalation as she jumped and backed away from the mirror. She stepped out of the half-bath and looked around. "Who's here?"

"Me. Quinn."

She looked all around her, then down at Quinn lying on the floor near one of the desks.

"You scared the holy hell out of me," she said.

"Sorry."

She squinted at him, then came toward him with a kind of broken gait, as if restrained by caution and curiosity. "You okay? What're you doing on the floor? How come you're here so early? How'd you get here?"

He found himself grinning. "Lots of questions, Pearl?"

"But you *are* all right?"

"Seem all right. Hell of a headache, though." He moved to sit up. "And my ribs are a bit sore," he added.

"Don't try to get up. I'll get some help." She moved toward the nearest desk and a phone.

"No, no." He raised a hand, stopping her.

Her hand came away from the phone, but she was staring oddly at him.

"I'll be fine, Pearl. Really. I just need a minute."

"Don't try to get up yet." She rolled a desk chair over to him and sat down in it, leaning forward and fixing him with an assessing stare. "Looks like you hit your head. What happened? You fall?"

"No. Somebody hit me in the head. Rammed his own head or his shoulder into my ribs first."

"Somebody attacked you in *here*? That's some nerve. This is a police facility."

"There's no sign on the door."

"Well, that's true."

"I didn't even get a chance to turn on the light," Quinn said. "We need to look things over, see if anything's missing."

Pearl glanced around. "Computers are still here. So's the coffee brewer. I was just about to make some." She paused. "Some of the desk drawers aren't shut all the way. And one of the bottom file cabinet drawers is hanging open."

Quinn gripped the desk corner and hauled himself to his feet. He was dizzy for a moment, and the headache was stronger.

Pearl stood up and held his arm. "You gonna be okay?"

"Yeah." He guessed he was. He looked around and saw what Pearl had seen. "I disturbed him. He was looking for something, on a fact-finding mission."

"Who we talking about?" Pearl asked. But they both knew.

"Tigers do that," Quinn said.

"Leave drawers open?"

"No. They double back on whoever's stalking them; then they lie in wait and become their most dangerous."

"I didn't know you hunted tigers."

"I watch the nature channel."

"Do we really think the intruder was the killer, trying to learn what we know so he can stay ahead of us?"

"It's a possibility. Let's look around and see if he was successful."

Pearl moved closer and put both arms around Quinn, steadying him. Of course that was when Fedderman arrived.

He stood inside the door with a surprised look on his face that needed to be wiped off with a napkin. "I'm interrupting. . . ."

"Don't be an asshole," Pearl said. "We were practicing judo."

Quinn moved away from Pearl and explained to Fedderman what had happened. Then the three of them, still silently absorbing the break-in and assault, examined drawer and file cabinet contents and decided nothing was missing.

"He might not have wanted to steal anything," Fedderman said, "just read things. Just learn."

"And we can't know how much he did learn," Quinn said.

Pearl went over and perched with her haunches on the edge of her desk. "Damn near everything's in the papers or TV news anyway."

"And now he knows that," Fedderman said.

"If he had time to examine everything."

Pearl pushed herself away from her desk and went around to her computer. She booted up hers, then the other two computers, and clicked on their histories. None of them showed any activity after yesterday afternoon.

"I don't think he learned much, if anything," she said. She sat back again on the edge of her desk and crossed her arms. "Maybe we're making this too complicated, Quinn. Maybe he just wanted to bash you in the head."

"And knew I'd be coming in at two in the morning?"

"So you interrupted a burglar, and he bashed you in the head," Fedderman said.

"Possibly. But he did a lot of snooping around and apparently didn't steal anything."

"Could he have gotten away after initially knocking you down?" Pearl asked. "I mean, did he have to also hit you in the head?"

"I'm not sure. It's still hazy."

"So maybe he was snooping, like we figure. A tiger."

"Huh?" Fedderman said.

Pearl gave him a dismissive wave of her hand to shut him up. To Quinn, she said: "And he was glad for the opportunity to bash you in the head."

"Can you think of anyone who'd wanna do that?" Fedderman asked. "Other than me and Pearl."

"And the killer," Pearl added.

"One person," Quinn said, "and I know where to find him."

48

The bottle or the gun?

Lavern Neeson, badly bruised from last night's beating by Hobbs, had risen at three in the morning in pain and this time had chosen both.

It was eight o'clock now, getting warmer and brighter outside. The bedroom was dim, though, because the shades were drawn and the heavy drapes pulled closed, so no one could have seen last night what Hobbs had done to her. It was an overly furnished, somewhat worn and chintzy room of the sort that held its secrets. On one of the walls was a discount store print of a flock of birds—crows, probably— rising as if startled from a wooded landscape. Lavern had never liked it, but never considered changing it.

She sat in a small chair near the bed, listening to Hobbs snore, holding the shotgun from the closet on her lap and casually aimed at him. He wasn't scheduled for work today and would sleep until well past ten. But Lavern liked to toy with the notion that he might wake up, and the first thing he'd see would be her and the dark muzzle of the shotgun.

He wouldn't know it wasn't loaded, but maybe he'd die on his own, of a heart attack.

More likely she'd simply scare the hell out of him, and then he'd beat the crap out of her for frightening and embarrassing him.

Still, just thinking about it afforded her some amusement.

In a little while, she'd get up from her chair, leave the bedroom, and return the shotgun to the back of the hall closet. Another day with Hobbs would begin. Fear would begin.

The faint noises of the city winding up for another busy day wafted in to Lavern, and she thought about all the women out there who weren't in any way dependent on husbands or lovers like Hobbs, women leading happy, pain-free lives, not afraid of making a wrong move that would lead to severe punishment.

Lavern envied those women, but joining their number seemed almost impossible.

She could think of only one way out of her predicament, and it terrified her.

If she left Hobbs, he'd surely come after her. It had happened once before, three years ago. If she tried to change him, he would beat her. If she changed herself, he would beat her. She knew that her friend Bess, who kept urging her to go to a women's shelter, was right. Not about the shelter—she couldn't stay there forever, even if Hobbs didn't simply come and get her. And restraining orders—she'd read the papers, seen the news, and knew how ineffective they were. What Bess *was* right about was that eventually it was almost certain that Hobbs would kill her.

Unless she killed him first.

Lavern thought she might possibly be acquitted if she did that. Other women had killed their abusive husbands and gotten away with it. But so many others hadn't. And even if she succeeded in avoiding prison, there would be the horrible publicity, the arrest, the trial. Who knew how a jury might find?

Killing Hobbs wasn't something Lavern actually saw as

an option, at least right now. But it was something she could consider, which she did more and more often. It wasn't illegal to think about it.

She moved the shotgun's long barrel slightly, so it was aimed at her husband's head, then traced an invisible line down along his body to his heart, then to his crotch.

Should I shoot him there?

The idea was intriguing. Just sitting there with Hobbs's life in her hands, without him knowing about it, intrigued her. At the same time, it scared her enough that she no longer could do it without first going to the bottle. If he ever woke up and caught her like this, or found out in some other way what she was doing, he'd be furious. Maybe murderous. He might actually kill her.

Unless she killed him first.

He was alone in the long, maroon-carpeted corridor as he waited for an elevator. Standing easily but alertly, he kept his head moving, glancing up and down the hall. Far down the hall and in the opposite direction from his own room a maid was parking her linen-laden cart near a door. That was all the activity he saw until the elevator arrived.

It was unoccupied but for an attractive blond woman in her forties who had the look and rolling luggage of an airline attendant. He saw by the illuminated button on the elevator's control panel that, like him, she was going to the lobby. She glanced at Dunn, smiled, and looked up at the LED floor numbers as the elevator descended. Dunn moved back and stood where he could also observe elevator etiquette and gaze at the numerals above the door, but at the same time see the woman in his peripheral vision.

He was 99 percent certain she posed no danger, but he'd been conditioned to assume that everyone posed some danger. That was the kind of perspective that would keep him alive.

Dunn wasn't nearly as nervous as last time, when he'd left his hotel on the first morning. He'd even enjoyed a room-service breakfast of waffles and bacon, with plenty of maple syrup. He'd downed two cups of strong black coffee to make him even more alert and aware.

When the elevator reached lobby level, the woman favored Dunn with another smile as she maneuvered her wheeled suitcase and garment bag out into the lobby. In another time and place he would have smiled back and assisted her with her luggage.

Concentrate! Be in this time, in this place.

He watched the woman begin to walk away and then exited the elevator himself.

The compact Quest and Quarry revolver was a reassuring weight in Dunn's blazer pocket as he pushed through the hotel's revolving glass doors and breathed in the warm morning air. He'd studied the company dossier on his quarry and decided on a more aggressive strategy this time. Walking to the next block, so he wouldn't be remembered by the uniformed doorman, he hailed a cab on his own and gave the driver an intersection near Thomas Rhodes's address. Then he settled back into the cab's upholstery and rode alert and mission-bent through the golden morning.

The game was on, his blood was up, and it occurred to him how much he enjoyed this.

Mitzi was still half asleep when she heard the knocking on her door. She reached over and felt a wide expanse of cool linen, and remembered that Mr. Handsome had left sometime after midnight.

More knocking. Not her imagination.

She made herself scoot over on the mattress and then maneuvered her body so she was sitting. The effort caused her head to ache behind both eyes.

Need more sleep. Definitely.

She groaned, explored with her tongue, and found that her teeth were fuzzy. Ah, well . . .

After drawing a deep breath, she stood up and lurched toward the living room.

When she opened the door to the hall, a man in a gray delivery uniform was standing there holding a long white box. His gaze took a ride up and down her body, and she realized she was wearing only her thin nightgown.

He smiled. "Flowers for a Mitzi Lewis."

"I am a Mitzi Lewis," Mitzi said in a sleep-thickened voice. She accepted the almost-weightless box and set it on a table near the door. Then she raised a forefinger in a signal for the man to wait.

It took her a few minutes to find her purse and wallet, then scare up a couple of dollars for a tip. When she turned around she saw that the deliveryman had minded his manners and was still standing politely on the other side of the threshold.

Mitzi handed him the tip, and he smiled again, making an obvious effort this time not to look at her below neck level. He tapped the bill of a nonexistent cap and turned around and began descending the stairs of her sixth-floor walk-up. It was an easier trek down than up, and Mitzi could hear him pick up speed, his shoes rapping out a machine-gun rhythm on the wooden steps.

She closed her apartment door, then carried the long white box over to the sofa and sat down.

When she opened the box she found a dozen long-stemmed red roses. There was a small, plain white envelope containing a white card with a brief message printed in blue ink:

> *Last night was more than wonderful.*
> *I'll call.*

There was no signature.

Mitzi placed the box next to her on the sofa, then sat slumped forward with her elbows on her knees, her chin resting in her right palm. *No signature . . .*

Christ! I slept with a man and don't even know his name. Oh, well, it was an interesting first.

49

Black Lake, Missouri, 1987

Marty had no idea what had awakened him.

He didn't think he'd been dreaming. But suddenly there he was in his bed, sprawled on his back, his eyes wide open and staring into darkness. It was hot in the room, and he was sweating, the sheet thrown off him and half jumbled on the floor. The luminous green hands of the big alarm clock on his dresser said that it was a little past three o'clock. He could hear katydids screaming away desperately outside.

He stood up, the floorboard creaking beneath his bare feet, and through his bedroom window he saw a yellow glow seeping through the cracks in the barn and spilling out around the uneven edges of its closed doors.

Lantern light. Somebody's out there.

Off in the distance a dog barked. Maybe that was what had awakened him. Marty couldn't be sure. What he did know was that something was happening in the barn.

Wearing only his jockey shorts, he crept from his bedroom so he wouldn't wake his parents. Either one or both wouldn't take kindly to him nosing around the house at this hour. Between the two of them, he guessed it was his father out in the barn.

He saw that their bedroom door, usually closed at night, was open. From where he stood he had a view of the corner of their bed, and when he moved so he had a better angle, he saw that it was empty.

Something involving both of them must be going on.

His heart was beating fast as he made his way across the creaking plank floor to the porch door.

Here was something else not right. The door was unlocked.

He went outside onto the porch. There was a half moon tonight, sketched on by dark clouds. It gave enough light to cast a glow on the bare yard and rutted driveway, and to edge the ragged line of trees on the ridge beyond the barn. The katydids were louder, and it was hotter outside than in the house.

Marty stepped down off the porch and began walking toward the big barn with its vertical cracks of faint yellow light. He couldn't hear his footfalls, and the dog was no longer barking in the distance. The only sound was the hopeless riot of the insects. Their ratcheting rasping was a mating call, Marty knew. Most of them would mate, and within a few days would be dead.

The barn's big wooden doors were closed but for an inch, and the long rusty hasp stuck out like a handle, inviting Marty to open one of the doors and find out about the mysterious light.

Marty gripped the hasp's rough surface and pulled the barn door open about two feet. It didn't squeal like it usually did, and he wondered if someone had oiled the hinges.

He held his breath as he entered the barn.

Marty's father hadn't heard him and stood continuing his work on Marty's mother, who was strung upside down so her nude body dangled from one of the barn's main rafters. On one of the other rafters perched a small barn owl. Without moving anything else, it swiveled its feathered head and stared at Marty as if he was intruding.

His father was shirtless and wearing an old pair of jeans and his leather work boots. He was facing away from Marty, and between his spread legs Marty could see his mother's upside-down face. Her eyes were open and her expression calm, though she seemed faintly annoyed by what was happening.

As Marty watched, his father raised the gutting knife in both hands and bunched his back muscles for strength. The knife descended and Marty's mother's insides fell out into a bloody pile between his father's widely spread boots.

There were streams of blood on each side of Alma's face now, and in her hair, but she held her calm expression. Marty saw that her throat had been slit and knew she'd been dead when he entered the barn.

His father continued his task, adroitly slicing here, occasionally hacking with the knife there, making sure the gutting was complete.

Then he stopped, stood very still, and turned around and saw Marty.

For a few seconds Carl Hawk looked embarrassed and ashamed. Then he looked angry and self-righteous.

Marty wasn't exactly frightened. He loved his father too much to fear him. But what felt from the inside like a poker face must have betrayed him and shown his confusion.

"There wasn't any choice," his father said. He was very calm and spoke patiently, in the tone of voice he used when teaching Marty to tie fishing flies. He held the bloody knife at his side, its blade pointing down. "She come at me with that axe an' tried to kill me." He glanced at a rusty long-handled axe lying in the litter of straw near one of the empty stalls, then waited for Marty to look in that direction.

Marty did, and nodded, confirming that yes, he saw the axe.

"Woman tried to kill me, son. Hell, she's been poisonin' me for months, anyways. You know that. Told you about it last winter and lots of times thereafter. Goddamned roach poison! Guess she got impatient about my dyin' so she took up the axe. You understand, once she killed me, you were gonna be next. She as much as said that. She went plain crazy. You understand?"

"I understand," Marty heard himself say.

"We all do what we gotta do," Carl Hawk said, "an' then we live with it. That's somethin' I thought I taught you."

"I understand," Marty said again.

His father stood there, studying him; then he wiped the knife on his jeans and stuck the point of the blade in a nearby wooden support pole, near where a kerosene lantern hung with its handle looped over a long nail. Below the lantern a metal pail, shovel, and a tow chain hung from hooks.

"It's done for now," Carl said. "Let's both of us go back in the house and see if we can sleep. Come mornin' we'll put the body down that old well back in the woods. The innards we'll feed to the hogs." He sighed and gave Marty a tight, humorless smile. "Then that'll be that."

Carl turned down the lantern wick, and the barn was in darkness except for what moonlight filtered in through the cracks and where the door stood open. He laid his hand gently on Marty's shoulder and guided him outside into the warm night. They began the slow walk toward the house.

"It had to be done," Carl said. "You know that, Marty. If it hadn't, you and me'd both be dead right now."

Marty didn't answer.

"When she was finished on me with the axe, she was gonna go on back to the house an' do you."

His father's boots made a creaking, leathery sound as he walked. Marty could barely hear it over the noise of the katydids. "You believe me, Marty?"

"I believe."

"You okay?" his father asked.

"I can do whatever you say," Marty told him.

His father stopped walking, closed his bloody hand tighter on Marty's shoulder, then drew him in close and hugged him.

Marty hugged him back.

50

New York, the present

The first thing Dr. Alfred Beeker saw when he opened the door to his office's anteroom at 9:45 A.M. was Beatrice with her blond head thrown back, laughing so hard that her fillings showed. Quinn was in Beeker's waiting room, charming the doctor's middle-aged, attractive receptionist, but he was sitting off to the right and not immediately noticeable to anyone walking in.

Beeker was a tall, broad-shouldered man in his forties, with thinning black hair combed severely sideways to disguise his baldness. His features were sharp, with dark eyes that appeared slightly crossed and lent him an expression of intensity. He was wearing a nicely tailored gray suit and carrying a beat-up black leather briefcase with a large tarnished brass clasp. Quinn wondered if the briefcase was an affectation. Or maybe that was where the good doctor kept his whips.

"Am I missing something?" Beeker asked Beatrice. Then he glanced to the side and saw Quinn.

Beatrice put on a straight, if twitching, face and stood up behind her desk. "This is Detective Frank Quinn."

Beeker didn't seem thrown by finding a cop in his office. He smiled at Quinn and looked at him curiously.

"I thought it best to catch you before your morning appointments," Quinn said, standing up. "It's become necessary for you and I to have a conversation. It won't take long."

"Am I under arrest?" Still the smile. A joke.

"Not yet," Quinn said. No smile. A joke, maybe.

"Come in and sit down," Beeker said, with a sideways glance at Beatrice, who was now engrossed in some kind of paperwork. He stepped past the reception desk and opened a plain oak door, then stood back so Quinn could enter first.

"Wonderful talking to you, dear," Quinn said to Beatrice, as he entered the office.

It was everything a Park Avenue psychoanalyst's office should be, restful and hushed. Very much like Zoe's office. Maybe they had the same decorator. Pale green walls, darker green carpet, lots of dark brown leather furniture, framed modern paintings that would scare no one. Centered in the room, facing the door, was a vast mahogany desk. There were matching file cabinets on the wall behind it. There was one very large window. Pale beige drapes lined in caramel-colored silk extended from the ceiling on either side of it and puddled on the floor.

The desk was uncluttered but for a dark brown phone, a freshly cut long-stemmed rose in a delicate crystal vase, and a gold picture frame. The wall to the right was floor-to-ceiling books, most of them medical journals. An ornate brass floor lamp near the desk was unnecessarily on and softly glowing. Apparently Beatrice had readied the office for her boss. *Have a nice day* hung in the air.

Beeker motioned for Quinn to sit in one of the sumptuous leather armchairs angled toward the desk. Quinn lowered his weight into the chair, which was even more comfortable than it looked. The seat cushion hissed as if it didn't like being sat on.

After waiting until Quinn was seated, Beeker walked around and situated himself in the high-backed leather chair behind his desk. He rocked back and forth a few times in the chair, and then sat forward and made a pink tent with his fingers the way Renz often did, which made Quinn distrust him. It wasn't hard for Quinn to imagine the doctor as his assailant in the dark Seventy-ninth Street office.

The doctor smiled faintly. "So how can I help you, Lieutenant Quinn?"

"Captain Quinn."

Beeker looked a bit surprised, as if he'd suddenly recognized Quinn's name from the news, though he didn't seem exactly thrown. His smile returned. Quinn might as well have been here to promote some sort of community action or to make a charity pitch. Beeker glanced at his watch, then touched the tip of the pink finger tent to the dimpled tip of his chin. "Well, Captain?"

"You don't have much time left," Quinn said.

"I know. My first appointment will be here in ten minutes, and I'll need to make a few preparations."

"That's not exactly what I meant," Quinn said. He thought he could smell the rose in the crystal vase. "If you ever lay a hand or any other object again on Zoe Manders, I'm going to kill you."

Beeker didn't change expression at first; then his intense dark eyes bored into Quinn. He lowered his hands palms down on the desk. He didn't seem afraid, only hyperalert. "Isn't it against regulations for an NYPD police captain to threaten a lawful citizen?"

"You aren't a lawful citizen. You're guilty of assault."

"This Miss Manders . . ."

"Dr. Manders. Zoe."

"She's filed a complaint against me?"

"No, and she won't."

"What makes you think I assaulted her?"

"She told me."

"Did she offer any proof?"

"No."

"But you believe her."

"Yes."

"I think I can guess why."

Guess away, asshole.

Beeker stared at Quinn for a while, obviously calculating. Then he stood up behind his desk. "Well, you've delivered your message. Now you can go about your business and I can go about mine."

Quinn didn't budge from his chair. "Where were you between one and three o'clock this morning?" *This morning . . .* had it been so recently?

Beeker smiled faintly. "Did someone attack Dr. Manders around that time? Or make a threatening phone call? Is that it? She thinks it was me?"

"Where were you?" Quinn asked again, calmly.

"Where any sane person who doesn't have a night job was—home in bed. And alone." He cocked his head to the side and gave Quinn an appraising look. "You have a personal interest in Zoe."

Quinn said nothing.

"I wouldn't believe everything Zoe says," Beeker told him.

"I don't believe everything anybody says."

"Zoe especially, you shouldn't believe."

"She said you threatened to put photographs of her on the Internet," Quinn said. "I believed that."

"There's nothing improper about those photos," Beeker said. He leaned forward, planting his hands on the desk. "But you can remind Zoe that she willingly posed for other photographs, and if she sends you or someone like you here again, they'll be posted on the Internet. She knows where." He leaned farther over the desk toward Quinn. "I won't be threatened. And I'd like to see your identification. I don't think you are from the police."

Quinn stood up, leaned across the desk, and shoved Beeker hard back into his chair. The chair was on rollers and shot back and slammed against the file cabinets, jolting Beeker. He remained seated, staring up at Quinn. He still didn't look afraid.

"I think you should reconsider posting photos of Zoe on the Internet," Quinn said.

"It was only a threat."

"Reconsider the threat."

"I could go to the real police," Beeker said.

"While you're there, you can read the assault complaint Zoe will file. And I'll get to interrogate you."

"Someone assaulted Zoe last night—earlier this morning?"

"Much earlier," Quinn said.

"Ah! Bruises fade with time. You must know that in your business. Zoe has no proof of anything."

Quinn walked around the desk and gripped Beeker by his shirt lapels. Some silk tie and flesh were pinched in with the material. He shook the doctor hard so that his head flopped around, bouncing off the chair's high leather back, and a few times off a filing cabinet as the chair rolled. Beeker's plastered-over hair rose on his head and stood high like a sparse rooster comb.

Quinn released him, but remained close, staring down at him. "You were right about me having delivered my message. Now I'll leave. Don't do anything that might prompt me to return. And remember what I said about those photographs."

Beeker was busy rearranging his shirt and tie, and didn't bother looking at Quinn.

As Quinn turned to walk past the desk, he glanced at the framed photo near the phone. He'd expected to see a family shot, or maybe Beeker's latest punching bag. Instead it was an outdoor photo of Beeker standing with three other men. They were all wearing mackinaws and boots and carrying shotguns or rifles. Beeker and another man were holding out what looked like dead rabbits they'd shot. Everyone in the photo, other than the rabbits, was smiling.

"You a hunter?" Quinn asked.

"Sometimes. Why do you ask?"

Ignoring the question, Quinn walked to the door, opened it, and went back out into the anteroom. The idea was to let Beeker stew, but Beeker didn't seem to be stewing.

"Is everything okay?" Beatrice asked. She must have heard Beeker's chair bumping around. Or maybe it was Beeker's head.

"Everything's violets and roses, dear," Quinn said, and smiled reassuringly at her on the way out.

But it wasn't okay. Beeker hadn't once seemed even slightly afraid during Quinn's violent visit.

That worried Quinn.

51

Sal Vitali sat at his desk in the almost-deserted squad room. All was quiet, except for a printer industriously buzzing away somewhere and an occasional muffled shout from the holding cells upstairs. Most of the detectives were out in the field. Only Don Mackey, a dogged old cop nearing retirement, was at his desk over near the window, working the phone.

Sal's partner, Mishkin, sat across from him. They'd cleared off most of the desktop, and on it, scattered over a pristine white sheet of printer paper, were the items the crime scene unit had vacuumed up from the Antonian Hotel corridor where Floyd Becker had been shot and killed before his body was dragged outside. There was lint, a bit of brown plastic that had come off the end of a shoelace (not Becker's, and probably not his killer's), lint, three human hairs, and more lint. None of the hairs was the victim's, but that didn't mean the killer's hair was there. The hairs could have come from anyone passing along the corridor.

Sal had read somewhere that the average person lost approximately eighty individual hairs per day. On most people that hair grew back, but on Sal's head, he wasn't so sure. It seemed to him that he left at least eighty hairs in the drain every morning when he showered. But maybe that was because he had so much of the stuff to begin with. The other detectives in the precinct kidded him sometimes about his hair, called him Columbo. Sal bore up under it and pretended to be annoyed. Like he had a choice.

Quinn might not approve of him examining the vacuum bag items, believing the Slicer and his gutted dead women, not .25-Caliber Killer victims, were Sal and Mishkin's bailiwick, but so what? This was supposed to be one case, with one psycho killer, so in Sal's view it was one big bag of shit.

What Sal really wanted to do was break both cases, collar two killers, show the bastards in the puzzle palace they were overthinking this thing. Renz and Helen the profiler figured there was one killer with two distinctly different MOs, who killed women one way and men another. Sal didn't see it as likely. They all must have fallen under the spell of Helen the profiler, who as far as Sal was concerned might be a female impersonator, with that lanky body, those long bony fingers, and that chin. Not a bad-looking one, though. Some of those transgenders could fool you.

"Nothing we might be able to use but the hair, Sal," Mishkin said, squinting down at the sparse assortment on the desktop. "And not even that unless we get a match."

"The little plastic doodad from the end of a shoelace," Sal said.

"If that's what it is," Mishkin said.

"Lab says that's what it is."

"Then when we get a suspect, we look close at his shoelaces. Especially if they're brown."

"And his hair," Sal said.

Mishkin sat back and wiped his hand down his face, then smoothed out his mustache as if it needed it. "That break-in at Quinn and his team's office, Sal—you think it's connected to any of this?"

"Doubt it," Sal said. "Probably just some asshole looking

for money to score some dope. Probably didn't even know the place was a cop shop."

"The guy did a neat job picking the lock."

"Smart asshole. Or maybe somebody forgot to lock the door when they left, and the guy walked right in."

"Happens," Mishkin said.

Very carefully, using tweezers, Sal picked up each item from the vacuuming and placed it back in its plastic evidence bag.

"Happens," he agreed, when he was finished.

"There were three hairs, right?" Mishkin said.

Sal looked at him. "Right."

"Just wanted to make sure," Mishkin said. "Wouldn't want one of your many hairs to get in with them."

Sal kept looking at him, wondering if he'd just been ragged, but Mishkin was wearing his usual bland and amiable expression.

"You want some coffee, Sal?"

"Sure."

You never could tell with Mishkin.

The man who'd broken into the Seventy-ninth Street office and knocked out Quinn sat at an inside table in the Aces Up diner on Amsterdam, sipping cold green tea and watching people and traffic stream past outside. Twin parallel lines of concern were etched vertically above the bridge of his nose. He was still unhappy about how his plan to become the hunter rather than the hunted had turned out.

The break-in had been easy enough. He smiled at the thought of it. How ironic that the police would take over office space and not concern themselves with the quality of the lock on the door. That was exactly how bureaucracies worked. Or didn't work. With a good set of picks in expert hands, the lock had yielded after only a few minutes.

The plan had been to enter and obtain information, then leave without any indication that he'd been there. He would then know what Quinn knew, and Quinn would be unaware of it. That might make the game somewhat less interesting, but definitely safer.

A waiter came and placed the tuna salad sandwich he'd ordered on the table before him, then topped off his iced tea.

He *had* been hungry, and as he replenished his body with food and energy, optimism gradually replaced his concern. Last night—or early this morning—might have gone a lot worse. The suddenness of Quinn's entrance and discovery of an intruder had surprised both of them. And in the ensuing struggle to escape, he had injured Quinn, given him something to think about other than his hunt.

Quinn wasn't a young man, but there was an obvious strength in him, and he knew how to fight, so it was lucky that he hadn't had time to set himself for the intruder's attack. The game might have ended right there. As it was, the break-in had been partially successful in that it might have thrown Quinn and his detectives off their game.

He took a sip of tea.

Yes, it could have been worse.

Now Quinn would walk with the added dimension of fear, the cold tingle up the spine that came with the realization that stalker might at any moment become stalked. The intruder smiled. He'd been in that position and knew how it felt. It seemed to turn the world upside down.

Not that it would keep Quinn subdued for long. He'd know how to handle fear. He was an old hand at his game, a seasoned hunter.

But now he was a hunter who would occasionally glance back over his shoulder.

What was that legendary baseball pitcher's adage? *Don't look back. Something might be gaining on you.*

One day Quinn might look back too late, and there would be what had been gaining on him, suddenly caught up.

* * *

Quinn was breathing heavily with the effort of keeping his weight off Zoe as he rolled from on top of her and onto his cool side of the bed. He blew out a breath toward the ceiling, then turned his head to the side to look across his pillow at her.

Zoe was still on her back, one of her bare legs gracefully bent at the knee. Her nude body was glistening with perspiration. She and Quinn were both sweating, but the ceiling fan was on and would soon cool their bodies. The fan made a barely discernable *tick, tick, tick* as the broad wicker blades rotated, as if to punctuate the room's isolation from the outside world.

Zoe noticed he was staring at her, and looked back at him with a kind of dreamy expression in her half-closed eyes.

"You okay?" Quinn asked.

"Men ask that a lot."

"How do you know?"

"My patients. I know a lot of secrets."

Quinn stared up at the ceiling, thinking about his visit with Alfred Beeker.

Tick, tick, tick . . .

"I am," Zoe said.

"Huh?"

"Okay. Better than okay." She reached over and gently touched his arm. "What are you thinking?"

"Women ask that a lot," Quinn said.

"Do men ever answer honestly?"

"Sometimes."

"So answer honestly now."

"I'm thinking I'm a little old for a nooner."

She slapped his arm, laughing. "Bastard!"

He leaned over, kissed her forehead, then climbed out of the bed. "If I can figure out how to open your fancy refrigerator, I'm going to get a beer. You want anything?"

"Right now," she said, "I don't feel as if I need anything."

Pretty sure that was a compliment, Quinn made his way into Zoe's state-of-the-art kitchen. The one she admitted she seldom cooked in. Quinn was sure she was telling the truth there. The gleaming white appliances looked brand new, especially the double-oven stove, which resembled the instrument panel of a jet airliner.

The built-in refrigerator door had so much weight and heft it felt like a well-balanced vault door when he opened it. There wasn't much in the fridge in the way of food—a small bowl of apples, something shadowy in the cheese compartment, an unopened carton of orange juice, six bottles of white wine, and half a dozen bottles of Heineken beer. Like the refrigerator of a supermodel, Quinn thought, though he didn't know one supermodel. He withdrew one of the green Heineken bottles and closed the refrigerator door. He used a bottle opener he'd noticed in one of the drawers rather than risk that the cap wasn't a twist-off, and then carried the bottle into the bedroom.

Zoe didn't appear to have moved. The warmth and scent of their afternoon sex was still in the air, not yet dissipated by the slowly rotating ceiling fan above the acre-sized bed.

Quinn touched the cold bottle to Zoe's damp forehead, and she smiled. He sat on the edge of the mattress, facing half away from her.

Before she got a chance to ask him what he was thinking, he said, "Why do you have so many damned pillows?" He was staring at the stacks of throw pillows from the bed that towered on the carpet.

"They're for show," she said.

"Ah. I know about that." He took another sip of cold beer. "I visited your doctor friend this morning."

Tick, tick, tick, went the fan.

Zoe was silent.

"He won't bother you again," Quinn said.

"He hadn't bothered me lately," Zoe said. "It was you he might have bothered."

"Yeah, with his anger issues."

"Do you think he was the one who broke into your office and assaulted you?"

"I still don't know what to think."

"So you talked to him mostly about me."

"I had to, Zoe."

"Because he might have attacked you, you were afraid for me."

"Anger issues are anger issues," Quinn said.

"Did you terrorize him?"

Quinn smiled. "I wouldn't say that. Whatever Beeker's faults, he doesn't seem easy to terrorize." He looked over at her. "You want a sip of beer?"

"No, thanks. Did you threaten him?"

"He threatened me. Us, actually. Said he had some very personal photographs of you and if we harassed him he'd post them on the Internet. He said you'd know where."

"I believe he might," Zoe said. "Those photos—"

"I don't care about them, Zoe. He won't post them."

"You said he didn't scare."

"But he knows what will happen to him if he posts those kinds of photos of you, if he ever bothers you again. He didn't have to be scared to understand."

"How can you know that?"

"I was emphatic."

He still didn't look at her, but he heard the sheets rustle as she moved closer on the wide bed. He felt her kiss his bare side, play her tongue over him. It was only slightly warmer than his flesh.

Tick, tick, tick . . .

"What did he say when you brought up the subject of the office break-in?" she asked.

"I didn't bring it up directly, but he doesn't have an alibi for its time frame. Says he was home in bed alone."

"Do you believe him?"

"I told him I didn't believe anyone about everything."

"Is that true?"

"It is except for you," Quinn said, twisting his torso so he could look into her eyes. "You're different."

52

Pearl dropped the mail all over the floor but didn't give a damn. She was too tired.

She closed and locked her door, then stepped over the clutter on the floor.

After another hot and unproductive day on the job, she'd finally found refuge in her apartment. She'd left the window-unit air conditioner on low so the place wouldn't preheat like an oven, but it still felt almost as hot as outside. Sometimes when she left the unit on like that it would freeze up and put out only brief wafts of neutral air while spitting occasional flecks of ice.

Like this time.

She switched off the struggling unit and turned away from it in disgust.

The bedroom was even warmer than the living room. She turned on that window unit, then went into the kitchen and switched on its smaller and almost useless air conditioner. The apartment's air conditioners looked about twenty years old. Where did the landlord buy this crap? If it kept up like this, she'd have to curl up in the refrigerator to find any relief from the heat.

She returned to the living room, slipped off her shoes and blouse, and slumped down on the sofa wearing only slacks and her bra, waiting for the bedroom and kitchen to cool down a few degrees. She'd have a snack and a cold beer, then go into the bedroom and stretch out wearing only her panties and try to read the latest *New Yorker*. For some reason she enjoyed reading about the Broadway plays she couldn't afford to see.

When she'd lived with Quinn they'd often gone to the theater. He was a Broadway buff and had turned her into one before they'd split up, leaving her with a habit she couldn't afford. He'd enjoyed Pinter and Stoppard, she *The Lion King*.

Quinn.

Pearl wasn't sure if it was the heat or lack of progress on the investigation that was keeping her in such a state of irritation, or if it was the knowledge of Quinn's affair with the psychoanalyst Zoe.

It wasn't that she had anything against Zoe Manders, but what the hell was Quinn doing sleeping with a shrink, anyway? If there was one thing their love lives should have taught both Quinn and Pearl it was that cops are best off mated with cops. They were the only ones who understood each other.

Shouldn't that also be true of psychoanalysts?

What the hell do Quinn and Zoe talk about over breakfast? While riding in cabs? When watching the sun set? After they screw?

Me?

The thought of being the subject of Quinn and Zoe's pillow talk brought a smoldering ember to flame in Pearl's stomach. She stood up restlessly and retrieved from the floor the handful of mail she'd brought up from her box down in the lobby.

Pearl carried the mail into the kitchen, where by now it might be a few degrees cooler.

Only it wasn't.

She went over and slapped the air conditioner, but it reacted pretty much the way Quinn did the few times she'd slapped him. It ignored her. She might as well have slapped a brick wall.

Screw it!

After getting a Budweiser from the refrigerator, she sat down at the small wooden table, took a couple of long pulls on the bottle, then turned her attention to the mail.

Jesus Christ!

Aside from the usual bills and ads, half of her mail—*half!*—was from doctors or medical clinics. Most of it wasn't even the kind of mail that required opening. Fanned out on the table was one color flier or brochure after another warning of the dangers of ignoring seemingly harmless growths anywhere on the body, advising routine searches for such growths, explaining the horrors that might evolve from such tiny discolorations or moles.

Moles!

Her mother! Her mother and that goddamned Milton Kahn! They'd prompted these to be sent, and perhaps sent some themselves.

Pearl's first impulse was to reach for the phone and call her mother, but she caught herself in time. That would only make things infinitely worse. And calling and dressing down Milt would do no good. In truth, he might not even know about her mother's efforts to frighten Pearl back into his arms. Maybe it was just her mother and Milt's aunt, Mrs. Kahn, out at the assisted living home in New Jersey, fighting boredom by becoming engrossed in matchmaking and medical terrorism.

Pearl took another long pull of beer and hoped the alcohol would soon calm her nerves. Pearl's mother, Mrs. Kahn, and Milton Kahn. Most likely all three were in on the sporadic, creepy mailings that had finally erupted into this postal bombardment. *This . . . this . . . !*

Take it easy. Don't assume. Best to give this some calm thought.

It was probable that Milt at least knew about the assault by mail and condoned it. But if Pearl called him, he'd deny it. And wasn't that what this was all about, getting her to call him?

She stood up from the table and threw the mail in with the kitchen trash. All of it. Including any bills that might have been hiding between brightly colored images of moles gone amok.

Then she finished her beer and went into the bathroom, where she stood before the mirror and took yet another long, long look at the mole behind her right ear, until the ear ached from being bent drastically forward to reveal the mole. She'd been examining the mole so frequently lately that her right ear appeared swollen and larger than her left.

Pearl splashed cold water over her face, patted it dry with a towel, then leaned on the washbasin with both hands and assessed herself anew in the mirror. The stress she'd been under since joining Quinn's investigation showed, the stress from worrying about murder and the mole. She leaned closer to the mirror to get a better look at the somber woman staring back at her.

You look like you've been run over by a subway.

Damn my mother! Damn Mrs. Kahn! Damn Milton Kahn! Damn Quinn! And Fedderman, too. And that bitch, Zoe. Look what they're doing to me!

"Enough of this bullshit," Pearl said to the other Pearl.

The other Pearl nodded, gave her a grim smile.

She would make another appointment with another dermatologist who wasn't Milton Kahn, and she would keep that appointment. She would have the seemingly harmless mole examined by an unbiased physician and put the matter to rest.

She was pretty sure she would.

* * *

Rhodes was too quick for him. Jerry Dunn had been following Thomas Rhodes for the last fifteen minutes, staying well back, waiting for Rhodes either to be relatively isolated, or surrounded by so many people that the bark of a shot would only serve to confuse them and the shooter—the hunter—could easily be lost among the milling humanity.

What Dunn liked was that Rhodes was carrying a black leather duffel bag slung from his shoulder by a thick strap. That meant he intended to run rather than try to turn the tables and become hunter rather than prey. Probably, Dunn thought, because Rhodes knew that if he couldn't successfully go into hiding he'd continue to be hunted no matter how this particular joust with death turned out.

What Dunn didn't like was that the duffel bag was only partly zipped, and Rhodes walked with one arm resting on the bag, his hand inside it. Dunn was sure the hand was curled around a .25-caliber revolver exactly like the one concealed in the fold of the morning *Times* he was carrying.

Rhodes was wearing brown slacks and a brownish tweed sport coat, warm for this kind of weather. Dunn figured that was so he could take all the useful clothing with him that wouldn't fit into the bag. It also meant he might be heading for a cooler climate. Not once had Rhodes glanced behind him, but Dunn didn't take for granted that his presence was unknown.

Suddenly Rhodes crossed Seventh Avenue in the middle of the block. At Fifty-first Street he jauntily descended the steps to a subway stop.

Dunn had to hurry. He followed down the concrete steps toward the platform, aware that his haste might cause carelessness. He might be entering a trap.

Ahead, beyond the turnstiles, he could see people coming up another flight of steps. Apparently a train had just arrived.

Dunn had a Metro card good for a week. He hurried through a turnstile, elbowing aside some of the crowd moving the opposite direction and pushing through the turnstiles to exit.

At the head of the steps he stopped.

He had a clear view down to a landing and a continuation of concrete steps, and saw no sign of Rhodes. Had he been tricked?

Damn it!

He glanced back toward the turnstiles and caught a glimpse of men's brown pants, as someone who might have been Rhodes jogged up the steps beyond the turnstiles and ran toward the street.

Rhodes?

The color of the pants was perfect.

Dunn ran toward the turnstiles, pushed through to exit, and dashed up the steps, taking them three at a time.

Back in the sunshine at street level, he looked in all directions.

No Thomas Rhodes.

Calm down, Dunn told himself. *Calm down!*

He didn't doubt Rhodes had known he was being tracked and had used the subway stop to slip away from his pursuer. He must have been waiting just to the side of the street steps so he could cut back the way he'd come after Dunn had hurried toward the turnstiles without a sideways glance. Now back up on the crowded sidewalks, Dunn had no chance of finding him again to resume tracking.

He moved back into a doorway and stood thinking, his eyes all the time moving, seeking another momentary glimpse of Rhodes.

Rhodes was wearing a heavy sport jacket and carrying a bag that could only be called luggage, so he was traveling. He might catch a cab and head for one of the airports, but his pursuer would figure him to travel by air, probably in first class.

Dunn knew he had to guess, and he went with the odds. What was the least likely way Rhodes would travel?

A bus.

Possibly a train, but less likely was a bus.

If that was the case, Dunn had a pretty good idea where Rhodes would hook up with his transportation. Where whoever was hunting him would have to make another choice. Port Authority Terminal on Forty-second Street, where a traveler could board either a bus or a subway train.

Rhodes wasn't carrying the duffel bag for nothing.

Dunn got out in the street and hailed a cab. He told the driver he was pressed for time and there was a twenty in it for him if he drove fast for the Port Authority Terminal, that he needed to hook up with someone he did business with and it was critical to an important deal for him to get there before a bus left.

All true. In its fashion.

It had been almost a week since Hobbs had laid a hand on her. Temporarily at least, Lavern Neeson was unbruised.

Often he'd call her from work to keep tabs on her, so she'd faked a doctor's appointment this time, knowing that since she was unmarked Hobbs wouldn't be interested. And she'd told him she thought she was coming down with a summer cold, not only to keep him away from her, but to give her an excuse for her sham appointment.

Where she'd taken her unbruised self was to the lounge where she'd almost been picked up by the handsome guy with the hooded eyes and jet-black hair. It was about the same time of day she'd been there last time, so he might well be there, too. She could picture him sitting on the same stool as before, hunched over his drink, and then walking toward her, absently spinning bar stools as he came. Then the change in his expression as he saw the bruises on her face, bruises that makeup couldn't quite conceal. She hadn't been able to get the man out of her thoughts, out of her dreams.

It could be different this time.

As she entered the lounge she blinked a few times to help adjust her eyes to the dimness, looking all around for the dark-eyed man.

He wasn't there.

Well, what did you expect? With your crappy luck.

But on the same stool where dark-eyes had sat was another man, in his late thirties, maybe forty. A nice-enough-looking guy wearing gray slacks and a shirt and tie. He was looking at Lavern and smiling. He had a lot of dark stubble on his chin, but that was the style, and maybe he was growing a beard.

When she got closer, she glanced at his left hand and didn't see a wedding band. For all that was worth these days.

Still smiling, he nodded to her and said, "You're late, but that's okay. We can make up for lost time."

Another bullshit artist.

"Do we know each other?"

"I've never before laid eyes on you," he admitted. The smile widened. Nice teeth, very white. "See, we're starting off honestly."

Lavern smiled back.

Why not? She could use a little talk, a little personal, painless attention.

And a drink.

53

". . . and they didn't know if the parrot was saying everything *he* was saying, or if *he* was saying everything the parrot was saying."

The crowd in Say What? thought about it, then with a
growing rush of applause decided they liked that one. They
cheered and hooted as Jackie Jameson waved his right arm
over his head in a circular motion, dipped low in his exag-
gerated bow, and trotted off the stage.

Mitzi and Rob (he had finally told her his name—Rob
Curlew) were seated at the table Rob preferred. It was barely
large enough for two, so they wouldn't attract unwanted
company. It was also at the very edge of the crowd, and not
far from one of the side exits. Not only could they look out
over the audience so Mitzi could judge crowd reaction to
particular jokes, but when the night of comedy and near comedy ended, they could easily slip outside and get away without having to talk to anyone Mitzi knew. Rob valued his privacy.
Mitzi understood that and accommodated him.

Tonight was different, however, because her boss Ted Tack

was holding her check from last week, and Mitzi needed the money. The rent was past due, and the landlord was pesky.

Jackie Jameson had been the final act, so Mitzi and Rob waited for the applause to trail off, then stood up from their table.

Mitzi started toward a side aisle so she could make her way to the stage and office. Rob closed his hand on her arm.

Mitzi explained that she had to pick up her paycheck.

"I can carry us till next week," Rob said.

Mitzi aimed her big smile at him. "In case you haven't noticed, you carried us all this week. You wouldn't want me sleeping with the landlord. I need my money, baby."

"You mean your independence."

"Up the rebels! Whatever it is they're against."

Rob smiled and kissed her cheek. "I'll be waiting right outside."

"It'll only take a few minutes for Ted to pay me or for me to punch him out," Mitzi said. She waved a small fist. "He always pays."

"Remember I'm nearby," Rob said, "in case there's any trouble." As if she was serious.

Mitizi wondered sometimes if *he* was serious, some of the things he said. Or maybe it was because he was normally so smooth that any slightly out-of-kilter remark seemed even more so.

As she moved away through the crowd that was gradually making its way outside, she wondered what kind of job Rob had, that he worried so little about money. Something to do with investments, he'd say, whenever she inquired, then he'd begin explaining things to her she didn't understand. There were lots of acronyms, but they all meant money. So maybe he was rich as well as handsome.

I am makin' out with The Man.

Somebody or something tugged at her right earlobe, and she turned, ready to cut some poor bastard off at the knees if she could figure out who'd been the tugger.

I better know you as a friend.

She did. Jackie Jameson was jammed up against her by the press of the crowd.

Her momentary anger was gone. She grinned at him. "Nice set, Jackie."

"Yours, too." He cupped his hands over his chest. "Wanna go lift a few, Mitz? Talkin' drinks here, not boobs."

"Sorry, Jackie, I'm going out with Rob."

Jameson made a big thing of looking all around. "So where is he?"

"Waiting outside."

"What is this guy, some kinda secret agent? You helping him hide?"

"He likes privacy, is all."

"Then he should like you. You're sure keeping him a big secret."

"I kinda enjoy that, him and me together, nobody around to applaud or boo."

"Oh, I'm sure they'd applaud, Mitz."

She grinned again. "I gotta go, get to the office before Ted makes his escape with my paycheck."

"Maybe Rob'd like to have a drink or two with us," Jackie said, as Mitzi was moving away in the general direction of stage and office.

"Oh, yeah, we'd both love having you around. In case conversation started to drag."

"I'm jealous, Mitz. You noticed?"

"Of me?"

"Of him," Jackie said. "I'm better for you, Mitz."

"It's illegal in this state for two comics to be that way with each other," Mitzi said.

"Is he prepared to be your love slave, like I am?"

"You're more a love jester, Jackie."

She was immediately sorry she'd said it. He turned away to hide the pain on his face.

When he turned back, he was smiling.

She bit her lower lip. "That was a horseshit remark. I didn't mean it, Jackie, honest."

"Sure you didn't."

"Will a blow job make it up?"

"I get the point," he said, "you say things you don't mean. Just be careful, Mitz."

"Of what?"

"Banana peels, that kinda thing." He gave her a wave and turned his back on her.

"Hey! Hey, Jackie! Don't go away mad!"

Even that had come out wrong. *Just go away* hung in the air. Two comics. Maybe it was a good law.

Jackie probably hadn't heard her anyway. He was deep into the crowd that was massing toward the street doors. She could just make out his dark head of hair with its bald spot, then he was gone. Hurt and gone, like so many people in her life.

Why am I always hurting people, or getting hurt?

Feeling paper-edge high, Mitzi continued her way to the stage steps and the office. She knew she'd deeply cut Jackie, maybe her only true friend and one of the last people in the universe she was willing to hurt, and she vowed she'd make it up to him. She wouldn't apologize—that would only remind him of what she'd so thoughtlessly said and embarrass him some more. What was needed here was a kind of indirect apology, giving away a piece of herself without it being obvious. Mitzi was good at that. She'd been doing it since she was a little girl.

Ten minutes later, her check in her purse, she met Rob outside in front of the club, beneath the lighted marquee. *Nobody looks that good in all that bright light coming from overhead*, she thought. *Not even me.* She clutched his arm, turning her head slightly away from him and the sickly light, as she led him out farther down the sidewalk.

* * *

They walked a few blocks to a small, dimly lighted sports bar they frequented. There were booths toward the back, where serious drinkers and lovers sat, leaving the front booths to the sports nuts who sat hypnotized by taped ball games while raising the alcohol level of their blood.

"You seem kind of down," Rob said, when they were settled in with their drinks. She had an apple martini, he a scotch on the rocks.

Mitzi told him what had happened with Jackie.

"I feel kind of sorry for him, too," Rob said. Then he smiled. "But I don't blame him for being jealous."

They sat for a few minutes in silence, sipping their drinks. There was cheering from the front of the bar.

"Home-run volume," Rob said.

"Maybe," Mitzi said. "I don't know how they can get so into it. Both the Mets and Yankees games have been over for hours. They already know who won."

"They like to pretend, like everybody else."

"What are you, running for political office?"

He gave her his hooded-eyes smile, melting her down. The bastard was into her even deeper than he knew, making her vulnerable. Vulnerability was something she loathed. "Mitzi, Mitzi . . . always the tough front."

She shrugged. "I'm just pretending, like everyone else."

"You should cheer up, sweet. You've got a birthday coming up next week."

"How'd you know that?"

Does he know how old I'm going to be? Twenty-five. Holy Christ! How'd that happen? Twenty-five already, and at a place like Say What? She didn't even have top billing

"You must've mentioned it," he said.

"Not me."

"Somebody else, then. Or maybe it was on your Web site."

"There is *nothing* true on my Web site."

He laughed. "I know that's your photo."

"It's my mother when she was my age."

"Can't you ever be serious, Mitzi?"

"Only when I'm being funny."

"We should celebrate your birthday."

"Day of mourning," Mitzi said. "Don't even think of buying me a present, Rob, really."

"No whoop-de-do?"

"Not even whoop."

He studied her over the rim of his glass. She couldn't read his eyes, so dark in the dim lounge, but with pinpoints of light or something else in their centers.

"Okay," he said. "But maybe I'll bring you flowers."

"That could work," she said.

54

Lavern Neeson sat in what had become her usual place, holding the shotgun from the closet loosely aimed at her sleeping husband.

The shotgun was exerting more and more of a spell on Lavern. She and Hobbs had argued again this evening about what for most couples would be nothing. They'd disagreed over who'd said what about some insignificant subject, and Hobbs, as usual, took the argument from the specific to the general. He accused Lavern of constantly saying things and then swearing she'd never uttered the words.

Lavern's friend and sometimes confidante, Bess, said that manipulating men claimed such things sometimes, for no purpose other than to instill uncertainty and guilt in a woman's mind. According to records at the Broken Wing Women's Shelter, it wasn't all that unusual for men to create devices that would make sounds in the basement or garage so that they could skeptically go investigate and then return to reassure and tell their frightened mates that they'd only imagined hearing something. If the sound came again, the abuser might simply claim he hadn't heard it, knowing full well it was real because he'd arranged for it.

Was it any wonder women subjected to that sort of treatment began to doubt their own sanity?

Something else: Lavern suspected that Hobbs might be moving objects when she wasn't looking, so she'd think she'd forgotten where she'd put things. Was she misplacing more and more objects lately—keys, her purse, half-read books, the cell phone—or was it that Hobbs was stepping up his program of shifting her reality so she could distinguish it less and less from her imagination? That's what Bess said it was called at the shelter: shifting the victim's reality.

Lavern knew the shotgun was real, even if it remained unloaded. If Hobbs were to awaken and stare into its dark muzzle, he wouldn't know the breach was empty. Lavern smiled. Let the bastard think he was a second away from death. Shift *his* reality.

Do I really want him to wake up?

She thought about what Hobbs would do once he realized she'd pointed an unloaded shotgun at him. Made him so frightened he'd pissed in his pants. Took away some of his manhood.

What would he do then?

Lavern knew, so as she sat alongside the bed fondling the shotgun and watching Hobbs sleep, she was very careful not to wake him.

It was exactly like that snob Thomas Rhodes to try leaving town in the means of transportation anyone who knew him would figure as his last choice. As for renting a car, Dunn knew that like many wealthy New Yorkers who'd moved to the city years ago, Rhodes had let his out-of-state driver's license expire. These days he traveled mostly by limo.

Dunn had studied the dossier on Rhodes with the utmost care and hadn't been fooled.

The hunter inside the mind of the prey. Two heads, one mind. Older than mankind.

Dunn's heart beat a stronger rhythm as his fingers caressed the compact .25-caliber revolver in his pocket. It was cool and heavy. Hefty for its size. Deadly.

Be careful, not cocky. Doing this wrong could cost you your life. You'd barely have time to realize you were the hunted instead of the hunter.

Every hunt should be like this.

While it scared the hell out of him, Dunn loved this part of it. He wasn't good ol' Jer' now; he was Thomas Rhodes's final nightmare walking.

Though it was evening, the Port Authority Terminal was crowded, which was exactly how Dunn preferred it. There would be a loud, echoing noise at the boarding gates, startling everyone, momentarily freezing them, and giving Dunn time to act while Rhodes was dying. To onlookers— those few who actually looked his way—the memory of what was about to happen would always at best be a series of mental stills, scenes like obscure slides or photographs that would, day by day, fade until they were impossible to interpret for sure. When it came to dealing this kind of death, there was, strangely enough, safety in numbers. So much to take in, so much sensory overload. Dunn was counting on it. He had only to act decisively, rapidly, and not waste motion.

Dunn had found a spot to watch the lower level, where tickets were sold by the various bus lines. There were boarding gates on several levels, but Rhodes would have to stop here first to purchase his ticket.

As Dunn had projected, Rhodes was attempting to flee the city by bus. After he'd bought his ticket, it had been simple for Dunn to follow him to the second level, where most of the gates were located, along with some shops and restaurants.

The "gates" were actually doors that led out to a concrete area where the buses came and went, disgorging and taking on passengers. Lines of people were standing or sitting on the floor, waiting for doors to open so they could board.

Rhodes made his way to Gate 322 in the North Terminal.

A bus was about to board, and another, nearby, was letting out passengers. According to the schedule Dunn had studied, the bus unloading was from Buffalo, New York. Thomas Rhodes had dipped into his duffel bag and changed clothes, then switched bags. He was now dressed in a hooded green nylon rain parka and carrying a backpack (another deliberately out-of-character affectation), and was about to board the bus soon to depart for Pittsburgh. Dunn figured Rhodes's ticket was a transfer and would take him farther away than Pittsburgh—if it were used.

This was good. The crowd was starting to coalesce and queue up for the boarding area outside Gate 322.

Staying to one side, and then approaching at a three-quarter angle so Rhodes wouldn't see him, Dunn walked directly toward the figure in the green parka. It was an obviously new coat, and though it was light and meant to protect only against rain, it was still too hot a garment for this kind of weather; Rhodes should have known better than that.

Or maybe the damned thing was made of Kevlar and bulletproof.

If you guess wrong . . .

Dunn almost smiled. Bulletproof or not, it wouldn't save Rhodes from fate in the person of Jerry Dunn. Rhodes was the one animal, and Dunn the one hunter. For both men, nothing else existed in the universe.

Rhodes was on the outskirts of the people about to board, when the door opened.

Some had made it through the door and a small crowd

was milling in the direction of the parked bus. Public address announcements no one on earth could understand floated and echoed in the warm air.

Dunn's mouth was dry. *Don't let him get outside. Take him inside. Take him inside.*

He was twenty feet from his quarry.

Fifteen.

If his wife and coworkers could see him now. Who of them would have guessed? Ol' Jer . . .

Make it right, a first accurate shot, then hammer back and a second quick squeeze of the trigger to make sure. Then claim Rhodes's gun for your trophy, stay calm, and walk fast from the scene.

Stay calm.

Closer, closer . . .

Six feet away.

The compact revolver came out of Dunn's coat pocket. His arm was pointed rigidly straight ahead, at Rhodes's right temple. He thumbed back the hammer. Rhodes seemed to sense Dunn's presence and began to turn.

Three feet.

He's turning! Squeeze! Squeeze!

Rhodes's eye that Dunn could see began to widen.

There was a sound like two loud, sharp slaps, very close together.

Thomas Rhodes dropped like an electrically powered being whose plug had been yanked. As he fell, Dunn was already moving to kneel in unison with his dead quarry's descent. Dropping with him in grotesque choreography, only alive and with a purpose. Slipping his own gun into a pocket, extending an arm.

Rhodes fell to his knees and flopped forward, his face making a nasty sound as it smacked nose first into concrete. Dunn was already reaching into Rhodes's right pants pocket for his gun.

It wasn't there. The pocket was empty.

Should have checked somehow. Made sure. Damn, damn, damn . . .

Dunn felt the outside of Rhodes's left pants pocket.

No gun.

He clutched and squeezed at the oversized green parka's pockets. A foul stench wafted up from Rhodes's body. He'd been sweating heavily in the parka, or maybe his sphincter had let loose as he died.

Blood now. On Rhodes's face. On the parka's hood.

Damn, damn, damn . . .

Still no gun. But would he be able to feel it under the coat's bunched and slippery material?

He wondered if the gun might be in a holster or tucked in Rhodes's belt in the small of his back. He began to feel, probing the wadded coat frantically, digging with his fingers.

And became aware of people around him watching. Beginning to stir.

Dunn knew his time was up. The opportunity to procure Rhodes's gun had passed.

He'd failed.

He stood up as planned and began walking swiftly away, feeling sweat trickling down his ribs. Down his forehead.

He walked faster, faster, and then began to run.

A man's voice shouted behind him, but the PA system was yammering at the same time, so Dunn didn't know what the man had yelled. He was aware of other people running now, but past him in the opposite direction to see what was going on.

Dimly he recalled passing one of the stairways leading down to the main level. He turned and ran in the same direction as so many others, blended with them for half a dozen strides until he reached the steps; then down he went as people continued to flash past on the periphery of his vision.

He made his way at a brisk walk through the crowded terminal and back out onto the sidewalk. He kept walking along Eighth Avenue, the gum-soled shoes he'd bought for his first hunt beating silently on the warm concrete, turned a corner, kept walking.

Away! Free!

After a while he slowed down. He was so hot. *Is it ever going to rain again in this damned city?*

His entire body was burning up and soaked in perspiration, as if with a fever. He clutched his shirt collar and yanked it to the side, causing one of the top buttons to fly off into the night.

Kept walking.

But without Thomas Rhodes's gun.

The man in the matching black outfit broke the connection on his cell phone and slipped it into his shirt pocket. He was at an outside table at a restaurant on Second Avenue, sipping a cold draft beer and watching pedestrians and traffic hurrying past. So many people in a rush, scurrying and self-important. So many ambitions, dreams, obsessions, depressions, so much tenderness and callousness . . . all those separate, personal worlds and worlds-to-be that could be obliterated in a second by a thousand possibilities. All those people . . . their disparate notions of reality didn't mean spit. Reality wasn't so different from dreams.

Dreams . . .

He knew as he watched a particularly graceful woman walking across the street that it was time for Mitzi. Not that the woman looked at all like Mitzi except for her erect and alert carriage. She was much taller than Mitzi. And of course she didn't have Mitzi's platinum spiked hair.

Mitzi the birthday girl. Thinking of her did bring a smile to his face. She certainly had the gift.

A waiter who'd just delivered food to a nearby table

paused on his way back inside the restaurant, noticing the almost-empty beer mug.

"Ready for another?" he asked.

"Sure am," the man in the black outfit answered, "I'm ready for another."

55

"Thomas Rhodes was a banker of no small reputation," Renz said. Quinn knew he'd picked up the phrase from this morning's *Times* account of Rhodes's murder at the Port Authority Bus Terminal.

Renz was leaning back in his leather chair behind his desk. The harsh morning sun highlighted his drooping features and pockmarks from old acne scars. It was already warm in the office, and there was the faint scent of stale tobacco smoke. Quinn thought that if Renz was going to continue his furtive cigar smoking he should buy some sort of deodorizer.

When Quinn didn't toss back the conversational ball, Renz said, "That puts additional pressure on thee and me, especially thee."

A bad representation of a Quaker, Quinn thought. "We did get a break, though. The gun."

Renz made his chair inch from side to side and nodded. "Ballistics make it out to be the same make and model that was used in the other Twenty-five-Caliber Killings." He leaned forward and extended the ballistics report to Quinn.

Quinn glanced at it, ignoring all the technical jargon about grooves and lands. Even the fact that the gun's serial number had been effectively removed with acid. What interested him was that the lab made it a dead certainty that Rhodes was carrying exactly the same kind of gun that was used on the previous victims. "A Springbok single-action twenty-five-caliber revolver," he said. "You have to pull back the hammer before each shot on that kind of gun, which means you have to make each bullet count." Without getting up, he placed the report back on Renz's desk. "I never heard of a Springbok."

"No one had. That's why the damned things were impossible to identify from their bullets. Springbok was a South African manufacturer that went out of business almost twenty years ago, not long after apartheid ended. The problem is, what with all the political and social turmoil in that part of the world, there are thousands of this cheap but reliable model unaccounted for."

"So someone could have bought a large lot on the black market."

"Or even legally, years ago, and simply kept them, and now he's found a use for them."

"So it's possible our killer is of South African origin," Quinn said.

"Or spent time in Africa."

"Hunting," Quinn said.

Which made it all the more likely that they were indeed searching for only one killer. Neither man pointed that out. Renz was still afraid he might be wrong about the politically convenient single-killer theory, and Quinn still had his doubts. The two types of murders—one clean and professional, the other bloody hell on a stick—didn't make sense. Unless of course Helen, the profiler, was right about one killer with two personalities. Quinn knew that was, in a way, true of most serial killers, though not to this degree. It was more a matter of them being accomplished actors who could present a benign, sometimes charming persona to the world in order to conceal the ugliness inside.

Quinn decided he'd ask Zoe's opinion. She was a psychoanalyst. Killers weren't her specialty, but she might well know more than Helen Iman about split personalities.

After all, she'd had experience with Alfred Beeker.

"I caught a snatch of radio news on the way over," Quinn said. "The media seem to be referring to the Twenty-five-Caliber Killer murders as duels. I take it that's Cindy Sellers's work."

"I've kept her up on things, including the Rhodes case and the fact he had a twenty-five-caliber gun," Renz said. He flashed his canine smile. "A deal's a deal."

"Until it isn't," Quinn said, knowing Renz.

"I saved the best for last," Renz said, showing the grin again. "About the gun. Ballistics doesn't have a perfect match, but they think the gun found on Rhodes is the one that killed Floyd Becker in the Antonian Hotel."

The real estate market in New York was almost as depressed as Berty Wrenner. He'd missed his sales quota again, and Home Away's sales manager, the sadistic Alec Farr, was making his life miserable.

Berty's employer, the Home Away Agency, specialized in selling small New York apartments to individuals as well as corporate buyers. Much of their business stemmed from Wall Street, and if the stock market was in decline and brokerage houses were laying off, Home Away's business was also in decline. The next step wasn't hard to figure out.

That was why Berty Wrenner hadn't made his sales quota this month. Or last. The other salespeople were making theirs, or at least coming close. The demanding Farr didn't consider close anywhere near good enough. Things were tight at Home Away. Like stomachs and jaw muscles. Lots of antacid tablets were being consumed. Daily lunchtime martinis were gaining on a few of the men and on Marlee Case, the only female agent not yet driven away by Farr. Lack of sleep accompanied by pressure from on high was a relentless destroyer of health, happiness, and sobriety.

The chesty, perpetually grinning Farr had held a sales conference at the beginning of the month and informed his six-agent team that it was crunch time (Farr was prone to clichés) so they'd better pull out all the stops, because, as Farr put it, "you gentlemen are in a goddamned fight for your lives, so you'd better not be gentlemen."

Berty, a middle-aged man who'd been a lot of things before he'd become a real estate agent, had a problem with that. He was, God help him, a gentleman in a cutthroat game. When he lied, his face turned a mottled red, and he couldn't look the target of his lie in the eye. His wasn't the face of a salesman or poker player, anyway. Berty looked as if one of his parents might have been a mole. Even Berty thought he looked like a balding, myopic mole, especially when he wore his glasses, which was all the time. Only Alec Farr didn't think Berty looked like a mole; he thought Berty looked like a rat, and often told him so.

The other five salesmen had made their quotas. Jeevers, the corporate client specialist, had barely made his by surrendering part of his commission to a major buyer. The stress of the contentious transaction showed on him. He appeared as though he hadn't slept the last three nights. His long, equine features were actually twitching. His thin body wouldn't be still where he sat poised on the edge of his desk, trying to maintain a relaxed posture; he was a man made to run who was forced to sit. Berty wondered sometimes if Jeevers was a reincarnated racehorse.

They were all lounging in postures of mock comfort in the outer office, waiting for Farr to react to the monthly sales figures he'd just received.

Marlee, a thickset, gray-haired woman with eyes like oversized blue marbles, glanced at her watch. "I wish he'd hurry up. I gotta get the hell outta here."

"You close that deal yet on West Twenty-fifth Street?" Joe Keller, the newest, youngest agent asked. He might have passed for twelve years old if it weren't for his shadowy beard that made him look perpetually a couple of shaves behind.

"Like I'm gonna tell you, you pathetic walking embryo."

Keller looked hurt, or he might have been putting them on. He would look boyish all his life, with a face difficult to read. A salesman's dream. Or a spy's. No one completely trusted Keller.

Jeevers flicked lint from his sleeve, though Berty hadn't seen any lint. "Keller wouldn't dream of yanking a deal out from under you," he said to Marlee. He gave her a horsy grin to show he was kidding.

"We'd all dream it, or we wouldn't be wasting our lives in this cutthroat business. Ask Farr."

"I wish he'd hurry up," Keller said. "I need to scoot my ass outta here, too."

"Got a girlfriend waiting?" asked Berty, who was long divorced and single. He hoped no one had noticed the note of envy in his voice.

Keller simply looked at him and shook his head.

"He don't wanna discuss his personal life, Mole," Marlee said. "How 'bout you, Berty? There a mole girl out there?"

"Somebody for everyone," Ned Nichols said.

Everyone looked at him in surprise. He very seldom spoke in the office, while in the larger world outside he'd wear his customers down by talking at them until they were numb and incapable of sales resistance.

All of these people knew even the most intricate and devious moves and could sell in any kind of real estate market except for the one they'd had the past six months. The crappy market was the reason why the firm was in trouble, and everyone in the office knew it, with the exception of Farr, who blasted blame around the place as if from the barrel of a shotgun.

The inner-office door opened, and everyone who'd been sitting or slouching stood up straight.

The office suddenly seemed smaller and ten degrees hotter. Alec Farr strutted into the room and filled it with his presence. He was a broad, solid man with a military posture, though he'd never served his country, anything, or anyone other than himself.

He grinned with perfect large teeth overtreated with whitener. It was not a reassuring grin.

"Gentlemen and lady," he said, "we are in a lifeboat, and it is sinking. I don't know if we can stop it from going down, but we are sure as hell going to try." He glared like a hungry lion at Jeevers. "How might we at least slow the vessel in its sinking, so a whimsical God might favor us with a miracle and save us?"

"Plug the leak?" Jeevers ventured nervously.

"Can't do that," Farr said. "Leak's too large, and there's nothing to plug it with."

"Bail water?" Marlee suggested.

"We've been doing that without a bucket. We're losing ground."

"In a boat?" Berty said, before he could stop himself. The words had simply slipped out on their own.

Farr jutted out his chin as if about to use it as a battering ram. His reddish monobrow formed a sharp V. Even the hairs protruding from his flared nostrils bristled. It was a frightening sight, especially to a man who hadn't made his quota.

"The answer to the question about the boat," Farr said in a calm yet threatening tone, "is that we throw someone out. Toss him—or her—over the side. The other question is, who's it gonna be?"

No one chanced an answer. The silence was like concrete hardening around them. Berty found it difficult to breathe.

"Maybe the mole," Farr said. "Of course, there's only so much food in the boat. We might want to eat the mole later, or use parts of him for bait. So who's it gonna be?"

Again the silence thickened around them.

Farr's terrible grin widened as he adjusted his tie knot and stared at each of them in turn. Then he rolled up the sales report in his hand and aimed the paper tube at them as if it were a gun.

"We'll all think hard on that," he said. "And see if individual sales figures improve next week. If they don't, a certain rat might leave a certain boat the hard way. Or maybe some even more useless piece of jetsam might be fed to the circling sharks. Am I understood?"

Everyone nodded. Marlee managed a strangled, "Yes, sir."

Farr fixed a burning stare directly on Berty, then turned and strode back into his office. The slam of the door was like a cannon shot.

"Jesus!" Keller said.

A pall of shame descended on everyone in the room.

"Why are we so afraid of that asshole?" Marlee asked.

Jeevers ducked behind his desk and picked up his leather attaché case stuffed with brochures and contract forms.

"Where you headed?" Keller asked. "Wanna stop off for a drink? It'd calm us down."

"Give you back your balls, you mean," Marlee said. "Glad I don't have to worry about that."

"I gotta make a stop on the way home," Jeevers said. "See a client."

"Over on West Twenty-fifth?" Keller asked.

Marlee gave him a look that scared Berty even though he wasn't the recipient. She was a woman who'd been known to throw a punch. Berty had seen and heard enough impending violence for one day.

"Once the mole goes, that's when we gotta start worrying," Nichols said.

Keller looked at Berty. "That the way you read it, Mole?"

Berty didn't answer. There was no other way to read it; he was a low producer, and in this game you produced or else. It was about time for *or else*. He draped his suit coat over his arm, picked up his scuffed briefcase, and headed for the door. Nichols and the others were already there, eager to be free of the dreaded office and the ominous Farr. Marlee and Berty were the last ones out.

"Farr," Marlee said *sotto voce*, and patted Berty's shoulder. "What an asshole he is."

Berty glanced at her and flickered a smile.

Marlee shook her head. "Somebody oughta shoot him."

All the way home in the hot, clattering subway train, Berty heard her harsh and fearful whisper over and over.

Somebody oughta shoot him.

"Shoot who?" asked the man scrunched in next to him on a plastic seat, and Berty realized he'd spoken aloud.

Berty could only shrug and shake his head, as if he hadn't clearly heard over the rush and clatter of the train.

"Somebody's always shooting somebody these days," the man said. He was a small man, like Berty only with a scraggly mustache, and didn't look unlike a mole. He held up the folded *Times* he'd been reading. "Sometimes it ain't the worst idea. The paper says, what with the Twenty-five-Caliber Killer, it's like we've gone back to the days of fighting duels to settle things."

Berty nodded wordlessly.

"Nothing wrong with that, I say," the man continued, "especially with that last guy got popped, Rhodes. A *banker.* They found a gun on him that was used to kill one of the earlier Twenty-five-Caliber victims. Looks like the two of them were going after each other even up. Fair fight, I say. Not murder. A duel. People'd sure as hell be more polite, nicer to each other, if they knew they might be challenged to a duel."

Thinking Berty might still be having trouble hearing him,

the man raised his hand and made a shooting gesture with thumb and forefinger.

Berty nodded and grinned.

A duel. Wouldn't that be something?

56

Pearl felt better, almost exhilarated. Finally she'd taken some action and stopped being a verbal punching bag for her mother, not to mention the target of harassment by Mrs. Kahn and her damned nephew Milton.

Unable to get a morning appointment with a new dermatologist, recommended by the phone book, Pearl had been pleasantly surprised when a Dr. Eichmann's assistant told her there'd been a cancellation and the doctor could see her late this afternoon if possible about the growth behind her ear.

Quinn, working hard at his desk, had been sympathetic ("Go. Then maybe you'll shut up about the damned thing."), and she'd left the West Seventy-ninth Street office early.

Dr. Eichmann, an affable older man with tousled gray hair, examined the subject of concern with thoroughness and care. He poked and probed and observed and told Pearl that what she was so worried about appeared to be a simple nevus, or mole.

"Has it changed shape or color recently," he asked. "Or grown larger?"

"I don't know for sure. I look at it in the mirror some-times and think it has."

"Where it is, I'm surprised you can see it in the mirror."

"It isn't easy."

"Uh-huh." He gave her a nice bedside-manner smile. "Melanocytes sometimes cluster and create moles," he explained, while Pearl stared at him blankly. "Some appear dysplastic and potentially dangerous." He patted her arm. "But this one is probably benign."

Probably? "So it's nothing to lose sleep over?" Pearl asked.

"Not unless you choose to. It shouldn't be a cause for concern. But since it obviously has been, I'll remove it and send it away for biopsy and you can know for sure and put any fears you might have to rest."

"I hope you don't think I'm a hypochondriac."

"You're a woman with a mole," he said.

He advised her that what he was going to do would hurt a little, and it did.

"Soon as the results of the biopsy are in, I'll contact you," he assured her. "Meanwhile, not to worry."

She thanked the doctor and paid at the front desk on her way out.

How simple it had all been. Now she had a square, flesh-colored bandage where the mole used to be, and she felt good about it. Felt good about herself. It was almost as if, somehow, she'd had Dr. Milton Kahn surgically removed from her life.

But on the sweltering subway ride to the stop near her apartment, squeezed into a seat next to a man who smelled as if he'd vomited on himself, Pearl began to worry.

Dr. Eichmann had said *probably*. No way was that the same as *definitely*.

And if the mole was so obviously harmless, why had he removed it and sent it away for a biopsy? Why had she chosen from the dozens of dermatologists in the phone directory one named Eichmann, the same name as that of the infamous Nazi who'd been executed for World War ll concentration camp horrors? What might her mother think about that? What might Quinn's shrink friend, Dr. Zoe Manders, think about it? Why should Pearl care?

What she should do, she told herself, as the smelly man next to her deliberately shifted his weight so his arm rested against her breast, what she should do is take Dr. Eichmann's advice and not worry about the results of the biopsy.

As the subway train growled and squealed to a halt at her stop, she freed herself from entanglement with the vomity-smelling man and elbowed her way off the train and onto the crowded platform. She joined the other sheep, herded by painted yellow arrows and habit, in their trudge toward the exit stairs ascending to dying sunlight and lengthening shadows.

It was amazing, she thought, how positive she'd felt when she'd left Dr. Eichmann's office and how depressed she felt now. What had caused such deterioration in her feeling of well being?

But she knew the cause. It wasn't the sweltering subway ride or the man who smelled of vomit, though surely he'd played a small role.

Though she might blame other people, the real cause of her depression of the last several weeks had been herself. Her *re*actions to their actions.

I did it to myself.
It wasn't them; it was me. I did it to myself.
They made me do it to myself.

Quinn and his detectives reinterviewed everyone connected to the Becker and Rhodes murders. They could find no connections between the two men, no connection between any two people who knew both men. *Had* the Becker and Rhodes murders both been hunts? Duels?

"Now we've got something," Fedderman finally said at the end of a dreary, unproductive day.

"What would that be?" Quinn asked.

"Whole bunch of questions," Fedderman said.

"Ballistics wasn't certain," Pearl said. "Maybe the gun found on Rhodes didn't kill Becker."

"The maid at the Antonian Hotel," Fedderman said. "Rosa Pajaro. She might know more than she's telling. She's scared. Maybe of something worse than losing her job or being deported."

"Think she's still working there?" Pearl asked.

"It's questionable," Fedderman said.

A phone call answered the question. Rosa Pajaro had collected her paycheck and disappeared from the Antonian without giving notice two days ago. A follow-up phone call revealed that she'd also left her basement apartment without bothering to notify the landlord.

"Scared, all right," Pearl said. "Probably all the way back to Puerto Rico."

"Mexico," Fedderman said.

"Probably happened when she saw Thomas Rhodes's photo on TV news or in the paper," Quinn said, "and she realized she was a key witness in a murder case."

"Can't blame her," Fedderman said.

"We don't know enough to blame anyone for anything," Pearl said.

Chain lightning danced in the darkening sky.

Lavern stood in the heat outside the Broken Wing Women's Shelter and felt a few droplets of moisture on her face, one on her eyelash, another on the bridge of her nose. Maybe it was going to rain and bring relief from the heat. Maybe not. The city might be once again toying with its people. The way Hobbs sometimes toyed with her.

She unconsciously raised a hand and felt the new bruises on her left cheekbone, another farther down on the side of her jaw. Hobbs hadn't broken her skin. He was good at what he did and didn't want to draw suspicion. Her makeup did a fair enough job of covering these latest of Lavern's facial bruises, from a distance.

Her left side hurt badly enough that she favored it and walked with a slight limp. When she'd left the apartment, she hadn't known where that limp would take her. Now, standing and staring at the shelter, she realized Broken Wing had been her destination from the beginning.

The sturdy brick building with its line of dormers seemed to call to her more strongly every time she passed it. It was like a fortress with a pale concrete stoop and solid wood double doors. Each door had a large brass knocker beneath a small leaded glass window. There was black iron grillwork over the ground-floor windows. The building didn't look as if it could be easily broken into. A person might feel safe there.

Lavern leaned against a NO PARKING sign and sighed. She knew that a person couldn't stay inside Broken Wing forever. That was the problem. She'd heard about women who'd found refuge there and stayed for months, and then left only to be reclaimed by their patiently waiting abusers.

Lavern knew Hobbs was patient.

He would wait.

She took a final glance at the thick wooden doors that would provide protection for only so long; then she limped away along the sidewalk. Lightning still flickered and charged patches of purple sky between the tall buildings, but whatever breath of air there'd been had now ceased. No more tentative raindrops found their way to earth. It wasn't going to rain this evening. It had been a trick. Life was a damned trick, a painful practical joke.

As she walked, Lavern tried to think of lots of things, but

found her mind focusing on the shotgun at home in the hall closet. The sharp pain in her left side whenever she took a step kept bringing her back to the gun. It was a twelve gauge, like the one her father had let her fire once in some woods behind a rented cabin. She remembered the deafening bark of the gun, the heavy recoil against her right shoulder. She'd fired at a paper target he'd nailed to a tree, and she'd hit it.

She'd hit it.

A pretty damned good shot.

I could do it again.

She couldn't stop thinking about the shotgun. It was unhealthy, a fixation like this, but she couldn't seem to control it. She guessed that was why they called them fixations. It was all Hobbs's fault.

Hobbs's damned fault.

He'd blocked every avenue of escape, made her into something that would have no choice other than to do to him what he might secretly want but not have the courage to do himself.

Suicide by wife.

I could do it again.

The pain in her side became more intense, and she wondered if Hobbs had cracked one of her ribs,

Traffic was backing up because the signal at the next intersection was red. A young couple, a tall man and a blond woman, climbed nimbly out of a stopped cab and disappeared into one of the buildings. They ran hunched over with their arms linked and their heads down, as if they were trying to get in out of the nonexistent rain or escape the paparazzi.

Their own dreamworld. Do they know, or even care, what's real?

Lavern felt a pang of envy so sharp it made her break stride.

She knew that inside the building the couple had entered was a small fusion restaurant with a bar, where she could get a drink. Alcohol would moderate her rage and dull the pain.

Every step was agony, but she began to walk faster. The shotgun remained on the edge of her thoughts.

I could do it again.

PART III

A few strong instincts, and a few plain rules.

—Wordsworth, "Alas! What Boots
the Long Laborious Quest?"

57

He would need a few things from a hardware store: a steel bicycle hook, a length of strong nylon rope, a roll of wide duct tape, a plastic drop cloth, some rubbing alcohol to clean flesh so it would dry fast and completely and the tape would be well bonded. He already had the rest of what he'd need—a portable electric drill to create a starting hole, so he could make sure he was fastening the hook in a solid wood joist capable of supporting body weight.

As always when collecting his materials, he acted circumspectly.

A short subway ride got him within walking distance of a big-box chain store in Queens, where he bought the required items. It might raise suspicion if he made his purchases in Manhattan, especially the steel hook, after all the publicity about Terri Gaddis.

Along with the hook he bought a bicycle tire pump, a diversionary item just in case the dazed-looking teenager behind the checkout counter was more alert than she appeared. On the way home, he stopped in at a Duane Reade and bought the bottle of rubbing alcohol. No danger there of arousing suspicion.

In a luggage shop on Third Avenue he purchased a cheap blue canvas carry-on to put everything in so that people glancing at him wouldn't fix him in their memories. He'd be merely a man in a hotel lobby carrying unexceptional luggage. One of hundreds of such men on hundreds of hours of security tape.

Once back in his room he'd phone Mitzi and tell her he'd reserved a table at Mephisto's for them tomorrow night. She was expecting that. It was her birthday. After drinks and dinner, he'd suggest they go to her apartment. He'd hint that he had a gift for her. She'd see the blue canvas bag and assume it contained her gift, and in a way it did.

He had something rare indeed to give her on her birthday—the perfect symmetry of time. Enter and exit screaming on the same date, though thanks to the duct tape, exit would be much quieter than entry.

Check the birth and death dates on a lot of tombstones, he mused, and you'd seldom see such ideal closure.

He was sure that Mitzi, if she could, would instantly come up with a joke about it.

Quinn was sure the reason why Renz had chosen the corner of Forty-third and Broadway for their meeting was so he could eat one of the knishes sold by the street vender there.

They had to move down the block and back into the display-glassed doorway of an electronics shop in order not to be buffeted by the tourists and various Times Square area characters streaming past. Renz's driver followed unobtrusively in Renz's long black limo, gliding from one illegal parking space to another.

Renz shifted the knish to his right hand. "This guy comes into the two-one precinct yesterday and complains he found a package on his doormat. It was wrapped in brown paper

and taped tight. His name was printed on it. Seems somebody left it there, rang the bell, and ran. Inside the package
was a revolver."

"A twenty-five Springbok?" Quinn asked hopefully,
watching Renz take a bite of knish while holding his free
hand cupped beneath his chin as a crumb catcher.

"I wish it wash sho," Renz said around the knish.

Quinn knew something must have come of the man's
complaint, or Renz wouldn't even have learned about it.

"Shmith an' Weshon," Renz said, and swallowed. "But
the meaning here was clear, so the guy was told what all
these poor schmucks are being told. There's no way to know
who put the gun there, and yes, he was probably being challenged to what the media and public are calling a duel, and
could he list any enemies who might have left the gun."

"Let me guess," Quinn said. "He didn't have any enemies."

"No! The guy listed over twenty people he thinks might
like to shoot him. He's sales manager at a real estate agency,
and apparently that makes for a lot of enemies."

"If you do it the wrong way, I guess."

"Oh, he even struck the detectives taking the complaint
as a prick. I'm sure he's a real bully. That's what everyone's
saying now, including Berty Wrenner." Renz took another
bite of knish. Half of it broke off and fell into his waiting
palm, and he flicked it away. Some of it got on the pants cuff
of a man in a suit walking past, and he glared at Renz.

Quinn waited until Renz had chewed and swallowed, so
as not to be sprayed by knish. "Who's Berty Wrenner?"

"The guy that shot the complainant," Renz said.

Quinn looked at him. "The guy who came into the
precinct house with the package and gun got shot?"

"Once, in the middle of the forehead," Renz said. "It did
the job, even though it was a twenty-two-caliber slug."

"Who's—who was the guy that got shot?"

"Name of Alec Farr. He was Wrenner's boss, and apparently rode the hell out of him, drove him nutty enough to kill. The other salespeople at the agency confirmed this. They didn't disguise the fact they were glad Farr was dead, said Wrenner was his favorite whipping boy."

"So you have Wrenner in custody."

"Yep. He was found sitting next to the body, sobbing."

"He's not our serial killer," Quinn said.

"Not a chance. Our problem, though. The mayor himself was on the phone this morning telling me these murders are out of control."

"He's just catching on to that?"

"He's had other things on his mind. But now we're on his mind."

"Why didn't Farr get out of town, if he took the threat seriously enough to go to the police?"

"Said he couldn't. He had a job, work to do here. He'd get fired if he left town just because some asshole threatened him. Besides, he was the stubborn sort."

Quinn thought that should be engraved on the tombstones of a lot of people he'd known: *He was the stubborn sort.* Maybe on his own tombstone.

"I'm getting pressure from on high you wouldn't believe," Renz said.

"Am I supposed to be feeling pressure here?" Quinn asked.

"That's the purpose of this conversation. Mayor told me to light a fire under you."

"Isn't that arson?"

"Unless you're protesting something. Like lack of progress. I know there's already a fire under you, Quinn, but that's because I know you, and the mayor doesn't. I'm simply delivering the message."

Quinn said nothing while Renz finished his knish, then produced a white handkerchief from a pocket and fastidiously wiped his hands finger by finger.

After stuffing the handkerchief back in his pants pocket, Renz reached into an inside pocket of his suit coat and brought out a folded *City Beat* and held it out to Quinn. "Sellers has got the exclusive on this; that's why it wasn't in the big papers this morning. It's on their Web sites, though, and radio and TV news is on the story heavy. Sellers painted Wrenner as a victim, said he shot Farr for the same reason women kill their abusive husbands. Wrenner was too dependent on Farr and his job to go out and get another job, just like wifey's too dependent to get another hubby and goes for the knife or gun instead."

Accepting the newspaper, Quinn said, "There's enough truth in it that in some quarters it might wash."

"That's what worries me, Quinn. The rest of the media's already spouting the same nonsense. They're making it look like murder's okay in certain circumstances. There are too many damned people in this city who think they're in those circumstances."

"Copycats with guns," Quinn said.

"Only nobody's got nine lives."

Quinn looked at a display of miniature digital cameras behind Renz. With all the electronic crap taking over the world, for all they knew they were being video streamed right now. Not that they had anything to hide, but neither one would want . . . say, the mayor, to see or hear their conversation.

Tucking the *City Beat* beneath his arm, Quinn said, "What would you have me do about all this, Harley?"

"Catch the bastard," Renz said, as if the answer was obvious and Quinn had somehow missed it.

"Uh-huh. Gonna have another knish?"

"One's enough. Moderation in all things. What I'm gonna have next is a cigar."

"Tell the mayor I'm on fire," Quinn said.

Renz smiled and motioned to his driver.

"Mission accomplished," he said, and got into the limo.

"Catch the bastard," Renz said again, and pulled the door shut so that all Quinn saw in the limo's tinted window was a bent-nosed, tough-looking guy with a thatch of unruly straight hair. Quinn.

58

Pearl told herself it was too early for Dr. Eichmann to call about her biopsy report, but she was nonetheless impatient. Quinn was off somewhere in a meeting with Renz, and Fedderman was trading briefings with Vitali and Mishkin so the left hand would know all about the right hand.

She'd been jumpy all morning, still angry at her mother and that prick Milton Kahn, anxious because she'd slept so poorly. She was jacked up on too much coffee and considering taking up smoking to calm her nerves, though she had never smoked. But most of all she was worried about the removed mole. Where was it now, somewhere out of state in a jar on some laboratory shelf? Being whirled dizzily in a centrifuge? Subjected to extreme light, magnification, and probing with sharp instruments?

For the past two hours she'd been seated at her desk, working on her computer because there was nothing more productive or distracting for her to do. Now and then leaning forward to sip more coffee, she played her fingers over the keyboard and jerked and clicked the mouse on its pad, trolling for information on any murders, anywhere, any time, that involved the hanging and disemboweling of the victims.

There was a case in Seattle two years ago, but they'd caught and convicted the guy, who'd turned out to be a former medical student and city employee. Another, five years ago, in California. In that one the killer was a mental case searching for a healthy kidney to be transplanted in exchange for his own diseased one. He'd been caught when he'd broken into a hospital to perform the surgery on himself. His motive was that he'd been unfairly kept too long on the transplant waiting list. He, too, was convicted, and died in prison.

That was it. This kind of murder was less popular than gunshots, stab wounds, poisoning, blunt instruments, or strangulation.

Pearl was about to give up, get another cup of coffee, and do some serious pacing, when on an obscure Web site about crimes against animals she discovered the case of a man named Dwayne Avis. Five years ago he had gotten a suspended sentence and paid a fine after torturing dogs on his upstate New York farm. Six of the animals had been found hanging and gutted in his barn.

Not quite the same thing as dead women, Pearl thought, leaning back in her chair and pressing a fist into her aching back.

But what other leads did they have?

She reread the small-town newspaper article on her computer monitor. Avis expressed no remorse, according to the reporter, and had threatened state police with a shotgun when they entered his property. When subdued and arrested, he stated that the dogs were his and what he did with them was his business. There was no photo of Avis accompanying the article.

Sick bastard, Pearl thought. Who'd do that to defenseless animals and then resist arrest and try to defend his actions? Or maybe he was simply evil. It might not be a bad idea to at least talk to him, make sure he wasn't getting away with doing the same thing again. After five years, people forgot.

After five years, people had moved away. It was possible Dwayne Avis was one of them. He might be gone or might even have died. Some dog lover might have shot him, and good riddance.

Or maybe he'd moved to New York City.

Pearl manipulated the mouse and made her way electronically to the paper's front page. It was the *Mansard Gazette*, headquartered in Mansard, New York. Pearl clicked back to the five-year-old news article about the slaughtered dogs. She printed it out to show to Quinn or Fedderman, when one or the other turned up at the office. Then she made use of the Internet to find out more about Mansard.

It turned out to be a small upstate farming town with a population of less than five hundred. Pearl figured most of that meager number lived on outlying farms. The Web site listed two phone numbers for the Mansard city hall. Pearl called the one titled "Public Relations."

She didn't introduce herself as a cop. Small towns could be gossip nests. If Avis did somehow turn out to be a suspect, she didn't want him alerted that the police were again interested in him.

A perky-sounding woman named Jane Ellen answered the phone and never even asked Pearl's name, but assumed she must be writing an article or doing a school paper on Mansard—maybe because Pearl led her in that direction.

Pearl listened to a lot about average rainfall and temperature, home prices, school ratings, and something called the Fall Apple Theater, before asking if Dwayne Avis still lived in or around Mansard.

"He's still on his farm," Jane Ellen said. Her tone had definitely become cooler.

"I met him once, and he told me about Mansard," Pearl said.

"Oh? He have anything good to say about it?"

Pearl laughed as if Jane Ellen were joking. "Of course he did."

"Dwayne is one who keeps pretty much to himself. Likes it out there on his farm, all secluded. Folks pretty much respect his wishes."

"Is his farm far from town?"

"'Bout ten miles."

"What's he grow?"

"Not much. Drives his old truck in and sells some tomatoes and corn at a local produce market the town has in season. Sometimes okra."

Okra? Haven't had that in years. Don't miss it. "Does he have any animals on his farm?" Pearl asked.

Jane Ellen was silent for a while. Then she said: "Not anymore. Had some kind of trouble years ago, but that's not for me to talk about."

But you just did. "What kind of trouble?"

"Oh, I don't know. There's just stories floating around. I don't pay much attention to them. Where do you know Mr. Avis from?"

"Oh, I don't know him at all. We just found ourselves sitting together on a bus once and got to talking. You know, passing strangers thrown together—and he started talking about Mansard, and I found myself getting interested."

Jane Ellen was starting to get suspicious. It wouldn't be good if Dwayne Avis learned someone had called and inquired about him.

"So tell me," Pearl said, "just what is the Fall Apple Theater?"

"I realize we're both usually free around lunchtime," Zoe said, "but we've got to do something about meeting like this."

"We need a bigger bed," Quinn said.

Zoe didn't seem amused. She was standing alongside her

bed, where Quinn still lay nude and perspiring and sexually sated. "You know what I mean," she said. "I'm going to have to hurry to be in time for my next appointment."

Quinn thought she sounded like a hotel prostitute, but he decided he'd better keep that to himself. He lay quietly and watched her dress. She'd showered, and her body was still damp despite all her toweling off, which made her clothes stick to her. He watched her wriggle into her panties, then her slacks. She smoothed material with her hands, tugged at it, rearranged it, glanced at her image in the dresser mirror and seemed dissatisfied by the way the slacks fit. Quinn thought they looked just fine. She bent down and picked up her bra from where she'd dropped it on the floor an hour earlier. He watched her extend her elbows out while leaning forward and reaching behind her to fasten the clasp. The movement reminded him of a graceful exotic bird flexing its wings.

"You sure you have to leave right away?" he asked.

"Oh, I'm sure." She reached for her blouse.

While she was standing at the mirror working a comb through her mussed hair, he sat up in bed and scooted his body so he was leaning with his back propped against the pillows.

Zoe was fully dressed now. As soon as her hair was to her satisfaction, she'd pick up her purse, kiss him good-bye, and be gone. They were both out of the mood now, even as they enjoyed the afterglow. Quinn knew he should follow Zoe's example and reset his mind for work. Noontime assignations were fun—more than fun—but you couldn't let them control your life.

Still, he enjoyed simply watching her.

She turned sideways and craned her neck, looking out of the corner of her eye to see if her hair was okay in back. For some reason, the gesture reminded him of Pearl. Then he knew why. It was reminiscent of Pearl examining her mole.

"You know Pearl?" he said.

She caught his eye in the mirror. "I feel that I do."

"She had this mole right behind her ear that kept worrying her. Worried her so much she had it removed and sent away for a biopsy. Now she's worried about what the biopsy results will be. So rattled she has a hard time even sitting still. Her concern is way out of proportion."

"And?"

"I'm afraid it's getting in the way of her work. I guess I'm asking you, as a psychoanalyst, if there's anything that'd ease her mind, make her revert to her old self on the job."

"Does she suspect the mole is cancerous?"

"I don't know what she suspects."

"She'll have the biopsy report pretty soon; then she'll know, and even if the news is bad, she'll find some relief from her immediate anxiety. Is there some reason for her to think she might receive bad news about the mole?"

"Her mother," Quinn said.

Zoe stopped teasing her hair with her wide-toothed comb and looked at him curiously in the mirror. "Some genetic problem?"

I'll say!

"Her mother's a pistol," Quinn said. "Pearl says she's trying to get her to go see this doctor Pearl used to date, get them together again. He's a dermatologist, and Pearl's mother figures if she can get Pearl worried enough about the mole, Pearl will make an appointment to see Milton Kahn—the dermatologist."

"That's horrible."

"Well, you'd have to know Pearl's mother."

"I know about matchmaking mothers, and Pearl's sounds like an extreme example."

"Anyway, Pearl saw a different dermatologist and is waiting for the results."

"Good for Pearl. But she's defying her mother. That might be leading to a heightened sense of apprehension.

Mother's always right. That phrase stays with many of us all our lives. Ruins many lives."

"So what should I do?"

Zoe finished with the comb, walked over, and kissed Quinn on the lips. "Wait," she said. "Like Pearl."

Then she smiled at him and hurried from the room.

Quinn lay for a while longer in Zoe's bed, feeling the rush of cool air from the window unit and listening to traffic below on Park Avenue, letting his mind wander. He could still feel the heat of Zoe from her side of the bed, still smell her and almost hear her moans of ecstasy.

An uneasiness crept into his state of quiet bliss.

Why did I make love to Zoe, then ask her about Pearl?

Why the hell did I do that?

But an old cop knew that just because there was a question didn't mean there was an answer.

59

Quinn was parking the Lincoln in front of the office when his cell phone chirped. He fished it from his pocket with one hand while spinning the steering wheel with the other to maneuver the nose of the long car toward the curb. Sometimes driving the Lincoln in Manhattan reminded him of captaining an ocean liner in a port crowded with smaller, faster ships.

He pushed the phone's talk button by feel, said, "Quinn."

"It's Feds," said the voice at the other end of the connection. "I got filled in by Vitali and Mishkin about the Farr shooting. They were close and heard the squeal on their car radio and got to the scene ten minutes after Farr was killed. The shooter, Bertrand Wrenner, was sitting on the front steps of Farr's building. The victim was sprawled half in, half out of the place, across the threshold. Wrenner was sobbing and still holding the murder weapon. The uniforms first on the scene took it from his hand, then read him his rights."

Quinn put the shift lever in park and turned off the engine. "He's confessed?"

"They couldn't get him to stop confessing."

"I already heard from Renz on the ballistics tests," Quinn said. He made no effort to get out of the car; reception was good here, and it was a comfortable, quiet place to talk on the phone. "Smith and Wesson twenty-two caliber. Not our gun. Not our serial killer."

"Another half-ass duel," Fedderman said, "only this time the winner got overwhelmed by what he did and broke down right there. Motive, gun, opportunity, witnesses, confession. No way not to get a conviction."

"Ordinarily," Quinn said.

"Renz is scared of this one, right?"

"You guessed it, Feds. The media's already casting the killer as a victim, comparing him to an abused dependent wife. Some T-shirt company is probably already printing FREE BERTY shirts."

"Berty?"

"That's what Bertrand Wrenner goes by." The sun was blasting down on the parked car, heating up the interior. Quinn was ready for the conversation to be over.

"Mishkin said you gotta feel sorry for the little shit," Fedderman said.

"Mishkin feels sorry for the world."

"Well, I guess the world could use it," Fedderman said. "I got copies on the specifics on this one from him and Vitali, crime scene photos, witness statements, the whole investigation so far. It's all a nice, neat bundle."

"Bring it to the office and file it, Feds, even though it's got nothing to do with our case other than it's the child of political expediency."

"Okay. Is Pearl with you?"

"No, I thought she might be with you. Maybe she's in the office. I just pulled up in front."

"She still worried about her mole?"

"She had it removed. They sent it away for a biopsy so they can let her know for sure everything's okay."

"Or if it's not."

"That, too."

"You think she's really got something to worry about?"

"Plenty, but not necessarily the mole." The parked car was really heating up. Quinn noticed that he was beginning to perspire. His shirt was starting to stick to him the way Zoe's clothes had when she'd dressed right after her shower.

"Funny," Fedderman said, "that was Wrenner's nickname at work—Mole."

"Funny old world," Quinn said, and pressed END. Fedderman was obviously about to get philosophical, and Quinn didn't think he could abide that.

He climbed out of the uncomfortably warm Lincoln and went up the shallow concrete steps to the office entrance.

The first thing he saw when he went inside was Pearl pacing in the middle of the room, carrying a coffee cup. There were spots on the floor where coffee had sloshed over the rim and dripped. Pearl's dark eyes were especially vivid in a way that for some reason reminded Quinn of when they'd had sex, and she was nervously flexing and unflexing the fingers of her left hand. Incongruously, she gave him a big white grin.

"You okay?" he asked.

"I think we should take a drive," she said.

Martin Hawk sat over coffee in the hotel restaurant and stared at his copies of the *Post* and *Times,* along with a copy of a much smaller paper, *City Beat.*

By all accounts, Bertrand Wrenner was nothing more than a common murderer. Certainly not a hunter. The media were referring to Alec Farr's murder as a duel, but Martin didn't see how it fit that definition. The victim had simply answered a ring at his door and been shot dead. A homicide. True, he'd been warned, as well as armed. Wrenner had delivered to him a gun with which to defend himself or go on the hunt for his potential killer. Judging by what fellow employees said, it was unlikely that, even afraid and on his guard, Farr could conceive of Bertrand Wrenner—Berty, as the papers called him—constituting a real threat. He hadn't thought Berty had it in him.

Martin Hawk could have told him that all cornered animals were capable of killing.

Again a server came by his table to make sure Martin didn't want breakfast today. He reassured her that was the case.

The thought of food made his stomach turn. That he was responsible for the series of murders labeled duels, which were now being cheered on by the media, sickened him and deprived him of appetite.

And filled him with contempt.

Dueling required anger or insult, a face-to-face encounter. A duel was an event brought about by hatred or disdain. But hunting was a pure and sacred tradition, an impulse in the core of all of us. The nearer to the surface it rose, the hungrier we got. Primal? Certainly. That was why it was the stuff of legend and religion. It required danger, a certain respect for one's prey, a contest of wiliness and wills.

It required stalking.

He set aside *City Beat* and reached for yet another newspaper he'd bought, a *London Times*. He leafed through it and found and opened the financial page.

There would be nothing about New York murders or duels in this paper.

Nothing to worry him.

60

True to their MapQuest directions, Quinn and Pearl drove on successively narrow roads for over an hour. They stopped to buy gas at a two-pump combination service station and mini-market outside Mansard, where Pearl used a horrific restroom. Then they bought a couple of bottle Cokes from a machine and got back into the Lincoln to drive some more.

Mansard itself wasn't much more than a few blinks on a loop off a state highway. Pearl leaned back in the passenger seat and watched about a dozen small, clapboard houses glide past. There were a few side streets where more houses might be located. She saw a green street sign and noticed that this stretch of the business loop, the main drag, had become Crescent Street. So named, she supposed, because it described a long, constant curve.

Quinn slowed the car to under twenty so they could take it all in. There was a seed and feed store, an auto parts shop, a hardware store, a small grocery store, a barbershop, the Crescent Diner, a boarded-up movie theater, and a white-frame and brick city hall, where Jane Ellen fielded phone calls. What looked like a World War II howitzer squatted next to a flagpole on the green space in front of city hall, elevated and aimed down the street as if to repel any invasion by the outside world.

Quinn's Lincoln was the only vehicle moving. On the sidewalks were about half a dozen people, mostly men wearing work clothes, and a couple of young boys who gaped at the car as if they'd never seen such a sight.

Pearl had been unable to find an exact address for Dwayne Avis. Quinn pulled the car diagonally across the street to the curb, where a tall, skeletal old man in jeans and a sleeveless black T-shirt was shuffling along at about half a mile per hour. He lowered the window.

"We're looking for the Dwayne Avis farm," Quinn said.

The man had scruffy gray hair pulled back in a ratty ponytail held with a rubber band. A faded tattoo of a nude woman twirling a hula hoop adorned his scrawny right arm. He smiled with a flash of gold tooth as he sidled toward the car and bent down so he could look Quinn in the eye.

"I know where that's at," he said in a low, whiskey voice.

"Might you share the information with us?"

"Nobody much goes there," the old man said.

"We're the exception."

The man leaned lower and peered past Quinn at Pearl. A whiff of gin and perspiration made its way into the warming car. "You two are cops."

"How'd you guess?"

"You didn't ask me why nobody much goes to the Avis farm."

"Being cops," Quinn said, "we usually sooner or later get what we ask for."

The gold-tinted smile widened. "Might as well make it sooner. You wanna visit Avis, you keep on the way you're goin' through town, then after about ten miles make a right turn on a dirt road dead-ends on the two-lane. Go left an' follow that road to the first dirt road, make another left, an' you're on the farm. That's Avis's driveway."

Quinn thanked him and started to close the window.

"You don't have to worry about me phonin' ahead an' tellin' Dwayne you're on the way," said the ponytailed man. "He probably wouldn't answer the phone anyway, an' tell you the truth, it don't mean shit to me why you wanna see him."

"I'll take you at your word," Quinn said.

"Don't count on a friendly welcome," the man said. He straightened up as if his back hurt and continued his slow, steady progress down the sidewalk.

"Me in ten years," Quinn said.

"You assume a lot," Pearl said.

The old man lifted a hand in a listless wave, but didn't look back at them as they drove away.

It wasn't much of a farm. The surrounding fields lay fallow except for near the back of the barn, where tomato vines wound their way up head-high wooden stakes. A small field of cornstalks off to the left appeared to be the only other crop. The rest of the farm was so neglected that the woods had taken over a large area of the fields. There were more trees near the ramshackle house and barn: a shade tree— looked like a maple—by the barn, and a huge willow whose graceful branches scraped the old house's second floor. In the shade of the willow a deteriorated wooden porch glider that didn't look safe to sit on had become the property of termites.

The house was sided with faded gray clapboard. The trim was dark green, but hadn't been painted in a long time. Here and there bare wood peeked through. There was a wide plank porch across the front. The wooden steps were painted gray and were rotted enough to be dangerous.

Pearl looked closely at the barn where the dogs had been found hanging and gutted. It was a leaning structure of weathered wood with horizontal streaks of old red paint still holding on. Its twin wooden doors were closed, and made to stay that way with a large padlock. The hinges on the doors were old and dusted with surface rust but looked strong. There was no sign of any animals.

As soon as Quinn and Pearl had climbed out of the parked Lincoln and slammed the car doors shut, a man in tattered jeans and a red shirt with its long sleeves rolled up to his biceps opened the front door and stepped out into the shade of the porch's sagging roof. He looked to be in his early fifties, had receded dark hair, and a hard, seamed face. Slung beneath his right arm was a double-barreled shotgun.

He stood casually observing Quinn and Pearl and said nothing.

"Dwayne Avis?" Quinn asked.

"Was when I woke up this mornin'."

He's going to be difficult. Quinn kept an eye on the shotgun.

Avis spread his feet wide and assumed an unyielding stance. His dark eyes were staring and unblinking, with a glint of arrogance in them.

"We're police," Pearl said. She'd had about enough of this backwoods bravado.

"State or local?"

"New York City."

"You got no jurisdiction here."

"We can get it in a hurry if we have to."

Avis stepped down off the porch, carefully holding the shotgun pointed at the ground. "Then why don't you hurry on away an' do that? Meanwhile," he said, raising the shotgun but aiming it off to the side, "get off my land."

Pearl thought she'd never heard that except in movies or TV.

Quinn thought this was a man who used his temper mainly as a weapon, not really losing it but pretending, showing it off as he did the shotgun, letting interlopers know what *could* happen if they took him lightly. Contrary to how they were portrayed in books and movies, this sort of person was dangerous. Pretending could turn real in a second.

"We only want to talk to you," Quinn said. "It'll be easiest all around if you don't make us have to leave and come back."

"I know what you wanna talk about," Avis said. "Them damn dogs. Well, I already been dealt with and consider that whole thing a closed matter. Dealin' with me next time won't be a pleasure. I swore that to myself."

"This isn't next time," Quinn said.

"We're not interested in dogs or anything related to them," Pearl said.

Quinn tried a smile on Avis. "Anyway, I don't even see any dogs around here." Playing dumb.

Avis knew better than to aim the shotgun anywhere close to them, but he pointed it farther off to the side, raised it, and fired one of the barrels. The noise was deafening, and Quinn could swear he heard pellets rattle through the branches of the willow at the side of the house.

"Shit!" said Pearl, instinctively dropping into a crouch.

Quinn remained upright and calm. "We're here as part of a murder investigation," he said. "And you're digging yourself a hole with that gun."

"*Murder* investigation? 'Cause of *dogs*?"

"Forget the goddamned dogs," Pearl said, straightening up, but not all the way. She seemed hyperalert. Her black eyes were fixed, unafraid and calculating, on Avis.

He seemed to see in her somebody maybe not so unlike himself. Somebody who might shoot him.

"Forget the dogs?" he said, showing her he was heeding her words.

"I'm a cat person," Pearl said, her bleak and menacing glare still trained on Avis.

"Well, I never killed any kinda person, nor animal I was never gonna eat."

Quinn swallowed a bad taste in his mouth and then very slowly removed a slip of paper from his shirt pocket. He read off a list of dates and times.

"I need to know where you were on those nights," he said.

"I was here."

"You remember all of them?"

"I don't need to remember any of 'em. I'm always here. And no, I don't have an alibi. I was alone. Didn't plan on havin' to prove I wasn't someplace else."

"You mind if we look in the barn?" Pearl asked.

"I do, but you will anyway sooner or later."

Seemingly ignoring them altogether, he turned his back on them and strode to the barn. He drew a ring of keys from a pocket of his threadbare jeans and unlocked the padlock, then swung both creaking doors open wide.

Pearl and Quinn stepped into the barn along with Avis. It was cooler in there, and surprisingly spacious and clean. Along one wall were wooden stalls, all of them empty. The bare dirt floor didn't look as if it had been disturbed. There was a strong animal smell in the barn, but no animals. There was no straw in any of the stalls or on the barn floor.

"Why no animals?" Pearl asked Avis.

"Too much trouble. Not enough profit."

Quinn and Pearl let Avis lead them out of the barn, keeping him ahead so they could see the shotgun.

"You gonna take me in?" Avis asked.

"That was never our intention," Quinn said.

Avis went with them, still slightly ahead and off to the side, as they walked over to the Lincoln and stood in the glaring sun. It was a hot place, Avis's farm, despite the shade trees. The breeze coming off the fields was warm and dry and carried the grit of dust.

"You comin' back?" Avis asked.

"Might," Quinn said. "And if I do and see that shotgun again, I'm gonna shove it up your ass sideways."

Avis showed a flicker of surprise, but not the slightest fear. He watched them without expression as they got into the car.

As they drove away, Quinn saw in the outside mirror that Avis continued to watch, unmoving, the shotgun's twin barrels still pointed at the ground.

"I really think he'd shoot somebody," Pearl said, when they were back on the dirt road leading to the state highway.

"If he had the chance," Quinn said, "and knew it wouldn't get complicated afterward."

"Not a knife man, though," Pearl said. "Maybe with dead dogs, but not with live people."

"That's the way I figure him, too, but he's hard to read."

"He obviously loves his gun. Penis substitute, maybe. Your friend Zoe could tell you. Guns or knives, those are the usual toys for boys. They tend to settle on one or the other."

"Usual isn't always," Quinn said tersely.

Pearl said, "Well, *duh!*" and turned on the radio.

He studied the items laid out on the bed and began methodically packing them into the blue canvas bag. The steel hook and portable drill were heavy, but he didn't want to take the risk of fastening the hook beforehand, as he had with Terri Gaddis. Terri had been of average intelligence at best, but Mitzi was sharp and observant. She might happen to look straight up while showering and see the hook set in her bathroom ceiling, or she might even notice its shadow and glance up at it out of curiosity.

She'd certainly be curious, like most intelligent people. She'd want to know what the hook was for and how it had gotten there. Or if it had always been there and she'd never noticed it.

He couldn't risk her asking a visitor, or the building super. So the hook would be installed just before it was needed.

Soon Mitzi would understand it all, when she could do nothing about it.

He smiled. Mitzi was smart, all right. His smartest so far. That made it all the better.

61

Quinn and Pearl got back to the city around five o'clock. Rush-hour traffic. Heat chimeras dancing in the lowering light. They were headed south on the Roosevelt Parkway on the West Side. The Lincoln's overworked air conditioner, its blower motor's bad bearing chattering, was fighting the summer heat to a draw.

"So Avis was pretty much a bust," Pearl said.

"Alphabetically, he's still first on the suspect list," Quinn said.

"Are you actually trying to make me feel better?"

"Like always," Quinn said, exiting the parkway. He had a dinner date with Zoe and didn't want to get tangled up with Pearl this evening. "Feds has got the unmarked. We're not far from your apartment. Why don't I drop you off? Save a subway ride."

"It's a deal if we stop someplace for dinner. Nothing fancy."

"I'll pull up someplace, and you can get some takeout," Quinn said.

Pearl said nothing for a couple of beats, watching the traffic, then: "We dealing with Zoe here?"

He laughed, understanding why she was so talented at her work. "We are," he admitted. "She and I have a dinner date this evening."

Pearl shook her head and smiled sadly. "A cop and a psychoanalyst. What must she think of you?"

"We have something in common. We both help people."

"She helps people like you, Quinn."

He held tight to the steering wheel and braked to avoid running up the back of a cab. "Like me?"

"Obsessive-compulsive personalities. Tunnel-visioned fanatics. Pathetic workaholics. Psychotic subterranean Rambos."

"At least I don't hear voices."

"You hear Renz," Pearl said. "There must be better choices."

"Who do you hear, Pearl? Dr. Phil? Your mother, telling you to get married to a skin doctor, a mole might be killing you?"

"I hear *you*, Quinn." *Goddamn you!*

They drove for a while in silence while Quinn negotiated heavy traffic on Broadway.

"If you listened to me," Quinn said after a while, "you wouldn't worry so much."

Pearl stared straight ahead and said nothing. Said nothing, in fact, until Quinn pulled the Lincoln to the curb in front of her apartment building.

Still not looking at him, she said, "You ever get the feeling Zoe's using you?"

"Using?"

"Observing. Studying. For God's sake, Quinn, she's a psychoanalyst on the make. And I don't mean the sexual make. Not only, anyway."

"We're not going to talk about Zoe."

"What, she might pick up vibes and get her feelings hurt?"

Pearl's pique was gaining on her. His relationship with Zoe was obviously hurting her, and that wasn't what he'd set out to do. "Pearl—"

"Someday you might be famous. Zoe's gonna put you in the academic book she's writing as a case study. You might be a whole chapter."

"Pearl, I didn't mean to insult you or hurt your—"

"I know the type. Screw and take notes, screw and take notes. Men are so damned unaware."

Quinn placed his arms on the steering wheel, slumped forward, and rested his forehead on the backs of his hands.

He sat with the engine idling, realizing that he felt guilty. He'd upset Pearl, which wasn't what he'd set out to do. He'd been defending himself—and Zoe—against Pearl's unreasonable invective and innuendo.

He sat up straight and was about to remark that they'd gotten off on the wrong track in this conversation.

But Pearl was already out of the car, slamming the door and walking away.

He watched her stomp up the steps to her building entrance and push inside, not looking back at him. Pearl in a snit. What the hell was wrong with her, born with a burr up her ass and making everybody around her miserable? Now she was going to walk down to that deli on the corner and get heated-up garbage for supper. She'd feel sorry for herself and then go to bed early and pissed off. That was Pearl. He knew her. She'd be hard on herself and make herself miserable.

Her own fault.

Why should I care?

He realized he shouldn't and drove away.

Screw and take notes. He had to laugh.

* * *

Quinn dropped back by the office to see what Fedderman had come up with in trying to find some correlation between the Slicer murders and the .25-Caliber Killer victims. Fedderman had left a report of his day's work, with and without Vitali and Mishkin, on Quinn's desk.

After sitting down behind his desk, Quinn fired up a Cuban cigar and leaned back. No matter what he'd do to eliminate or disguise the tobacco scent, Pearl would notice it tomorrow morning and bring it to his attention. He wouldn't tell her his conversation with her in the car was what made him want to smoke a cigar and relax, get his nervous system back together. That might give her some satisfaction. He blew smoke and smiled. *Pearl.*

Halfway through his cigar, Quinn finished reading Fedderman's report. He wasn't surprised to learn that Feds hadn't found a thing connecting the murders. Neither had Vitali or Mishkin. Quinn knew these were three people good at their jobs. If they couldn't see any parallel, maybe there wasn't any. It seemed the more they looked for one, the further away they got from Renz's very political reasoning that there was only one killer committing both series of murders.

Of course, Renz might be a political animal, but he wasn't a bad detective, and he still had his cop's instincts, even if they weren't as honed as before he'd become commissioner. Then there was Helen. She didn't think it was impossible that both impulses, both MOs, could exist in the same person, the same twisted and compartmentalized mind.

Don't we all compartmentalize? Isn't that what keeps us sane? Or makes us part of the majority insanity that passes for normal?

Quinn drew on his cigar, rolled the illegal smoke around in his mouth, then exhaled. He set the report aside.

By way of twisted minds . . .

He booted up his computer and keyed in Dr. Alfred Beeker's Web site.

There was no mention of Beeker being a doctor there, and he didn't appear, unless he was one of the men wearing leather masks. There was lots of S&M literature, some of it amateurish and full of bad grammar. Then there were the photographs. Women in various poses of restraint, some of them not poses. Leather restraints, chains, elaborately knotted ropes. The women were mostly in their twenties and thirties, but some appeared younger. Probably they weren't younger. Beeker was smart enough not to have shots of minors on his Web site.

Quinn clicked from one photo spread to another, scanning the thumbnails.

And there was Zoe, just as Beeker had said.

The poses were mild, without leather, chains, or whips. More like the sort of thing you'd see in *Playboy*. A younger Zoe who looked amazingly like the fifties pinup Bettie Page, mostly because of her similar hairdo. Zoe in a bikini, making a perfect O with her lips and pretending to be shocked and afraid. Zoe with her breasts exposed, smiling seductively and hugging a pink sheet to her lower body. Zoe seated nude in a wicker rocking chair, pretending to knit. Zoe wearing nothing but high-heeled shoes and bending gracefully to touch her toes. *Zoe, Zoe, Zoe . . .*

Quinn realized he had an erection. That bastard Beeker. What if his patients knew about his kinky other self? Or maybe they did. Maybe because of his predilection for kinky sex he crossed the line with his patients. Maybe those were his patients in his photographs.

Maybe they're his patients. Jesus!

Quinn's cigar, propped in the ashtray, had gone out. He relit it and shut down the computer.

He sat smoking for a while, thinking as he stared into the haze of his exhalations, as if the smoke were made up of his musings and might reveal some meaning.

He wanted to see Zoe and knew that if he called her she could be talked into inviting him to her apartment. But he didn't want Beeker to be a part of their relationship in any way. Better if he waited a while, until the photos he'd just seen had faded in his memory.

He could wait for a while to see Zoe again. Certainly until dinner.

Later on, he'd see Beeker.

62

As soon as Lavern carefully and quietly closed the door behind her, she heard her husband's voice: "You're late and you're drunk."

"I was with Bess." The first person Lavern could think of who'd back her up. "We sat in the restaurant after dinner and talked, and time flew."

"You were drinking."

She knew there was no way he could know for sure if she was drunk, as she'd just come in and the living room light hadn't even been turned on. She was facing absolute blackness and could only be a dark silhouette against the dim light of the hall. Hobbs was completely invisible in the dark. "We had wine for dinner, then a few drinks afterward. That's all."

She didn't tell him she'd skipped dinner and drunk alone, and then with a man in a lounge far from the neighborhood where she might have been recognized and word might get back to Hobbs. Nothing had happened between her and the man (*Victor something*, she thought, *but maybe not . . .*), and in fact both had been too drunk to do anything about it if they'd felt any real sexual attraction. They'd been asked to leave and objected mildly, then were actually hurried and pushed from the place by a burly bartender.

Victor (or whoever) had thrown a punch at the bartender that was so ineffective it had been ignored, and there they were out on the sidewalk, barely able to stand.

Lavern had leaned back against a streetlight, closed her eyes, and almost passed out. Or maybe she had briefly lost consciousness. When she opened her eyes, Victor was gone. A man who might have been Victor was crossing the street at the intersection half a block down.

Too far away for her to catch up with him. All that effort . . .

Well, the hell with Victor.

So Lavern had walked, too, in the opposite direction, weaving noticeably at first and attracting attention. People slowed when they saw her approaching and veered out of her path. They seemed to be ashamed of her, embarrassed for her.

Screw you! All of you!

A woman in a gray business suit gave her a disdainful glance. A teenage boy with baggy pants low on his pelvis kept a hold on his fly and grinned at her as he bopped past. *Fellow clowns and rebels.*

After a few blocks she began to sober up; she could feel it.

On the cab ride home she'd impressed the driver with her terse and logical conversation about everything from politics to professional basketball. *Pretty damned good!* She was sure she'd reached the point where it wouldn't be obvious that she'd been drinking.

She'd been wrong. Hobbs must have smelled liquor on her breath, maybe on her clothes.

"Shut the goddamned door all the way and come in here," he said.

She obeyed, and at the click of the door latch the lights winked on in the living room, temporarily blinding her.

She gasped. Hobbs was standing ten inches from her and had flipped the wall switch.

The punch came out of the blinding light, smashing into her left ear and sending her reeling against a table, overturning it.

Hobbs was on her so fast she didn't have time to think about the pain. His initial punches were wild. Then his fist landed on her ribs, which were still perhaps cracked from her last beating. *That* pain jolted through her, and she was sitting on the carpet, unable to breathe. Hobbs rested a foot on her shoulder and shoved her down so she was lying on her side.

He stood glaring down at her with his fists propped on his hips. "Goddamn lush. You're screwin' around on me, too, aren't you?"

"No! Never!"

"Boozin' and screwin' around!"

He kicked her hard in the upper thigh and she rolled over onto her stomach.

This is going to be bad. Worse than usual. I have to get through it. No choice. Have to . . .

"Into the bedroom," he said, and began kicking her repeatedly, not hard now. He wanted her able to crawl, and in the right direction. Her bare left elbow bumped a table leg.

"You're too drunk even to crawl straight," he said in disgust.

And she was. Lavern had to admit he was right. Were it not for the persistent guiding probes of his shoe she wouldn't have been headed for the hall and the bedroom door. The door seemed so distant now.

Has he somehow injured my sight?

He kicked harder, hurting the base of her spine, and she crawled faster, shredding her panty hose on the carpet and skinning her knees, scraping the heels of her hands on the rough fiber.

He had to help her into the bed. She flopped back onto the

soft mattress, watching the rectangular white ceiling spin up and away, and wished she could keep falling, falling . . .

Hobbs began to undress her. She didn't resist, but he lost his patience with buttons and snaps and started ripping off of her clothes.

It proved to be more difficult than he'd thought.

He gave up completely and stalked off into the hall. Steel clattered in the kitchen, and he returned to the bedroom holding a carving knife.

He began slicing not flesh, but material with the knife. So expertly did he use the knife on her resistant clothing that it made her afraid of what he'd be able to do with such expertise to her flesh.

Amazingly, considering his frenzy, the blade didn't so much as touch her.

Lavern clenched her eyes tightly shut and sent herself somewhere else, somewhere where this was happening to someone else.

You can be two people if you must. You really can. One afraid and in pain, and the other drifting and unfeeling . . .

Right now, the choice of which to be was easy.

With the morning already heating up like hell, Hobbs left for work without disturbing her where she lay in bed pretending to be asleep, the thin sheet pulled up over her face as if it were a shroud.

Beneath the taut white linen, her eyes were open and afraid.

63

They'd begun to gather in the park before dawn, and now there were hundreds of them.

At eight o'clock, New York One estimated the crowd at a thousand. It sure looked like a thousand massed on a TV screen. Traffic on Central Park West had to be diverted when their numbers spilled out onto the street.

They carried identical neatly produced FREE BERTY signs, and some wore T-shirts bearing the same demand in large black letters.

The event was large enough to disrupt traffic patterns throughout Midtown Manhattan, and made Quinn late on his way to Alfred Beeker's Park Avenue office. He wanted to get there by nine, before Beeker's first patients began to arrive.

He wanted to be in a room alone with Beeker.

Quinn sat as patiently as he could, draping his right wrist over the Lincoln's steering wheel, watching the brown UPS van ahead of him advance along the street ten feet at a time. His right foot moved automatically between accelerator and brake pedal, advancing the Lincoln along with the van. The car's air conditioner was sucking in some of the van's exhaust, so Quinn dropped the driver's side window about six inches. Heat rolled in, along with more exhaust fumes. The metallic chattering emitted by the air conditioner was louder with the window down. Too loud.

The window was gliding back up when Quinn's cell phone chirped. He leaned to the side and worked it out of his pocket, flipped it open, and pressed the button to answer.

"That you, Quinn?"

Renz's voice.

"It's my phone," Quinn said.

"That might not mean shit. You mighta just lost it, and I'm talking to some clown pretending to be you."

"I'm me, and not pretending."

"What about the clown part?"

"It's what I don't want to waste time on now, Harley."

"I tried to get in touch with you yesterday afternoon to tell you this movement to sympathize with Berty Wrenner is picking up steam, and you know what goes with steam."

"Pressure," Quinn said, trying not to yawn. The hot sun beating through the windshield was making him sleepy.

"Where were you yesterday, Quinn?"

"Pearl and I drove upstate to investigate a lead. Guy named Dwayne Avis. Nothing came of it, but I'll get a report to you so it's in the mix."

"Seen TV news this morning?"

"I managed to avoid it."

"Berty's due to be arraigned today, so his supporters are having a big demonstration in the park. Signs, songs, the whole shebang."

"You don't hear that word very often anymore," Quinn said. "Shebang."

"Parse it," Renz said, "and you got sexism." He seemed to mean it. There were times when nothing seemed too trivial for Renz to worry over.

"I won't mention you said it," Quinn assured him.

"Thanks. The news says the shebang is growing larger."

"That must be what's causing the traffic mess I'm stuck in. So what does Berty's army want?"

"Freedom for Berty."

"Despite the murder charge with evidence and a confession to back it up?"

"All that doesn't seem important to them. You know how it goes, Quinn. The little guy's perfect to play the poor schmuck who's a victim of the machine."

"We the machine?"

"We're part of it."

"So you wanna turn Berty free?"

"Not me. But if certain politicians could think of an excuse, they'd be out there marching with Berty's army."

"You're about the most opportunistic politician I know," Quinn said, "and you're not out there marching."

"I'm also first and foremost a cop, or I wouldn't associate with you and your fouled-up crew."

"You including Vitali and Mishkin?"

"Mishkin's Barney Fife with a brush mustache and Vitali's turning into Columbo."

"Television again," Quinn said.

"Between the Slicer, and the Twenty-five-Caliber Killer, and this dueling bullshit, this friggin' city's gone nuts."

"Always has been. That's why we love it."

"So you on your way to the Seventy-ninth Street office?"

"I've gotta make a stop first; then I'm going there."

"Keep me better informed, Quinn. Give me some raw meat now and then to throw to the people who want to turn *me* into raw meat. You know how the game is played. That's the reason why I hire you when we run into this kind of shit storm."

"Would you throw them Vitali and Mishkin?"

"I can promise you they'll go before you do."

"You're an honest evil man, Harley. That's so rare in this world."

"I'm working on the honest part."

"And making progress. I'll fax you that report."

"You do that, the whole shebang. Whenever you find time in your frenetic schedule."

That sounded like an exit line to Quinn. He broke the connection and stuck the phone back in his pocket.

The NYPD must have been getting the "Free Berty" demonstration under control. Traffic was creeping ahead steadily now, without the nerve-racking stop and go.

The city had caught its breath and was moving on.

Lavern removed the sheet from over her face and found a lance of sunlight aimed at her head, illuminating her pillow and igniting the pain in her ear where Hobbs had struck her last night. She moaned and glanced at the clock near the bed. Almost nine o'clock.

She recalled last night and shrank within herself. The apartment was quiet. Hobbs had left for work over an hour ago. At least there was that. She had some peace for a while. Some freedom from fear and fists.

And knives. Something new from Hobbs.

As she sat up in bed the pain in her ribs flared, and she drew a sharp breath. Her injured ear began to ring. She got both bare feet on the floor and stood up, dizzy at first so that she had to stoop slightly and touch the edge of the mattress to keep her balance. Then she worked her sleep shirt over her head and removed her panties. Every move hurt. It was as if she'd been in a terrible auto accident the day before and the pain and stiffness had caught up with her overnight. Knowing she was stooped like an old woman, she made her way toward the bathroom.

In the full-length mirror on the bathroom door she was

shocked by how relatively unmarked her body was. Though her ear and the side of her head ached, there was only a slight discoloration at her temple and around the corner of her eye. Her sides were red and turning purplish and would be colorfully bruised, but not for a while. The bruising would be vivid but limited, and not visible when she was dressed. But if she looked as bad as she felt, someone would rush her to a hospital.

She was still proud of her body and thought that, considering what she'd been through, she looked all right, even sexy, though it was obvious something had happened to her ribs. As long as they were covered, she could pass for one of the world's uninjured. Hobbs had it down to an art.

Lavern sometimes wondered how many other bruised but seemingly uninjured women she passed every day on the street, concealing their pain, holding it inside.

As she turned on the shower, she heard the rasp of the intercom. After hesitating a few seconds, she swiveled the white porcelain faucet handles to off. She dried her hands on a towel and put on a robe. Her hair looked like a birds' nest from sleeping on it, but it would have to do.

Yanking the robe's sash tight about her waist, she hurried from the bathroom and answered another, longer intercom buzz.

A metallic male voice from the lobby said there was a delivery for Lavern Neeson in 5C. She told the deliveryman she was the recipient and buzzed him in.

A few minutes later he was at the door, a young, acne-cursed man wearing dirt-crusted jeans and a gray T-shirt. The shirt had FLORA DORA lettered on it. Lavern knew it was the name of a small florist shop in the next block.

She accepted the narrow white box from the man, told him to wait a minute, and then dug a few dollars from her purse to tip him.

When he was gone, she carried the box to the coffee table

and sat down before it on the sofa. Her ear began to ring louder, and her headache was pulsing. When she was finished here she'd take two Aleves with a glass of water, see if that helped.

She leaned forward in the quiet apartment and opened the box.

It was full of pink and red roses. There was a small white card affixed with a delicate pink ribbon to one of the stems. Lavern opened the card so she could read the blue-ink scrawling inside it and recognized the handwriting.

The roses were from Hobbs. The writing on the card proclaimed that he loved her.

The sad part about it, Lavern thought, was that he really did.

Martin Hawk sat back, sipped his espresso, and idly watched the pigeons scratching out their brief existence on the sidewalk outside the restaurant where he'd just enjoyed a delicious breakfast. He mused on how his life had changed for the better. Had it been luck? Fate? He preferred to credit it to design, but he was a realist.

At sixteen his intelligence had been obvious, especially in his knowledge of the outdoors and in the scores he accumulated on various tests meant to measure scholarly potential. Yet he'd been a hopeless student. His father had become concerned, and when Alma's widowed and childless sister, Adriella, offered to take the boy into her home in Little Rock and see that he was enrolled in a better school and tutored, Carl thanked her for her generosity and told Marty it was time for him to become a scholar. Education was important, and he'd be a neglectful father if he didn't see that Marty obtained some.

Marty didn't like leaving Black Lake, but to disobey his father was unthinkable. So he lived with Adriella and struggled along in Little Rock, not exactly a top scholar, but getting by.

Three weeks before his high school graduation, fate intervened. Adriella, who was much more attractive and personable than her late sister, met and married Lloyd Barkweather.

Barkweather was a large, bluff man with shrewd gray eyes. He was moderately wealthy. And he was British. He'd been spending a month in Little Rock to consider Arkansas as a contending state in a search for the site of a new Rolls-Royce jet engine plant. Barkweather had said no to Arkansas, and a love-struck Adriella had said yes to Barkweather.

An ardent big game hunter, Barkweather had soon taken a shine to Marty. When he and Adriella moved, Marty went with them to London, where he continued his education, doing only marginally better as a scholar.

But he did marvelously well as an outdoorsman, going with Barkweather on hunting expeditions in faraway countries whose names Marty could barely pronounce.

When Barkweather and Adriella were killed in a motorcar pileup on the M23, Marty was surprised to find himself the sole heir to a modest investment portfolio.

Still without his degree, Marty left school at the age of twenty-one. He placed the portfolio in the stewardship of the investment department of Barclays Bank and traveled to Africa, where he went to work as a guide for a British company offering safaris. Mostly they were photography safaris, but Marty did hunt on his own with a rifle that had been a gift from Barkweather.

His reputation as a hunter grew, as did his reputation with women. The first had been the lonely wife of a Canadian client. Then local wives and daughters of civil servants fell one after another as victims of his charm.

Marty found courting and bedding women much like stalking and bagging game.

But not quite. There was some trouble about an unwanted pregnancy that became a miscarriage, then a suicide, and he left Africa to hunt in India.

He thought less and less about the disconsolate African woman who'd leaped to her death from a bridge out of love and remorse.

When a tiger in the Sunderbans became a man-eater, it was Marty who was hired to track and kill it. Within the week the tiger was dead, and Martin Hawk was something of a hero.

After that kill, he returned to Africa.

A month later he was sitting in a camp chair outside his tent when he noticed a slow whirl of vultures circling a distant creature almost dead. Martin Hawk raised his binoculars and saw that the doomed animal was a male lion that had perhaps been fatally injured in a fight for dominance of the pride.

He leaned back in his chair, still with the binoculars pressed to his eyes, and became fascinated not by the lion, but by the huge birds gliding and soaring on the warm air currents off the veldt, patiently waiting for the lion to die.

It was then, for a reason he didn't understand or try to analyze, that he felt the need to return to his home country and his father.

The time Martin Hawk had chosen to return was fortunate. His modest portfolio in euros had, due to the rate of exchange, become considerably more valuable in dollars.

After his plane landed at Kennedy in New York, he canceled his connecting flight and took a cab into the city.

New York City. He wanted to see it.

It might be the perfect place for a unique and profitable business he'd long considered while enjoying the hunt.

So far it had been exactly that.

Martin Hawk had never gotten beyond New York.

He raised his hand to get the waiter's attention and ordered another espresso.

64

Dr. Beeker knew how to play the role. He looked like a high-priced psychiatrist this morning. He was wearing a brown suede sport jacket with a yellow and black tie, darker brown slacks, and brown loafers. His glasses were dangling from a cord around his neck, nestled against his chest next to a gold tie clasp. His damp, thinning hair seemed longer and was curled above his ears and at the nape of his neck, reminding Quinn of a nest of snakes.

When he entered and saw Quinn in his office anteroom his features tightened and his intense dark eyes darted to his receptionist, then back to Quinn.

"Detective Quinn insisted on waiting," Beatrice, the middle-aged, attractive blond woman behind the desk, said in her defense.

Without smiling, Beeker nodded to her.

Quinn stood up from the black leather sofa that seemed to have grown to him. "We need to talk."

"I have appointments soon," Beeker said.

He strode into his office and left the door open. Quinn

took it as an invitation and went in, noticing that the doctor had left in his wake a lemony scent of cologne or shaving lotion. He closed the door behind him.

Beeker was sitting behind his desk, doing the tent thing with his fingers.

Quinn remained standing. "I visited your Web site," he said.

Beeker smiled slightly. He had a slow way of smiling that seemed to give his expression added meaning. "I'm sure you enjoyed it."

"The photos of Zoe—"

"Aren't bad, are they?" Beeker shifted his weight slightly in his chair so it tilted backward, but not so far that he had to remove his elbows from his desk. "Zoe's a beautiful woman. But you knew that."

"I'd like you to delete the photos of Zoe," Quinn said.

"If Zoe makes that request, I'll consider it."

"I'm making the request for her."

"I don't accept that." Beeker leaned forward again. "You might not like it, Detective, but Zoe enjoyed posing for those photos. She's proud of her body and doesn't mind revealing it. The shots I'm sure you'd find the most disturbing aren't on the Internet. She enjoyed posing for those, too."

"It was another time, another place," Quinn said.

"But not another Zoe. She doesn't necessarily fit your concept of her, Detective Quinn. You don't really know her at all. I'm not sure I do. Like each of us, she's many different people wrapped in the same skin."

"I didn't come here for psychobabble," Quinn said, and moved closer to the desk.

Beeker didn't react. "You don't intimidate me, Detective Quinn."

"I'm not interested in intimidating you. I'm simply telling you to delete the photos."

"If Zoe calls me, I'll do that. It's a part of our former relationship that's between the two of us."

"If I don't intimidate you, why are you agreeing to delete the photos?"

"I'll delete them if Zoe requests it. Not you."

"I'll let you keep that distinction," Quinn said.

"Our Zoe has sides to her you've never seen. As you have sides she's unaware of. Wouldn't you say that's so, detective?"

"Not everyone goes around pretending to be what they aren't," Quinn said.

"You mean like a sexual deviant pretending to be a respectable Park Avenue psychiatrist? Overcompensating behavior used as a disguise? I'm not putting up any kind of defensive subterfuge, and neither is Zoe. The idea of either of us living secret lives is all in *your* mind. She posed for photographs often and willingly and knew what I was going to do with them. What we've done and photographed is all legal, Detective Quinn. You can check with the vice squad. Zoe and I were part of a club whose members share certain modes of impulse and behavior. It's the other photographs that might worry you. The ones with the interesting props. They're the real Zoe, too."

Quinn was fighting to keep his temper, but at the same time was somewhat surprised. Beeker was taunting him now, daring him.

"The most outwardly respectable people are the most likely to have diametrically opposite components to their personalities, Detective. Surely you've noticed that. The reformers who consort with prostitutes, the Bible-thumpers who steal from the church, the gay-bashers who are latent homosexuals, the upright family men who are serial killers." Beeker gave his slow smile again. "Then there is the healer of the mind, Zoe, who accepts and lives with her own various facets of self-identity. Her other sides, but not her secret sides."

"I get it, already," Quinn said. "We're all two people."

"No, no, no. We're all many people. We simply have to accept and integrate our various selves. I help people to do that." Beeker stood up behind his desk. "But if someone does have a *secret* self, Detective Quinn, you might do well to look for it as the opposite of their public self." He walked out from behind the desk. "A zealous cop crusader, for instance, might also be a serial killer. Hasn't that happened in our fair city?"

It had. And Quinn had been fooled by it too long and people had died. Beeker must know that.

"You seem to have researched me," Quinn said.

"Somewhat. I'm interested in whoever's interested in Zoe. As you are. Why pretend otherwise?"

"I do believe you're practicing your dark art on me, Doctor."

"I specialize in dialectical behavior therapy, Detective Quinn. It requires the cooperation of the patient. I don't believe you're capable of that."

Quinn knew it was time to go. He hadn't come here to physically assault Beeker, but things were moving in that direction.

He moved toward the door. "Delete the photos, Dr. Beeker."

"Have Zoe call me."

"You're a stubborn one."

"Notice I'm not the type," Beeker said.

The slow smile was forming as Quinn turned away.

Quinn was perspiring when he left Beeker's office. He knew he'd lost a round, and he didn't like it.

He didn't like it that there were more, and more explicit, photographs of Zoe. He didn't like what Dr. Beeker had told him, which was, in effect, the same thing Helen Iman had told him about contradictory behavior.

If they were right about reformers, Bible-thumpers, and gay-bashers, were they right about serial killers?

And weren't serial killers supposed to be *his* area of expertise?

65

Renz had Quinn, Pearl, Fedderman, and Helen the profiler in his office. The door was locked, and Renz had left
word not to be disturbed unless it was urgent.

When everyone was more or less settled, Renz sat down
behind his waxed and uncluttered desk. "I have an idea," he
said.

Quinn was seated in one of the chairs facing the desk. He
could think of several things to say to Renz's statement, but
he chose the relatively safe, "And you want to try it out on
us."

"Exactly," Renz said. "I will say before I go into it that
Helen approves."

"I think it might work," Helen said.

"Helen thinks, and I think," Renz said to Quinn, "that the
killer sees you, even *wants* you, as his opponent. The bond
that sometimes forms between serial killers and the lead detectives who pursue them is strong here. We think we can
take advantage of it. We want to place a letter from you to
the killer in the newspapers—*City Beat* first, of course—in
which you taunt the killer. I think we know how he'll react."

Renz glanced at Helen, as if they'd rehearsed this and she'd missed her cue.

"We think he'll challenge you," Helen said. "And in some manner give himself away."

"And if he doesn't give anything away?" Pearl asked.

"Then it's up to Quinn whether to accept the challenge."

"If the killer's smart," Quinn said, "he'll simply ignore the letter."

"He's smart and mentally ill," Helen said.

"When do you want this letter?" Quinn asked.

Renz leaned over his desk, a folded slip of paper extended in his right hand. "With Helen's help, I've already written it."

Quinn accepted the paper and looked at it.

To the one who kills from shadows and secrecy:

It is time for honorable men to stop the wave of murder that is washing over the city. But there is only one man who—if honorable and a man—can stop it. The .25-Caliber Killer must come forward. The fact that he cooperated will be considered in his sentencing. If he ignores this opportunity, when my hunt for him ends as it must, he will feel the full weight of the law.

Captain Frank Quinn

"It's not so much a taunt," Quinn said, "as an offer of a deal."

"Believe me," Helen said, "he'll consider it a taunt, and he'll respond as he must. There's always the chance that unforeseen circumstances might interfere with this plan, but the psychology of it is sound."

"And if he doesn't respond," Renz said, "we've lost nothing. Those are the kind of odds I like."

"You're not the one taunting a maniac with a gun," Pearl said.

Quinn gave her a look that was obviously meant as a caution signal, but Pearl saw green lights where others saw red.

"The letter doesn't mention the Slicer," Quinn said.

"We're trying to appeal only to the hunter side of the killer," Helen said. "The sportsman with a code. That's the part of him that will respond to the letter."

"It isn't in our contract with the city that we fight duels," Pearl said.

"It would be more like a hunt," Helen said. "That's the point."

"And hunting is in your contract," Renz said, "however it might be phrased. Hunting is what we do."

"We?" Pearl asked.

"I'll do it," Quinn said, before Renz could answer Pearl. He smiled at Renz. "It's true that we have nothing to lose if the killer doesn't respond."

"We knew you'd want to do it," Helen said.

Pearl gave her a dark look. Helen seemed unimpressed.

Renz took the letter back from Quinn. "I'll fax this to Cindy Sellers at *City Beat,*" he said. "Give them a shot at a special edition. The other papers won't be far behind."

"They'll all be behind the Internet and cable news," Fedderman said. They all knew how newspaper offices, as well as the NYPD, sprang leaks.

Renz shrugged. "That's the plight of print journalism. Sellers will have to understand it."

"I hope the killer doesn't respond," Pearl said, as they were standing up to leave the office.

Renz began to fume. His jowls actually shook.

Quinn raised a hand before Renz could speak. "Let's all keep this running smoothly," he said, looking at everyone but Renz.

"Helen knows the mind of the killer," Renz said, as they were filing out.

"It will work," Helen added.

Quinn turned to look at her. "Do you guarantee it?"

"No," Helen said. "There are no guarantees in what we do. This is more like an extended warranty."

"My new idea for some fresh material," Mitzi said. "Two serial killers, married to each other."

Mitzi and Jackie Jameson had run through their routines and were killing time sitting and sipping cold drinks in what passed for Say What?'s green room. It was a twelve-foot-square windowless room with a few old easy chairs and recliners, some gray steel folding chairs, mirrors and more mirrors, and an old refrigerator. Nothing in it was green. The two comics faced each other in opposite threadbare easy chairs. Jackie was drinking a Coke in intermittent gulps. Mitzie, one Levied leg thrown over a chair arm, sipped bottled water.

"It could be funny, Mitz," Jackie said. "But keeping a marriage like that together could be murder."

"In sickness and in health," Mitzi said.

Jackie grimaced.

"See what I mean?" Mitzi said. "Possibilities. Grim, so probably funny. And I could recycle some of the old husband-and-wife jokes in a new context and they'd seem fresh."

"I dunno, though," Jackie said. "Considering what's going on out there these days, will people think you oughta be joking about serial killers?"

"I'm not sure. Whaddya think?"

"Yeah, it might go over okay. Take it from a guy who's got no taste."

"That's why I sought your advice."

"If you do decide to go in that direction, maybe you oughta learn some more about serial killers, give your material more edge."

"Talk to a few serial killers?"

"Might be easier to talk to a guy named Quinn," Jackie said. "He's—

"I know who he is," Mitzi said. "I read the papers every day for material. Oh, that Middle East."

"So give him a call. He might help you out."

"In his spare time," Mitzi said.

Jackie grinned at her. "You scared to call him?"

"He's a scary guy."

"He'd be awed to hear from a celebrity like you."

"I could tell him I'm Whoopi Goldberg."

Jackie dug his cell phone from one of his pockets and tossed it over so it landed on what there was of Mitzi's lap, the way she was sprawled in the chair.

"So call him," he said, and threw back his head to drain the rest of his Coke. He bent a kink in the empty can and tossed it into a plastic-lined trash receptacle.

"You into throwing things?" Mitzi asked.

"It's a kind of therapy. Helps me to let loose. Go ahead and call him."

"Anybody ever tell you, Jackie, you're kinda pushy?"

"You got nothing to lose, Mitz. He might surprise you. Serial killers might be a barrel of laughs."

"They've got other uses for barrels," Mitzi said. She flipped up the lid on the phone. "Whaddya think, nine-one-one or information?"

"I dunno," Jackie said. "They're both a bundle of giggles, but nine-one-one tends to take things more seriously." Looking at her, he thought, *that law against two comics, what a shame.*

66

Martin Hawk sat that evening in the bar of his hotel and watched the reflection of a television screen on the glass partition of his booth. The TV was over by the cash register. Its sound was down, but volume wasn't needed for what was being shown. It was a big mob scene somewhere in the park. Backward in the screen's reflection Martin could see the lettering on the signs and shirts. He mentally flipped the letters: FREE BERTY.

So it was about the latest in the series of murders in the city, all inspired by the honorable blood sport that Martin had perfected and developed into a profitable business. Bertrand Wrenner, a feckless little man who under any other circumstances wouldn't have dreamed of shooting anyone, had taken the media's interpretation of Quest and Quarry's unintentional consequences to heart. The fool actually thought he was dueling, that somehow what was happening in the city put the stamp of respectability on unadorned murder.

Berty Wrenner, Martin was sure, had never gone hunting. A bowl of peanuts and Martin's drink sat untouched be-

fore him. What was going on now in the city had deprived
him of appetite and thirst. Somehow noble opportunity for
his clients had been turned into complicity in murders. He
knew the crowds demonstrating in the park, the masses
plodding to their jobs and then back home every day, wouldn't
understand his goals or accomplishments. They might regard
murder as dueling now; and for a while if Quest and Quarry
were exposed, they might even regard what its clientele did
as hunting. But Martin knew the fickleness of group thought.
He might well become a reviled and shunned, not to mention
imprisoned, member of society.

And of course there was Quinn, himself a hunter, a man
Martin had no choice but to respect. Quinn was always out
there trying to track him, thinking about him, attempting to
get into his mind and motives. Stalking him.

Martin felt a powerful need for understanding, to set the
record straight. To deal with the hunter who hunted him.

He could think of only one way to do that. For the record.
For his record. For the fortification of his soul.

He laid some bills and a tip next to the peanut bowl on the
table and started to stand up. The news was going to a commercial break, but in the instant before the picture went to a
shot of luxury autos driving in formation, the backward
crawl at the bottom of the screen said there'd been a new de-
velopment in the latest series of murders in New York City,
involving a letter.

Martin sat back down.

The next morning, Pearl and Fedderman had stopped for
doughnuts, just like cops in books and movies.

"Krispy Kreme," Fedderman said. "How can their doughnuts be so delicious and their stock so lousy?"

Pearl looked over at him. "You in the stock market, Feds?"

"No. It was either that or the supermarket. I never had the
money for both."

They actually tried to pay for the doughnuts, but the guy behind the counter said they were free in return for the protection the cops gave his store. They thanked him and got their coffees refilled in to-go cups. The doughnut guy told them to be sure and come back, and they said they would, meaning it. Sometimes the world felt right.

They got into the unmarked parked illegally at the curb. Fedderman drove. They were on their way to put their heads together with Vitali and Mishkin to see if they could break the logjam in their investigation. Neither of them mentioned the letter Helen the profiler had composed that was released under Quinn's name. Pearl hoped the killer would ignore the damned thing.

The pressure from on high was real and growing, exacerbated by the Berty Wrenner case. Quinn hadn't demanded action, as Renz had demanded of him, because he knew they were all pros and treated them as such. But pros felt the pressure just like everyone else, only they could shrug it off. Most of the time.

It was obvious that the stress was wearing on Quinn. His eyes were often bloodshot, as if he wasn't getting much sleep, and his craggy features had taken on an expression of weary determination. He seemed to be taking more desperate measures, like having Nancy Weaver interview Wrenner's fellow employees at the real estate agency where Wrenner worked. Everyone there seemed to have hated Alec Farr, so there was a remote possibility Wrenner had had an accomplice.

Pearl and Fedderman didn't say much as they finished their coffees and left the foam containers in the car's plastic cup holders.

They were on Broadway, driving north in heavy traffic, when Pearl said, "Hang a left at the next corner."

"Why?" Fedderman asked.

"I need to make a quick stop."

"What is this, you gotta pee?" *With all that coffee in her, it figures*, Fedderman thought.

"Just make the turn, Feds. Please."

Astounded by the *please,* Fedderman steered the gray Ford into the turn. They drove for a while. Fedderman could smell something unpleasant now and then, as if someone had vomited in the car and it hadn't been thoroughly cleaned. Maybe a suspect. They did that sometimes. He'd have opened a window, but the air conditioner was having enough of a problem keeping the summer heat outside.

"Any more instructions?" he asked.

"I just want to—"

"I know where we're going now," he said. "Your apartment." He glanced over at her. "I guess you're desperate for my body."

"It *would* require desperation," Pearl said.

When he'd parked in front of the brick and stone building, she told him she'd only be a minute and got out of the car. Her slacks felt tight and constricting, as if they'd contracted in the heat, and clung to her lower body. She was aware of Fedderman watching her as she took the front concrete steps and entered the vestibule. She wondered what he was thinking, but she knew. What all men thought.

Showing herself off, Fedderman thought. Tight pants and a flight of stairs; women couldn't resist the opportunity—if they had it to show. Pearl had it.

Ah! She saw right away that there was something white visible through her mail slot. The postman had been here.

She keyed open the box and withdrew the day's mail. Only one envelope, and a colorful flier from a new Thai restaurant that had opened in the neighborhood. The flier slipped from her grasp and fluttered to the tile floor. She ignored it and turned over the envelope.

In the top left corner was Dr. Eichmann's name and office address.

Since Pearl had paid her bill, she knew what must be in the envelope. The pathology report for the biopsy of her mole. It had to be!

She moved over to a corner near the windowed door—where the mingled scents of cleaning solvent and urine were stronger, but the light was better—and started to tear open the envelope.

Then she stopped.

She had to work today, as usual, and there was no way to know how this report would affect her, one way or the other.

Pearl stared at the sealed envelope and decided it was too delicate a matter, too intensely private, to share with Fedderman, and he was waiting out in the car. Probably about to lean on the horn. She didn't want him to see her reaction to the news, either way.

She stuffed the envelope in a pocket and went back outside, trying to forget it for the time being. It wasn't going anywhere, and whenever she decided to read it, it would say the same thing.

Live or die, she had to concentrate on today.

She wouldn't admit that she was terrified of what she might learn, and now that she had the envelope whose contents she'd been so eager to read, she'd delay opening it as long as possible.

Martin Hawk had spent most of the morning on his reply to Quinn's letter, cutting and pasting from a *New Yorker* he'd bought at a kiosk several blocks from the hotel.

When it was finished, he decided not to mail it. Instead he took it to a Kinko's, where he ran a copy of it.

Then he faxed it.

67

They weren't sorry he was dead.

Nancy Weaver sat in Alec Farr's office, in the large black leather desk chair that had been Farr's, and read over the notes she'd taken on the interviews with the employees of the Home Away agency. Though some of the employees were at least polite, including Farr's personal assistant, a weepy-eyed woman named Gloria Ann, most of them clearly disliked Farr to the point where they were glad fate had stepped in and removed him from their lives.

Mention of Berty Wrenner's name brought praise and distress. Praise because Berty was such a quiet, thoughtful, warmhearted man. Distress because Berty was in a pickle for killing Farr. Weaver knew how, once they became causes célèbres, the oppressed and imprisoned could grow in everyone's estimation, but this was ridiculous. Berty Wrenner should be in line for sainthood.

The last name on her interview list was Adam Hastings, the owner of Home Away. He entered Farr's office without knocking, a tall, slender man in his sixties, with gray hair, glittering blue eyes, and the face of a sly reptile. He sat down in the straight-backed wooden chair where employees must have sat to be excoriated by Farr, smoothed the creases in his neat gray suit, and smiled at Weaver.

"I'm here to tell you what a prince Bertrand Wrenner is and what an asshole Alec Farr was," he said.

Weaver's face showed nothing, but she kind of liked the way the interview was starting. She was dealing with the alpha of alpha males here. This could be exhilarating.

"Is that how you really saw it?" she asked.

"I told a half-truth," Hastings said. He had a smooth, cultured voice, like a late-night DJ on public radio classics. "Bertrand Wrenner is an incompetent little twit, and Alec Farr was a son of a bitch."

"Did you know that when you hired them?"

"Not entirely. I thought Wrenner might be able to sell, but he turned out to be a wimp. Farr, I knew was a son of a bitch. That was the reason I hired him. I knew he used steroids, not because he was an athlete, but so he'd be more intimidating and aggressive. We're not in an easy business, Detective Weaver, especially in these times."

It was *Officer Weaver,* but Weaver didn't correct him. "So what your salespeople are saying is true—Farr was a slave-driving prick."

"Quite so. He demonstrated it on a daily basis. Several of our people quit because they couldn't take the pressure. Boo-hoo. They were replaceable, and Farr got results."

"Not lately, he didn't."

Hastings smiled again. It was a scary sight. "It's a punishing economy out there, Detective. You should be glad you're in public service. When people need a house or a new car, they can delay buying them. When people need a cop, they usually can't put it off."

"You make me glad I'm not on commission," Weaver said.

"You should be glad. But if you ever need a job, consider contacting Home Away. There's something about you that makes me think you'd be a fit."

"If ever I start using steroids," Weaver said.

Hastings stood up. "I've told you all I really know. I don't spend a lot of time on the premises. I hired Alec Farr to run this end of the business, and he did it his way."

"Like in the Frank Sinatra song," Weaver said, "only it got him killed."

"And now I have to replace two employees." Hastings sounded self-pitying and mildly piqued, as if some triviality had tripped him up and now he had to waste his valuable time dealing with the consequences.

"Mr. Hastings," Weaver said, "is that the only reason you're sorry Alec Farr is dead?"

"Of course it is. He was a valuable employee."

"Did you like him?"

"Not at all. No one could like him."

"What about Berty Wrenner?"

"Didn't really know him, and he can be replaced."

Everybody's epitaph, Weaver thought.

"Anything else, Detective?"

"Not at the moment, sir."

Why did I call him 'sir'? Did Farr feel intimidated by Hastings, even in his own office? Is that the kind of pissing contest game they played around here? A game that became more than a game to Berty Wrenner and drove him to murder?

Hastings nodded a good-bye and went out the door.

Weaver stood up from Alec Farr's chair and glanced around the office. There were a few awards on the walls. Top salesman of this year or that, and a nineteen-year-old business administration diploma from someplace called Pierpont College. Above the black file cabinets was a bad painting of a bald eagle soaring against the background of an American flag. At least Farr had been a patriot. No photographs of wife or kids, as Farr had been a divorced man without children. No shots of any other family members. No Elk membership certificate, mounted trophy fish, personal mementos, or souvenirs from tourist traps.

Weaver decided that Farr had been a lonely man. His job must have meant everything to him. That was the reason he'd stayed instead of run. Not courage, but lonely desperation. She decided that maybe she thought more kindly of Alec Farr than anyone else who'd ever been in this office. Still, she wouldn't have enjoyed working for him, and she couldn't say she would have liked him. In fact, she didn't really like anyone she'd interviewed today.

Feeling a sudden urgency to get out of the office and away from the Home Away agency, she headed for the door. She knew the air would be better outside, uncontaminated by Machiavellian maneuvering and raw ambition. Not to mention fear.

The place was toxic. The toxicity could be fatal.

68

"A woman named Mitzi Lewis called," Fedderman said, when he checked in by phone with Quinn. "She does stand-up comedy and wanted to talk to you about serial killers. She's got some kind of routine in mind."

"Comedy? About serial killers?"

"That's what she said."

"Jesus, Feds!"

"I know. She sounded nice, though."

"Call her back and tell her I'm too busy now, but I'll give her an interview when all this is over."

"Seems the thing to do," Fedderman said.

"And Feds, tell her it'll be over soon."

"We hope."

"Leave that part out," Quinn said, and broke the connection.

Mitzi said it aloud to see how it would sound: "There *is* a smoking section, but it's not exactly *in* the plane."

No, that one wasn't funny, and it reminded passengers

they were in an aluminum tube six miles up going five hundred miles per hour. No laughs to be mined here.

Her cell sounded the five key notes of *Comedy Tonight*, and she yanked it from her pocket. Ah! Fedderman was calling. The cop.

She listened to his message from Quinn, then she sighed and thanked him. He said he was really sorry, and she believed him.

Okay, she thought, putting the phone back in her pocket. She'd forget about the married serial killers idea until later, and if it still seemed workable she'd see if she could talk with Quinn.

Meanwhile, time to get back to work.

Mitzi continued strolling in Washington Square, paying little attention to the many pigeons strutting and flapping around her feet. The day was another incineration, and she was wearing baggy shorts and a sleeveless T-shirt. Several homeless people were lounging in the park, one of them curled in the fetal position on a bench she was approaching. In the shade of a tree, two heavily bearded men were using an upside-down cardboard box for a table and were deeply involved in playing chess. Tourists were ambling about, as were students, artists with sketch pads, and various Village types. Mitzi, with her Doc Martens boots and spiked white blond hair, guessed she was one of the Village types. She seemed to be attracting no attention whatsoever, and found herself rather grateful for that. It made it easier for her to think. To work.

Which was what she'd been doing when she received Fedderman's call. She sometimes sold jokes to the airlines. It seemed that all of them were incorporating comedy into their welcome and safety spiels. It was good PR, and the informality of comedy helped to soothe nerves and put passengers at ease. Other than comedians, few people died in the middle of a joke. But with all the passenger traffic and frequent fliers, airborne comedy ate up material in a hurry. The airlines depended on people like Mitzi to provide them with a steady supply of humor. Reassuring takeoff and landing humor in particular was in high demand.

Despite the warm temperature, the direct sunlight on Mitzi's face made her smile. Her twenty-fifth birthday was today, and she felt good, as long as she stayed away from thoughts of getting older and more wrinkled. Crow's-feet were beginning to form at the corners of her eyes—she was sure of it. If the light was right and she smiled wide, people must be able to see them. If she dwelled on it too much the truth was undeniable and unbearable: time was marching all over her.

On the plus side there was Rob. They were going out for dinner tonight, and, knowing Rob, he'd have some kind of birthday gift for her.

As she passed the bench with the homeless man curled up on it, he mumbled something she couldn't understand, then turned his head away, as if she'd impolitely disturbed his sleep. An empty wine bottle was on the ground beneath the bench, along with a used condom. Mitzi guessed the bench had seen a lot of action last night. The man mumbled again in his sleep, something unintelligible about flying or dying.

When she was well past him, Mitzi slowed her pace.

I walk down the aisle to the only empty seat in the plane, and this drunk sitting next to it says . . .

'Would it embarrassh you if I shang?' I say 'not at all,' and then I find out that in his language shang *means . . .*

The pigeons waddling about on the pavement, pecking at minute bits of whatever, parted way for Mitzi, but never moved more than a few feet. They didn't seem to sense anything imminent. Mitzi caught a shadowy movement in the corner of her vision, and a large dark bird—a hawk— swooped down, used its fully spread dark wings as brakes, sank its talons into a white and gray pigeon, then regained height, carrying the helpless pigeon away. It had all happened so suddenly and noiselessly that it might have been an illusion. As if she had the Discovery Channel on with the sound off, only it was real.

Mitzi looked around. No one else in the square seemed to have noticed what happened. The pigeons, pecking away at miniscule edibles, went on about their business as if nothing had occurred and one of their number weren't missing.

Poor pigeon.

You're shanged, pal.

Mitzi stood staring up at the sky, but the hawk and its prey were nowhere in sight.

Had she imagined it?

She didn't think so.

A peregrine falcon. That's what she must have seen. She knew they were in the city, and that they hunted pigeons, but few people had actually seen them in action.

Now Mitzi was one of those few. Seeing it had, in a way, been exhilarating. In another way, disturbing. Whatever it was, it had sure put the cap on comedy.

She picked up her pace and walked toward one of the park exits, unable to shake the image of the large dark bird suddenly appearing and deftly using its powerful wings to entrap the pigeon while it gained a grip and managed to lift off with its stunned prey. She couldn't get over how it had all happened so abruptly, disturbing nothing around it, and then it was over. It was the way fate sometimes dealt with people.

She understood then what was making her uneasy. The strike of the falcon seemed so incongruous as to be prophetic. *She* had seen this rare and startling sight. Mustn't that mean something? Hadn't she somehow been *chosen*?

Don't be so childish and self-absorbed. Everything that happens to you doesn't have to be infused with hidden meaning and great gravity. God, fate, whoever, whatever doesn't telegraph his, her, its moves. Prophecy before tragedy? Ask the pigeon.

The oversized leather boots she was wearing were starting to give her a blister. Mitzi concentrated on that. It was a real and imminent problem.

She walked more carefully on the hot pavement, scrunching up her toes and trying to keep the boots from rubbing, as she left the square and made her way toward her subway stop. On the subway she was still trying to put the incident with the pigeon out of her mind.

But she couldn't.

She knew she'd probably dream about it tonight.

But she wouldn't.

69

Pearl hadn't slept more than an hour straight last night. This was insane. She was torturing herself. She knew it had to end, and only she could end it.

Finally she'd worked up the courage to read Dr. Eichmann's pathology report.

She sat on the sofa with a knife she'd gotten from the kitchen to use as a letter opener. But when she inserted the narrow blade into the corner of the envelope, the flap popped open of its own accord. It had been barely sealed.

How dare they send a document like this in a way that allows anyone to read it!

Had *someone read it?*

In her anger Pearl imagined some ham-handed postal employee noticing the unsealed flap and checking to see if there might be money in the envelope. Then, disappointed, reading the results of her biopsy. Sharing the information with fellow employees, all of them making a big joke of it.

Calm down, idiot!

Postal employees were no more likely than cops to behave that way. And the envelope *was* sealed, only lightly. It didn't appear to have been tampered with, and probably had found its way, like thousands—*millions*—of letters, to its proper recipient unread.

She withdrew the single white sheet of paper from the envelope and unfolded it. Held it in a trembling hand and read . . .

She couldn't concentrate. Her eyes skipped from line to line, from checked box to checked box, always focusing on the word *benign*.

Breathing more easily than she had for weeks, she leaned back in the sofa cushions and looked at the ceiling, saying the word aloud: "Benign."

She read the pathology report again. And again. Each time liberated her anew. It was actually true that the mole had been benign, had been . . . a beauty mark.

Yes, a beauty mark!

But something was impinging on her binge of relief, on her new freedom from impending fatal illness, and it didn't take Pearl long to figure out what it was.

She felt herself getting angry. *Those, those, those* . . . she would never be able to forgive her mother, Mrs. Kahn, and most of all that bastard Milton Kahn, for deliberately frightening her about the mole.

About death.

She knew exactly what she would do. She'd make copies of this pathology report, with the word *benign* underlined wherever it appeared. She would mail copies to her mother, to Mrs. Kahn, and to Milton Kahn.

She would do it immediately.

Then, maybe, she'd feel better.

Her cell phone vibrated in her pocket and made her jump. She pulled it out, flipped it open, and saw that Quinn was calling her.

"Pearl," he said, when she'd made the connection and said hello, "Feds isn't coming by for you this morning. He's going to meet with Vitali and Mishkin alone. I'm on the way to pick you up. Should be there in about five minutes."

"This a date?" she asked. *Why am I always such a wise ass?*

"Yeah. We're gonna double with Renz and Helen the profiler."

"I'm trying to imagine them as a romantic couple," Pearl said.

"Don't. Please. Just be ready."

"Okay. I'll be waiting out front."

"You read the *Times* this morning?"

"No. I usually get one out of a machine."

"Well, you can read mine on the way to see Renz."

Pearl felt her pulse pick up. Her anger, the pathology report, were forgotten. "Something moving?"

"Something's moving," Quinn said, and ended the conversation.

Renz, in his overheated, tobacco-scented office, had today's *Times* lying on his desk, flipped to the open letter from the .25-Caliber Killer to Quinn.

The reply to Quinn's letter was short and to the point:

Captain Quinn:

What is happening now in this city isn't hunting, isn't dueling, isn't sport. It is murder. We are both civilized men. We are both, in our own ways, hunters. As it was probably destined to do since the beginning, our contest has developed into a mutual hunt. In the stalking of truly dangerous game, hunter and prey become indistinguishable. You will soon receive a package from me. It contains a .25-caliber Springbok revolver. We both know what it means.

I wish you luck.

   The .25-Caliber Killer

Renz passed copies of the page around so that everyone else in the office—Quinn, Pearl, Vitali, Mishkin, and Helen the profiler—could read it, whether for the first time or again.

Helen smiled and said, "It worked."

Renz looked at Quinn from behind his desk. "Are you ready for this?"

"Of course I am."

"You shouldn't do this, Quinn," Pearl said, ignoring the astounded look Renz gave her.

"We didn't set this up to waste time," Renz said. "He has to do it, for his own reasons."

"He's right," Quinn said. "And I have to do it without NYPD protection the killer might spot. This is an opportunity we can't risk screwing up."

"You're playing a game with your life, Quinn!"

"It's a game I'm forced to play."

Pearl gave him a dark, probing stare. "This is some kind of honor thing with you, right?"

"Not entirely."

"Don't take the honor part of it lightly," Helen told Pearl.

Pearl ignored her. "Your job is to catch a killer, Quinn, not risk your life in some archaic macho game that you have to play by the rules."

"It amounts to the same thing, Pearl. If the killer realizes I'm not playing the game honestly, he'll simply back off and continue what he's been doing. I have to do this on the up and up with him, and alone."

"That's how it is, Pearl," Renz said.

Pearl looked at Sal Vitali, who shrugged. His partner Mishkin did the same.

"Bullshit! Mano-a-mano bullshit!" Pearl said. She looked at Renz appealingly. "At least give him some protection."

"I can't do that," Renz said. "If protection was spotted this would all be for nothing."

"He really can't," Helen added, defending Renz.

"Listen—"

Quinn rested a big hand on Pearl's shoulder and gave her a warning look. She was losing this argument and knew it, and fell silent.

"I'll issue the order," Renz said. "No one is to talk to the media, or to interfere in the hunt. I mean *no one.*"

"Male-pattern madness!" Pearl said under her breath.

"Something more than that," Quinn told her.

After leaving Renz's office, on the walk back to where the Lincoln was parked in the sun, Quinn said, "Whatever happened with that mole of yours, Pearl?"

"Mole? It turned out to be nothing. No big deal."

"Good. I figured that's how it'd go." Not even breaking stride. Making business-as-usual small talk.

Pearl stepped out and moved around to block Quinn's path.

She looked him in the eye the way she sometimes regarded suspects.

"You can't actually do this thing with the killer," she said.

"I agreed to it."

"Oh, so what? At least take an extra weapon. Something more than that ancient South African peashooter."

"Time to drop the subject, Pearl. I mean it."

She stalked off, bouncing in a way that attracted a lot of male attention.

"Pearl! Get in the goddamned car."

She stopped and turned. There was a stiffness to her features caused by more than anger. She was almost, but not quite, crying. "I'll catch up with you later."

"Where you going, Pearl?" Quinn's tone was softer now.

"To copy and mail something. I feel I have to do it. No choice. It involves life instead of death."

Quinn watched her walk away, wondering what she'd meant. Then he opened the Lincoln's door and felt heat roll out. He got in and sat with the engine running and the air conditioner blasting, watching Pearl through the windshield until she disappeared among a throng of people who'd just crossed with the traffic light.

Pearl talk, he figured, and fastened his safety belt.

70

Quinn sat with Zoe at a corner table in Hammacher's, a German restaurant on the East Side. It was a place that afforded privacy, with high-backed wooden booths and lots of cloth and green carpeting to mute sound so voices wouldn't carry. Deals legal and illegal were made here.

Quinn had courted some of his upper-echelon snitches in Hammacher's, but hadn't visited the restaurant in over a year. Nothing had changed. Still the hushed ambience, still the elderly waiters who kept their distance unless summoned, and still the indefinable mingled scents of spices, boiled sauerkraut, and something else that almost made the eyes water.

They'd both ordered German draft beers with unpronounceable names and the sauerbraten special and were waiting for their food to arrive, their gigantic frosted mugs of beer in front of them. No one was seated within twenty feet of their booth.

Zoe had on one of her psychoanalyst outfits. A light gray blazer over a white blouse, a blue skirt of modest length. She wasn't wearing much makeup, which only tended to make her look younger. There was a frankness and receptiveness about her features. Patients might tell her everything.

Quinn explained to her about the plan to lure the killer into the open by agreeing to what he, the killer, regarded as a hunt.

Zoe listened carefully, then took a sip of beer. The foam left a slight mustache, and Quinn resisted the impulse to reach across the table and touch it, touch her lips.

"So the sport is that the two hunters are evenly matched," she said. "Sometimes one is stalking the other; sometimes it's vice versa."

"That's pretty much it," Quinn said. "Usually the participants are accustomed to hunting in the wild. I suppose the urban setting is supposed to negate any advantage one might have over the other because of familiarity with certain types of terrain."

Zoe gave him a slight smile. "At least the prey gets to shoot back. That's what the anti-hunting movement has always dreamed of."

"Are you part of that movement?"

"I'm not terribly zealous about either side of the argument," Zoe said. "But two human beings stalking each other, and then one of them dying—that's something different from hunting."

"I'm not so sure it is," Quinn said.

"This is a male thing. Is that why it appeals to you?"

"I don't know that it appeals to me," Quinn said.

Zoe smiled at him. "But it does."

Quinn regarded his oversized beer mug. "Yeah, I guess on a certain level it does."

Zoe reached across the table and touched his hand. "I do understand, Quinn."

"And you approve?"

"If it's something you feel you have to do, I'm behind your decision."

"A friend of mine described it as . . . what did she say . . . 'mano-a-mano bullshit.' "

Zoe leaned back. "Well, it is in a way. But your *friend* simply doesn't have a great enough understanding or appreciation of the compulsion to adhere to the male code. If she knew you at all, she'd know that you *have* to do this. Not only do you see it as your job, but you see it as your destiny. You are what you are. It's a challenge between your ego and your id, and you must accept it to retain your manhood."

"I suppose that's true," Quinn said. He hadn't really thought it out. He'd simply known within seconds that to accept the killer's challenge, to play the game by his rules, was the honorable thing to do. "Honor," he muttered.

"That's exactly what it is," Zoe said. "Your honor. That is not a small thing, Quinn. And I think it's important that you know I appreciate that and I stand behind you."

"The classic male and female roles," Quinn said.

"That's true. They're roles that are ancient and deeply rooted in human experience. Remember all those medieval tales about dragon slaying and rescuing the princess?"

"Enough of them," Quinn said. "So you're my princess?"

"Sure am," Zoe said. "After dinner I'll show you."

For her birthday dinner, Rob took Mitzi to Mephisto's, a marvelous restaurant in Lower Manhattan. It wasn't where you'd go to dine economically. Mitzi was impressed by the fact that Rob would spend so much simply because she was turning twenty-five. She sampled her marinated mushroom appetizer and glanced around. Of course she knew no one. This wasn't the kind of place her friends from the club would frequent.

Mitzi smiled across the white tablecloth and glittering crystal at Rob. It was obvious that he wanted to make this an occasion. He'd worn a perfectly tailored blue suit, a white shirt, and a silky floral pattern red tie with a gold tie clasp. There was a gold pin in the form of a soaring bird on his suit coat's left lapel. Mitzi had to admit she'd never expected to dine in this kind of place with a man so perfect for her on her birthday. And he'd brought a gift for her. At least he'd intimated that it was a gift. It was in a blue carry-on bag that sat beneath the table. She'd tried to pry out of him what the bag contained, but he wouldn't say anything other than that he wanted it to be a surprise. Men liked to play games. They made games out of just about everything they did. Mitzi had an entire routine about it.

Rob raised his champagne glass to her and fixed her with a smile that dazzled like the crystal. She reached across the table and clinked her glass against his, but not hard. The thing must cost a fortune.

"To Mitzi at twenty-five," he said. "May you always remain so young."

She grinned and sipped champagne from the delicate stemmed glass. "If only that were possible."

"Maybe it is," he said, "if you believe hard enough."

"No," Mitzi said. "Mother Nature's a joker, just like me."

"Then you and Mother Nature should be friends."

"We are," Mitzi said, "but she's a bitch sometimes. Like most of my other friends. She seems to get a laugh out of women growing old and men getting tired of them. Look around. You see it happen all the time."

"You don't have to worry about that with me, Mitzi. I promise."

She stared hard into his deep dark eyes and rested her hand gently on his. "For some reason," she said, "I believe you. More importantly, I think *you* believe you. But don't you see that's the joke? You'll change your mind. Lovers do. They honestly think they won't, but they do."

"Not me," Rob said. "I'll love you for the rest of your life."

With the polished toe of his wingtip shoe he nudged the blue canvas bag beneath the table.

Mitzi sipped champagne and continued gazing into his eyes. Despite the mystery there she decided to believe him with every beating cell of her heart, at least for tonight. If he wanted to make tonight her night—their night—it was fine with her.

How many Robs were there?

How many nights like this were there?

Carpe diem. Seize the day. Like in the Robin Williams movie. How would you say *seize the night* in Latin?

There had to be a joke in there somewhere. Maybe even in Latin. Latin could be a terrifically funny language.

71

When they left the restaurant after dinner, Mitzi knew she was a little drunk. During the coziness of the cab ride to her apartment, she tried to tease Rob, get him to reveal what was in the blue bag.

Instead of telling her, he teased back, sitting close and keeping the bag well on the other side of him on the back seat. Some of the teasing became sexual, but Mitzi didn't mind. The cabbie was from some Middle Eastern country, listening to low-volume but insistent Arabic music. He seemed uninterested in what his passengers were doing and might not understand much English.

Rob didn't direct the cabbie to stop in front of her building. Instead, they got out at the corner, leaving a short walk. That was okay. The night was still warm, but pleasant because of a slight breeze. As the cab drove away, Mitzi hoped she'd be able to walk all right after all the mixed drinks and wine she'd consumed.

She leaned in close to Rob and he put his arm around her, supporting her. Her legs felt all right, but there was an alcohol-induced numbness in her cheeks. And the sidewalk seemed to be moving around a bit on her, like a funhouse floor. She wasn't sure if she could navigate a straight line without his help. Mitzi walked with her head resting against his shoulder until they had to climb the steps to her building's entrance.

No one had passed them on the sidewalk, and they rode the elevator by themselves up to her floor. Just before the door slid open, he leaned over and kissed the side of her neck.

Mitzi did have trouble finding her apartment key in her purse, and when she did finally close her fingers on the key chain, it slipped from her grasp. Maybe she was drunker than she thought.

Rob helped her, fishing the key from her purse and placing it in her hand so she had a firm grip on it. He was smiling down at her as she fumbled to insert the key in the lock.

She did manage to do that without his help. She unlocked the brass knob lock, then the deadbolt above, and pushed the door open.

To blinding, flashing brilliance winking from cameras.

Behind the flaring lights she could glimpse figures of at least a dozen people, all facing her. Most of them held cameras high in front of them or in tight to their faces so they could use viewfinders.

Mitzi was stunned. She felt Rob's grip tighten on her arm so she wouldn't fall.

"Surprise!" everyone shouted in imperfect unison.

Still stunned, but grinning, Mitzi looked up at Rob. "You! Did *you* know about this?"

Rob was smiling, yet he did seem genuinely surprised.

"I didn't," he said. "I swear it!"

"He's telling the truth, Mitz." Jackie's voice from somewhere over by the sofa. "We didn't have a chance to tell him. You haven't been around the club lately, Rob, and Mitzi's the only one with your phone number, so we had no choice but to surprise you both."

"More fun that way, anyway," Ted Tack's voice said.

Rob's grip tightened again on Mitzi's arm, but this time in a gentle signal to gain her attention.

"See, darling," he said. "I'm honest to a fault."

"Get them some champagne," Jackie said. "It's time for a toast!"

"More champagne," Mitzi said. "Yeah, I could use that."

72

Quinn thought that for Zoe's safety he shouldn't spend the night. He didn't tell her that was why he was leaving, but after they'd made love in her bedroom he showered, dressed, and kissed her good night. She seemed to understand why he was going and kissed him back with a special passion.

Quinn smiled down at her. "You make me want to stay."

"But you can't," she said.

"You're ahead of me."

"There's no ahead or behind. I understand you, that's all."

"Your job," he said.

"No, darling. It's more than my job."

He kissed her again and didn't look back at her as he left.

When he got to his apartment building he was surprised that there wasn't a package waiting for him in his mailbox. He was sure there was room for it, but he found only the usual fliers and bills.

But when he went upstairs there was the package in front of his apartment door. It was about six inches square, tightly encased in brown wrapping paper fastened with heavy tape. There was no label. Quinn's name and address were printed in black ink directly on the wrapping. He knew there'd be no fingerprints to be found, and the name and address lettering looked as if it had been done with a ruler and would provide no basis for comparison. The wrapping paper, too, would be a common brand and untraceable.

Still, when he got inside the apartment he put on latex gloves before carefully opening the package.

Inside the wrapping paper was a white box of the sort a large piece of jewelry might come in. Inside the box was a small .25-caliber Springbok revolver. It was loaded. Its barrel was almost short enough to be called snub-nosed, colored a dusky blue steel like the rest of the revolver except for its checked wooden grip. It looked cheap, like the kind of piece that might blow up in your hand, but Quinn knew it was simple and effective. A close-in weapon. It would be easy to conceal and make very little noise, but it would do the job.

He called Fedderman, who came within fifteen minutes with a guy from the lab named Peterman, who looked about sixteen years old and was all business. Peterman dusted the revolver for prints and found none. The box, paper wrapping, and tape he put in a plastic evidence bag. He and Fedderman took the bag with them when they left. Quinn knew the contents of the evidence bag would provide about as much workable evidence as the revolver. None.

As they went out the door, Fedderman gave Quinn a sad backward glance that had a disturbing finality about it.

Fedderman and Peterman had been there less than twenty minutes. Time seemed to be running faster now, at least for Quinn. As if it might be running out.

He found a clean, soft rag under the sink and wiped print dust off the revolver, then checked it to make sure it was in good working condition. He felt secure in his apartment, but he tucked the gun in his belt anyway, then went into the kitchen and poured himself two fingers of Famous Grouse scotch in a water tumbler.

He made sure the apartment was securely locked, then sat for a long time at his desk, sipping scotch.

When he finally went to bed, he placed the gun beneath his pillow. Being an old single-action revolver, it would have to be cocked by drawing back the hammer before it could be fired. There was little chance of that happening accidentally. It was a good under-the-pillow gun.

The scotch relaxed him enough that he could get to sleep, but a small corner of his mind remained awake.

Lavern Neeson sat in the chair by the bed for hours, cradling the shotgun almost as if it were a child. She listened to Hobbs snore and to the familiar sounds of the building, the steady hum of the air-conditioning, the faint pop and rattle of pipes, the occasional muffled crack of wood expanding or contracting. In the kitchen, the refrigerator cycled on and off.

Shortly before dawn, she stood up from the chair and replaced the shotgun in the closet. Before closing the closet door, she stared for a long time at the box of shells on the top shelf. Such potential for destruction in such small items. Such potential for change with the simple squeeze of a trigger. Instantaneous, irreversible change. Like being yanked with a bang from one world and dropped into another.

The prospect was intimidating, but with every passing day it was less frightening than the world she lived in.

She stood with her bare feet on the cool wood floor, her face buried in her hands, and began to cry. Her sobs were almost silent, and no one was there to see her shoulders quake.

It didn't take long for her to get herself under control. She'd become an expert at modulating and manipulating her emotions. Her expression was calm. Only her reddened eyes and the tear tracks on her cheeks remained of her violent fit of sobbing.

Peace and rest. She was beginning to associate the shotgun with peace and rest. That was dangerous and she knew it, but she couldn't stop it.

Less than a minute later she was back in bed with Hobbs, feeling the heat emanating from his muscular body. He lay on his left side, facing away from her, unmoving and unaware, snoring away.

Lavern drifted into an uneasy sleep for a short while, and then the alarm went off.

The sun had barely risen when the landline phone on the table next to Quinn's bed rang.

He woke slowly, not sure how many rings he'd missed, and tried to get his body to respond to the urgency he felt to answer the phone.

Finally his partially numb right hand found the receiver and clumsily removed it from its cradle.

Lying on his back, he pressed the receiver to his ear, said, "Quinn," in a sleep-thickened voice.

The voice on the other end of the connection sounded wide awake, crisp, and authoritative.

It said, "Listen carefully. Don't talk. These are the rules."

73

The bedroom was bright with fragments of early morning sunlight when the man Mitzi Lewis knew as Rob Curlew observed her as she slept.

Standing nude, he leaned over her and listened closely to her breathing. She was still sleeping soundly.

Careful to make no noise, he gathered up his clothes and carried them into the bathroom. He ran no water and made little noise getting dressed.

He didn't want to leave Mitzi, didn't want to lose this one. But her surprise party last night had been a surprise for him, too. Now almost everyone she knew had seen him and would be able to supply police with descriptions, could identify him. Many of them had photographs of him with Mitzi.

He simply couldn't take the chance. Sometimes the best of hunters came up empty.

When he was dressed, he found the blue carry-on that he'd promised Mitzi he'd open this morning, and walked softly back to her bed.

He stood very still and listened to her breathe, watched her sleep. She looked so innocent, so unknowing.

She would never know the pivotal moment in her life, the moment that had saved her life. Perhaps the great joke of her life. Being Mitzi, she might very well have looked at it that way.

He wanted to kiss her, but knew that might be a mistake. Instead he left the bedroom quietly, left her apartment, and disappeared into the city that was not yet all the way awake.

At 8:00 A.M., after a breakfast of eggs, sausage, and toast, Quinn phoned Renz and described his dawn phone call from the killer.

The rules were simple enough. At nine o'clock this morning the hunt would begin. It was limited to the island of Manhattan. Both men were to be armed only with their identical .25-caliber revolvers. Quinn was safe in his apartment until nine o'clock, but not afterward. From that point on, he was safe nowhere, nor was his opponent.

"He knows where you live, but you don't know where he does," Renz pointed out.

"That's why I'm probably safe here," Quinn said. "Our killer's the sort who'd rather make it a sporting proposition. He wouldn't consider it cricket to shoot me in my bed."

"Cricket . . ." Renz repeated thoughtfully. "He use that word?"

"I don't think so," Quinn said.

"But you just used it," Renz said. "Maybe because he did."

"Maybe," Quinn said. "Maybe he watches the BBC."

"There you go," Renz said. "He also knows what you look like."

"Only from newspaper photos, and they don't do me justice."

"He's really not as cricket as he'd like you to think," Renz said. "Let's not forget he's just another psycho asshole who makes his own rules."

"There's nothing in those rules about leaving my apartment *before* nine o'clock," Quinn said. "That's what I'll be doing after I hang up on you."

"Okay. I'll issue the order again that no one is to interfere with you or the kil—your opponent."

Both men were silent for a while, knowing this might well be their final conversation, and that there simply wasn't any more to say other than everything, and that was impossible to put into words.

"Luck," Renz said simply, and hung up.

It was when Quinn replaced the receiver that he remembered something. Maybe. It was possible the .25-Caliber Killer *had* used the word *cricket* in their phone conversation. He might have a touch of British accent.

Bloody hell!

Not that it changed anything if the killer did happen to be a Brit. He was soon going to find himself in a sticky wicket.

Quinn finished his coffee; then he hand washed and dried his breakfast dishes before leaving the apartment.

He figured a man who'd done the dishes in preparation for his next meal was unlikely to meet death until then. Surely if you planned for the future it was more likely there would be one.

Think alive, stay alive.

But he didn't intend to spend the day simply trying to stay alive while keeping an eye out for the killer.

He had a destination.

Quinn left his apartment via the fire stairs, then he did a turn around the block to be reasonably sure he wasn't being followed. It was possible, maybe likely, that his opponent had his apartment building already staked out though it wasn't yet nine o'clock.

He entered an office building whose lobby, lined with closed shops, ran through to the opposite block. Without pausing, he walked though it and out the opposite tinted glass doors, then doubled back outside, observing all the way. He was reasonably sure he wasn't being followed.

What he wanted to do was lose himself in the city before nine o'clock.

The morning was warm and still, and with a slight overcast that would burn off by noon. Right now shadows were muted and the light seemed evenly distributed. Shooter's weather. As he strode along the sidewalk, Quinn was aware of the weight of the Springbok revolver in one suit-coat pocket, his cell phone in the other.

Mustn't get them confused, he cautioned himself with a smile.

My God! Helen and Zoe are right. At least a part of me is enjoying this.

Though he didn't think he was being followed, the tension was still there. His back muscles were tight, and his antennae were out for anything unusual, anything that might spell danger. He was moving through the city in a kind of hyperawareness. It was a strain that would eventually take its toll.

The trick, he soon realized, was to stay among people, but not so many that they provided cover to fire from and then escape into.

Stop thinking defensively. You be the one to use crowds for cover, to look for the killer and apprehend him, to take him down if necessary without killing anyone else.

Quinn was just beginning to realize how difficult that would be.

He didn't want to keep pounding the pavement wearing himself out, and just in case he *was* at the moment being stalked, he didn't want to become a still target, whatever the time.

On First Avenue he saw a bus preparing to stop for a knot of people standing in front of a bank. At the last second, he boarded and fed in his change. He found a seat away from the window, near the back of the bus, and settled in for his ride uptown.

The roar of the bus's engine, the rhythm of accelerating and stopping, allowed him to relax. Manhattan was a big island. It wouldn't be easy for hunter and prey to come together. The killer would be waiting and watching at points where his quarry might show—workplace, apartment, the near proximities of friends and associates, known haunts. That was part of the problem. Quinn knew practically nothing about his prey, and didn't know how much his prey knew about him. He was beginning to catch on as to how this game was played. He would at some point have to actively hunt. Hunter could become prey in an instant.

He glanced at his watch. Almost nine o'clock.

He was fair game.

74

Dr. Alfred Beeker's blond assistant Beatrice was on duty behind her desk in the anteroom when Quinn arrived at the doctor's Park Avenue office. She was the only one in the room. A mug of coffee and a half-eaten cinnamon roll sat on a white paper napkin on her desk. The whole place smelled like cinnamon.

She looked up at Quinn and appeared frightened. Had Beeker told her about Quinn? Was Beatrice herself part of the S&M lifestyle that Beeker embraced?

"Is Doctor Beeker in?" Quinn asked.

"I'm sorry," she said, "the doctor's with a patient." Doing a nice job of pretending not to remember Quinn.

"In his office?"

"Of course."

"I'd like to look in on him."

Now Beatrice looked alarmed. Beeker must have put a word in her ear about Quinn. She glanced back at the door, then at Quinn, weighing her chances of stopping him from barging in on Beeker and not liking them.

"I need to see him," Quinn said.

"I told you, he's—"

"You don't understand," Quinn said. "I only want to *see* him. I won't even say hello, if you don't want me to."

She stood up and faced him with her arms crossed. Quinn admired her spunk.

"I'm not going to go away until I see him," Quinn said. "Which way would be less all-around trouble? If you called in and asked him to step out here for a moment, or if I barged in while he's in the middle of a session with a patient?"

"What if I call the police?"

"You remember me, dear. The police?" He showed her his shield, though he was sure she already knew who he was.

"Why didn't you say in the beginning this was police business?"

"I wanted to see how cooperative you'd be."

"I'd say you just like to play games," she said. Not angrily, though.

"You've got me there."

She sat back down, plucked the receiver from her desk phone, and pushed a button. Then she turned her back on Quinn and talked softly enough that he couldn't understand her.

A few seconds after she'd hung up, the large door on the wall behind the reception desk opened, and Beeker stepped into the anteroom. He glared at Quinn, and his face turned a mottled red. Plenty angry, Dr. Alfred Beeker. Again, though, Quinn noted the doctor was unafraid.

As he stood looking at Beeker, Quinn became acutely aware of the compact revolver in his pocket. In an odd way it wasn't at all like the gun he usually carried holstered, his old police special revolver. That gun was used to maintain order, to protect people, or to use in self-defense. This gun was for a separate and distinct purpose—for stalking and killing another human being. Quinn couldn't help imagining Beeker in his black leather outfit, standing and holding a whip, with Zoe . . .

"Make this fast," Beeker said.

I'd love to.

Beatrice took a large bite of cinnamon roll. It released a surge of sweet scent in the office.

Quinn nodded to Beeker, smiled and nodded to Beatrice, then turned and walked out the door.

He'd learned what he wanted to know. The doctor was in. And not outside in the city streets, stalking him.

75

Quinn soon learned the rhythm of the hunt.

He moved along the sidewalk at the speed of pedestrian traffic. The knack was in being careful to stay near other people, but at the same time avoid becoming part of a crowd that might shield the killer's approach. He knew that a larger crowd tended only to mean more confused and conflicting witnesses. After shooting him, the killer might even become part of the swarm of onlookers.

It was no good to think of yourself as only the prey. Quinn knew that to survive he'd sometimes have to become the hunter. He crossed streets often, and every half hour or so doubled back. Sometimes he'd find a concealing doorway, or some other quiet corner from which he could observe. There he would wait to see who was walking in his wake. He had no idea what his pursuer looked like. What he wanted was to see the same man twice, to judge his bearing and attitude. He was pretty sure he was being followed, and that he'd be able to spot the killer. At that point Quinn would become the stalker. Quinn figured he had a chance here. He was good at spotting tails, and at shaking them. Why not at arresting them?

Or, if necessary, at killing one of them?

In truth he was almost positive that was what he'd have to do, that this was a serious game played to the death.

But the morning wore on, and whoever was following Quinn—*if* there was someone following him—remained anonymous and all the more dangerous.

It was almost eleven o'clock when Quinn decided he should have lunch. He'd stop at a diner, someplace he'd never been before, where it couldn't be predicted he would go. The noon lunch crowd was still an hour away, so the restaurants shouldn't be crowded yet. He could get a table or booth where he'd be facing the door, away from a window through which he might be seen, or even shot.

It all seemed so incongruous at that moment. So unreal. The morning, the street, the city seemed so normal. Was he really taking part in some madman's deadly game?

He knew that kind of thinking could be like an opiate, dulling alertness. He was in a game, all right. A hunt. And he'd damned well better remember it.

About a hundred feet ahead, a knot of pedestrians waited at an intersection. People were standing on and just off the curb, impatient for the light to change so they could cross. Quinn thought about hurrying to join them, then became aware that his right shoelace had come untied and was flopping around. He was passing a low stone wall running parallel to the office building on his right, and he didn't want to catch up to the people at the corner *too* fast. It was a good time to tie the shoelace.

He stopped, braced his foot up on the low wall, and quickly retied the brown lace.

When he straightened up to continue walking, he saw that the light at the intersection had just changed to walk. The knot of pedestrians had surged forward and dispersed. Most of them were almost halfway across the street. All of them were gone from the corner and the curb.

All but one.

He was a medium-height, well-dressed man in a dark blue suit, coat open, tie flapping in the breeze. He had neatly trimmed dark hair combed straight back, and looked fit and handsome.

Quinn remembered the blue suit, the head of thick black hair. The man had been part of the knot of people at the corner, waiting to cross the intersection

Only he hadn't crossed. He'd turned around and was now walking toward Quinn.

None of this might have seemed real a few minutes ago, but it *was* real. And coming at him. *It was happening!*

The man's smooth, athletic stride didn't slow or in any way change as he slipped a hand into his pocket. The movement hadn't seemed fast, but it had been fast.

Faster than Quinn could reach his own pocket.

The man had stopped now and was standing in shooting position, his body turned sideways, his right arm extended and holding a small revolver pointed at Quinn. The dark eyes sighting over the barrel at Quinn were somber and intent and without fear.

Quinn was fumbling his own revolver out of his pocket, knowing even as he did so that it would be too late. He'd simply tied his shoe, briefly let down his guard, and he was dead.

He braced himself to dive to the side, but he was only going through the motions, giving himself a slim chance.

Before he could move he saw the man's extended arm suddenly drop.

Quinn stared, confused.

He's dancing!

That was Quinn's first thought as the man shuffled his feet, snapping his head this way and that. Then he became aware of the noise, a roar of gunfire.

He looked in its direction and saw Pearl standing in the middle of the street with her feet spread wide, holding her big nine-millimeter Glock in both hands and blasting away.

Then came a sudden, vibrant silence.

Quinn looked away from Pearl, back in the direction she'd been shooting.

The man in the blue suit lay motionless on the sidewalk. There was blood spreading out from beneath him. A lot of blood.

Quinn knew Pearl had disobeyed Renz's instructions. She must have been tailing Quinn, perhaps even tailing his pursuer, the man in the blue suit.

The .25-Caliber Killer.

Aware of his heavy breathing and the blood pulsing in his ears, Quinn stood and watched Pearl approach the downed man to make sure he was dead. After kneeling briefly beside the man, she stood up and walked toward Quinn. Her features were calm, unsmiling, the composed face of a woman at peace with the knowledge that she'd done a difficult job successfully.

Quinn felt beads of sweat running down his ribs beneath his shirt. Pearl had acted on her own and saved his life.

He couldn't yet calculate the cost she'd have to pay, but he knew it was nothing to how much he owed her.

76

Throughout the next day they learned about Martin Hawk, saw where he'd been staying in Manhattan, where he lived in Stamford, Connecticut. They learned how he lived, what he read, whom he knew, and in a sense came to know him.

In his Manhattan hotel room they'd found a blue carry-on containing a large bicycle hook, rolls of duct tape, a coil of nylon rope, and a sharp knife. Everyone there was relieved, even the SCU people. No one was more relieved than Quinn. There was no doubt about it now. Renz and Helen's single-killer theory had been on target. They'd gotten the right man, and he'd left them no choice but to take him down perma-nently.

Hawk's house and its contents were even more revealing.

In Stamford, he'd lived alone in a ten-room brick and stone house on a wooded piece of property large enough to be called an estate. He'd lived and been educated in England for a while, and had indeed been a hunter. His big game tro-phies attested to that. According to neighbors he was friendly, even charming, but was somewhat aloof and had lived a lonely life. On his walls hung valuable abstract art. In his refrigerator were gourmet foods. In his garage were a two-year-old Jaguar and a three-year-old Land Rover. In his office and his bedroom were framed photographs of two attractive women, but there was nothing in the house to identify them.

Hawk's office yielded the most evidence. A concealed safe contained client names and a set of books for a company referred to as Quest and Quarry.

All in all, the suspect's hotel room and home were mines rich with the ore of evidence. If he'd been alive to stand trial, the outcome wouldn't have been in doubt.

But Martin Hawk would never stand trial, and soon the case would be officially closed.

Quinn and Pearl were still decompressing from the action that took Hawk's life, and had almost claimed Quinn's. Fedderman had taken the time to call the airport and check on flights back to Florida. Cindy Sellers had her scoop and was no longer hectoring Renz, who was basking, even romping, in favorable publicity. Mitzi Lewis couldn't stop walking around smiling and marveling at her good luck. It was easy to be funny when you were so grateful to be breathing.

The pressure was off all around.

Quinn spent most of his time at Zoe's and slept there to avoid the media wolves. He and Zoe would make love, and afterward it would be hours before he'd fall asleep. Maybe the cause of his sleeplessness was the lasting exhilaration of still being alive, along with the residue of fear. He'd experienced these emotions before. It took a while sometimes to come down from the adrenaline and cortisone high of taunting death and winning.

But he knew that wasn't what was disturbing his sleep.

Something barely beyond his consciousness wasn't right.

77

The morning was cooler than most, and golden with sunlight.

Zoe skipped their usual grapefruit, toast, and coffee in the kitchen and left the apartment early to deal with her appointments. Quinn showered and dressed, then went out to buy a newspaper and get some breakfast.

The television mounted high behind the counter of the Lotus Diner was tuned to the news, and the news, of course, was still about Martin Hawk, Renz, Quinn, and Pearl. But mostly about Martin Hawk.

Thel the waitress came over and cleared the dishes, then topped off Quinn's coffee.

"You didn't bring the check," Quinn said.

"This one's on us," Thel said. "Just this once. Don't get used to it."

That was about as civil as Thel got. Quinn thanked her, and she ignored him and returned to stand near the coffee urn behind the counter.

Quinn sat for another half hour reading the news, an ear cocked to the softly playing television.

Reading and hearing it made things suddenly come together.

He realized what had been disturbing his sleep. What was still bothering him.

A very large piece of the puzzle was missing.

He got his cell phone from his pocket and started to peck out Zoe's office number. Then he changed his mind and called Helen the profiler.

Helen, like Quinn, did contract work for the NYPD and had a home office. It was a converted second bedroom of her apartment in the Village, and it had French doors that led out to a small brick courtyard surrounded by foliage, an ancient brick wall, and a high wooden fence that looked ready to collapse from the weight of the vines growing up it. Helen had coffee made, and she and Quinn sat in wrought-iron chairs at the small round metal table in the center of the courtyard. They were in deep shade, and the sounds from the street were curiously muffled yet nearby.

Helen was wearing some kind of kimono, brown leather sandals, and no makeup. Her ginger-colored hair was combed back and held by a tan elastic band. She looked younger than usual, like a lanky athlete who'd just come from a women's college basketball game.

Quinn sipped his coffee from an old cracked mug lettered THIMK and glanced around. "Nice back here."

"Private," Helen said. He knew it was an invitation to talk in confidence.

"I have a feeling you know why I came," Quinn said.

"Yeah, but you go first."

"I know we were dealing with dual and possibly conflicting personalities in the same person, but now that we know more about Martin Hawk, I'm having a hard time buying into the notion that he did those women."

"You think Pearl shot the wrong man?"

"Not exactly." Quinn reached for words he couldn't find. "I'm not sure what I think."

Helen leaned back and crossed her long legs beneath the silk kimono. Her well-pedicured feet looked huge and reminded Quinn what a large woman she was.

She said, "Martin Hawk turned out to be an educated and sophisticated opponent who was obviously upset about the dearth of tradition and sportsmanship in society, depressed over what his life's love and endeavor had become. You're thinking that whatever duality he might have contained, it's unlikely that a man like Hawk, obsessed with fairness and honor, the regimen of the hunt, would simply slaughter unsuspecting helpless victims."

"You've been giving this some thought," Quinn said.

Helen nodded. "As have you."

"Have you spoken to Renz?"

Helen smiled sadly. "He wouldn't want to listen. Wouldn't believe me if he did listen. There's a narrative fixed in his mind and in the media. It's all working for him now, and he wouldn't want to change it. And I have to say he'd have a point. What about the stuff they found in the bag in Hawk's hotel room?"

"I don't know about it. I thought maybe you might explain it."

"I can't," Helen said. "It's compelling evidence. It would have taken down the suspect in court if Pearl's bullets had missed."

"You and I both think there's something more to this case. The only problem is, we don't know what."

"That's where we stand," Helen said.

"So what do we do?" Quinn asked.

"I'm not certain we're correct. But *if* we are, at this point I'm not in any position to do anything."

"You could risk your job and professional reputation by backing me up," Quinn said.

He'd thought Helen would laugh or at least smile, but she didn't. Instead she said, "Bring me something, and I'll back you."

Then she smiled. "If there is something."

78

Quinn knew that if he went to his apartment or to the office there'd be media types there. The Manhattan paparazzi.

He drove the Lincoln to First Avenue and found a parking space near East Fifty-fifth Street. He got out of the car and fed the meter, then began walking south on the sunny, crowded sidewalk, cloaking himself in the anonymity of the city.

As he walked, he thought about the way the Slicer victims were killed. Displaying the victims was almost like a desecration of the hunt, and the hunt had been Martin Hawk's quasi-religion. It seemed impossible, at least in Quinn's mind, that the .25-Caliber Killer and the Slicer were the same man.

Then who was the Slicer?

Alfred Beeker? Could he kill in such a grisly manner? Perhaps. His was a profession that delved into sadistic and tortured souls. Maybe some of what he'd encountered had rubbed off.

Or maybe limiting the suspects to men might be where things had gone wrong. It wasn't only men who sometimes hated women. Plenty of women still had enough pent-up rage at their mothers or sisters to compel them to kill.

And what about Dwayne Avis, prime suspect alphabetically but not in any other way? Quinn realized with a jolt that identification with the prominent rental car agency had diverted his attention from the fact that *avis* was Latin for *bird.*

Apropos of nothing. But still . . .

On the other hand, Avis was unlikely. He was in his late fifties, in the outer range of age for serial killers.

Still, it was possible. While the psychologists might be right and it was a long leap from torturing and killing animals to torturing and killing women, maybe it worked in the other direction. The dogs might not have been first. They might have been used as some kind of stopgap between human victims. Grisly offerings to relieve the compulsion to kill.

Quinn had to do *something,* and he needed his computer and directories, the files on the women's murders.

He got back into the car and drove toward the office on West Seventy-ninth Street. The hell with the media.

There were only about a dozen of them outside the office, perhaps because they thought the main narrative of the story they were simultaneously following and creating was over. Quinn brushed past them with relative ease, smiling and no-commenting every third step.

When he was inside, he ignored frantic, loud knocking and locked and chained the street door. This wasn't a regular precinct house; there was no reason to keep it open when most of the neighborhood didn't even know it existed.

He switched on the office lights and sat down at his desk, then booted up his computer. He ignored it while it was activating its underlying software, and instead turned his attention to his phone directories and the Dwayne Avis file.

There was plenty to be found on the arrest and conviction of Avis in Browne County in upstate New York for cruelty to animals.

It took Quinn about fifteen minutes to contact the Browne County Sheriff's Office that had apprehended Avis. The officers who'd been involved in the case were no longer with the department, but the undersheriff (which Quinn figured was some kind of deputy) Quinn talked to had, like Quinn, a voluminous file on Dwayne Avis.

The undersheriff's name was Tom Hazelhoff, and he held a dim view of Avis. "Guy's quite an asshole," Hazelhoff said, "but he don't give us much trouble anymore. Keeps to himself, and the neighbors don't call in about some poor dog yowling all night. Guy who'd do that to dogs . . ." Hazelhoff's voice trailed off in disgust.

"I hear you," Quinn said. "I'm a dog man myself. Your files'd be more extensive than ours, since he was in your system and went to trial there. What I want to know about Dwayne Avis is whether that's his real name. "

"Hold on," Hazelhoff said. "Lemme look."

He was gone more than ten minutes. Quinn almost hung up.

Then his patience was rewarded. Hazelhoff came back on the line.

"It's his real name, all right," Hazelhoff said.

Quinn's heart became a weight in his chest.

"He had it legally changed to Dwayne Avis twelve years ago when he came here from Missouri," Hazelhoff continued, "from his Native American name, Wild Sky Hawk. It says here for reasons of convenience."

That was when the building collapsed on Quinn. Or was it the truth and full understanding?

Dwayne Avis was Martin Hawk's father.

It was the son who procured victims for his father, repaying old debts, or perhaps even out of twisted familial love or obligation. The son, Martin, had nothing to do with the actual slaughter. Martin Hawk had personally killed no one.

Suddenly it occurred to Quinn that Dwayne Avis must be aware of the barrage of media attention being given to the .25-Caliber Killer case and the death of Martin Hawk, his son. Avis was isolated on his remote farm, but he surely had a generator, electricity, a radio or television.

"Quinn? You still there?"

"I am. Thanks, deputy."

"Undersheriff. I hope I was of help."

"Oh, you were. Can I ask another favor?"

"Sure can."

"Get someone to Dwayne Avis's farm soon as you can and hold him for questioning."

"In regards to what?"

"Murder," Quinn said. "Not dogs this time."

"I'll go myself," Hazelhoff said.

"I were you, I'd take backup."

But Hazelhoff had broken the connection and was gone.

79

An hour later, Hazelhoff called back.

"Avis wasn't there," he said. "There are indications that he's fled. Couple of long guns are still in his farmhouse, and there's a box, opened, with half a dozen twenty-five-caliber Springbok revolvers and ammunition. Ain't that the kind of revolver was used—"

"It is," Quinn said.

"Well, my guess is he mighta taken one or more of those guns with him. He's probably headed someplace where you can't walk around with a rifle or shotgun, but he'd still wanna be armed."

"Agreed," Quinn said. "You sure he's fled, not just out somewhere and he might come back?"

"His dresser drawers are hangin' open an' there's signs he's grabbed some clothes from his closet. Half a carton of milk's settin' on the kitchen table, like he took a drink an' didn't bother to put the carton back 'cause he knew he wasn't comin' back. Didn't even put the cap back on. The milk's still cool, so he couldn't have left very long ago. Also, you can see where he musta dragged somethin' large an' heavy off the closet shelf, left a big space an' knocked a few things onto the floor. There's an indentation on the mattress where it looks like a suitcase sat. Top of all that, that old truck of his is gone from behind the house. He's fled, all right. No sign of where, though."

Quinn thought he might know where. To New York City, to avenge his son's death by killing the woman who'd caused it.

He hung up on Hazelhoff and called Pearl.

"Quinn," she said, when she answered. "What's up?"

"I don't want to take time to explain, Pearl, but I want you to leave your apartment right now. Don't take anything with you, just hang up the phone and go."

"Go where, Quinn?"

"To the corner deli down the street from your apartment. Stay there till I show up."

"I don't understand this, Quinn."

"Do you have to? Right now?"

"Damned right I do."

"Can't you trust me, Pearl?"

"Do I have to answer that?"

"Damn it, Pearl!" He surprised himself by how anguished he sounded.

"I can trust you," she said, hearing the same thing in his voice. "Quinn—"

"Go, Pearl. Please! Go now!" Quinn broke the connection.

Quinn immediately phoned Renz and explained the situation, then asked Renz to send radio cars to intercept Avis if he happened to show up.

On the way outside to climb into the Lincoln, Quinn phoned Fedderman on his cell and told him what was happening.

Then he drove fast toward Pearl's apartment.

* * *

It had been damned hard work. Must've been, or Hobbs wouldn't be so winded. And his right arm was sore, as if he might have messed up his rotator cuff again.

He'd been drinking a while and figured he must have a snoot full, the way the room was tilting this way and that, making it difficult not to bump into things as he made his way toward the bed. It was like being on a boat in the middle of the ocean.

Hard work, but worth it. Teach the bitch a lesson.

After beating Lavern harder than he ever had, Hobbs staggered across the bedroom and fell onto the bed. He snorted a couple of times and then let out a long sigh. He lay there in peaceful drunken slumber as she crawled from the bedroom, certain that this time he'd broken one of her ribs completely. More than one. He had to have, the way he'd hit and kicked her.

As she crawled, one of her elbows felt wobbly and kept giving, and she dragged one knee.

Damn him, damn him, damn him . . .

She crawled off the bedroom carpet, onto the hardwood floor of the hall, then onto the softer hall runner. Every inch she crawled brought pain. Lavern had been warned that Hobbs would go too far and kill her some day. Maybe this was the day. Maybe he had killed her. Maybe this was an exercise in revenge and not prevention.

If that's what it is, so be it!

Damn him, damn him, damn him . . .

When she reached the closet, she opened the door, felt around behind the coats, and closed her hand around the shotgun.

She used the gun as a cane to aid her in struggling to her feet, where she could reach the box of shells on the closet shelf.

Leaning against the wooden door frame, breathing hard and hurting with every breath, she slipped a shell into the breech.

80

As soon as he turned the Lincoln onto Pearl's block, Quinn knew he was too late. Police cars were angled in at the curb in front of her building. Several uniformed cops were standing outside the building but up close to it. Quinn could guess why. They didn't want to be visible from an upstairs window and become targets. They were talking with a man in a brown suit. Quinn recognized the blocky form and head of tousled black hair. Sal Vitali.

Quinn parked the Lincoln fifty feet away from the nearest police car, then climbed out, stayed inside the protective angle of vision, and jogged toward the knot of cops and Vitali.

"What've we got?" Quinn asked when he'd joined the group. He glanced over. Fedderman had arrived out of nowhere, shirt cuff flapping like a signal flag.

Vitali pointed to a uniformed cop, a skinny guy in his forties with a long, pointed nose. "Everson here was first on the scene," he said. "Officer Cullen, who's inside helping clear the building's tenants out the back fire stairs, showed up a few minutes later. Cullen used the elevator, and Everson took the stairs. Everson won the race and got to Pearl's floor just in time to see the suspect back up with her into her apartment and close the door. He had an arm around her neck and a gun held to her head."

Quinn looked at Everson. "What kinda gun?"

"Small handgun of some kind," Everson said. He had dead-looking brown eyes.

"Revolver?"

"Coulda been. Blue steel, I think. He was jamming the thing in her ear, and her hair kinda blocked my view."

"He display any other weapon?"

"None that I could see."

"Got a 'scrip of the suspect?"

"Medium height, black hair, muscular build, maybe fifty."

Quinn nodded. "Nice work."

"'Nother thing, Captain. He didn't look scared at all. A real calm one."

"Drugged up?"

"No, not that kinda drowsy calm. He's plenty alert."

"Hostage team's on the way here," Vitali said.

Quinn knew what that meant. SWAT sharpshooters, a hostage negotiator. Somebody else in charge.

Fedderman was thinking the same thing. "Let's go in and get her," he said.

"Get her shot, maybe," Vitali said in his gravel-pit voice.

Fedderman looked from Vitali to Quinn. "If what you say's true," he said to Quinn, "he's got nothing to lose. He won't negotiate. He's just playing out the string."

Quinn knew Fedderman was right.

Mishkin came out of the building, staying in tight to the brick and stone front. When he knew he was safe, he straightened up out of his protective hunch and walked over to them. He was wearing a tie and a white shirt with the sleeves neatly folded up to reveal thin wrists. He was sweating and looking like a harried accountant.

"We got everybody but Pearl and the suspect outta the building," he said.

"I think we oughta go in fast," Quinn said.

"Not 'we,' " Mishkin said. "You."

Quinn looked at him.

"You alone, or he swears he'll shoot her and then himself."

"Why me alone?" Quinn asked. But he knew why.

"He says you killed his son," Mishkin said.

The other men stared at Quinn, saying nothing. Sirens sounded, blocks away but getting closer.

Quinn said, "Make sure nobody interferes, Feds." He set off toward the building's entrance.

"Like Pearl did," Fedderman said when Quinn was out of earshot.

Lavern Neeson made herself crawl.

She made it into the bedroom with great difficulty and a lot of pain, dragging the shotgun by its long barrel. At some point the sleeping Hobbs must have awakened enough to use the remote to switch on the TV. It was flickering without sound beyond the foot of the bed. Closed-caption yellow letters crawled along the bottom of the screen, the words of a man and woman arguing in dead silence about where the stock market was going.

She waited a few minutes until she'd caught her breath, then reached out and gripped a chair leg and dragged the chair closer to her and to the bed.

Using the shotgun and chair for support, Lavern made it to her knees. When she thought she was steady enough, she leaned the shotgun against the mattress. It wouldn't do to pull herself up onto the chair and then not be able to reach the shotgun where it lay on the floor.

It took her about five minutes, but she did manage to reach an awkward sitting position on the chair. She stretched out her right arm and pulled the shotgun to her. She sat very still because even the slightest movement of her body brought pain.

Lavern was proud of herself. She'd made it here, to her chair by the bed, with the shotgun. She was well on the way to what she'd decided to do. Hobbs continued snoring lightly, unaware of the monumental struggle so near him. One that would change his and Lavern's world forever.

Lavern moved the shotgun's safety to the off position. It was ready to fire. This close to her target, she wouldn't even have to aim it.

But she would aim the gun. She wanted to be responsible for her decision and what would happen in the future. In the meantime, she'd endure the present with at least a modicum of comfort and a certain nostalgia. A sad glance over her shoulder before turning a corner. She knew she was second by second living out what remained of her old life.

The room seemed to block all sound from outside and become very small. Automatically, her breathing found the tempo of her husband's as she sat and watched him sleep. They were both on the edge of an abyss. One difference between them was that she knew it. Another was that he had put them there.

It would be easy for Hobbs, Lavern thought. She'd squeeze the trigger and he'd simply slip from one dream to another. She'd be the one left with the blood and the mess and every kind of horror.

The reality.

It wasn't fair, but it never had been.

81

Quinn nodded to the uniformed cop in the lobby, who tried to look blankly at him, then gave it up and nodded back, wishing him luck. He was still watching as the elevator door closed, and then Quinn was on the way up.

He drew his old .38 revolver and held it tight against his thigh as he stepped from the quiet elevator into the silent hall. The building even *felt* empty.

Quinn advanced along the carpeted hall that smelled of time and dust and saw that the door to Pearl's apartment was standing open.

Feeling fear that was on the edge of nausea, he moved closer to the doorway so he had a narrow view of the apartment's interior. He saw a corner of the sofa, part of a lamp table, half of Pearl's framed museum print of Munch's *The Scream.*

He swallowed to make sure his throat wasn't dry. "Dwayne Avis?"

"I'm here with your lady love," Avis said in a calm voice. "I ain't so sure she's a lady, though. Why don't you come on into the apartment, Captain Quinn, so we can see each other?"

Quinn took a deep breath and willed his legs to move. He tasted bile at the back of his throat.

There was Avis, standing near the opposite end of the sofa, holding Pearl in front of him with one arm tight around her neck. The other arm was crooked so the .25-caliber Springbok revolver in his right hand pointed straight into Pearl's right ear. Pearl's eyes met Quinn's. She looked afraid but calculating. She hadn't given up and was trusting him to figure out something. To try, anyway. They both knew that the only way Dwayne Avis was going to leave the building was dead or in custody.

Avis seemed almost unconcerned by his predicament. He was simply using what leverage he had and was prepared to cope with whatever came of it.

Quinn moved away from the doorway, closer to them. Avis watched him, his hooded dark eyes unblinking, the gun steady against Pearl's ear.

"That'd be near enough," Avis said.

Quinn stopped and stood still.

"He's gonna shoot you," Pearl said. "Then me."

"Or you and then him," Avis said.

"What are your demands?" Quinn asked. But he knew Avis didn't have demands. Pearl had it right. Avis simply wanted Quinn and Pearl, in whatever order, to leave this world before he did. Even if Avis by some wild chance was able to kill Quinn and make his escape, he'd still shoot Pearl.

Quinn tried to figure what he had to work with. Avis was skilled at using Pearl's body as a shield. He was crouched with his head behind and slightly to the side of Pearl's so that he was peering over her left shoulder. Only his left eye and the left side of his forehead were exposed. Quinn hadn't actually shown his revolver to Avis, but he was sure Avis knew it was there in Quinn's right hand, alongside and slightly behind his right thigh where it couldn't be seen. If Quinn's right arm began to rise to point his weapon, the bloodbath would begin.

Then Quinn saw the one possibility Avis had left him. Quinn was more familiar than Avis with the old Springbok revolvers, which had been used probably exclusively by Avis's son Martin and the Quest and Quarry clients. Most likely the ones at Avis's farm were simply stored there. The revolver in Avis's hand wasn't cocked. The hammer was still forward and would have to be thumbed back before the gun would fire.

The amount of time it would take Avis's thumb to cock the revolver and for Avis to squeeze the trigger was the amount of time Quinn had to act and make whatever he did work. Seconds.

And the slight exposure of Avis's eye and tanned forehead was a difficult target, even in these close quarters.

Seconds.

Seconds that might save Pearl's life or end it. That might be ticking away now in Avis's head.

Quinn knew that if he did chance it and take the shot, he'd have to move first in order to have time.

He did move first. Instantly and decisively.

As his hand came up with the bulky old .38, Quinn saw Avis's stubby thumb moving toward the Springbok's hammer.

Seconds.

Quinn turned off every other part of his mind, took aim, and squeezed the trigger.

The room rocked with the deafening blast of gunfire.

One shot. Before either Avis or Pearl could react.

Quinn saw a red mist appear like a halo around Avis's head, saw a fragment of skull and hair spin back and away. Avis's arm fell away from Pearl. They both toppled backward.

Avis lay still on his back. Pearl rolled to the side and

scrambled to her feet. She was trembling, and there were flecks of blood and what looked like gray brain matter on her left cheek.

Quinn had moved forward after the shot without realizing it. He and Pearl stared down at Avis's motionless figure. A large piece of Avis's skull was missing above his left eye. Without the vitality of life he looked diminutive and harmless.

Quinn and Pearl noticed at the same time how close it had been. Avis had managed to cock the pistol in the second before he'd died.

Instinctively, Quinn kicked the gun away from the dead hand, halfway across the room.

The bullet that had taken off part of Avis's skull had also broken a window, allowing the breeze to enter through the shattered pane. A curtain blown in the wind momentarily created a shadow on the wall that looked like a huge feathered wing.

For the first time in her life, Pearl fainted.

82

Perhaps it had been the pain that made her lose consciousness. Or maybe Lavern had simply fallen asleep.

It was the pain that had awakened her. With each breath, the ribs on her left side seemed to catch fire. She was still holding on to the shotgun barrel, the butt of its wooden stock resting on the bedroom floor.

She had no idea how long she'd slept or been unconscious. From where she sat she couldn't see the clock.

Hobbs was still snoring, but not loudly. The TV was still on beyond the foot of the bed, tuned to the news, still muted. Yellow closed-caption letters crawled past at the bottom of the screen while an impossibly beautiful blond anchorwoman mouthed each syllable with red, red lips.

Lavern looked beyond the TV, saw light edging the drawn shades, and knew it was morning. Early morning.

Hobbs suddenly snorted and coughed, then resumed snoring. He was sleeping more lightly now. He might wake up soon.

Something on TV caught Lavern's attention. The closed-caption lettering indicated that the anchorwoman was talking about the Slicer being shot to death in some woman's apartment. It had turned out that he wasn't also the .25-Caliber Killer—but the man gunned down earlier by the police was his son, who'd procured the victims for his father. The son, who'd arranged urban 'hunts,' had apparently killed no one directly, but had seduced and prepared women for his father to murder and butcher.

Suddenly the screen was split, and another woman appeared, a lanky redhead. The blond anchorwoman was on the other half of the screen, interviewing her. They were discussing the reasons why the father-son team of killers acted as they had. Lavern would have turned up the sound so she could hear their voices, but she was afraid to risk waking Hobbs.

The redheaded woman, Helen something, was explaining the emotional trap the son had been in, and the societal, sometimes-ancient forces that had acted upon both father and son. Reasons and motivations stemmed from all of this. Motivations to kill. Excuses for killing.

None of it sounded like justification to Lavern.

Yet here she was with a shotgun beside her, waiting for her husband to wake up so she could kill him, so she could do to him what he would otherwise eventually do to her.

I have the courage to kill him, but not to leave him.

But did she really believe that? And wasn't there more to it?

She understood for the first time that she might leave Hobbs and learn how to live without him, but if she killed him he'd be with her always.

Always.

She made sure the shotgun's wooden stock was firmly planted on the floor, then used the gun as a cane to help her stand up from her chair.

Lavern took a few careful steps. It hurt, but she could walk.

She leaned the shotgun against the bed, where Hobbs

would see it when he woke up and think about what might have happened.

Then she limped from the bedroom and went outside. Lavern was still wearing yesterday's clothes, carrying yesterday's pain, but right now she didn't care.

It took her twenty minutes to hail a cab and tell the driver to take her to the Broken Wing Women's Shelter.

83

Quinn would have smoked one of the Cuban cigars he'd recently bought from Iggy, his supplier, but he knew it wasn't worth the disapproval and barrage of air-freshener bombs hissing their incense all over his apartment. As if it weren't *his* apartment.

He stared at the ceiling and considered how things had worked out.

The case had become clearer in the light of further research, as they all did in the post-arrest phase. The evidence was being added to, reexamined, reclassified, and analyzed. There would of course be no trial, with Martin Hawk and his father both dead.

This one had what the pop psychologists called closure.

Fedderman had returned to Florida, where he thought he could live cheaper and there were a few places that served what tasted like New York deli food. He'd said he might take another fling at golf.

Renz's reputation was at its high point. A mayoral bid didn't seem so far fetched at the moment. He and Quinn talked frequently, still arranging and organizing material to

develop the full story of what had happened, how this familial team of killer and enabler had evolved. But much of the
story was lost in the past and the wooded hills around Black
Lake, Missouri, and would never be known. From time to
time Renz would mention that someday he might write a
book about the case. Being a published author was important in politics, locally or nationally.

Berty Wrenner, as well as most of the surviving Quest
and Quarry clients, had been tried and convicted, and the
rash of modern-day duels in the city had soon abated.

Quinn's reverie suddenly ended with the grating ring of
the intercom. He glanced at his watch and climbed out of
bed.

Pearl identified herself, and he buzzed her in, then unlocked the apartment door and returned to the bedroom to
pull on some pants.

He was sitting on the bed working socks on his feet when
Pearl walked into the room. She was wearing jeans, black
boots, and a black leather jacket. She had a folded *Post*
tucked under one arm.

She said, "You're running late, Quinn."

"I took a shower last night," he said. "I'll get dressed, and
we can get right outta here." He'd promised Pearl he'd go
with her to visit her mother at the Sunset Assisted Living
home in New Jersey. She had to appear there at least every
month or so to keep the staff on their toes. She felt it was her
duty. She hated to go alone. Quinn understood why, but on
another level he kind of liked Pearl's mother.

Pearl sniffed the air. "You been smoking, Quinn?"

"Not in months," he lied.

"Smells like smoke."

"It lingers." He nodded toward the folded newspaper as
he struggled to put on his shoes. "Anything going on?"

"Nothing unusual. A guy on the Lower East Side killed
himself with a shotgun outside a women's shelter. Put the

barrel in his mouth and used a bent wire hanger to push the trigger. Made a big mess in the street."

"You're right," Quinn said. "Nothing unusual."

He went into the bathroom and peed, washed his hands, used deodorant, splashed cold water on his face, then combed his hair. It stuck up kind of funny on one side, but what the hell. He went back to the bedroom and found a clean shirt. Added a conservative blue tie. Pearl's mother would like that.

Within a few minutes they were in the Lincoln and on their way, driving through a light snow that the weather forecasters swore wouldn't amount to any measurable accumulation.

"We can stop at that place across the bridge and get some doughnuts and coffee," Pearl said.

Quinn nodded, concentrating on his driving and wondering if he should use the wipers. "We can take some to your mother."

"Whatever," Pearl said.

The sky seemed a darker gray, and the swirling snowfall thickened. There was no doubt now about using the wipers. Quinn switched them on, and they settled into their metronomic *thumpa . . . thumpa . . . thumpa,* spanning most of the wide windshield. The sound was conducive to thought.

As he did from time to time, Quinn wondered what Zoe Manders was doing these days.

Not that he cared a great deal.

After what had happened with Martin Hawk, Quinn realized that Zoe had been prepared to let him die, while Pearl had saved his life. After all the soul searching and mental machinations, it had come down to that simple truth. It meant something.

So Quinn had left Zoe and resolved to rekindle his relationship with Pearl.

Pearl knew exactly what was going on and why, and she didn't allow much reason for hope.

But some.

The big car sped on through the snow-roiled cold air, toward an uncertain future. Quinn turned on the headlights so he could see the road ahead more clearly, but they didn't do much good.